W9-DGM-953

HAMILTON STARK

Also by the Author

Family Life
Searching for Survivors

HAMILTON STARK

A NOVEL

Russell Banks

HOUGHTON MIFFLIN
COMPANY

BOSTON 1978

Library of Congress Cataloging in Publication Data

Banks, Russell, date
Hamilton Stark.

I. Title.
PZ4.B2175Ham [PS3552.A49]
813'.5'4 78-4960
ISBN 0-395-26471-5

Printed in the United States of America

S 10 9 8 7 6 5 4 3 2 1

Chapter One, "By Way of an Introduction to the Novel, This or Any," was originally published in slightly different form in the anthology *Statements II*, Jonathan Baumbach and Peter Spielberg, eds., Fiction Collective/Braziller, New York, 1977.

The author wishes to express his gratitude to the John Simon Guggenheim Memorial Foundation for its generous support while this novel was being completed.

for Mary — still, and again

"The individual has a host of shadows,
all of which resemble him and for the moment
have an equal claim to authenticity."
— Kierkegaard, *Repetition*

Contents

HAMILTON
STARK

CHAPTER ONE

By Way of an Introduction to the Novel, This or Any

IT DIDN'T OCCUR to me to write a novel with A. as the prototype for its hero, Hamilton Stark, until fairly recently, a year ago this spring, when I drove the forty miles from my home in Northwood across New Hampshire to his home outside the town of B. Upon written invitation (via post card, as was his habit), I was on my way to visit him for the afternoon and possibly the evening. The post card read:

4/12/74. If you don't show up here Sat. with a fifth of CC and a a case of Molson I'll stop up your plumbing with my toe. Number 5 has gone back to Mother and I've gone back to my old habits. Bring me a box of 30.06 rifle shells too. We'll do some shooting. A.

Typically, he had typed his message, and the four-color photograph printed on the reverse side was of a building he had helped construct, in this case a Tampax factory in the southwestern part of the state. A. was a pipefitter with a wide range of practical engineering skills, and on that job he had been the foreman for all the plumbing, heating and air-conditioning systems.

After leaving my home around noon, I stopped in Concord, the state capital, and as instructed, purchased a fifth of Canadian Club whiskey and a case of Molson ale, which also happens to be Canadian. A. loved practically everything Canadian and thought Canada a truly "civilized" country, especially its far northern regions, where no one lives. "Up there," he once told me, "there's so many rocks and so few people, the people act like rocks. There aren't even any goddamn trees up there, once you get far enough north! Now that's *class*," he pronounced.

I had nodded my head in agreement, as was my habit, but I wasn't actually sure — wasn't sure that I agreed with him, of course, but also was not sure that he had meant what he had said, that he hadn't been criticizing the Canadian landscape and people rather than praising them. I didn't bother to pursue the subject; I knew my confusion at his ambiguous tone would only have been compounded by the further, inclusive, ambiguously hostile pronouncements that he would have heaped upon my head. He was like that. Once he perceived a crack in his listener's confidence in the meaning and intent of his remarks, he gleefully hurled himself like a boulder against the crack until he had split the egg of assured understanding wide open and had it lying in pieces like Humpty Dumpty at the bottom of the wall. And like a fallen Humpty Dumpty, the listener always felt foolish and guilty, as if the fall and the consequent shattering were all his own fault, a just punishment for his exceeding pride.

In many ways, A. was a peculiar man.

I was saying, though, that I had left Concord, and a half-hour later, as I was driving past the pink and aqua house trailers along the road, the two-room shacks with rusted stovepipes poking through the roofs, the old farmhouses boarded up or half-covered against the winter with flapping sheets of polyethylene, the fields compulsively cleared by long-dead generations of Yankee farmers gone now in this generation to scrubby choke-cherry and gnarled stunted birch, saw the gap-toothed children with matted hair and dirty rashes on their round faces playing by the side of the road, glimpsed in windows the blank, gray faces of young women and the old men's and old women's faces collapsing like rotted fruit, the broken toys and tools and ravaged carcasses of old cars lying randomly in the packed-dirt yards, the scrawny yellow mongrels nastily barking from the doorsteps at my passing car — as I drove through this melancholy scene and thus neared the home of A., it occurred to me for the first time that I might write a novel with A. as the prototype for its hero.

I will tell you how I arrived at such a notion.

It fascinated and amazed me that a person born into squalor such as this could grow to his adulthood in that same neighborhood and yet could possess qualities which, upon close examination, could be seen as both wisdom and passion.

How was that possible? I asked myself.

And then I asked myself if A. possessed these qualities (wisdom and passion), in fact, or if he were merely peculiarly mad. But on the other hand, I countered, even if he *were* peculiarly mad, and if his peculiar madness, which sometimes took forms that could be construed as wisdom and passion, happened to be a condition necessary for the man's mere survival — after having been born and raised in social circumstances that ordinarily dun a human being to death, turning him wormy with passive, quiet desperation long before he reaches adolescence — why, then madness was indeed wisdom, and to cling to such madness was passion!

That way, spiritual survival became, in my eyes, self-transcendence, practically an evolutionary move on the part of the organism. The question of love, its mere possibility, a question that had haunted me in my long consideration of A.'s character, thereby became wholly irrelevant. He was beyond offering love, above it and superior to it — at least the kind of love that I, from my indulgent background, had learned long ago to value in myself and seek from others.

This was, for me, a welcome series of insights, and I felt greatly relieved, as if from a dreaded, demeaning chore, like cleaning out a septic tank. I thought: Any person whose life provides us with that particular relief is worth writing a novel about. For who among us has not wished to be freed of his need to love and be loved?

It was with considerable excitement, then, that I approached the turnoff from the paved to a dirt road, practically a trail, that led through a quarter-mile of approximately flat and unkempt fields to A.'s home. The fields on both sides of the deeply rutted road, lined with slowly collapsing stone walls, had retreated to furzy bushes and scrambling tangles of wild blackberries, sumac, and poison ivy. Scattered over the fields in no discernible pattern were ten or twelve rusting shells of windowless cars and trucks, some of them further decomposed and more nearly destroyed than others, also several farm vehicles — harrows, plows, cultivators — a one-handled wheelbarrow, an outhouse lying awkwardly on its side, rusty bedsprings and swollen mattresses spitting yellowish stuffing onto the ground, a pile of fifty-gallon oil drums, an engine block and a transmission housing, both lying atop a child's crushed red wagon which lay atop an American Flyer sled in splinters, next to a refrigerator (with the door invitingly open, I noticed), and a red, overstuffed couch which had been partially destroyed by fire. None of this wreckage was new to me. I had observed, enumerated, and reflected on all of it many times, both alone and with friends, especially with my friend C. (about whom more later).

The fields and the road were all part of A.'s property, but a stranger, noting the broad, carefully maintained lawns, gardens, house and outbuildings which spread out from the closed gate at the end of the cluttered fields, would surely infer two separate and probably quarreling owners, one for the fields and badly maintained roadway, another for the house and grounds. But that was not the case. A. was fastidious and energetic, even compulsive, about the maintenance of the house and the yards, gardens and outbuildings that surrounded it. The region that lay beyond the white, iron rail fence, however, he cared for not at all, even though some seven hundred acres of that region was his private property, had been deeded to him with the houses and outbuildings by his parents.

Actually, it was fortunate that so much of the world beyond the fence was A.'s private property, because for years he had been tossing his garbage over that fence, throwing his rubbish, all his used-up tools, vehicles, furniture, even his old newspapers, over the fence and into the field. Every now and then, perhaps once a year, depending on domestic changes, he rolled out his bulldozer, took down a section of the fence, and shoved the rotting garbage and trash roughly toward the main road and away from the house, to make more room near the fence. It was a casual operation. The vehicles stayed pretty much where he had left them, and he usually left them where they had got stopped, either because of running aground on a huge boulder, of which the field had an abundance, stalling or coughing out of gas, getting stuck in the mucky, tangled ground, or ramming into another car or truck from a previous year's trash. He used his vehicles until they were too weary and broken to drive any farther than to this odd burial ground, and he always tried to make that last drive as exciting as possible. Then he would hitchhike twenty miles to Concord, where there were half a dozen automobile dealers, and buy a new vehicle, usually a different type from the one he had just interred — a pickup truck if last year's had been a sedan, a station wagon if a convertible. Because of the intense way he drove them, his new vehicles rarely lasted longer than a year.

Similarly, whenever he disposed of furniture, tools, garden implements, waste or rubbish of any kind, he took from the act whatever last pleasure he could wring from it — making bets, and usually winning them, that he could lift and throw a sofa over the fence, or hurl a transmission housing from his pickup bed onto a pile of old toys, and then an engine block onto the transmission housing; or that he could carry a refrigerator in a broken wheelbarrow for a quarter of a mile over a rough surface under a hot August sun. Afterward, to complete the act, he liked to sit up on his porch, usually in the admiring company of a friend or one of the local adolescent boys he permitted to hang around him, and while guzzling Canadian whiskey and ale, fire his rifle at the new trash. He shot his rifle at many things, animate and inanimate, but he always seemed to enjoy it most when he was shooting at the things he had used up and thrown out.

On this particular day, a blotchy, glutinous gray afternoon with a cold rain lightly falling, as I neared the gate where the road ended and A.'s wide, paved driveway began, I noticed a high, wobbling stack of what appeared to be new furniture — a Formica-topped kitchen table and four chairs, a double bed with bookcase headboard and matching dresser, several table lamps, and two or three cardboard cartons filled with pastel articles of clothing and possibly curtains and bedding. This carefully constructed stack, with all the articles balanced and counterbalanced, was located a few feet from the fence and about twenty feet from the roadway, and I had never seen it before. I assumed, therefore, that these were his fifth wife's leavings, her effects, an assumption which later proved correct.

I got out of my car, walked up to the gate, unlatched it, and swung it open. I could see A. in the distance, sitting on the porch of the house at the far side, swinging slowly in the wood glider. Neither of us waved or signaled to the other. That was customary. I returned to my car, drove it through the gate, got out again, and closed the gate behind me, as I knew I was supposed to do, and then drove up the long, curving driveway past the smooth, freshly greening lawns to the house, and parked next to the house on the side opposite the porch, where the driveway ended, facing the entrance to the small barn, which under A.'s care had been converted after his father's death into a modern garage and workshop. Behind the house loomed the humpbacked profile of the mountain, Blue Job, adding its shadow to the day's gray light and casting the darker light like a negating sun across the house and onto the fields in front.

It occurs to me that I really needn't bother with all this. Certainly not at this point. Perhaps later in the narrative such descriptions will be of significance, but here, now, I'm merely attempting to explain how I came to write a novel with a hero whose real-life prototype is my friend, my own "hero," as a matter of fact. And though that notion had *occurred* to me barely moments before, by the time I had parked my car and had started walking around the front of the house to greet A. at the porch, I had already completely forgotten the idea. I was worrying over whether or not I had properly secured the gate at the end of the driveway.

We spent the remainder of the day and most of the evening cheerfully drinking, first out on the porch, where until dark we sat and took turns shooting at the furniture A. and his fifth wife had bought as newlyweds the previous November. After dark, we lurched into the house and sprawled on the floor of the kitchen (the chairs and table were all in the field, ripped apart by high-powered rifle slugs), finishing the bottle of whiskey and the case of ale. I remember that A. had recently installed a central vacuum-cleaning system in the house, so that one could simply plug the hose into outlets located in the baseboard of every room without having to drag a heavy cannister or tank along from room to room, and he was quite proud of the system. He said to me, "I've got a dishwasher, a clothes washer and dryer, and a microwave oven that bakes a potato in forty-six seconds. And now I've got this vac' system. Now, you tell me, what the hell do I need a *woman* for?"

I said nothing. I was too drunk to speak clearly, and also, his question had seemed rhetorical.

Then he said, "I can get laid when I want to get laid. And if the day ever comes when I can't get it, it'll only be because I don't want it enough."

This last statement seemed wise to me then, and it does now, too.

I was quite drunk, naturally, but I somehow got myself safely home, and that was the end of the day last spring when it first occurred to me write a novel about A., or rather, about someone very much like A., so much like him that I would have to give him the name of Hamilton Stark, or A. would know that the novel was about him, a thing he would hate me for. I did not want A. to hate me. Luckily, he is no longer alive, or naturally, I would not be writing this introduction.

(I should say that I *believe* he is no longer alive, and although technically he does not exist, that is, his body has never been located, it would certainly be strange and ironic if the publication of this novel brought him out of a hiding place. I can imagine the letter I would receive, postmarked in some tiny, far-northern Canadian village where he is thought of as a hermit:

The only reason I'm not suing you is that a lawyer would cost me more than you could make from such a piece of crap as your so-called novel. Just know that if I ever run into you I'll run right over you. You are an asshole. And a lousy writer too. You're going to get everything you deserve, you faggot.

And then, for the rest of my life, silence. Cold, stony silence. It would be a hard thing to bear.)

It wasn't until almost a full year later, a Sunday early in February of this year, that I again thought of writing about him. This is how it happened.

I was in the neighborhood, as they say in New Hampshire when you are within ten miles of a place, photographing birds in winter scenery at a state park not far from A.'s home, and as it was still early in the afternoon when I finished, I decided to stop by for a brief visit. I rarely visited him unannounced or uninvited, but for reasons too vague and smokily intuitive to go into here, I decided that this time it would be permitted and perhaps even welcomed.

When I arrived, I noticed immediately that he had parked his car in the driveway outside the garage, which was not his habit. At that time he was driving a pale green Chrysler. It was an airport limousine, an unusually long vehicle that he took considerable pride in being able to park wholly inside his garage. Swinging open the garage door, raising it like the curtain at a stage play and revealing the blunt green tail of an automobile that, like a dragon, seemed to go on forever, disappearing into the far, cavernous darkness of the converted barn, was an exquisite pleasure for him. As a matter of fact, on several occasions I myself, as the audience, had found the experience oddly satisfying and had broken spontaneously into applause.

But on this day the car was parked outside the garage, and the garage door was locked. I walked quickly around to the side door at the porch, knocked, and then called. That door, too, when I tried it, was locked. It was a cold, diamond-clear day, with about eight inches of dry, week-old snow on the ground, and there were hundreds of footprints in the snow, most of them probably A.'s. But fresh prints could not be distinguished from week-old ones. A narrow path had been tramped from the porch down to the fence in front of the house, and on the other side of the fence was a waist-high pyramid of the last week's garbage and trash, most of it frozen solid. Across the snow-covered, bumpy fields in front and into the woods behind the house and on either side were numerous chains of footprints — but it was impossible to tell when in the previous week any of the chains had been laid down. Beyond the woods hunched the mountain, mute, seeming almost smug.

It wasn't so much that I couldn't understand A.'s absence as that I could not understand both his absence and the car's presence. Except under severe duress or drunkenness, he never rode in anyone else's vehicle. I knew he must still be on the premises. On the other hand, if he were just out for a walk in the woods, a normal activity on such a crisp, clear afternoon, why did he leave his car parked outside the garage? That was not normal. (Rather, it was not *usual*. Nothing about A. was normal.)

I decided to examine the car more closely. Perhaps there

was a note, or a clue. After circling the enormous green Chrysler twice, I finally noticed the three holes in the front window on the driver's side, holes surrounded by interconnected cracks, like spider webs, holes that could have been made only by high-powered rifle bullets.

This was certainly a curious, if not ominous, development.

I called out his name several times, doubtless with fear in my voice and surely with urgency. No answer. Silence — except for the whisper of the cold wind riffling through the pines and the distant, harsh cries of a pair of crows from somewhere in the woods behind the house.

What could I do? I couldn't ask any of A.'s neighbors, those folks in the trailers and shacks back along the road, if they had seen him recently. The mere mention of his name and myself as a concerned friend would have invited any of those folks to slam his door in my face, or worse. Years of living in A.'s proximity had aroused in his neighbors a certain amount of anger. I couldn't call the police. To a stranger, especially to a law enforcement official, the circumstances simply weren't that ominous. The police chief, A.'s brother-in-law, but no help for that, doubtless would have advised me to drop by again in a day or two, and if A. still hadn't moved his car, then perhaps an inquiry could begin. And though at this time his divorce from "Number Five," as he called her, had been legally consummated, A. nevertheless was still living alone, so there was as yet no new spouse, no proper "next-of-kin" to alert and interrogate.

Feeling puzzled, helpless and, increasingly, alarmed, I got back into my car and started the long drive home to Northwood. I had not gone many miles when I imagined, successively, three separate events, or eventualities, which, successively, I believed true — that is, I believed in turn that each event sufficiently explained the peculiar circumstances surrounding A.'s absence.

Event #1: Upon arriving at my home in Northwood, I built a fire in the library and was about to fix myself a cognac and soda when the phone rang. It was A. His voice was sharp, harsh, annoyed with me, as if he had been trying to reach me for several hours.

I tried to explain that I had spent most of the day photographing jays and chickadees in the snow and had stopped by his house on the way home, but he interrupted me, barking that he didn't give a damn where I'd been; he'd been arrested by his own brother-in-law, Chub Blount, and had been charged with the murder of Dora, his fifth wife. He told me that he'd been permitted one call, and he'd called me, and then, when I hadn't answered the phone, he'd decided I was probably in on the arrest somehow, so now he was calling to let me know what he thought of that kind of betrayal.

I was shocked. I assured him that I was shocked. "I didn't even know Dora was *dead*, for God's sake! And you know what I think of your brother-in-law," I reminded him. "If I had known that Dora was dead, murdered, I mean, and if for whatever reason I had thought you were responsible, you *know* I'd never have called Chub in. I probably would have called the state police, not *that* idiot," I reassured him. "Assuming, of course, that I would've called anyone. I mean, what the hell, A., you know what I thought of Dora," I said.

Apparently my words soothed him, as good sense inevitably did. Above all else, even in distress, A. was a reasonable man. In a calm voice now, he said that he wanted me to hire a lawyer for him.

"Did you do it? I mean, you know, kill her?" I asked. Perhaps he'd shot her with his 30.06 while she was sitting in his car — though I could not imagine any circumstance under which Dora might have ended up sitting in the driver's seat of A.'s Chrysler while he stood outside with his rifle. But I did want those bullet holes explained.

For several uncomfortable seconds A. snarled at me, literally snarled, like a bobcat or cougar interrupted at a meal. Then he shouted that he hadn't called me so he could confess to me, and he hadn't called to protest innocently that he was being framed by his brother-in-law. He'd called, first, to tell me what he thought of me if I had been a party to his arrest, and then to instruct me to hire a lawyer for him. Not a shyster, a *lawyer*, he bellowed. He figured it was a job that fitted my natural and acquired skills rather well. (A.'s sarcasm rarely failed to make a point, though often an obscure one.) As to whether or not he had in fact murdered his ex-wife, A. told me that if the lawyer I hired was able to convince a jury that he didn't do it, that would be the truth. If he failed, that would be the truth too, A. explained. That was why he wanted the best lawyer in the state of New Hampshire, he shouted. Did I understand?

"Yes, I understand. How do you think it happened, though? I mean, how do you think Dora was killed? How does Chub, the police, explain those bullet holes in the Chrysler?"

A. uttered a low, sneaky-sounding giggle, almost a cackle, except that he was genuinely amused. He was intrigued, he said, by my knowledge of those holes. Until now, until I had asked about them, he himself had wondered who killed Dora. But now . . . and his voice drifted back into that low, sneaky giggle.

"Now, look, A., you don't think that *I* . . ."

He assured me that he thought nothing of the kind. Besides, he pointed out, it didn't matter *what* he thought, *who* he thought had killed her. All that mattered to him was getting his case presented to a jury by the best damned lawyer in New Hampshire, and if I could find him the best damned lawyer in New Hampshire, he'd forget all about my knowledge of the three bullet holes in the Chrysler.

I agreed to the terms. I had no choice. But who could such a marvelous attorney be? I wondered. In a backward state like New Hampshire, how could there be a barrister sufficiently gifted to create the kind of awful truth A. had defined? The task of locating and hiring such a person frightened me. I am an ordinary man. I felt alone, young, inadequate.

Event #2: I departed from A.'s house, driving carefully along the rutted, rock-snared path to the main road, where I turned left, and in a moment I was beyond A.'s property and was passing the battered house trailers, tarpaper-covered shanties, and those all but deserted farmhouses. Then there was a stretch of road where for about a half-mile there were no dwellings and the dark spruce and Scotch pine woods came scruffily up to the edge of the road, darkening it, creating the effect of a shaggy tunnel or a narrow pass through a range of craggy mountains. As I entered this stretch of road, I saw a young woman standing by the side and was about to pass her when I realized who she was and what she was carrying in her arms.

It was Rochelle, A.'s twenty-six-year-old daughter, his only child and at that the child of his own late childhood. A lovely red-haired girl with long thin arms and legs, dressed in a forest green wool parka, hatless, with the hood laid back beneath her dark, tumbling, red river of hair — she was a startling figure to behold, especially when she was the last person in the world one expected to see out here, and even more especially when one realized that she was carrying a rifle, which, because of the telescopic sight attached to it, I instantly recognized as A.'s own Winchester 30.06. She had the rifle cradled under her right arm and across the front of her flat belly, with her left hand gripping the bolt as if she had just fired off a round, or was about to. She seemed distraught, shaking, green eyes darting wildly, roughly, and in the direction of the woods on the left side of the road. She did not seem to notice my car as I slowed, crossed over, and stopped beside her.

Leaning out the open window so she could recognize me, I cried, "*Rochelle!* What's the matter? What are you doing out here?"

"I'll *kill* him!" she screamed into the woods, as if I were located in that darkness rather than behind her in my car. "I'll *kill* the bastard! I'll *kill* him!"

"Where is he?"

"In there someplace," she said in a hoarse voice, as if she had been screaming for hours and had exhausted all her vocal resources but the roar. All she had left was her maximum effort; anything less collapsed of its own weight. "I know he's in there," she croaked, motioning toward the woods with the tip of the barrel. "I think I hit him once, maybe twice, at the house when he drove up. When I chased him down here, I could see he was bleeding, his face was bleeding, all over his lousy face, the bastard!"

Her own face was gathered up like a fist, her green eyes agate-hard. Her fine, even teeth were clenched, and the muscles of her long jaw worked ferociously in and out. Her delicately freckled hands had turned chalk white from the force of her grip on the rifle.

Though she had acknowledged my question by shouting her answer into the woods, she had not acknowledged my presence yet and continued to stare searchingly into the tangled darkness. With extreme care, moving slowly yet smoothly and, I hoped, gently, I got out of my car. She seemed not to notice, so I took a single step toward her; then she wheeled about on her heels and swung the gun up, slapped the butt against her right shoulder, and pointed the tip at my heart. She sighted down the barrel with care, focusing the telescope with her left hand as if she were tuning in a distant radio station.

"*Don't!*" she ordered.

I froze, one foot held delicately off the ground, both hands palm down and off to my sides, as if quieting an orchestra. "Rochelle," I said in a calm voice, "give me the gun. C'mon, honey, let me have the gun now, you don't want to kill your dad. I know you're mad at him, I know he's upset you, but you don't want to *kill* him for it, now do you, honey? C'mon, honey, let your ol' buddy have the gun, then we can sit down and talk about it." I had slowly let my foot descend to the ground and had taken a second step.

I was terrified — the sight of one of the most stable creatures I had ever known, one of the most admirably predictable and rational women I had ever met, standing wild-eyed before me with a high-powered rifle zeroed in on my thundering heart, so upset my notion of the real and expected world that anything could have happened, anything, and it would have seemed appropriate. Rochelle could have broken into a Cole Porter song and started tap-dancing her way down the road, using the rifle as a cane, waving over her shoulder at me as she pranced out of sight, the end of a musical comedy based on the exciting life of a girl revolutionary. Or she could have suddenly opened her mouth wide, as if to eat a pear, and shoving the tip of the barrel in, jammed her thumb against the trigger and blown the top of her lovely head away. Or she could have simply squeezed one finger, nothing more than that, just wrinkled her trigger finger one-sixteenth of an inch, and I would have heard the explosion, possibly would have smelled the fire and smoke, seen a shred of the narrow belt of blue sky fall into my face as I was blown back against the side of my car, my chest an erupting volcano for no more than a split second, and then Nothing, unimaginable Nothing.

With a shudder, I decided it didn't matter what happened so long as anything could happen. I took another step, then yet another, and gradually, as I neared her, she lowered the barrel of the gun until, by the time I could reach out and touch her shoulder, it was pointing at the ground. With my left hand I took the gun from her, and with my right I reached around her shoulders and drew her to me.

Suddenly she was sobbing, her bony, fragile shoulders hunched and twitching with the sobs. And then it all came out, what he had said in his answer to her letter, what her letter had said about her mother, A.'s first wife, until finally she was blubbering wetly against my chest. "Oh, I don't understand, I just don't *understand!* Why does he have to be that way, why is he so *awful? Why?*"

I sighed. It was not going to be easy for me to explain. After all, she was his daughter, his only child. And she loved him.

Event #3:
(From The New York *Times*, Wednesday, May 1, 19——.)

ABERDEEN LAKE, Dist. of Keewatin (AP) — On and off for the last twenty-four years a man with a long gray beard has lived in an empty tomb in a little used cemetery in this tiny (pop. 49) village one hundred miles below the Arctic Circle. He says, "It's nice and peaceful.

"Well, it's waterproof and nobody is going to trouble a fella living in a tomb," says the sixty-five-year-old man, who goes only by the name of Ham.

"They call it a receiving tomb. They put the bodies in there until the ground thaws and they can bury them. But they haven't used it in a long time," says the old-timer, an American who refuses to talk about his past.

He considers himself a retiree and draws a $62.50 monthly Social Security check. Does it bother him living in a cemetery?

"No, I kind of like it," he says. "You know, we all got to die sometime, and this just helps a fella get used to the idea. Besides, it's kind of nice here."

Where did he come from? What kind of life did he lead that brought him to this end. "I'm luckier than most," he says. "I got what I wanted, not what I deserved."

I read the article with slight, barely conscious interest, prodded by my daily habit of reading every article in the newspaper from beginning to end diligently, regardless of the content, but perhaps also prodded by the vaguely familiar tone of the somewhat cryptic remarks attributed to the old man, an assertiveness tempered by a strangely familiar form of personal humility, a kind of matter-of-fact pride and wisdom that I had not heard in many years. There was a small wirephoto of the graybeard above the article, and when I studied the blurred face, I recognized, in spite of the long beard, the hair, the stooped posture and the obvious aging that had taken place, my friend of long, long ago. It was A.

And thus, once again, after a lapse of what seemed an entire lifetime, I began thinking obsessively about the man. "*Where did he come from? What kind of life did he lead that brought him to this end?*" I chuckled to myself at the poor, befuddled reporter's questions and imagined A. frustrating the fellow with half-truths and outright lies, flattery and aggression. The reporter should not have been talking to A., I snorted, but *me!* He'd never learn the truth from A., not in a million years.

Believing as I did that each of the above three events, taken separately, could explain A.'s peculiar (to me) absence that Sunday afternoon in February 1975, I had reached a point in my relation to him where almost anything could happen and where whatever did happen would be believable. It would seem "natural," "right," consistent with all I had known of him before. In other words, the man had become sufficiently real to me that I could, and therefore should, write a novel about him.

It was almost four o'clock by the time I arrived at my home in Northwood. The sun was setting coldly behind the low hills, dragging a darkening gray blanket across the snowy fields and woods while the temperature tumbled fast toward zero and below. Then, as the sun dropped wholly behind the farthest hill, leaving only a sky fading from red to peach to sooty gray to deep, starry blue, a low cold wind cruised across the snow, from the colder, eastern horizon to the slightly less cold western, as if following the waning light. Then the wind was gone, like a pack of silent dogs, and the night settled motionlessly down to its business of making the icy lakes creak and boom, of making the trees snap, the streams whimper, the hibernating animals underground turn worriedly in their sleep, of making the rocks beneath the snow concentrate their mass.

Inside my house, as soon as I had built the fire to blazing in the library, I sat down at my desk, plucked my pen from the holder, and, opening a blank notebook before me, wrote in large letters on the first page, HAMILTON STARK, A NOVEL. I turned the page, and continued to write.

CHAPTER TWO

The Matrix: In Which Certain Geographic, Historic, Economic & Ethnic Factors Get Described and Thence Enter the Drama; Also Flora & Fauna & Other Environmental Marginalia; Some Local Traditions; A Fabled Place & an Early Murder There

matrix (mā′triks, ma′), n., pl. **ma-tri-ces** (mā′-tri-sēz′, ma′), **ma-trix-es.** **1.** that which gives origin or form to a thing, or which serves to enclose it: *Rome was the matrix of Western civilization.* **2.** *Anat.* a formative part, as the corium beneath the nail. **3.** *Biol.* the intercellular substance of a tissue. **4.** the fine-grained portion of a rock in which coarser crystals or rock fragments are embedded. **5.** fine material, as cement, in which coarser material in lumps, as of an aggregate, are embedded. **6.** *Mining.* gangue. **7.** *Metall.* a crystalline phase in an alloy in which other phases are embedded. **8.** *Print.* a model for casting faces. **9.** master (def. 18). **10.** (in a press or stamping machine) a multiple die or perforated block on which the material to be formed is placed. **11.** *Math.* the rectangular arrangement into rows and columns of the elements of a set or sets. **12.** a mold made by electro-forming from a disc recording, from which other discs may be pressed. **13.** (on a circuitry of an electronic computer) an array of components, diodes, magnetic storage cores, etc., for translating from one code to another. **14.** *Archaic.* the womb. [<L: female breast kept for breeding (LL:

register, orig. of such breasts), womb, parent system (of plants), deriv. of *māter* mother]

From *The Random House Dictionary of the English Language, The Unabridged Edition* (New York, 1967).

1.

How far back in time is it reasonable to push, before one detaches himself from the near bank and poles himself, guiding the drift back downstream, home again, by straddling the current at midstream, stroke over stroke down to the present? Eh? Back there the stream had narrowed, had run with a swiftness that increased geometrically with each mile as one returned to the source. There were rapids, low overhanging trees with dangerous strange beasts residing among the dark foliage; there were hidden shoals, sudden waterfalls, mythical creatures drinking at the edges of eddies and pools, caves along the banks, dawns savagely bright and silent, dusks that fell in seconds and released at their fall the cacophony of nighttime hunts. And the farther back one poled his fragile craft, the closer one came to the source (that high clear spring where a mountain toad bejeweled by sunlight squats upon a thick pelt of moss and sleeps), the more trivial seemed whatever quandary, shame, or project that characterized one's present.

How, then, to justify the well-known practice of understanding one's present by going into the past, when the farther into the past one travels, the more trivial seems the present? For if such understanding is available there, its nature at bottom would seem to be that the present is of no special significance. Why stay down there, it (the past) asks you, in that mucky, mosquito-infested, broad delta region where the muddied waters mix turgidly with the green and blue of the sea? Why indeed, when you have seen the flumed waterfalls here inland, the crystalline streambed glittering in noontime sunlight, the exotic beasts and highland orchids where the stream curls farther and farther into the mountains, through the mists to the mossy crags and the lichen-covered high plateaus?

For just look at where we, reader and writer of this book, stand now. Look at our quandary, our shame, our project. A mere crank, questions of his intentionality, of the quality of our love for him and possibilities of his love for us — that's what's got us down! A rube! A citizen of the provinces, a man whose life may well be incapable of offering posterity a single slice of cheese more than his particular sociology! How mere. Especially when to speak of love, or of cruelty, or of "demons" and the possession thereby (as indeed we must and shall), we are in all probability speaking solely from our private and peculiar, narrow versions of our very own lives. Worse, of our lives as *children!* Brats, puling, polymorphously demanding dependencies, social and genetic accidents dropped into an inappropriate time and place. We are so used to our own whining about how we never *asked* for our parents, their limitations and friends, that we forget how little our parents and their friends had to do with requesting *us.* We weren't exactly what was wanted — unteethed, limp-limbed, blind, bawling, caul-wrapped, hungry and without gratitude. What would any poor people, poor and therefore leisureless, in bad health and nasty-tempered, want with children? Or at least with children such as we were? A poor people, if, as a consequence of the quick and cheap pleasure of copulation with sick and tense bodies, it must produce children, wants them to be born fully grown, strong, intelligent, useful and filled with abiding gratitude. No people is in such dire need of a healthy slave population as a poor people in a poor land. But one of life's great ironies is that all these people get are children, and more of them than anyone else. If the reader does not yet agree, let him read some population statistics. It's enough to make a sensitive man weep and think longingly of infanticide.

But despite the irrelevance and the triviality of the place where we are standing now, it does have historical background. This poor mongrel has a pedigree. Several of them, in fact. We might prefer running with a blooded hound, but we cannot have one; perhaps we'll accept the run with our own mangy cur, even learn to admire him, if we can know something of his ancestry. For it is true that — though he may seem it and though we sometimes despise him for seeming it — he does not come wholly from nowhere out of nothing.

He springs from the Valley of the Suncook, so named for the ululating river meandering gently southerly and westerly to the Merrimack, which is, in turn, a larger, coarser stream that poles the region south of the granitic mountains and widens and fills across bumpy flatlands all the way to the sea of Massachusetts, where at last it empties its finely ground contents onto the outflowing tide and adds yet another petulant lip to the North American continental shelf. To speak solely of the Suncook River, however, is to speak, at its head, of a man-stride-wide rill that breaks across boulders thrown in springtime thaws and by snowmelt from the sides of glacial morraines. It is to speak then of a confluence of brooks, streams, creeks — the Webster, the Perry, the Crooked Run — all of them southern outlets of muskegs, ponds, small lakes, with names like Halfmoon and Brindle, Huntress, Upper Suncook and Lower Suncook. Thus, in referring to the Valley of the Suncook, and specifically to its northern terminus, one is referring to the beginning of a system, if he follow nature's path, and the end of a system, if he follow a manmade map, which inevitably traces the path of white settlement. These two paths, that of nature and that of white human settlement, and the particularities thereof, are what determine the affective history of a people springing from that region, or any region, for hundreds of years afterward, long after the paths have been worn smooth and straightened with machinery, widened and bridged, overpassed, clover-leafed and median-stripped.

It is tempting to make much of the observation that the essential movements of nature here have been from north to south, while those of white neo-European society have been from south to north. Regard the prevailing wind and water systems, the tendency of erosion to flow inevitably to the sea. What are now called the White Mountains were then ten-thousand-foot-high upthrust blocks of granite, stocky mountains in the prime of life, the craggy head of the robust Appalachian chain. In the blond valleys and sun-warmed plains below the peaks, herds of gigantic bison with horns like barrel hoops grazed peacefully, while lions the size of modern horses loped lazily along behind, keeping to the shadows of the briars and the low nut trees, waiting hungrily for a straggler or a fat calf to wander from the herd's protection. So far as is now known, this was a region without bipeds, human beings.

Then the first signs of the glaciers — lingering winter snows, each summer shorter than the one before, streams and lakes that fail one spring to boom and break from ice to water and thus they complete a full year icebound, and winds, high, relentlessly cold winds, carting across the mountain barrier moisture-laden clouds from the snow blanket of the farther north, blotting out the sun for month after month, then year after year. The herds shift the loci of their grazing circles farther south, on to the Carolinas, and even through the gaps and west into the Valley of the Mississippi. Until there comes a time when the hard icy tongue of the glacier has carved a notch in the mountain wall and has extruded enough of its body through that notch into the soft valleys beyond to drag with it a never-melting pelt, finally covering even the very peaks with a mantle of ice, accelerating its march now by making its own weather unimpededly. And as the glacier, conjoined with several separate glacial forays from the two far sides of the mountains, crunches its way across those upthrust blocks of granite and the bumpy flats beyond, great wads of earth are scraped away, huge chunks of stone are ripped free of the mountain wall, deep trenches are gouged through the effluvial plain, and all the matter, stone, till, boulders, billions of tons of black earth, all of it, is plowed ahead or is eaten by the ice and as if being digested is passed along and ground finer and finer as the head moves southward and is at last spat out at the sides or lodged deeply beneath the grinding white belly. What escapes being eaten by the glacier gets shoved ahead of it, all the way to the sea, where great blocks of ice laden with soil and rock torn from the continent hundreds of miles away crack and break of their own weight and fall tremendously into the storm-tossed sea, where as icebergs they bob and float southerly, gradually diminishing in size, eventually melting, crumbling apart like saturated lumps of sugar somewhere off Hatteras.

The glaciers are not driven back from the south. No, under the influences of forces centered deeply behind them in the arctic thermal systems, they retreat. This is not the nice distinction employed by military strategists trying to save face with an angry and hurt civilian population from which future infantries must be drawn, but rather, in the case of glacial movement, "retreat" is a scientifically descriptive term. For, truly, what could stop a glacier's scourging march across a whole continent if it did not entirely of itself slow its march, hold, and then begin to withdraw? So, too, with the glaciers that covered what is now known as New England. Simply, they began to retreat, and as they did so the skies began to clear, for weeks, then whole months at a time, while below, dark patches of wet ground showed, and then whole soggy regions, vast swamps near the coast, huge deltas, and above the deltas, gradually rising fields stuffed and swollen with smoothly ground boulders, stones, streams of gravel and sand. In the low places, there were deep cold lakes filling rapidly with fresh icemelt, spilling over the till deposited like dams at the ends, making streams that gushed with clear waters toward the plains and the sea. And as the sullen glacier moved still farther back, beyond Massachusetts, deep furrows and mile-high moraines were revealed, here and there an isolated monadnock, dripping wetly in the sunlight as if just disgorged, too tough to chew and too bulky to swallow whole. Until, finally, the White Mountains themselves stood revealed, humbler now, lower, scraped clean and smoothed, gouged with new deep valleys and notches, yet still obdurate, still planted deeply below the earth's crust, altered, yes, but not moved. While beyond the mountains, its noise daily diminishing, the glacier still retreats, leaving behind long lakes, swamps, rivers, a tough-skinned corrugation of hills and low mountains, a topsoil of gravelly land and a subsoil of boulders, clay, sand and shale. The winds die down, and for the first time in ten thousand years there are low and warm winds for a full half-year. And then the grasses appear, the low berry bushes, the fruit and nut trees, and the taller, straighter conifers. Come the forests, come the birds and beasts of the forests, for now there is plenty again — the fruits and the sorrels, the produce of the yamboo, the blooms of the yulan, all the bear-loved blood-gutted berries and wrinkled cresses, whole heavy branches of juice-slimed sloes and ferns, whortles and plums, the speckled eggs of daws, the roe of the dee, the milk of the dameen. Thickly mottled with dark shapes are the skies, for now have arrived the crested cormorant, the heron, the melancholic loon, the sharp-eyed hawk and the eagle, the sun-blotting geese, the starling, the lowly wren, the jay, and the chickadee. Churning silver are the waters of the lakes and the streams, for now spawn the salmon, the blood-flecked pike, the turgid bass, the muscular trout. Great-bodied shad surge upstream from the low warm waters near the sea, followed by waves of alewives, bream and pout. Flushed are the dark new forests with the footfall, bark and cough of the brawny bear, the roar of the urinating cougar of the claws and fangs that rend, the pad and nighttime howl of the timber wolf, the scowl of the badger, the sneak of the lynx. Add to these the fox who deceitfully reasons and stays forever hungry, the dutiful beaver, the martin, otter, muskrat and mouse — all the wee new beasties of the wood. Add to these the white-tailed deer, the rabbit, the moose with gobs of saturated moss dripping from its great jaws. Add to these the names of the hundreds not named, and fill the air with the buzz of bees, hornets, deerflies, blackflies, butterflies, the nighttime moths, dragonflies, and below, all the newts, toads, grackles, salamanders, snakes and centipedes that populate the ground beneath the great trees and the grasses, stones, logs and sweetly moldering leaves.

Now, curl a pair of great, god-sized arms and lift these names of creatures great and small, finny and fur-warmed, feathered and scaled; hold and heft all the names of the mast-high pines and spruce, the straight and the gnarled sword-hard woods, the fruit-laden, the briary, even unto the lacy ferns and maplike lichens; and cart in the god-arms all the names to the ovoid valley bisected by the stream later to be named the Suncook, barred on the south by the moraine later to be named the Blue Hills, on the north the Belknap; and here, scattering them as if sowing seeds, set the names upon the ground. Now, standing back a few leagues, see what you have made.

This is what it is: a good place for creatures capable of hunting game year-round. And a good place for creatures that are at least capable, if they cannot hunt year-round, of gathering nuts and berries and fruits and storing them against the barren winter. Creatures that must graze on long or even short grasses cannot live here, nor can creatures unable to endure long cold winters. Hummocky, rock-laden, tree-covered land bound by steep hills and potted with small shallow lakes and narrow, rapidly coursing streams, with a thin, swiftly eroded topsoil and a subsoil of sand, clay and yellow shale — this place is good only for tough, heavy-coated, pugnacious, stubborn animals, and also for birds that travel south in winter, and too, all hibernating creatures. No others can prosper and multiply under such harsh conditions. They might try it for a few generations, but sensing the approach of specieswide depletion, they inevitably drift to the south and west.

This is the pattern followed by the first bipeds, the first human beings, to appear in the region. They were, of course, Indians, coming, like the glaciers, from the north, walking down from what is now called Quebec and New Brunswick, first in small foraging bands following deer herds and moose, then in larger groups, families, groups of families, and finally whole tribes. They were from the Algonquin nation of Indians, these first arrivals — Penacooks, Pemaquids, Sasquatches, Deemolays, Awtuckits, Ogunquits, Kanvasbaks, Katshermits, Merrimacks, and so forth, one band after another, passing into the Suncook Valley from the north, usually following the valleys southward from the large lakes in the north, the Winnepesaukee, the Squam, the Ossipee, along the banks of the rivers that drain them.

But all these people, one following upon the moccasined heel of the other, after entering the Suncook Valley, soon departed for the broader, more bountiful valleys to the south, saving this region up north where the streams narrow for when, late each summer, the alewives run or a week in spring when the salmon spawn and can be easily snared in wicker weirs set into the shallow cold waters or even speared from the shore by boys. For the rest of the year, these tribes, the Narragansett, the Penacook, the Pemaquid, and so forth, lived in relative peace and ease, cultivating corn and tobacco, fishing from the rocks along the bays and estuaries, hunting deer and other sweet-tasting game like turkey and rabbit, along the coast of what later came to be known to the English as Massachusetts and Rhode Island.

The only tribe that made do with life year-round in the small northern valleys like the Suncook was the Abenooki, late arrivals from New Brunswick, a short, slightly bent, flat-nosed people who spoke an Algonquin dialect. They, unlike their neighbors to the south, were strictly hunters and gatherers. They did not make any attempt to cultivate the soil, which is just as well, given the poor quality of the soil and their lack of modern farm implements.

The Abenooki, because they were the first group of human beings to make a more or less permanent settlement in the Valley of the Suncook, are of interest here. As their economy was essentially that of hunting and gathering, with no trade for leaven, their existence was what has been called "marginal." They lived in huts constructed from birchbark, moss, leaves, and muddied grasses tied with thongs to a frame of saplings which they had broken and beaten down with stones.

Their clothing was not woven but rather made from the tanned hides of animals, deer mostly, laced loosely together with tendons and ligaments torn from the animals. They were not potters nor even weavers in any sense, nor did they possess the skills one usually associates with eastern woodland Indians, such as canoe-making, weir-weaving, tobacco-growing (though they seem to have participated in the custom of *smoking* tobacco, apparently acquiring the substance by stealing it in the summer from wandering members of the more agrarian tribes to the south and west of them), body decoration, and organized warfare. Their religious life seems to have been an extremely simple one, based on a belief in the Great Spirit as the Creator and first principle of both the visible and invisible worlds (between which worlds they made awkwardly few distinctions). Additionally, they believed in the existence of numberless woodland gnomes and minor good spirits, evidently guardians of places thought to be especially beautiful and, therefore, lucky. Similarly, places thought to be especially ugly and, therefore, unlucky were watched over by "devils," minor evil spirits. Except for these devils, there does not seem to be any larger dark spirit, or negative principle, to oppose and thus define their belief in a Creator, their so-called Great Spirit (elsewhere named Mannitoo). It does not seem that any rites were associated with the minor deities, whether to propitiate, charm, or merely to honor them, nor, surprisingly, were there even any rites associated with their belief in the Creator. Therefore, though they certainly believed in the existence and power of these several deities, the Abenooki cannot be said to have worshiped them. And while it can be said that they had numerous *customs* associated with religious life, because of the absence of ritual they cannot be said to have had a religious life as such.

Their social structure was extremely loose, based as it was

on a male-dominated family unit and sexual promiscuity. Although incest was a taboo, it was nevertheless practiced extensively, especially in winter. There seems to have been no established rite for selecting leaders, no council of elders, no father-to-son descent of authority. Simply, the largest and strongest male was usually accepted as leader until such time as he was replaced, in hand-to-hand combat or through manipulation and deceit or by simple assassination, by a younger male. The old, when they became ill or infirm, were allowed to freeze to death, usually by the others' refusal to allow them to come into the huts when the weather turned cold in mid-October. With a like tough-mindedness, sickly infants or badly injured children were drowned by their own parents. Cross-eyed children, especially females, were highly prized for their beauty, and female obesity, when limited to the lower trunk and legs, was regarded as sexually provocative. Large breasts were also praised.

Most of this information, incidentally, comes to us by way of a small body of chants or song poems, for the Abenooki, as much as they loved hunting and torture, also loved singing. Consequently, we have (from the first white explorers in the area) a number of songs, and while most are concerned exclusively with hunting and torture, a few reveal homely details of the day-to-day existence of the Abenooki. For instance, a "Hunger Chant":

Wa-wa-wa-wa-wa-wa! Wa-wa-wa!
A belly full of smoke
Turns to stone.
Ribs try to cut it
But keep on breaking off.
Wa-wa-wa-wa-wa-wa! Wa-wa-wa!
I'd chew my hands off
If I knew how to grab and hold them.

I'd eat my dog and baby boy
If they weren't so scabbed and thin.
Wa-wa-wa-wa-wa-wa! Wa-wa-wa!
(repeat)

The entire corpus of the Abenooki chants and song poems were transcribed phonetically by a pair of Jesuit missionaries, Fathers Michel LaFamme and Bruce Brôlet, who traveled in the region in the late seventeenth century, investigating reports then circulating among the Canadian Algonquin residing along the Saint Lawrence River that there were in the forests to the south of them small bands of "angry people who know nothing of a life." From the name, the Jesuit fathers had speculated that these might possibly be remnants from the voyages of the Irish monks, meditative men who supposedly had sailed across "the northern mists" in the eleventh and twelfth centuries. Naturally, when they discovered only the scattered tribes of the Abenooki scratching a living from these valleys, the fathers were disappointed, for they had hoped to locate a native brethren in Christ. Nevertheless, the two priests lived for a winter among the Abenooki in the Valley of the Suncook, studying their customs and manners, such as they were, learning their language, such as it was, and taking down, as well as they could, the Abenooki literature. This was made difficult because Abenooki, although an Algonquin dialect, is a wholly uninflected language spoken in a low, nasal monotone. There is no sound for *R* and none for *W* or *L*—so that, for instance, the phrase "drifting over the waters in a sloop" would come out: "difftingova-thatazinna-soup" (which is one of the reasons that so few Abenookis ever learned English, French or Latin). It is, of course, not a written language in any sense of the word. To complicate matters further, there are no obvious rules of syntax, and though a sharp distinction between nouns and verbs is held, none is held between adjectives and adverbs, nor are verbs declined beyond the present tense. But since verbal communication between the Abenookis surely took place, one must assume that there are whole phonemes that simply are not heard by the non-Abenooki auditor.

Against such formidable obstacles as these, LaFamme and Brôlet nevertheless were able to notate and eventually translate into Latin seventy-three entire songs, plus one hundred and forty staves from what appears to be a half-forgotten epic of creation, certain elements of which suggest a linear kinship from ancient times with the Indians of the Labrador flatlands, the so-called Graelings of the early-arriving Norsemen. A few typical selections from that long poem (called by the Abenooki "Stone-People-Long-Song") might be of interest:

Stave 12
Seal mother, take from me the sharp-toothed cold!
Take from me the deep-chest cough!
Take from me the ice-toed feet that bleed!
Take from me the banging-hard fingertips!
Let me lie here in the snowfield and die warm!

Stave 37
Ninnomakee chews on the ear of Gan the Wolf,
And Gan cries out, "Let go, Tooth-faced One!
My father is your father's only son!"
But Ninnomakee does not stop his biting mouth
Because of his far-sung thunder-like rage,
Which covers his eyes like a bloody hide,
Which stops up his ears like a lump of marrow,
Which fills his throat like a gob of seal-fat.
And when he has chewed off the ear of Gan the Wolf,
Ninnomakee of the Terrible Teeth bites Gan's face twelve times.

Stave 114
Ninnomakee's fat wife gives him the bear-coat and the grease,
And he slaps her twice and smiles the big love-smile.

"You are twice the wife the thin girl-woman makes,"
He tells her. "I slap her one time and she breaks!"

Stave 122
The time for drinking the honey has arrived again!
Ho-h-ho-h-ho-h-ho-h-hee-hee-hee!
We cook it and wait, full of jokes and wrestling.
Then we open our big mouths and pour it down,
And for five nights and days we are crazy.
Ninnomakee breaks more big trees than anyone else.
That is why the women love him and are so afraid again.

As mentioned earlier, the Abenooki, because they were the first group of humans to make a more or less permanent settlement in the Valley of the Suncook, are of interest here. One should not make too much of it, but nevertheless it does seem that, as as a society, they were preeminently well adapted to the harsh and selfish environment, its parsimony and the cruelty with which it protected itself against human exploitation. It would be a long wait before a second group of human beings would appear who were so well adapted. And as the reader has doubtless guessed by now, foremost among this second group of humans (anthropologically speaking) would be the pipefitter A., or Hamilton Stark. As a matter of fact, one might properly think of him as the single most evolved instance of a type or class of human beings which, as type or class, had made an astoundingly successful adaptation to an environment that had successfully been turning other groups away for well over a thousand years.

One additional peculiarity of the Abenooki. They were the only people to have resided in the several hinterland valleys north of the coastal plain of Massachusetts, west of the coastal plain of Maine, south of the great barrier range of mountains that crosses from Vermont through New Hampshire well into

Maine and terminates at Mount Katahdin, who were willing to defend their valleys against incursion. They defended them against the remnants of the southern tribes when these tribes began to be pushed northward by the English; they defended them against the Algonquins who, in the employ of the French, ranged southward and attempted to set up bases from which they could harass English settlements farther south; and they defended them against English and later Irish Protestant colonists who came tramping northward looking for cheap land to speculate with and sometimes even to farm. No one else, before or after, bothered to defend these lands against newcomers. It's almost as if the Abenooki knew that, because of the subtlety and the peculiar extremity of their adaptation, they were unable to live at anything approaching their present low state anywhere else. They were like duck-billed platypuses, or giraffes, or strange top-eyed fish able to survive only in extremely cold waters at great depths with very high atmospheric pressures against their bodies. Remove them from what had become a "natural" state and they would gasp for air, their eyes would bulge, their skin would dry and crack open, fissures and large warts would appear, and flopping pathetically in the mud of a truly foreign shore, they would slowly, painfully, die.

Their violence, then, their pugnaciousness and witless recalcitrance, when, for example, they were offered the alternative of removing themselves to the rich forestlands of Nova Scotia, seem to have been deeply instinctual responses to their real situation, responses prompted by a sense of themselves more subtle and perhaps more profound than any native history, oral or otherwise, would have permitted expression. They were called "irrational," "savage," "suicidal," even, by the chroniclers attached to the military forces sent out from the large coastal settlements to pacify and, if possible, remove them from their valleys — lands which, according to royal grants, charters, contracts and deeds, now belonged to companies of white Englishmen. One studies the response of the Abenooki to this particular stimulus, hoping to learn from it, and one more or less successfully draws several generalizations from that response. The difficulty is in knowing what those generalizations should be applied to. To Hamilton Stark? His family, friends, neighbors?

Perhaps, perhaps — but if so, one must also remember that there is more to explaining a single human being than the ancient history of his region allows.

Ergo: some observations less anthropological, less geographic, less distant from the true object of our study than the foregoing; by the same token, however, observations, now following, which are as wholly from outside the conscious life of the true object of our study as have been all foregoing observations.

2.

Moving northward now, from the third, fourth, and fifth generations of families of Europeans who had settled in Boston, Newburyport, Salem, Gloucester, Charlestown, Cambridge, Belmont, Concord, and on and on — the small, yet crowded, cities and villages clustered close to the coast, bays and estuaries — all those seventeenth-century business communities with theological interests and connections, whose interests and connections, of a business as well as of a theological nature, had begun to jam harshly against one another by the end of the century. Second sons often went unemployed, and third sons came up landless, too. And there seemed to be an excess of ministers and schoolmasters. What to do? What to do? One of the nicest things about being an American in that century (or in the two centuries that followed, for that matter) was the literal plenitude of land not yet populated by white people. This, of course, is an old story, well known. The second sons and their younger brothers pack up wife, ax, gun and bag of seed, and they head out for the back country, the far outback, the territory, the hinterland, the boonies.

Lemuel Stark, aet. twenty-four, out of Newburyport, Massachusetts, in 1703, with his wife, Eliza, and son, Josiah, in a company of thirteen men and twelve women and seventeen children of various ages, went forth from Newburyport on 22 April to clear and establish residence upon certaine lands near the headwaters of the Suncooke River which had been properly surveyed and marked the previous year by a party of engineers sent out for the Newburyport Northern Regional Development Association.

There they met the resident Abenookis, who, innocently, the previous summer had traded forty freshly speared salmon and twelve maple-cured cougar skins for a knife and hand mirror offered by members of the surveying party. The leader of the Indians in 1703 was a tall (for an Abenooki), muscular man named Horse. His name had been given him by a wandering Cree from the far northwest, a man who enjoyed the luxury of having actually seen horses and so knew what they looked like, which of course the Abenooki did not. It was rumored among the Abenooki that sometimes the white people stood upon and even had sex with enormous, long-tailed, big-nosed beasts, but the Abenooki word for the animal was Kiyoosee-hi-yi-ho-yo ("enormous, long-tailed, big-nosed beast that gets screwed by the white man"). When the wandering Cree had told them, first, that the animal was called by his people a "horse," and second, that the white people were in many ways dependent upon the "horse's" good nature and great strength, and third, that the tall (for an Abenooki), muscular, big-nosed boy before him looked something like a horse, the boy's family immediately changed his name from Water Lily to Horse. When later, after having passed many trials of strength and courage, he became the leader of the Abenookis residing in the Valley of the Suncook, Horse was very proud of his name, for among the Abenooki, while there were many who were named Water Lily, there was but one named Horse.

Horse, as noted above, was a physically gifted man, but he was also known to be shrewd and inventive, and among his people he was regarded as a driver of hard bargains. For instance, to their endless wonder and admiration, it was he who had succeeded in convincing the surveying party to give up the mirror and knife for a bunch of fish and furs. This is leading up to the moment, probably anticipated by now, when it can be announced that Horse was a proper match for the similarly gifted, shrewd, inventive and careful man Lemuel Stark. A classic confrontation.

It was atop Blue Job Mountain, supposedly, that the two finally met, at the end of a long chase, a foot race with a bloody dying for the loser that had begun at sunrise on the mist-blanketed bank of the Suncook. Lemuel had left the safety of the camp for an early morning leak in the bushes, and Horse, with three comrades, had surprised him at it. Lemuel ran, stuffing himself frantically back into his trousers. Horse gave chase. The others, as Abenooki are wont to do, melted back into the forest to await the outcome of the chase. If Horse lost and were slain by the white man, one of his three comrades would be able to take his place as leader of the Suncook Valley Abenooki. If, on the other hand, Horse either captured or killed the white man, all Abenookis would benefit alike, although obviously Horse would benefit the most. Even so, the Indians reasoned, it wasn't a bad idea to melt into the forest and meet back at camp and sit around all day beneath the balsams, drinking fermented honey and waiting for the race results to come in.

Lemuel ran armed with his unloaded musket. Horse was armed with the knife and mirror he had obtained the previous summer by smart swapping. Lemuel had the advantage of height and probably good speed. Horse had the advantage of knowing the country, especially the Indian paths that followed the meandering shore of the river. Both men were in excellent physical condition. The race was a toss-up.

They ran along the river, following the narrow pathway through what is now called Center Barnstead. Here Lemuel stumbled and fell, skinning his knee. Horse, not believing his good luck, hesitated, just long enough for Lemuel to scramble to his feet and speed away southward, running slightly downhill, to what's now called Barnstead Parade. Lemuel was beginning to enjoy the race, was gaining slightly on his pursuer, and was probably reaching that point of exhaustion where lightheadedness and exhilaration replace fatigue and anxiety. Horse, on the other hand, having finally realized that he was alone in his pursuit of the white man, was beginning to understand the political implications of the chase. He had to catch the white man now. If he did not, he would be humiliated in front of his people and would lose his position of leadership, probably to someone named Water Lily. Horse had a fairly well developed sense of irony.

What the author would like to do here, but because of his respect for historical truth cannot, is to describe the awful death of Lemuel Stark, suggesting, through metaphor, symbol, and literal utterance, the effect of that death on Lemuel's son,

Josiah, who, under the understandably careful care of his mother, Eliza Stark, grew up (1) to hate "Injuns" (and all other non-Caucasian racial groups, whether minorities or not), (2) to resolve personal conflicts by the use of personal violence, and (3) to adore his mother, mainly because it was through her that he received first-person testimony as to the heroic stature of his lost and long-grieved-for father. Thus her testimony:

"Your father, my son, loved you. He loved you perhaps too well, and as it turned out, not wisely enough, though that, of course, is not for me to judge, Heaven forgive me for presuming, I was not presuming, Father, it was a figure of speech, and it's just that you, Josiah, and I, my son and I, Father, it's just that we both have lived here so long, except for Thee and Thy everlasting comfort, that sometimes in our frailty we wonder and ask, Where has he gone, my husband and my son's father, why did he not come back to us, why did he leave in the first place? . . . when of course, Father, we know all the answers to those questions, don't we, Josiah? it's not easy for us, the weak and fragile vessels of Thy everlasting love, to keep ourselves from crying out in the long night of our solitude, is it, Josiah, my son, my dear sweet boy, my beloved boy, you do so resemble your father, Josiah, his black hair, and his eyes, eyes the color of Irish peat, the clear white skin, the smile, the teeth, the tiny ears . . . thank Heaven I have you, my son, else my grief for your lost father would surely break me, I fear it, I'm ashamed for it, but I am a weak woman, my son, your mother is weak, son, but you shall be strong, I know it, as your father was strong, a tall, muscular, energetic man, who loved you, my son, oh, yes, he surely loved you, and if I say he did not love you wisely but too well, I say it only because his love for you, his *love*, was what made him run from that pitiless Indian chief, that Beast of the Forest, the one they call Horse — the ugly one you have seen in the village, the same who now claims he is Christian, yes, but who cannot be, or he would confess publicly what he did to my husband, your father, and be hanged for it or thrown in a pit and slowly pressed by stones until he is crushed beneath them, forgive me, Father, for the force of my anger, I know that revenge is Thine, yet I cannot bear that the savage who slew my husband, the father of my son, I cannot *endure* that the murderer is allowed to walk easily about the village and forest like any Christian and loyal subject of the king, and if I cannot have revenge, and I know, Lord, that to continue lusting after it would only lead me sinfully to envy what power is rightfully Thine, but if I cannot have revenge, if I cannot see that savage pressed to death by stones, cannot throw the final, crushing, bone-snapping stone upon him myself, then I shall at least make sure that you, my son, know the truth, that you know your father loved you and was no coward, that you know he was not afraid, no, and that you know he now resides in the bosom of the Lord and is looking down on us, surely, and weeping at our plight and the way his good name has been smeared with mud and filth by that savage, the one called Horse, yes, my son, he would weep to see us now, his good wife and baby boy living alone on the land below the very mountain where he was cruelly slain, here on the plot of land he purchased with his honest toil the year before you were even born and a full year and a half before I myself even saw this place, this bleak and ungiving plot of earth, this scab, this mountain-shaded rockpile where the winds come all year long and bring us disease, chills, agues, where we must wake every gray morning and look out onto the mountain where your father ended his all too brief life in courageous defense of your life and my honor, for that is how it truly happened, my son, not as the savage, the heathen, Horse, would have it, no, and not as those in the village would have it, those who wish to believe that the heathen is converted so they can gain credit for it in Heaven, we both know who they are, my son, and why they choose to believe the Animal instead of the knowledge that God Himself has placed into their darkened hearts. They choose Satan, and God will surely loose His rage upon them for it, my son, just as surely as He will protect and comfort thee and me in our distress and despair, here in this tiny cabin where very morning we must wake to shade, winter and summer, shade cast by the heathen as much as by that mountain. You must not cry, Josiah, for the Lord is our shepherd, He will comfort us, the Lord and His truth, and the truth of your father's love for us, his bravery, and the treachery that followed, what we should expect from Savages but not what we should have expected from our neighbors, our friends, *Christians*, men and women who knew your father from his childhood and who chose to believe a heathen Indian chief, an Animal, a Dusky Beast of the Forest, one of Satan's own henchmen, before they would believe the Lord Himself, before they would believe even the wife of the slain man, for I told them, Josiah, just as I am telling you, have told you, will go on telling you, for I must strengthen you against the burden you will have to bear in this village as you grow into your boyhood and young manhood, strengthen you with the truth, so that someday when you are grown you will be able to redeem your poor father's stained memory and return his name to its rightful place of respect and honor among Christians, and though the people of this village choose not to believe me, I know that you will believe me, and thereby will come to know the truth of your father's life and the grandeur of his death, for I am the only one who saw it, I and the Beast who slew him, we two are the only ones who know what happened that morning, yet people have chosen to believe him because they wish to believe him converted, they wish to obtain credit for his conversion, when in fact it's *he* who has converted *them*, and they know it, they must, they cannot truly believe your father would leave his wife and son, his infant son, alone in the wilderness, just disappear into the woods, like a fox, the Indian said, that's how he said it when they asked him, What happened to Lemuel Stark? they asked when the Heathen had learned to speak a few words of English in that *awful* way of theirs, enough to pretend he had converted to Christ, and he told them, Like a fox, into the woods, we talk and him go like fox into woods, gone, big smile on face, smile like fox, Horse told them, and they all looked at each other and nodded, yes, how true, how sad for his wife and son, to desert them at their hour of greatest need and dependency, but they *forgot, they forgot that I saw your father leave*, Josiah, that morning, the dawning of our second day in this wilderness, for we were all camped out on the shore of the river, near where Dame Edna now lives, very early in the morning, just at sunrise, and the mist was floating low over the dark, nearly still water, and I opened my eyes and saw your father rise from his pallet beside me, and before he left my side, he whispered that he wanted to look at the mist and the still water and watch the light change as the sun rose, for your father was a tender man, not a coward, a deeply tender and God-fearing man, though he was not a man who talked easily of his Love of God, not like these others who now surround us, he was a *true* Christian, a quiet man tender enough to wish to see the sunrise his second day in the wilderness, in the valley where he had chosen to build his home and live out a peaceful God-fearing life in the comfort and love of his family, and so eager was he to watch the light change as the sun rose over the river that he walked away from the camp alone, carrying only his musket, doubtless in the event that he saw some game, a deer or rabbit, that he could bring back to share in camp with the company of people he thought were his friends, all of them people from the town he had been born and raised in, people he had known all his life and with whom he had joined in this venture into the wilderness, and I lay there next to his pallet with you at my breast, and I smiled up into his broad face, and surely, as surely as God is in His Heaven, as surely as anything on this earth exists, I would have known if that man was going to leave us, was going to walk off and disappear into the forests, leaving behind his wife and baby, alone, without money or possessions, with nothing but a seven-hundred acre plot of rock- and tree-covered land in the wilderness, I would have known that, such things cannot be hidden, they are too horrible, too inhuman, for me not to have known that, a man's wife knows certain things about him that no one else may ever know, and oh, Josiah, oh, my son, I would have known if your father, that early morning when he stepped into the bushes at the edge of the clearing by the river, were deserting us, were leaving us here to choose between scratching pitifully in desolate and deprived isolation on this land or enslaving ourselves to the charity of a village that would sooner believe an Indian's version of a tale than a man's own true wife's version, and I saw his face as he left my side, Josiah, *I saw his face*, remember that, for that's how I know the true story of what actually happened once his square-shouldered form had disappeared into the tangle of bushes at the edge of the clearing, I know what happened then, I know that he was set upon in cunning silence by Horse and a band of bloodthirsty Abenooki, and I know that your father, instantly deciding that the Indians would be able to overcome and slay the party of sleeping Christians, chose to run instead of fight, chose to lead that pack of savages as far as he could from the place where his friends, his young wife, and most important, his baby son, lay sleeping, and so, indeed, he ran, a strong young man who, you may enjoy knowing, was a well-known runner, once said to be the best long-distance runner in the entire colony of Massachusetts, a man who could run all day long, from Hopkinton Green all the way to Boston Common once in only a little over two hours, thought by some to be a miracle, thus when your father decided to run from those savages, he was not behaving in a cowardly manner, oh, no, he was instead choosing to employ against them the strongest weapon he owned, his ability as a runner, which he was to use so effectively that no one would ever know of his decision, of his great bravery and love, so that the very people he saved from death, and worse, were later to deride your father's memory and to pity me, *pity*, pity a woman and child they should *honor* instead, as the wife and son of a hero, the only hero this village has so far produced and probably the only one it ever will produce, unless it be a son of Lemuel Stark or a son destined to spring from that seed in some future time, a hero who will know the truth of Lemuel Stark's life and death and therefore will not believe the fiction, who will know instead that Lemuel Stark courageously led the ravening pack of Abenookis along the river and away from the camp all the way to Blue Job Mountain, where, tireless, he ran ahead of the savages, who, like hounds with one replacing the other as the lead hound grew tired, pursued screaming behind with axes and knives and other murderous devices brandished above their heads, led that pack up the side of the mountain that towered above the very plot of land he had chosen for a homesite, led them up the tortuously brambled and tangled path to the craggy top, where no trees grew, where the cold winds scraped every living thing away, scourging it, leaving only boulders, crags, and the sky above—and there, at last, he turned and faced his pursuers, for there was nowhere farther to run unless he could leap into the sky, and to accomplish that, he needed his murderers' aid, which they eagerly provided, first the brutal, sly Horse, then each of his followers, like Brutus and the vicious Romans, one after the other sinking his dagger into your father's body, a dozen, a hundred blows, each of them mortal, so that after the first blow your father's soul had flown away to Heaven, releasing him from his torn and bleeding body, leaving behind, atop the mountain, a pack of satanic savages tearing at a mere chunk of flesh, while far below, by the river, a gathering of Christians were beginning to wonder where their friend had gone, and a wife was beginning to worry that something terrible had happened to him, and an infant son was beginning to wake hungrily from his peaceful sleep . . ."

CHAPTER THREE

Three Tales from His Childhood

TRUTHFULLY, I PLANNED from the beginning to bring into the narrative at precisely this point Rochelle's version of three tales told to her by her father when she was a child. Or at least that is what she claims. It's quite possible that she invented them herself (quite unlike her, however; her methods of composition depend heavily on observation and memory; she leaves formalism, fantasy, hallucination, meditation, etc., to others).

Let us think of this sequence of tales as coming from Rochelle's own novel about her father, a project I will describe and speculate on in some detail later. At this moment I am concerned with her lovely, fragile ambivalence toward her father, a man she believes is either a demon himself or is merely possessed by one. I am also concerned that she believes it was not always true that her father either is a demon or is possessed by one. She believes that when she was a child, a young child, but one of indeterminate age, it seemed to her that her father loved her. That's very important. It may be the hinge of her ambivalence. These tales are important to her (important to me for other reasons, which doubtless will soon become apparent) because it seemed to her that her father never loved her as much again as when he would take her like a flower into the curl of his huge arm and, at her urging, tell her tales from his childhood. Or so she believes.

Only three of those tales from the many that he told her remain with her today, perhaps because, above all his other stories, it was these three that bore significance for him, telling them, as he apparently did, three and four times over, when he never repeated any other tale even once. And too, it may be only that these three bore significance, later, for Rochelle herself, when, as emblems of an as-yet-unrevealed future, they foretold either the name of the demon he would become or the name of the demon who became him. Regardless, it was with stories such as these, tales from his childhood, that she first learned to perceive her father's present perfected state (her very words), and that is the context in which, in her attempt at a novel, she offered them to others. It is not, of course, the context provided here, in spite of the fact that the prose style and narrative form are strictly Rochelle's. The context offered here, my personal contribution, is merely the frame.

The Fighting Cocks

Every morning Hamilton Stark [In Rochelle's ms., this character is named Alvin Stock; for obvious reasons, I have substituted the name of the person she was really writing about. More on this later. The author.] fed and watered his father's fighting cocks. His father had told him that it was his "job," and for doing it Ham received every Sunday a small amount of money, which his father told him was called an "allowance."

Ham also had to feed and water the chickens, but because he enjoyed doing that, he didn't consider it part of his "job." He had chosen a name for each of the ten hens, and whenever he discovered a gravel-colored egg in one of the nests, he thanked whichever bird had laid it, saying quietly in the dusty light of the henhouse, "Thank you, Amy. Thank you, Jane. Thank you, Harriet."

Living in the henhouse with the hens was a fat old rooster named Henry. He was a Rhode Island red, like the hens. To Ham, Henry seemed shy, especially compared to the fighting cocks, because he only crowed twice a day, at sunrise and sunset, and quietly at that (unlike the fighting cocks, who crowed loudly and constantly). Ham liked Henry, and in spite of his shyness, Henry seemed pretty friendly toward Ham too. Not as friendly as the hens, maybe, but surely more friendly than those fighting cocks.

They were bantam fighting cocks, half the size of Henry and the other Rhode Island reds, but so fierce they had to be kept inside wire mesh cages in their own special corner of the henhouse. Also, they had their own caged sections of the henyard, which they got to in warm weather by way of their own little doorways. There were only two of them, and Ham's father had named them Jack and Gene, after two famous boxers. "All these guys know is fighting," he had said. "You wouldn't want me to name them after a couple of violin players, would you?"

The fighting cocks made Ham's father happy. He had brought them home with him, their cages stashed in the back of his pickup truck, early one summer evening, after having spent several hours in Pittsfield at the Bonnie Aire Café with some friends. He had bought them from a man he had met there, a lumberman from Canada who was going out west by train and couldn't take them with him.

That first night Ham's father had talked excitedly about staging cockfights with Jack and Gene. Even though he'd never actually seen a cockfight, he figured there wasn't much to it once you had a pair of fighting cocks. Ham's mother said that she really wasn't interested in anything that had to do with animals such as that, and she had gone into the kitchen to wash the supper dishes. Then Ham's father had fallen asleep in his chair by the radio.

As soon as he realized that his father had fallen asleep, Ham crept over to the cages, which his father had placed on the floor next to his easy chair, and he studied the strange-looking birds. The one named Jack was red, the one named Gene was yellow, and they both looked fiery — fast, sharp, sudden little birds with wildly round eyes, short orange combs, beaks like the points of scissors, and long knifelike spurs attached to the backs of their legs. They reminded Ham of snakes — their cold, unblinking eyes, the way they held their bodies motionless while they watched him, always from the side, turning only their wedge-shaped heads as Ham moved in a careful circle around their cages.

Finally he sat down on the floor next to the cages. His father was snoring. Reaching out one hand, Ham brushed the top of Jack's cage and quickly yanked his hand back. The bird didn't move. Trying the same thing with Gene, he joggled the cage a bit, knocking the bird off-balance for a second, but getting no other response from it. Moving back to Jack's cage, he once again reached toward the mesh, and just as he felt the touch of the cold wire against his fingertips, he realized that the bird had lanced the palm of his hand with its beak, and a hot flower of pain filled his hand and shot up the length of his arm.

He screamed, and his father woke up, and his mother came running in from the kitchen. Blood was pouring from a small hole in the palm of his hand all over his flannel pajamas and bare feet. Ham kept screaming and slapping his hand against himself as if a tiny spot of fire were stuck to it.

Wrapping his hand with the dishcloth she had been carrying, his mother hurried him upstairs to the bathroom, where, after a while, she was able to calm him and wash and dress his wound. Then she took him into his room and helped him put on a clean pair of pajamas and tucked him into bed.

Kissing him good-night, she said, "Don't be afraid," in a voice that helped him not to be afraid, because it was a voice that told him she was not afraid.

Then she went downstairs, and he could hear her talking to his father, though he could not hear the words. Several times his father interrupted her, but she quickly resumed talking.

After a few minutes his father started talking, and his mother began to interrupt, but he kept on talking in his low, steady voice. And when he finished, he left the living room and came into the hall and started up the stairs.

He came into Ham's room and sat down at the foot of the bed. "Let me see your hand, son."

Ham extended his gauze-wrapped hand to his father, who examined the dressing for a second, then returned it. "Still hurt?"

"A little," Ham said somberly.

"A lot, I bet."

"Yes, a lot."

"Did you learn something?"

"Yes. I guess so."

"What?"

"To stay away from your fighting cocks?" he tried.

"No, not exactly," his father said to him. "I don't want you to be *afraid* of them, boy. And if you just stayed away from them, that's all you'd be. Afraid. I want you to *respect* them. Do you understand the difference?" his father asked. "Respecting something that can hurt you is different from just being afraid of it. And to respect the fighting cocks you're going to have to deal with them face to face. Maybe that way you'll get over being afraid of them," he promised. "Do you understand?"

"No . . . not really. Maybe I do."

"Well, it doesn't matter. You will," his father told him. And then he told him that he had a "job" for him. Every morning from then on Ham would have to feed and water the hens and rooster, including the fighting cocks. He would start the next morning, when they would do it together, so he'd know how much corn to give them and how to handle the fighting cocks so they wouldn't hurt him or escape from their cages. But after that he would have to do it alone. It was a "job," his father explained, because he was going to be paid for it — fifteen cents a week, every Sunday morning before church.

But Ham could not stop being afraid of the fighting cocks. He might have if one morning early that first week Gene, the yellow one, had not nipped off a piece of the meat of his hand between thumb and forefinger. After pitching corn into Gene's cage, Ham simply had not been fast enough in pulling his hand away, and the bird had got him.

His father had showed him how to do it, but true safety depended on speed, so he was not sorry for Ham. "If you'd done it the way I showed you, he never would have got you. You've still got to learn how to respect those birds. It's not *fear* that'll get your hand out of that cage in time. It's respect."

So Ham had concentrated on speed that he believed was derived from respect rather than from fear. He practiced on old Henry, the Rhode Island red, whom he knew he respected and of whom he had no fear whatsoever. He would walk into the henhouse carrying a can of corn, and extending a handful of it, he would call, "Here, Henry! Here, Henry! Corn, Henry!" and the bird, head cocked to one side like a partially deaf old man, would stalk somewhat wobbly toward the boy, and when his beak was a few inches from Ham's hand, the boy would throw the corn onto the cold, bare ground, and Henry would dive for it.

If that's what respect feels like, Ham thought, I like it. I especially like it better than being frightened.

Nevertheless, when it came time to feed the fighting cocks, the only speed Ham developed seemed to depend on fear. He was terrified of the birds — their endless anger, their suddenness, the weapons they carried. Whenever he neared their twin cages in the corner of the henhouse, his hands started to throb, his arms grew weak, and his back and shoulder muscles stiffened. One night he dreamed that as he opened the sliding door to feed Jack, both cocks had flown out and had furiously attacked his face, hunting madly for his eyes, and he had awakened screaming. When his mother tried to get him to tell her about the dream that had frightened him, he had refused to tell her. "I can't remember," he had lied.

Throughout the fall, Ham struggled to overcome his fear of the fighting cocks. The birds had grown used to his feeding and watering them every morning, so they no longer treated his arrival as a chance to attack or escape but instead waited patiently for their food, which, as soon as Ham had slid back the door to their cage, they greedily devoured, swinging their heads like short hatchets swiftly chopping the corn to bits.

In spite of this change in the birds' expectations regarding Ham's arrival, a change that in some sense gave them a measure of reliability and even a type of kindness toward him, he was still frightened of them, and he continued to move his hand with the food or water dish in and out of their cages as if he were plucking hot coals from a fire. He tried to respect them for their new restraint, but he couldn't. He knew that the reason they were no longer flying at him was merely because they were hungry and had realized that it was his job to feed them.

They didn't like their cages, especially when every day the hens and old Henry left the henhouse to scratch in the fenced-in yard outside. Also, the daytime proximity of Henry and his harem amiably socializing together seemed to enrage the fighting cocks, and every hour or so the pair would crow angrily at the other birds. As always, Henry continued to crow only at sunrise and sunset.

Ham's father no longer talked about arranging cockfights and making lots of money from Jack and Gene. Ham's mother explained that it was illegal anyhow. "And with good reason," she had said angrily, but that was as much as she would say.

Every Sunday morning, before Ham and his mother got into the pickup truck and drove to the church in the Center, his father, who never went to church except at Christmas and Easter, paid Ham his fifteen cents — a dime and a nickel. "Put the nickel in the collection plate. Save the dime," he told his son each time he paid him.

And Ham did save the dimes. The first Sunday he had been paid, he had taken the calendar down from the kitchen wall, and studying it a while, had calculated that by Christmas he would have saved almost two dollars, which, he decided, he would use to buy Christmas presents — for his parents and his cousins. Until then, he had been too young to have any money of his own, and he had not been able to buy any presents for anyone. Like a baby, he had been forced only to accept. But now that he had a job, he was not a baby anymore.

Then one Sunday morning in early December, after it had snowed heavily all night long, the milky, overcast sky in the morning and the dense silence of the first snow caused everyone in the family to sleep a few minutes later than usual. Even old Henry overslept and didn't crow until almost eight o'clock — a half-hour late at that time of the year.

In a rush to feed and water the birds, Ham neglected to close the door to Jack's cage with the snap that locked it. He hurried back through the foot-deep snow to the house, and while his father shoveled out the long driveway to the road, he gulped down his breakfast and got dressed for church. Before he and his mother left, his father paid him.

Later, when they returned from church and walked into the kitchen, his father said somberly to Ham, "Leave your coat on, boy. I want you to come out to the henhouse and see something." He got up from his chair, put on his own coat and hat, and led his son outside and along the narrow path he had shoveled to the henhouse.

At the door to the henhouse, his father stopped and lit a cigarette. Then he said, "Go on in," and Ham swung open the door and stepped inside.

The cold-eyed fighting cocks, locked inside their cages, were striding rapidly back and forth. Across from them, in the farthest dark corner of the henhouse, the hens were huddled silently together in a rippling mass, all of them facing the wall. And in the center of the packed dirt floor lay the body of old Henry, shredded at the breast and head, with a flurry of blood-tipped feathers scattered about it on the floor.

Ham turned around and stepped back outside to where his father stood smoking and waiting for him. The sky had begun to clear, and the snow glared brightly in the sunlight, so that for several seconds Ham could not see.

He heard his father say, "You know what happened, don't you?"

Ham tried not to cry and finally succeeded and answered, "The fighting cocks killed Henry."

"You forgot to close Jack's cage this morning, and after you and your mother left, all hell broke loose. By the time I got out here, Jack had killed the rooster and scared the hens so bad they probably won't lay till spring."

Ham said that he was sorry. He said it several times because it felt strange to him when he said it, almost as if he didn't mean it, as if somehow he were glad that Henry was dead and the hens wouldn't lay.

His father told him that being sorry never changed anything in this world. Never. "So the first thing you're going to do is buy a new rooster for those hens. If we're lucky we'll get them laying again. It'll probably help if we put the fighting cocks out in the barn right away, so this afternoon I'll build a couple of coops for them out there. Up to now I kept them in here because it was easier for you to feed them all at once. Now it'll be harder for you," he said grimly.

"How much will a new rooster cost?" Ham asked, knowing the answer even before he heard it.

"Two or three dollars," his father said, flicking his cigarette butt into the snowbank and heading for the house.

Ham stood there alone for a few seconds and then started running to catch up to his father, who had almost reached the house.

The Drunken Pigs

In certain years the family raised a pig. Always Poland China pigs. But there was a period of about five years when they were raising two pigs, every spring butchering the older of the two and replacing it immediately with a young one. In two years that pig would weigh one hundred and fifty pounds or more, and its turn, as the older of the pair, would have arrived.

By that time Ham, whose responsibility it was to feed them, would've grown attached to the bristly, pinkish white beast, so he was grateful that every time his father and Archie Carr, the butcher, packed one of the pigs into the back of Archie's truck and drove off with it, they left behind a football-shaped and -sized piglet, so small it had to be fenced separately for a while to protect it from the clumsy, thrashing bulk of the remaining adult pig.

"Pigs don't get along until they're about the same size," Ham's father had explained. "Like people." Then he had laughed down lightly at his son, and touching the boy's coal black hair with his enormous fingertips had said, "Naw, not like people."

Ham knew that they raised the pigs to kill and eat and that it saved them a lot of money. It was wartime, and even though his father worked hard every day as a plumber, Ham knew that they were poor, so he tried to think about the pigs the way he thought about the vegetable garden.

It wasn't easy. The pigs themselves made it difficult for him. They had too much character for it. Certainly they rooted like potatoes in the dark ground of the pigpen, but sometimes Ham would stand on the rough board fencing of the pen and watch them snuffle through the dirt, and when the pigs realized that he was there, they'd stare up at him and wrinkle the loamy surface of the dirt with their buried noses, as if signaling to him. Besides, the pigs *ate* potatoes — or at least they ate the peelings, whole buckets of them, left over from Ham's mother's cooking at the end of each week.

And yes, it was true that the pigs were in fact shaped more like a summer squash than anything else — they surely weren't shaped like animals, or people. Rounded at the ends, long and smooth-sided, so fat their tiny legs in soft ground were almost invisible, with a tendril-like tail at one end and leafy ears at the other, it should have been easy to think of them as nothing more than gigantic pinkish summer squashes. Except of course that they ate squashes, ate greedily the seedy cores that Ham's mother scraped away when she was canning for the winter.

Another thing that made it hard for Ham to think of the pigs in the same way he thought of the vegetables from the garden was that the pigs made noises, grunts and loud, high squeals, which Ham thought he understood. One time the pigs broke loose from the pen and were very hard to find and catch because, once loose, they remained silent and out of sight. But when Ham's mother discovered one of them rummaging noiselessly through her geranium bed over on the shady side of the house, the pig had started squealing loudly and had headed straight for the pigpen. The other pig, the older one, had wandered out behind the barn and had fallen through the wooden platform that covered an old unused well back there. Twelve feet down, standing in a foot of water in total darkness, the pig remained silent until Ham and his father, seeing that the cover had been broken, walked over to the well and peered down, and only then did the pig begin to squeal for help.

Also, the pigs liked Ham. Or at least it seemed to him that they did. They let him scratch their dry, scaly backs and smooth foreheads and often came to the fence when they saw him there. In calm silence the beasts would poke their snouts between the slats, and he would scratch them. One pig would even let Ham place two fingertips of one hand a short ways into its nostrils, dime-sized openings, as long as with his other hand the boy kept scratching the bony ridge of the snout.

They tried not to name the pigs. His father had pointed out that if they didn't give them names, it would help Ham avoid becoming too fond of them. "They're not pets. Remember that. No more reason to name a pig you're going to eat in a year or two than name a damn apple tree," he had explained.

Ham's mother had agreed, but later, when Ham accidentally revealed to her that on his own he had secretly continued naming the pigs year after year, she had merely smiled. Because he had referred to only one of the pigs by name, Anne, she asked him the name of the other.

"Tricksie. I named her that because she looks like the one we had two years ago, and her name was Tricksie too," he told her, pointing out the pig's unusually long snout and small ears.

"Tricksie and Anne. Why Anne?"

"I don't know. It just seemed to fit her," he said. Then he asked her not to tell his father that he had named the pigs, and she assured him that she wouldn't.

The September that Tricksie began her final season as a pig and Anne was more than half-grown, Ham and his mother harvested an unusually large crop of grapes. They were Concord grapes, large and purple and darkly sweet, that grew from several clusters of vines in front of the garden and along the south-facing side of the road.

For a week, every afternoon when school was out Ham would step down from the school bus and walk to the grapevines and work alongside his mother until suppertime. These were warm, pleasant afternoons for him, picking the dusky grapes in the golden September sunlight, talking quietly with his mother as they worked, chatting of school, his friends, his new teacher. He also liked asking her about what he was like when he was a baby, and she apparently enjoyed telling him. He asked her why she didn't have another baby, and she said, "Maybe I will," in such a way that he figured it was a decision. And that turned out to be the year before his sister Jody was born.

When he and his mother had finally picked all the grapes, having stored them each night in close-woven baskets in the cellar, his mother started making jelly with them. She'd never made grape jelly before, had never gathered a large enough crop, and she was excited at the prospect. She washed the grapes, and squashed them, and separated the skins and seeds from the pulp, the pulp from the juice. She saved the juice in Mason jars and used the cleaned pulp for the jelly. The skins and seeds, sloshing thickly in a five-gallon tub like a purple stew, she decided to feed to the pigs.

That afternoon when Ham got home from school, she asked him to carry the tub out to the pigpen and leave it for them. He dipped his fingers into the gooey mass and tasted it: sweet, and a little bit sour at the edges. But he was sure that the pigs, after a daily diet of grain mash and water, would consider it a treat.

Eagerly, he dragged the heavy tub across the back yard to the end of the barn where the pigpen was located, swung back the gate, and slid the tub inside. Closing the gate, he climbed up on the fence and watched Tricksie and Anne hungrily shove their snouts into the mushy substance.

After a few moments, the animals' rapid eating began to slow, and Ham, bored, left them alone and returned to the house. He wondered if, after such a huge afternoon meal, they'd be hungry again in the morning, and he decided yes, because, after all, they were pigs, weren't they?

The next morning, as he always did, Ham got up, dressed, came downstairs, and while his mother made breakfast, he went out to feed and water the hens, his father's fighting cocks, and the pigs. These were his daily chores. It was a sparkling clear morning, cloudless and dry, with a light frost that silvered the grass and made it crackle under his feet as he walked. He went to the henhouse first, completed his tasks there, and went on to the pigpen, lugging the bucket of watery grain mash he had made up in the barn.

As he rounded the corner of the barn and neared the pen, he started to call, "Soo-ee! Soo-ee! Here, pig-pig-pig!" Then he saw them. Tricksie, the larger of the two, was lying on her side near the fence, facing away from it. Anne was also lying down, a few feet beyond Tricksie. Ham thought they were sleeping, so he called again, expecting them to scramble awkwardly to their feet and rush to the trough. When they failed to respond to his second call, he thought, They must be full from yesterday's extra meal.

But then, coming closer to the fence, he realized that both pigs, though still the same size in relation to each other, in fact had nearly doubled in size. They both seemed as large and as round as hills, and as inert.

He put the bucket on the ground, reached around for a stick, and after a few seconds found the long, pointed maple branch he sometimes used to prod the pigs away from the trough while he filled it. Reaching through the slats of the fence with the stick, he poked Tricksie on the back, but got no result. She lay there as if she were a huge pile of sand.

Again he poked her. Nothing.

He then saw a purple trickle, like a string, from the pig's fig-shaped anus, and he knew that she was dead. He looked over at Anne and saw the same purple string dribbling down the inside of one of her hams, and he knew that both pigs were dead.

Grabbing the stick firmly, he started whacking it against Tricksie's hindquarters, her back, her swollen belly, swinging the stick in as long an arc as he could, whacking the pig's body all the way up to the head, which he couldn't quite reach, so he pitched the stick into the pen, climbed over the fence and jumped down into the muck, where he picked up the stick and resumed beating the carcass, swinging the stick from over his head, bringing it down hard against the pig's ears, eyes, and snout.

He moved to the other pig and began to thrash its belly and head, too, again and again, when at last the stick broke off in his hand. He threw the piece of wood away and stood there in the deep, dark mud, weeping, and through his clenched teeth brokenly cursing his mother, calling her stupid, stupid, stupid.

The Erotic Mouse

The winter that Ham's sister Jody was born, his mother asked him from then on when he was playing in the house to please play in the front room. He was nine that year, and because he liked building things, he took up a lot of room when he was playing and usually left a great clutter behind him. This was why his mother, still tired from having the baby and too busy with feeding and caring for her to cope with Ham's expansive play and the resulting mess, had insisted. "You never pick up after yourself, so from now on all your puzzles and model planes, *all* of it, gets done in the front room!"

The front room was an unfinished first-floor room to the right of the stairway as one entered the house, opposite the living room. In an earlier time it would have been a front parlor, a room set aside for special social events only. In size and window arrangements it matched the living room. It was almost exactly twenty feet square, with two windows on the front wall and two on the side, a door that led from the front hallway and another that led directly into the back downstairs bedroom.

A standard Cape built late in the eighteenth century, the house, essentially foursquare, was filled to the eaves with symmetries. Downstairs, one could go from any one room to the fourth by walking in a circle centered on the chimney. Upstairs, the four small bedrooms, one of which Ham's father had converted into a bathroom, fanned out from the chimney like the arms of a Maltese cross, all four equal in size and placement. Ham's mother and father slept downstairs in the large bedroom, and Ham slept alone upstairs — at least until his sister Jody was no longer an infant, when one of the small bedrooms would be hers.

For years, ever since Ham could remember, the front parlor had remained empty, cold and unused — except when his cousins from Massachusetts came up to visit in the summer. Then, because of the mess and the noise of the three children, Ham's mother had insisted, as she would later for Ham alone, that they play there. Which they did, happily. It provided them with the privacy and freedom to make their noise and clutter uninhibitedly.

But now, for reasons Ham could not identify, he was reluctant to use the front room. For a long time he had avoided even entering the room. Unable to explain his reluctance to himself, he surely was unable to explain it to his mother, and all he could do was shrug off her questions and say, "I don't know, I just *hate* that room."

Eventually, however, he relented. One March afternoon he moved all his puzzles and games, his Erector set and tools, his model airplanes and his drawing pads and crayons and watercolors, into the front room, one thing at a time, slowly, as if he had been ordered to move out of the house altogether.

The following afternoon he returned home from school,

and while he was sitting on the floor in the middle of the bare room, working on a balsa and tissue paper model of a P-47 Warhawk, he remembered the last time he had spent an afternoon there. It was when, the previous summer, almost a full year ago, his two cousins from Massachusetts had been "sent to the country" by their parents. Ham liked his cousins, especially the boy, Daniel, who was his age. But he also liked the girl, Virginia, even though she was older than the boys by four full years. Her parents had nicknamed her Ginger, and Ham had always assumed that it was because of her reddish hair, which somehow reminded him of what ginger looked like. She was a good-natured and attentive girl, and she never seemed to object to keeping company with two boys four years younger than she. She was able to lead them without necessarily dominating them, achieving a balance that pleased all three and, for Ham's mother, making the chore of suddenly having to care for three children less strenuous than it might have been.

But the last time they had come up to visit, Ginger had changed. Sullen, withdrawn and aloof from the boys, she had preferred staying in the kitchen with Ham's mother to playing in the front room or, on sunny days, out in the barn and yard with the boys. Ham saw immediately that she had changed. She spoke to him in a voice heavy with sarcasm and condescension, and she treated her brother Daniel with outright contempt.

"What's with her?" Ham asked Daniel after Ginger had sneered at the boys' request that she join them in a game of Monopoly. It was raining, and the boys were sitting by a window in the front room, slightly bored, watching the rain dribble down the glass.

"She's big stuff now," Daniel explained. "She thinks she's Miss America. All she does at home is look in the mirror. At night she locks herself in her bedroom and studies her titties in the mirror. No kidding, I seen her. I looked through the keyhole once an' saw her doing it."

"Doing what?"

"Looking at her titties."

"Her *titties?* Has she got *those?*" Ham didn't remember noticing any pointy things protruding from her chest when she arrived.

"Yeah, little bitty titties!" Daniel laughed. "I seen 'em, lots of times."

"How? Does she show them to you?"

"Naw. But I look at her through the keyhole in her bedroom door, and sometimes I walk in on her when she's taking a bath or getting dressed or something, like it was an accident. Boy, she hates that. And sometimes I sneak up on her from behind and yank up her shirt or sweater and take a look and run away before she can even hit me. She doesn't run as fast as she used to, so it's real easy."

"Yeah?" Ham was astonished by these turns in his cousins' lives, and he was equally astonished by Daniel's boldness.

"You want to see 'em?"

"See what?"

"Her boobs, the titties, stupid!"

"Sure," Ham quickly answered. "How?"

"Easy. You call her in here, tell her you want her to explain something to you, something like about the Monopoly rules, and I'll circle around through the living room and sneak up behind her and yank up her shirt. Okay? Got it?"

"Sure."

"But when I do, you better be ready to take off, because she really gets mad," Daniel warned.

Ham said he'd be ready, and Daniel went out of the front room into the living room. Then Ham started calling Ginger to come and explain something to him. "A Monopoly rule!" he yelled.

She sighed, got up from the kitchen table, and strolled through the downstairs bedroom to the front room. When she appeared at the door and asked, "Okay, what is it?" Ham momentarily lost his courage and was about to say "Never mind," when he saw Daniel tiptoeing out of the bedroom behind her, his blue eyes gleaming excitedly, his fingers and hands poised to grab her shirttail, which he did, snapping it up to her armpits and exposing to Ham's amazed eyes a tiny white brassiere strapped across her chest. Then, as she screamed, Ham started running, backward and out the door to the living room, through the living room to the kitchen and into the bedroom, where he ran into Ginger, who had remained standing in the doorway, her arms folded defiantly across her chest. Daniel, who had first fled into the kitchen and then had turned to follow Ham as he passed through, bumped into his cousin from behind and yelled, "Hurry up! Get going!" And then he saw her too.

They started to spin around and head back through the kitchen again, but she said, "Forget it, Daniel! I'm through chasing you. If you two want to be disgusting little sex fiends, go ahead. Here, take a good look," she said, and she lifted her blouse and showed them her brassiere. "Satisfied?"

Ham felt his ears redden at the sight, and he turned around and ran from the room, all the way upstairs to his bedroom, where he sat down on the bed and waited for Daniel to come looking for him. While he waited, he promised himself, over and over, that he'd never look at Ginger's titties again, no matter what her brother said, never.

Except when he happened to be in the front room, he hadn't thought about it since it had happened. It was like almost forgetting it, or like having only dreamed it, parts of it — the part where Daniel sneaks up behind her, his eyes gleaming, his fingers outstretched and hooked a little, like Dracula's, while Ginger stands in front of the door to the bedroom, talking peacefully to Ham about the Monopoly rules, when suddenly she bares her breasts to him, stands there leering, calling him a disgusting little sex fiend. That's what he remembered whenever he had to spend more than a minute or two alone in the front room.

And inevitably, if he remained there, he remembered two other things, both of which caused him discomfort that was extreme and similar in feeling to the discomfort caused by the first memory. Like the one, the other memories were of events that had taken place in the front room. In one of them, he is with Ginger. She is about ten, and he is only six, and they are looking at each other's genitals, touching them with fingertips, prodding, pulling tissue back, scrutinizing with excrutiatingly gentle curiosity their respectively tiny organs.

They were not found out. No one burst in on them and pointed a huge finger and called them disgusting little sex fiends. Yet the memory gave Ham terrible discomfort, a deep sense of shame, and always, if at that moment he did not leave the front room, he would remember the other event that had taken place there. He would remember one spring morning, a Sunday before church, going into the front room from his parents' bedroom, taking a short cut to the stairs, and as he runs through the room, he glimpses a tiny mouse huddled on the fireplace hearthstone, a brown mouse the size of a man's thumb caught in a brick-walled corner. Ham stops and tiptoes over to the mouse, which cannot escape its corner and, as a final ruse, is stilled, trembling, waiting. The boy leans to his left and with his two hands removes a brick from the stack of a dozen or so that his father placed there, probably for some intended chimney repair, and the boy drops the brick onto the mouse, crushing its body but not killing it, so that it squeaks wetly, like an orange being squeezed for juice, and the boy must retrieve the brick, hold it up to his chin and drop it a second time, and then a third, and finally a fourth, when the mouse is dead.

Ham slowly got to his feet and walked from the front room to the kitchen, on his way passing through his parents' bedroom, where the new baby slept in her white, gauze-shrouded basinette. His mother was resting. She was seated at the kitchen table looking at her fingernails. When he came into the room, she smiled and said hello to him and asked him to come stand next to her.

While she stroked his hair back with her hands, he asked her one more time if he had to play in the front room. She relented and said no, he didn't have to.

But she wanted to know why he hated that room, when he used to love it so.

He was going to tell her about the mouse, but when he opened his mouth to speak, he remembered that she already knew about it. It had never been a secret. He had run proudly from the front room to the kitchen and had brought both parents back to see the dead animal. They had been pleased and amazed. His father had patted him on the head and had said, "Good boy," and his mother had said, "I never would've been able to do that. I just would've run for the cat and let him do it!"

So he said nothing to his mother, nothing of the mouse and of course nothing about his cousins. He shrugged his shoulders and looked at his feet.

"You're a strange one, Ham," she told him, smiling. "But

if you want to be here with me and the baby, I guess I'll just have to give in and let you."

After that he forgot about the mouse and did not remember it even when, now and then, because of some errand or helping his mother or father, he could not avoid going into the front room. And when he had forgotten about the mouse, he no longer remembered staring and poking at his cousin's body, or her hands on his. And eventually he forgot the day she pulled up her own blouse and exposed her breasts to him.

If it seems strange that the daughter of a man like Hamilton Stark should treasure and retell in literary form these three tales of his childhood, the reader might remember that it's only in the light of these stories that she is able to justify her love for the man. Otherwise, she might be forced to regard her love for him as perverse, lost, tangled in ropes of ritualized grief and re-enacted trauma, possibly for the rest of her life, and certainly his.

And if it seems strange that a hero's childhood should be described in this manner, please remember that my hero is both controversial and enormous, and therefore whoever would attempt to describe him objectively (excluding from his description the narrator's personal sympathies and antipathies for the subject) runs the risk of being dominated by the subject. That is the reason for the mask, the format of the tales, the realism, the lack of realism.

There will be other masks, other formats, other castings of reality. You may continue to call this one Rochelle, if you wish, and of course she will continue to play a major role in the events being described. She is, after all, Hamilton Stark's only child, and despite her having been deserted by him, she is crucial to our understanding of him. Actually, her absence from his life, because it was willed by him, is more revealing than her presence would be. I hope you like her. I do. She's twenty-six years old, a long-boned, precisely featured, red-haired young woman with green eyes and clear white skin that's almost translucent. She moves quickly but with grace and elegance. True elegance. If I were a younger man, I would court her. I would pursue her ceaselessly. For though she's the kind of young woman who tends to draw organized, purposeful, self-centered men into changing their lives suddenly, radically, and, very often, disastrously, she's also the kind of woman who's astonished when it actually happens — though, to one not so affected by her charms, it's never clear that she did not secretly desire the disaster.

But, to continue:

CHAPTER FOUR

Her Mother Speaks to Her of a Man She Calls "Your Father"

No, really, dear, I mean it. It's time everyone stopped all this dancing around the few trivial facts of the man and got right down to where you can stick your nose up against them, so to speak. Forgive me for saying it this way, but the man, your father, is a despicable man. Always was. Despicable, pure and simple, and everyone who's ever had the misfortune to know him knows at least that much about him, and especially everyone who's ever been married to him, among whom I count myself the first, as you know.

But you're his only child, dear, you've never been married to him, of course, so that's probably why you keep going through all this hero-worshiping nonsense with the man. But only child or not, don't forget the facts you have to ignore. Life's like that, it'll let you keep on ignoring the facts, practically forever, if you want to go that far, but eventually it'll make you pay for it — or your children, or your wife or husband, or maybe even your grandchildren. Anyhow, *somebody* ends up paying, and I don't plan on being that somebody for you. No, you're practically grown now, old enough to know the truth about your father. You think now that he's somebody to imitate, someone to admire and recommend to all your friends, someone who'll defend you against your enemies, a confidant, an advisor, a teacher, a chum. When I get through, dear, you'll know better than to imitate him. You'll know not to expect him to defend you against anything. Hah, you'll need someone to defend you against *him!* A chum. Some chum.

You're probably wondering why I'm telling you all this now, why I waited so long to turn you against him. Well, blood is thicker than water, that's how I always reasoned about the matter, and besides, I never wanted him coming back at me that I turned you against him, you his only child, the one he probably claims to love so much, but of course, only later, when you're practically all grown up and it's *easy* to love you, *easy* to be your father now — not that you weren't a lovable child, no, of course not, you were a wonderful, cuddly, curly-haired little thing, everyone loved you, especially me, and I didn't want your father claiming that I had turned you against him by only telling you the bad things about him, or only telling you things in a light that would make you think badly of the man your father. Let the child find out for herself, that's what I always said, when people asked me if you knew what kind of a man your father was, and believe me, they asked, oh God, did they ever ask. They couldn't believe it when you talked about him the way you did, when you bragged about his being a pipefitter, when you told people what a big shot he was, how he built the U.S. Air Force Academy all by himself, that place in Colorado, as if that weren't one big lie. Brother, the things that man could tell a child. I remember my eyes filling with tears when I would hear you out on the back steps telling your little friends how your father had been a champion boxer. And when you told them he was a champion runner. And when you described his cars. His ability to play the saxophone. His enormous bicep. His black and thick hair. The curly mat of black hair on his chest. The broad shoulders, the hard-muscled back. The rocky thigh.

Well, you asked me for my thoughts and opinions and my memories of the man, and I'm going to give them to you, no matter what they do to your version of him. I know you'll be asking the same of his other wives — or, I should say, ex-wives — so I won't bother with what I know to be true of him after we got our divorce, because you'll get plenty of that from the women who knew him later and better than I did during those particular years of his life. And who knows, maybe he's changed. It sometimes happens. But even so, above all, I want to be fair to the man, because from what I've heard, he's been fair to me. From what I've heard, he's actually told people he still loves me, and that he loved me best of all, that I was his "true love." I can understand that. I mean, it doesn't surprise me. We were so young, and you know what they say about young lovers, first lovers. Oh, I've gotten over him, all right, I mean, I can admit now that he was my first love, my true love, all that sort of thing, but I'm over him now. Because after all, you must remember *he* was the one who left. Not me. *He* was the one who walked out. Not me. *He* was the one who wanted the divorce, the one who got himself a lover while he was still married to me. Not me. I never did any of that. It makes it easier to get over someone if you've never done anything wrong to him. You can understand that.

But I'm sure that when he says I was his first love he's telling the truth. I don't think he lied to me about that, and maybe even after all these years he still does think of me that way. It wouldn't be the strangest thing about him. You know what they say about first loves. We were young. I mean *young*. I was a fashion model then, for the Globe Department Store right here in Lakeland. A small-town girl, sure, but pretty. Some people said pretty enough to succeed as a fashion model in New York, even. You know all this, you've seen pictures, snapshots, and of course, you've talked to people who knew me then. Anyhow, that's not important, except that naturally it helped me land your father.

He came south to Florida that winter, it was the winter he thought he murdered his father, your grandfather. Someone'll probably go into all that in detail, so I won't bother here. It's a fascinating story, though. Whenever I tell people about it now, they simply refuse to believe that I believed it then, that he had killed his own father, I mean. But I always say, "Listen, if he believed it *himself*, why shouldn't I believe it too?" Not many people can come up with an answer for that one.

Anyhow, it was the winter he thought he murdered his father that I first met your father. He came south to Florida, hitchhiking, with nothing more than what he could put in a single battered suitcase. Why he chose Lakeland I'll never know for sure, but I think it had something to do with a construction job that was going on then. A lot of plumbing was involved, connecting up a couple of lakes in the area for a town water supply, something like that. I never paid much attention to the jobs he worked on, never really understood them very well, though of course I was a good listener and always made sure to praise him highly for his work, both to his face and behind his back.

He chose to stop running in Lakeland, after running all the way south from his family home in New Hampshire in the middle of the winter, hitchhiking on trucks, sleeping alongside the highway in places like Red Bank, New Jersey, and Raleigh, North Carolina. He had just turned twenty-two years old, big and strong and not afraid of anything or anyone, except the police, of course. I often think of him, now that you are doing the same thing at almost the same age, hitch-hiking all over the country, sleeping by the side of the road and all, not afraid of anything or anyone, and you aren't even afraid of the police, naturally, because you don't think you have killed your father. Anyhow, I often think of your father during those years, and it gives me some slight comfort, because after all, he did the same thing, and no harm came to him for it.

I did say that he was big and strong then, didn't I? Well, indeed he was. Never in my life had I seen a man as big and strong as your father was then. It's where you get your height. He was wearing a T-shirt that showed all his muscles, and work pants, and he had come into the Globe to buy some underwear. He had just gotten off work at the pumping station. They were building a new pumping station that year and he had walked up to the foreman with his suitcase in his hand, and the way he told me later, he just said to the foreman, "You probably need pipefitters, and I'm the best damned pipefitter you're ever going to get the chance to hire, so you ought to hire me whether you need pipefitters right now or not." The foreman, who later tried to become your father's friend, Bucky Walker, you remember him, he said, "Anybody thinks that high of himself is either so damned good I can't afford to let him go, or so damned bad it'll be a pleasure to fire him. So you're hired, pal." That's how your father told it, and later, when Bucky told me the story, it was the same story, and Bucky had no reason to lie about it, because by that time your father had gone back up north and had left me with you as a baby here in Lakeland. Actually, Bucky was kind of interested in me then. He was hanging around the apartment a lot after work, drinking beer and talking about your father, wondering why he had gone and done what he had done. I often wonder what would have happened if I had gone along with Bucky the way he obviously wanted me to and had even married him after my divorce. And after he had divorced Sally, naturally. I mean, he was kind of a sweet man, and God knows, he was in love with me. I guess I never really told you much about all that, did I? Well, it doesn't matter, because I was still so in love with your father that I couldn't see the good side of any other man, even a man as sweet as Bucky Walker.

But I'm getting away from the thing I wanted to describe to you, how your father looked to me when we first met. I was modeling a pink one-piece Esther Williams bathing suit in a swimwear fashion show on the mezzanine of the Globe, and I had just started down the ramp when I caught sight of him coming up the stairs from the first floor, where he had bought some underwear. He told me later that, noticing a sign about the swimwear show upstairs, he'd decided to come and take a look. There wasn't a beach at Lakeland, as you know, it's so far inland, and at that time he had been in Florida for over a month and hadn't seen a single woman in a bathing suit, and as he always said, that's what Florida was to him, "Women in bathing suits and Coney Island with palm trees." He'd seen the Coney-Island-with-palm-trees part, but so far he hadn't seen anything of the women in bathing suits. So he decided to walk up the stairs to the mezzanine and take in the fashion show. Your father was always like that, very direct and not at all self-conscious. It didn't matter to him that he was the only man in the place, or that he was dressed in a construction worker's clothes, all dirty and sweaty and everything.

I was walking down the platform, with mostly older women shoppers seated around the platform, my boss, Polly Prudhomme, describing the bathing suit I was wearing to the shoppers while I walked along, turning, strolling, kneeling, and then I saw your father's head as it came over the top of the stairs. Oh, I couldn't believe it. It was like a dream. A huge, smiling, suntanned face, a great toothy grin, tiny ears, dark eyes twinkling, a mass of black curly hair, a neck like a tree, and then his broad shoulders, thick chest, great brown arms swinging as he came up the stairs, and then that tiny waist of his, the long muscular legs, until finally he was at the top of the stairs, standing there with his legs apart, his hands in fists on his narrow hips, a big smile across his face, good-natured like a boy's, only somehow hungrier than a boy's could be. I was so taken by his appearance, especially the way it had gradually come to me, piece by piece like that, like a mirage floating up from the floor — first the head, then the torso, then the legs — until at last standing there before me was a grinning giant, the handsomest man I had ever seen. Anyhow, I was so taken by his appearance that I stopped midway down the ramp, stood still, and stared straight at him, and I smiled. I smiled! All the women in the audience and all the girls waiting to come behind me and even Polly Prudhomme herself followed my gaze until they too were staring straight at him, most of them with their mouths open. Polly had stopped describing the bathing suit I was wearing and was gaping like the rest of us. It was a strange moment, silent, no one moving, your father standing at the top of the stairs, grinning, while maybe fifty women stared back at him, with me motionless up there on that ramp, smiling at him, as if I was a slave girl or something being auctioned off and he had suddenly appeared from the desert to save me from a fate worse than death. It was like the movies!

Well, like the old song says, those may have been the best of times, but they were the worst of times too. At least for me they were. Your father, when he wanted to be, was the most charming, thoughtful, witty — oh God, could he be funny — intelligent, tender, sexy, and all-around *interesting* man you'd ever want to meet. And when he was, those were the best of times. I was never a happier woman than I was then. I sang all day long until I got off work and could meet him at the door of the Globe, where he'd be waiting for me, standing there in the late afternoon sun, dirty from his job at the pumping station, chatting with the janitor, old Eddie Coy, who locked the door after the store employees had left. I'd come out the door, and your father would see me, and holding his lunch pail under one arm, he'd whip the other arm around me, and he'd lift me right off the ground and spin me in a half-circle and set me down again, and then he'd stare down into my eyes, and he'd say, in that deep, throaty voice of his, "Hi."

It was really something. I get a little weepy just remembering those days, the best of them. When it comes to the worst of them, though, all I have to do is remember a single one of them, just one of those days, and my eyes clear up pretty fast, let me tell you. There were Friday nights back then before we were married when I'd get off work and would come out the door, expecting your father to be there, as he'd promised, to take me out to dinner, and not finding him, would ask Eddie Coy if he'd seen your father, and Eddie would shake his head, No, not yet, so I'd wait and wait and wait, a half-hour, an hour, an hour and a half, until finally I'd know that he wasn't coming, and I'd walk on home to my apartment, fix myself some supper, take a long bath, and try to sleep — until along about one in the morning, when I'd still be awake, tossing and turning, and there's come a loud banging on the door. Jumping out of bed, I'd rush to the door, and when I opened it, I'd see him, standing there, a vicious snarl across his face, bloodied lips and cut eyes, bruises and scrapes, torn clothing, with a half-emptied bottle of whiskey in his hand. "Ran into a little bit of trouble down at th' Tam," was how he'd explain all the cuts and bruises. Then, using nothing but the foulest language, he'd describe in gory detail how he'd single-handedly beaten up half a dozen sailors or brickmasons or electricians or "crackers," though I was never sure what he meant by the word, who he was referring to, exactly. Probably just anyone he couldn't identify any other way by uniform and such. Anyhow, he'd stagger into my apartment, brushing off my foolish attempts to clean him up and bandage his cuts, pushing me and any sympathy I might have away, physically shoving me into a corner of the room, where I waited, slowly growing frightened of him, as he talked to himself, only to himself, and drank the whiskey from the bottle, growling like a dog, literally growling and curling his lips back and showing his teeth, snapping and snarling, rambling on about his "enemies," turning everyone into an enemy—his parents, his sisters, his friends in New Hampshire and the people he'd met here in Florida, and of course, even me. Then, after a while, especially me. I was becoming his worst enemy. Everytime he came in that drunk and torn up from fighting in the taverns, he would end the night by cursing at me, spitting out horrible names, a little more horrible each time it happened, a little more personally cutting, slicing into the parts of me that were the tenderest parts, taking the cruelest advantage of whatever fears and secrets I might have revealed to him some other night when we had been holding each other tenderly. Teasing and mocking me for my fears, threatening to expose my secrets, he'd call me "stupid" and "idiotic" and "sentimental" for a while, and then "selfish" and "insensitive" and "cruel," and finally "whore" and "leech" and "nag"—those last three, it always came down to them, whore and leech and nag. That's what probably made them hurt so much, the fact that it always came down to the same three names. If he had just been lashing out at the world in general, he might've ended up calling me lots of awful things, sure, but all different. But because he always called me only those three, and all three, never one without the other two, he made me think that he really believed it about me, that even when he was sober and being kind to me, he still thought of me as a whore, a leech, and a nag. And of course, because I loved him and he was a man, I started seriously wondering if I was a whore or a leech or a nag, and there was just enough guilt for my own sexual interests in life, just enough dependency, and just enough nagging for me to slip slowly into believing that I *was* those things he was calling me, until I too thought of myself as a whore, a leech, and a nag. I even felt sorry for him for having to put up with me, for having fallen in love with me. So when he asked me to marry him I was so grateful, and so eager for the chance to prove by my loyalty that I wasn't a whore and by my wifely support and devotion that I wasn't a leech and by my trust and obedience that I wasn't a nag, that I said, "Yes," I said, "Oh, yes, yes, oh God, yes! Yes, yes," I said, "yes."

Well, that's way behind me now, and I've forgiven him, forgiven him for all of it. Really. I have. Part of it was my fault, I'm sure. I mean, I didn't understand him very well, so it was hard for me to give him what he really wanted and needed — though I'm not sure any woman would have been able to give him what he wanted and needed. He was lonely, terribly lonely, I could tell that much. I could understand that. A stranger in a strange land, like they say. No friends, except the few rough pals he made at work. No family, and unable to be in touch with his family in New Hampshire because of what he was sure he had done to his father. And

Florida was just not the place for him — he said he was a man of cold winds and ice and snow. I remember him telling me that, very serious, as if he was telling me he was Catholic or Methodist or Episcopalian. He hated the heat, the sun, the white light of noon, said it made him shrivel up inside, said it made him feel closed off from the world. He was always complaining about the palm trees. "They're not trees. Why d'yer call them trees? They're giant weeds, that's what. *Weeds*," he called them. And he disliked the people who lived here, called them "crackers," even when they were from places like New York and Ohio. "Life in Florida," he would grumble, "is like living in a motel full of crackers." So actually, I wasn't surprised when he left Florida. I expected it. What did surprise me, though, was that he did it alone, that he didn't take the two of us along with him, his wife and his baby.

We hadn't been getting along for quite a few months when he left — not since I first told him I was pregnant, as a matter of fact, and you were three months old when he left, so that means we hadn't been getting along for about a year. But I had blamed that pretty much on myself, on the pregnancy and all and the way I was right after you were born, the way I was all wrapped up with being a mother. Like I said, he was lonely, and after I got pregnant it was hard for me to help him not be lonely.

Oh, what am I doing this for? What's the matter with me? I sat down here to tell you the truth, and I'm not doing it, I'm lying, sliding over things, leaving important things out. I'm not telling the truth at all. It's just that I don't want you to be hurt by him any more than you already have been. But I can't keep on lying to you.

Life with your father was horrible for me right from the

start. First there was that affair with Polly Prudhomme. Then there was the drinking. And after that there was all the violence, the fighting, the times he actually hit me. Then came the silence. He went silent on me. Shut everything down and just sat in his chair, reading sometimes, or looking out the window, or leaning back, his hands behind his head, and looking at the cracks in the ceiling. When you were born, he would come into the room where I was sleeping you, and he would stand over your little bassinet and stare silently at you, no expression on his face at all. It was the strangest, scariest thing I had ever seen. It was as if he had died or something. I started going a little crazy from it. You can imagine the pressure it created, that silence, his expressionless face. I'd sob, "Do you love me?" and he'd say, "Sure," just that, as if he was answering a question about a new hat I'd bought. "How do you like this one, hon?" "Fine," he'd say. Except that I'd be sobbing, "What do you *feel* about me? What do you feel about the *baby?*" And he'd look up from the newspaper and say, "Fine." No expression at all on his face, no depth in his voice. Well, I know I went a little crazy from it. I'd sometimes find myself in the middle of the night lying on the bathroom floor, my face pressed against the cold tiles of the floor, sobbing hysterically, "Why don't you *leave* me! Get out! Get out!" And he'd be at the door, leaning casually against the frame of it, looking down at me with a strange curiosity in his eyes, and he'd say, "Fine." The next morning, silence.

It went on like that for many weeks until finally one morning I got out of the bed I slept in, looked over at his bed and saw that it was already made, thought I'd overslept, and rushed out to the kitchen to make his breakfast. He was gone. He never left before seven-thirty. I looked at the clock on the wall. Seven o'clock.

He never came back. He didn't love me. He didn't love you. You were only a baby. He never even told you any nighttime stories or sang you any songs. You were only a baby. He should've loved you for that at least. But he didn't. I loved him. He might have loved me back a little for that. But he didn't. So he left us. Packed a suitcase, walked out, got on a bus, disappeared. He left me with some money in the bank, and once he wired me a hundred dollars from Colorado. Six months later, I got a typed post card from him. It said:

Better get a divorce under way. I'll pay. My father is alive and well. Your lawyer can reach me c/o my parents, Barnstead, New Hampshire. Everything's going to be all right for you now. The hard part is over. For you. I do feel guilty, if you're wondering, but it won't do you any good. It doesn't even seem to do me any good either, so I won't be feeling it for long. As ever,

H. Stark

That was all. Six months later we were legally divorced, and I never saw your father again, though, as you know, I did hear from him again, numerous times. But I was lucky enough never to have to see him again.

There were the post cards he sent you, but you also might as well know that your father called me for years afterward, usually late at night, often on a sentimental occasion, like our anniversary or my birthday or yours. He was always drunk when he called, and because I would be less than enthusiastic, he'd turn sour and angry almost immediately and would hang up on me. I never bothered at the time to tell you of these calls because you were too young to have understood, and he eventually stopped calling, probably when he was with his second wife, whom, I'm told, he loved intensely for a while, though frankly speaking, I don't believe it.

Your father beat me at least fifteen times in the year that we were married and living together. By "beat me" I mean hitting me more than once on any given occasion. I'm not counting all the times your father hit me only once.

Your father swore and cursed at me constantly. He mocked my clumsiness when I was great with child.

Your father lay in my own bed with my best friend, Polly Prudhomme, who also happened to be my boss until I was too pregnant to model even the maternity dresses and had to quit my job at the store. He told me about it after everyone in the store and practically everyone in town already knew about it, and then when he told me about it, he gave me all the details of their times together. He praised her especially for her skill at giving him what he called "head," which meant sucking on his penis (you're old enough to know all this by now) and letting him ejaculate into her mouth and, he said, she swallowed the semen, though that's a little hard for me to believe. Yet he insisted that's what she liked to do and that she did it so well he almost became addicted to it. He told me they even had a code worked out so that he could make an appointment with her by teasing her in front of me, and I remember, when he came to the store to get me after work, his saying to Polly, as if he was teasing her about her name, "Polly want a cracker? Polly want a cracker?" And she'd laugh and say, "Naw, not tonight," or, "Later, maybe, after supper for dessert." I would scold him afterward for making fun of her name. "Besides, she doesn't know what you mean by 'cracker,' " I would say to him, and he'd just laugh, knowing that actually I was the one who didn't know what "cracker" meant.

Your father drank whiskey until he passed out on the floor, and he always did it on nights when he had promised to take me out to dinner and dancing.

Your father had a fistfight with my only living relative, my Uncle Orlando — beating him senseless in his own front yard in front of his own wife and horrified children — all because Orlando had enough courage to stand up to your father and tell him what a selfish and cruel man he was to be treating me the way he was then (this was only a week before your father left me).

Your father bragged about his abilities as a pipefitter. He had no humility. He was convinced that, compared to him, all the men he worked with and for were stupid, lazy, and unskilled.

Your father was frequently impotent, sexually inadequate. I won't go into it any further than that because there may well be reasons for it that we can never really know about, matters outside my experiences with him, childhood experiences and that sort of thing, but your father, I thought, was not quite right sexually. He talked too much about some of his friends' (men friends, mind you) muscles. Also, he seemed to enjoy a certain kind of intercourse which, I'm told, only homosexual men do regularly. You know what I'm talking about.

Your father hated cats. I won't tell you about how one time he killed a whole litter of kittens. It was horrible.

Your father cheated at cards. Even bridge.

Your father stole government property.

Your father lied about his taxes. He also told strangers that he made more money than he really did make. Sometimes he even told them he was making money on the side by playing the stock market, betting on the horses, betting on dogs, winning sports pools, bowling. He had me believing (until I had my lawyer check it out later) that he owned a lot of real estate in New Hampshire. "Half the side of a mountain," was how he put it, but my lawyer told me that your father's parents owned an old rundown farm, and your father owned nothing.

Your father thought all flowers were ugly, though he once admitted he liked blue hydrangeas. "Mainly because they don't look like they're real," he explained to me.

Your father didn't know how to swim. He said it was on principle, but of course it was because he didn't want to be in a position of having to learn something that most people already knew about.

Your father didn't know how to ride a bicycle, either, and that too he said was on principle. I could never understand that.

Your father hated people of all races, creeds, and colors. He was an extremely prejudiced man, the worst I have ever known, even after living my whole life in the South. He would make fun of a person's background, no matter what it was. "Stupid Polacks." "Grabby Jews." "Dumb niggers." "Drunken Indians." "Thick-headed Irishers." He hated them all — even what he himself was, which he referred to as "common white trash" or sometimes "snot-nosed Yankees" and "backwoods New Hampshire shit-kickers." But whenever he used these terms, he somehow said them with a certain note of endearment. Somehow these slurs became affectionate nicknames. Not so for the others, though.

Your father could play the saxophone well, but he only played it when he was alone or thought he was alone. He did not, as he claimed, play in the Guy Lombardo orchestra. He often referred to himself as "one of Guy's Royal Canadians" when people asked him about his saxophone, which he displayed ostentatiously on the coffee table in the living room of our apartment.

Your father had a smile that people loved, and when, because of their love for his smile, they got close to him, he stopped smiling and never allowed it to be seen again. I cannot recall his smiling at me after we were married, and actually, I can't recall his smiling at me from the moment I told him that I was falling in love with him, which happened the fourth time I went out with him. Of course I know he must have smiled at me then, many times. It's just that I can't recall it.

Your father told wonderful jokes, but only to strangers. When he told jokes to people who were not strangers, the jokes were cruel and dark and only funny in a way that made you feel guilty if you laughed.

Your father would sneer at old people on park benches as if they disgusted him.

Your father kicked dogs and dared them to bite him for it.

Your father was a jaywalker.

Your father growled. Like an animal. At night, if a car drove up, or if someone knocked on the door, your father would start to growl, low and deep from way back in his throat.

Your father often ate the same thing for lunch that he knew I was fixing for supper.

Your father lied about having been a champion boxer. He was, however, a very good, that is, a successful, barroom brawler.

Your father lied about having been a champion runner, though he did have very muscular legs and seemed never to be physically tired, so he probably could have been a champion runner if he had tried. But he never even tried.

Your father thought he had killed his father, but he never confessed to having any guilt for it. He blamed it on his father. Otherwise, he never talked about it with me. I'd ask him to tell me about it and he'd say, "It was all my old man's fault," and then he'd roll over and go to sleep.

Your father talked incoherently to himself when he was drunk, and he was drunk at least one night a week, usually Friday night, after he had gotten paid.

Your father had piles, which was unusual for a man as young as he was then.

Your father was too big.

Your father was afraid of going to the dentist. Also, he refused to see a doctor when he was sick or for his piles, and he refused to take medicines of any kind. Even aspirin. He was convinced that it would only make things worse. He always said, "If things can get worse, they will, but there's no reason to make it easy for them."

Your father was afraid that his penis was too small, and in a way he was right, because, while his body was unusually large, his penis was normal-sized. Unfortunately, because he asked me, I told him that one night. He never made love to me afterward, but that came fairly late in the pregnancy anyhow.

Your father said he loved his mother, but once when he was drunk he started to cry and roll around on the floor, yelling about how much he hated her.

Your father was not a happy man. But he said it was on principle, and that it was for him a moral principle, what he called a "moral imperative," and that was why he tried so hard to make other people unhappy too. I could never tell for sure when he was joking, but I think he was joking then. But he may not have been. He certainly acted as though he thought everyone should be unhappy, that it was for him a moral thing and, therefore, by making people unhappy he was somehow making them better.

Your father was the worst thing that ever happened to me.

Your father refused to admit that he was lonely, even though he had no friends he could confide in. But he said that was on principle, too, I mean the part about being lonely. I think he would've liked to have had a few friends, so long as he could've kept on being lonely at the same time. But he had too many principles.

Your father hated me.

Oh, God, how he hated me.

CHAPTER FOUR

Addendum A

THROUGHOUT THE PRECEDING monologue, Rochelle listened attentively to her mother, motionless and almost completely silent. Or at least that is how she would later describe herself. She smoked cigarettes one after the other. When she had smoked one down to the filter, she would crush it out in the seashell ashtray on her mother's Danish coffee table. Crossing and uncrossing her long legs with that unself-conscious, almost inevitable grace of hers, she never once took her alert eyes off her mother's expressive, changing face. The only sounds in the room were the continual drone of the air conditioner and the soft, southern voice of Rochelle's mother and now and then the noise of a car in the midday Florida heat slipping past the apartment building.

It's difficult to know how the content of her mother's jeremiad affected Rochelle. We have only her self-description, offered much later, when her attitude toward her father had been altered considerably by the things she had heard from her father's four other wives, from the testimony of numerous people, including myself, who had known him over the years in one capacity or another, from a lengthy interview with his dying mother and another with his sisters and a brother-in-law, and when she herself had, as they say, "gotten in touch with her anger."

One could easily speculate about Rochelle's reaction to the news (and at that time it *was* news) that her father was in many ways a self-centered, immature, violent, cruel, eccentric, and possibly insane man. But I'm afraid that in my own case any speculation would be influenced by my personal relationship with her, and thus, however innocently, I would tend to work toward evoking in the reader deep feelings of pity and admiration for this amazing young woman. Also, I'm not at all familiar with the nature of Rochelle's relationship with her mother and therefore cannot confidently say that she did not have some secret use for refusing to believe her mother, i.e., that she did not, perhaps, need to think of her mother as a liar, as a bitter, middle-aged woman filled with self-pity, a mother in need of a villain to justify the absence of her husband throughout her daughter's childhood and adolescence.

Suffice it to say, then, that I'm not the best person to be in the position of presenting, with anything that approximates objectivity, Rochelle's emotional reaction to her mother's testimony concerning the character of her father. Frankly, I am too much in love with Rochelle to be of much good to anyone in this particular matter, except possibly to Rochelle herself, and probably not even that. I admire the woman, and I say it with practically no qualification whatsoever, and because I am aware of how deeply and sharply she has suffered and how she has endured with intelligence, dignity and selflessness throughout, I am filled almost to overflowing with compassion for her. Also, I confess that for several years I have desired her love in return, have sought her favor in every way I could imagine, taking advantage of every slight opportunity to court her that has come my way — and as a result, I have had to watch myself lie for her, to know that I was, on certain occasions, violating all principles, even those few principles I had once thought inviolable. I say this without apology. I offer it merely as a warning.

My vulnerability to a woman like Rochelle is well known. Or at least it's well known to me. Many men have a weakness (I should say, a "weakness") for women with long, wildly flowing, deep red hair. And many men have a similar "weakness" for women who are tall, as tall or even taller than they themselves are, and who are thin without being gaunt, large without being big or heavy in any way. And, too, many men have a "weakness" for women who are well shaped, neatly and symmetrically proportioned. I am surely one of each of these types of men, and if that were all there was to my beloved Rochelle, I would be safe, as it were, and could report to you anything I might believe to be true of her without having to feel that I might be deceiving you to further my own rather special interests. But Rochelle is so much more than merely a tall, well-shaped woman with long red hair, that I am consequently that much less a reliable witness to her words and feelings.

I realize that so far I've not said a thing about Rochelle's character or her spiritual nature or intellect. Nevertheless, I would like to linger a little longer on what might be called her "body." She has skin on her body that is as smooth and white as a fine young onion, or as the flesh of an apple, or as an abalone shell worn smooth by a century's tides. Dark green (blue-spruce green, actually), her eyes are tear-shaped, slightly downturned, with long, dark lashes. Her nose is long, straight, slender, the vertical arc that insists on the perfect symmetry of her face. Her mouth is neither large nor small, but full and expressive nonetheless, with a sharp, slightly protruding upper lip, a pouting lower lip, and large, white, even teeth that seem as ready to nibble as quick to bite. Her forehead, cheeks and chin are smooth, symmetrical, but at the same time sharply defined by angles which are clearly visible in all but the severest light. Ears — small, a happy maze of tender and delicate whorls, full-lobed. Throat — slender, long, white, and at the base, a mauve birthmark the size and approximate shape of a candle flame. And I have kissed that flame.

(Please note that I do not believe it would be appropriate for me to speculate on, or even to report what I know to be the case with regard to, Rochelle Stark's character, her spiritual nature, or her intellect. It seems to me that these attributes would be better portrayed, more interestingly and realistically portrayed, in action, *in medias res,* as it were, and therefore I will put off such portrayal until later in the narrative, when my beloved Rochelle's developed inner life can be made manifest more naturally and convincingly.)

CHAPTER FOUR

Addendum B

In Chapter Four proper, Rochelle's mother — whose name, by the way, is Trudy Brewer Stark (she retained her married name after the divorce) — mentioned in passing that her daughter Rochelle was at present "hitchhiking all over the country, sleeping by the side of the road and all, not afraid of anything or anyone. . . ." From the text, it's also apparent, or should be, that at the time of the mother's speaking the daughter is approximately twenty-two years old. As it happens, this interview was made four years ago, which would make Rochelle twenty-six now, a figure that is consistent with the information she has personally made available to me on different occasions.

It is true, as her mother claimed, that when she was twenty-two Rochelle was traveling about the country in a somewhat casual manner. Or so it seemed. She carried all her worldly goods on her back in a large Kelty expedition pack, slept in a sleeping bag at the side of the road or wherever she happened to find herself at nightfall, and after a fashion "lived off the land" by shoplifting at supermarkets and fruit stands, stealing from gardens and orchards, and, whenever possible, picking wild berries, fruit and nuts.

She lived this way for about a year, most of which she spent retracing the footsteps of her father's fearful flight from

New Hampshire, his wanderings that followed the desertion of his wife and infant daughter in Lakeland, Florida, and, when he discovered that in fact he had not killed his father and that his long hegira had been essentially in vain, his swift return home to New Hampshire.

Rochelle's journey, a fact-finding tour more than a hegira or pilgrimage, was not in vain. She returned home to her mother's apartment in Lakeland with the information she had gone out for. Essentially, the information was geographic and social, material that would help her realize her ambition to write a realistic novel about a man who was very much like her father, Hamilton Stark. She was young, and she had not traveled much, and naturally she had felt somewhat intimidated by the task she had set herself, especially when it came to writing about a character who had traveled rather widely in his youth and had spent most of his life locked inside the social confines of the working class. But her year-long note-taking journey reassured her that she would have little difficulty handling the geographic and social realism that her novel, as she had conceived it, would require. This was the point at which she began her series of interviews with her father's five ex-wives, several of his friends, and his mother, sisters and brother-in-law. As I have mentioned, the interview with her own mother was the first in this series.

CHAPTER FOUR

Addendum C

In Chapter Four, which was narrated by Rochelle's mother, Trudy Brewer Stark, there were numerous references to Hamilton Stark's belief that he had murdered his father. Naturally, this belief was of considerable moment and consequence to Hamilton, a fact not lost on his daughter, Rochelle, when, some twenty-two or more years later, she began to write a novel about a man based closely on her father.

Therefore, since this episode has considerable bearing on the meaning of this, my own novel, and since Rochelle has evidenced herself to be an author far more naturally gifted than myself in portraying the circumstances, characters, emotions and actions that comprise the episode, I am including here her Chapter Eight, entitled "Return and Depart," which concerns itself most particularly with the events and circumstances that led up to Hamilton's "murder" of his father.

Note: There have been obvious name changes, as mentioned briefly in my Chapter Three, "Three Tales from His Childhood" — her Alvin Stock is actually my Hamilton Stark, who is, of course, my friend A. Rochelle's Feeney in "Return and Depart" is Hamilton's friend, a man who in my novel remains nameless; he is not, as might be thought, the character C., nor is he myself; simply, I do not have a character in my novel who corresponds to Feeney, nor do I have such a person in my life. Nor does A. have one in his. In fact, Feeney may be a pure invention. The girl named Betsy Cooper is my Nancy Steele; in A.'s life, her name is B. Crawford is Rochelle's name for the place I have called Barnstead, which in A.'s life is the town of B. All three places happen to be located in New Hampshire. Rochelle's Loudon is the state capital, Concord, called that both in my novel and in A.'s life. As the chapter begins, Alvin (Hamilton, A.) has been discharged from the Air Force (the Army Engineers Corps, both for Hamilton and for A.), is twenty-one years old in 1963 (1948 for Hamilton and A.), and is returning home from Vietnam (Fort Devens Massachusetts) to Crawford (Barnstead, B.).

A further note: The reader may wonder why I did not include with my earlier selections from Rochelle's novel (specifically in Chapter Three, with the three tales from his childhood) a schematic breakdown of the name and place correspondences between the two novels and "reality," such as I have included here in the note above. My decision was essentially founded on stylistic premises, but also I did not want to introduce too many characters into the novel too early for even the most organized and devoted reader to keep separate from one another. But the reader might well ask why, then, didn't I choose simply to continue here with my earlier practice of using the same names, the same as in my novel, for the excerpts from Rochelle's novel? Yes, I would answer, but then the reader might tend to believe that both Rochelle and I were writing about the same character, Hamilton Stark, when, of course, nothing could be further from the truth. Therefore, I reasoned, at some point I would be obliged to make the distinctions explicit, and this seemed to me the appropriate point for it.

CHAPTER 8

Return and Depart

Alvin came home to Crawford, a veteran, not a hero, for there was no war just then. He had spent all his discharge money traveling east and slowly north across the country, seeing his friends home, visiting a few days with each, eating large meals with the family, meeting the girlfriend, taking her friend to a movie or on a blind date, drinking afterward with his buddy until the local bars closed, and then catching the morning train, bus or plane as far as his next friend's home town, where he would repeat the ritual. It was a casual yet methodical itinerary, one the group of young veterans had worked out together with affectionate care during their last few weeks in Vietnam. Its logical and necessary conclusion, that Alvin would arrive home in Crawford, New Hampshire, last, alone, with no one left to pass through his home town on his way to someplace farther east or north, was a geographical accident. Consequently, when finally Alvin had been greeted at the Loudon bus station by his own family and in Crawford by his local friends, had put away his blue uniform, and had unpacked his duffel, his entire experience as an American soldier abroad as one of the military "advisers" in Southeast Asia was placed neatly into his past, as if into a trunk, and was stored away with his uniform in the attic.

This act, however, was not solely the result of an accident of geography (his having been discharged on the West Coast and returning home to a place farther north and east than that of any of his friends), though that was of course of some importance. But rather, it was also something he himself desired — to compartmentalize his past. He did not want any of his old Air Force buddies dropping by to spend several days drinking and talking about the past. He did not want any of his previous life overlapping his present and smearing onto his future. In a way, it was how he made himself available to himself: he now consciously thought of his past as a batch of differently shaped and variously colored boxes or blocks, all strung together in simple chronological order, like a chain of islands that happened to fall along a single meridian or degree of latitude. Among these blocks, Alvin numbered: Early Childhood; Early Adolescent Period of Self-Recrimination; The Religious Conversion Period; The Two Years He Wanted To Become a Minister; The Year He Wanted To Go to College; Giving Up; and In the Air Force.* To Alvin, no coherent relationship existed among these blocks of time except, of course, that of simple sequence. And by the time he was twenty-two, he was beginning to feel comfortable with that absence of relation. In fact, he was learning how to utilize and even to depend upon it — just to keep moving.

"Well, what d'you plan on doing now?" his father asked him across the table.

It was at breakfast, Alvin's first morning home. Having served him bacon, fried eggs, orange juice and coffee, his mother was now bustling silently, smilingly around the kitchen. "I don't know," Alvin said. "I just thought I'd call up a few people, maybe go see some old friends. You know . . ."

"I don't mean this morning."

"Oh."

---

* These comprise the sequence and subjects of the first seven chapters of *The Plumber's Apprentice*, the novel from which "Return and Depart" is drawn. It also marks one of the few places in the book where the narrator self-consciously becomes "the author."

"I mean, *do*. For a living. Or are you just up early because it's a nice fall day?"

Alvin wasn't sure he understood. "Where are the girls?" he asked his mother.

"Oh, they're still sleeping, Alvin. You forget, they're teenagers, and this is Saturday. No school." She smiled apologetically.

His father snorted.

"Yeah, well, I guess I'm just excited about being home and all."

"What're you planning to *do* now?" his father asked again.

Alvin put down his coffee cup and lit a cigarette. Inhaling deeply, he stared down at his half-emptied cup. "Pa," he said, "I don't think I know for sure what you're asking."

The older man looked straight ahead, across the table and out the window. "For *work*. A man has to *do* something. You're a *man* now, aren't you?"

"Yes."

"All right, then. What're you going to *do*?"

Alvin's mother had stopped her busy movement and now, looking down at her hands, stood motionless by the stove. None of the three people in the room was looking at any of the others. A gust of wind cracked against the house and whistled along its sides from north to south. Outside, the sky was stone dry and blue, a cool, windy, October morning. The ground was gone all to browns and yellows, and the trees had turned violently red, orange, yellow, purple. The dry leaves, about to fall from the branches to the parchmentlike ground, were clattering noisily in the wind and could be heard even from inside the house.

"Well," Alvin began, "I've thought about it. A lot. And I thought I'd drive over to Loudon on Monday and see if I could get a job working for the state. Department of Public Works, maybe. Then I'd take it from there — I mean, about where I'd be living and all, and when." Alvin spoke slowly, with care, obviously tense, as if he were lying.

"Okay. But before you do that," his father said, "I want you to consider this." The older man was still staring out the window. "Say you come to work for me again. But not part-time, not as a helper. As a pipefitter this time. Gradually, working together, we can take on a few bigger jobs. Schools. Maybe a hospital or something. Apartment houses. You know a few things about engineering now, and I know a lot about installation." He paused, as if waiting for Alvin to answer.

When his son remained silent, he went on. "We can get capital from the bank or the government. In a few years we can turn this one-man plumbing business into a regular contracting outfit. Fifteen, twenty, thirty men laying pipe. Maybe doing some good-sized jobs all over the state."

Again, the older man paused, as if to gauge his son's response, and getting none, continued speaking, but more rapidly. "Here's the deal. You go to work for me on Monday, day after tomorrow, as an apprentice pipefitter. I can get you into the union. Easy. The Loudon local. I've already talked to the business agent over there. I'll pay you apprentice wages, what anybody else'd pay you. It'll take you five years before you can get your journeyman's license. If you're still at it then, and if you've given all you've got to make this into a solid, medium-sized plumbing and heating company, I'll make you an equal partner in the business. Where it goes from there depends on what we both decide. Together. In fifteen years or so I'll retire. Then the whole thing'll be yours. Assuming you're still at it and want it." He finally looked over at Alvin's face. "How does that sound to you?" he asked somberly.

Alvin sighed and rubbed his cigarette out in his saucer. He looked up and saw that both his parents were looking down at him, waiting for an answer. "Starting Monday, eh?"

"I already spoke to the union brass over in Loudon. They've got a couple of openings for new apprentices coming up this month. They'll hold one of them for you, if you want it."

"Five years?"

"Five years. On the job as a pipefitter early every morning. But doing a hell of a lot of estimating, too. And paperwork, engineering at nights and on weekends, too — making this operation into a regular contracting business. You can go on living here if you want to. Or you can get your own place. Up to you."

"Can I have till tomorrow, before I give an answer?"

"Sure. Take all the time you need. Between now and Monday morning." That was a joke, and Alvin's father smiled to indicate it.

Alvin laughed. "Ha!"

Then his father got up from the table, put on his old green cap and coat, and went out the door. After a few seconds, Alvin heard the pickup truck start and rattle past the house, down the dirt road toward town.

"Has he been planning this a long time?" Alvin asked his mother, who had gone back to work, this time at the sink, washing dishes.

"A *long* time," she answered over her shoulder

He accepted his father's offer. It didn't appear to him that he had much of a choice, so he accepted the offer with a certain reluctance and with the type of resentment that gets felt by everyone concerned but never expressed by anyone at all. He worked for his father — dutifully, methodically, punctually — but never more than was specifically required of him. His father told him, "Far as I'm concerned, you're just another apprentice pipefitter. A helper. And I'll treat you the same's I treat anyone else I hire out of the local. And if you don't do your job, pal, you can pick up your pay and head on down the road. Either you cut it, or you're down the road. Agreed?"

"Agreed." Alvin thought that was fair enough as long as he, for his part, was free to treat his father the same way he'd treat any boss he happened to be working for, any foreman whose crew he ended up on. He thought that, he decided it, but he never mentioned it to his father, his employer, his foreman.

The offer, then, almost as soon as it had been made and accepted, was corrupted. The bargain, sealed, was instantly broken open again — with the father treating his son like an employee but demanding in return filial loyalty and commitment, the son treating his father like an employer but resenting any demands placed on him which were not covered specifically in the union contract. Neither party, naturally, was satisfied. Each felt he was being cheated by the other.

Throughout the fall they worked together this way — father and son, boss and helper. Most of the work they did was small repair jobs, the kind of work Alvin's father had always done, jobs which Alvin hated because the work was often difficult, usually dirty, and frequently unacceptable to the customer. They replaced burst water pipes, cleaned out the drainage system in a supermarket, and installed several new oil burners in old furnaces. They repaired half a dozen water pumps, countless leaking faucets, clogged traps and toilets; installed washing machine drains, garbage disposals, drainage vents, lavatories, laundry tubs and bathtubs. They built furnace fireboxes, set toilets, installed radiators, piped up hot water heaters, and repaired sump pump systems. And in practically every case they were working on the plumbing or heating system of an old house, renovating or, worse, often merely repairing facilities, fixtures, equipment and pipes that had been used for several generations. Consequently, the work was filthy — in cobwebs, dust, soot, mucky water, shit and garbage. And it was always difficult, exacting work, trying to make an old piece of equipment work like a new one, trying to install pipes and fixtures where an architect had planned a closet or a stairwell, trying to run sharp-edged metal heating ducts where there was no basement, no light, and barely enough room between the floor joists and the cold ground for a man to crawl in. And because it was repair or renovation work, it inevitably took more time than the customer expected it to take, the equipment never functioned quite as well as it did when it was brand-new, and more parts and material were used than the customer had thought necessary. "Why can't you guys use more of the pipe that was already *there?*" was the typical complaint. And of course the bill always came to more than the customer thought the job was worth. Exhausted, filthy, Alvin would write out the bill and hand it to the customer, who would look at it, cluck his tongue, and say, "Jee-*suz!* I used to want my kid to grow up to be a doctor, but now I think I'll tell him to become a *plumber!*" In a way that Alvin couldn't quite name, conversations like that always left him feeling slightly humiliated.

Two or three nights a week Alvin and his father pored over blueprints, specifications, price books and long columns of figures, estimating and bidding on the kind of work they both wanted to do, each for his own reasons — shopping centers, filling stations, apartment houses, small schools, small-town office buildings. For Alvin, new construction meant work that was not dirty and was difficult only in a technical, interesting way. It was also somehow less demeaning than repair work. For his father, no such nice distinction seemed to exist. For him, the difference was strictly money. "All you can make on a repair job is your time and maybe a few pennies on the materials," he would grumble. "And for every job where you make a little more than what the job costs, you have two more that you lose money on, because either you took the job too cheap in the first place or the damn customer's a deadbeat."

On new work, however, there was a clear profit to be made. The two men would estimate all the costs, materials, time, overhead — and then they'd add up the figures and tack fifteen percent on top. That fall the Stock & Son Plumbing & Heating Company put out bids on six jobs — a school in Gilmanton, a filling station in Laconia, two garden apartment buildings in Loudon, and two ski lodges, one in Belknap and one in North Conway. But they were too high on all six. Not by much, but enough to be out of the running and in no position after the bids had been opened to bargain secretly with the general contractor against the other subcontractors, as was the practice. "Those fuckers all play footsie with each other," Alvin's father explained to him. "And the only way to get in on the game is to get in on the game fair and square. On your own. Prove you can do the job on time and for what you said you could. Next time, the big boys, the general contractors, will know to play footsie with you, too. But you still got to get that first job or two on your own. After that, you're golden." So they continued to estimate and bid for jobs two or three nights a week, Saturdays and Sundays, working the rest of the week "out of the pickup," as his father put it.

Alvin was a reasonably good plumber. He was extremely

large and strong, close to tireless unless he got bored. And he was basically skilled — after all, he had worked for his father after school and summers since he was fourteen years old. On the other hand, he was more adept at estimating new work than his father was, because he was better able to read blueprints and to work rapidly with numbers. Nevertheless, he was paid only for the time he worked as a pipefitter, at a first-year apprentice's rate, and paid not at all for the time he spent estimating. To his father, that was part of the deal, the offer. To Alvin, it was not. But he said nothing.

He didn't gripe or grumble about it to anyone, not even to his friend Feeney, whom he saw frequently — whenever he wasn't working for his father. His social life then was actually not much different from what it had been during his last year of high school, four years before, except of course that he didn't attend any of the school functions and no longer could avail himself of the company of Betsy Cooper, his high school girl friend, who, then in her senior year at Mount Holyoke College, was engaged to marry a medical student at Columbia. Alvin drove around with Feeney, drinking at bars and in cars, picking up girls at roller-skating rinks, roadhouses, country-and-western dances, and drive-in restaurants. He often successfully made love to these girls (in the car, or sometimes at Feeney's house, now that Feeney's father had left), and he usually got boisterously drunk, and he inevitably got into a fistfight with a stranger. These three activities he had rarely, if ever, indulged in as a high school student, and, therefore, people concluded that Alvin Stock had "changed" since coming back from the service. It was a reasonable conclusion.

His father told him, "I don't give a shit what you do on your own time. As long as you get to work on time in the morning and your hangover don't slow you down any. And as long as I don't have to bail you out of jail. Far as I'm concerned, you're free, white, and twenty-one. Except when you're working for me." He smiled quickly, the movement almost unseen, like a lizard's tongue. It was a joke. Alvin was supposed to laugh.

His mother was not as sanguine, however. Every night when he went out, dark hair combed slickly back, clean T-shirt and khakis, loafers shined, Feeney outside in the car rapping impatiently on the horn, she would watch him leave and then would sit down and wait for him to return, no matter how late. In the kitchen, seated at the table, working a crossword puzzle and listening to the radio (turned low, so her husband, in the bedroom adjacent, could sleep), she would wait for her son to come home, and finally, at two or three in the morning, she would hear Feeney's car drive up, and she'd snap to attention in the chair, her eyes dry and red from sleeplessness and fatigue, and when he entered the house, usually by the front door, she'd call to him. "Alvin!"

"Whut."

"In the kitchen. Come in here, I want to talk to you."

He would tip and stumble through the living room and take a seat opposite her at the long table. "Whut." Sometimes he would be wearing a bruise across his face and lipstick across his shirtfront. Sometimes one or the other. Rarely neither.

Then she would begin: "Alvin. Son. You've got to get hold of yourself. Look at you. You can't *be* this way, you can't become the kind of person who . . . acts this way all the time. I'm worried about you, son."

"Well, don't. I am who I am. That's all," he'd answer, lighting a cigarette.

"You're unhappy, aren't you?"

"I wasn't . . . until I come in here and started gettin' nagged at." He looked her in the face, blew smoke at her. One mean bastard, he thought.

She coughed, got up abruptly, walked into her bedroom. "Good night. Shut off the lights before you go up." Angrily. It ended this way every time she waited up for him. She wasn't ever going to do it again.

"Yes, *ma'am.*" Sneering. Rubbing out his cigarette in the saucer of her cup. Sliding away from the table and standing up. Going from the kitchen through the living room to the stairs and up to his bedroom, having left the lights on behind him. On purpose.

Whose purpose? He didn't know. He sat in darkness on his bed, kicking his shoes slowly off. Oh, what the hell, she was right, right about everything, for God's sake. The nights he turned into a bum, a nothing, a big slob screwing every whore in Belknap County, brawling in every bar and roadhouse, drinking himself sick all the nights he didn't have to work for his father . . . And she knew it, knew that these were the nights he turned into a bum, a slob, broke, drunk, fucked out, the taste of vomit on his teeth, his knuckles scraped, nose swollen, half the preceding six hours completely blacked out, erased from conscious memory, the rest remembered only in terms of sudden movement and roaring . . . And it was all her fault, his goddamned, sweet, nagging and high-falutin' mother's fault. She should've left him the hell alone, or else helped him get away to college, anywhere, just away . . . And it was all Betsy Cooper's fault too — that touchy, virgin, cock-teasing bitch, and all her ambitions, her promises to write letters to him, all her lies to him, how she didn't care what he did with his life, she would love and respect it . . . What a pile of crap that was! In a week she'd be home from college for the Christmas break. He'd go over to that big white barn of a house on the hill, and he'd tell her what the hell he thought of her, and then he'd fuck her, right in front of that big living room mirror, and she'd watch, and she'd love it, but she'd hate herself for loving it, and when he'd fucked her, he'd get off and stand up and laugh, laugh like a loon, laugh and laugh and laugh, God damn it. God damn it. Damn it. It was nobody's fault — but his own. He knew that. Impossible to deny. Impossible to blame anybody else, least of all his mother, least of all Betsy Cooper, both of whom were guilty merely of having thought him better, stronger, smarter, than he was, both of whom loved him — or had once loved him. He deserved himself. Everyone else deserved someone better. Only he was bad enough, weak enough, dumb enough, to deserve being who, in the final fact, he was . . .

It was mid-December, a blowy, snowy, Friday evening, cold enough that the wind crackled against the windshield of Feeney's Dodge, and the snowflakes, dry and hard as salt crystals, blew against the car and swiftly away from it, finally settling in long, wind-carved drifts along the sides of the road and edges of the woods and against the buildings they passed, as they drove back from Pittsfield to Crawford.

Feeney wanted a drink, had pulled a pint bottle of rye from the glove compartment as he drove, and poured a few ounces into his mouth, passing it across to Alvin when he had finished. Alvin silently recapped the bottle and replaced it in the glove compartment.

"Whassamatta, doncha wanta leetle drinkee?" Feeney teased him. Looking over at his dark friend, Feeney grinned, showing his small, brown teeth, and he wet his thick lips like a horse.

Alvin said no, explaining that he was tired tonight and just wanted to be out of the house, not out of his head, for chrissake.

Feeney chuckled salaciously and asked for the bottle again. Alvin passed it to him.

"You're just pissed we didn't scarf any quiffs at the fuckin' movies," Feeney said seriously, trying to be sympathetic. He noted the car's rapid slide toward the side of the road and whipped the wheel to the left, spinning the vehicle back into line, just missing a two-foot snowdrift.

"No," Alvin said. "Nothing like that. It's hard to get too down when you strike out with a batch of fuckin' sixteen-year-olds giggling in the back of a fuckin' small-town moviehouse. Besides, I really liked the movie," he added. *Picnic* it was, with Alvin played by William Holden, Betsy Cooper by Kim Novak in a sexy lavender dress, the plot basically a brief, melancholy meeting between a hungry, lonely, trapped woman and a profound man, the meeting borne in conflict between the characters, carried to tragic, compassionate fruition by sex and coincidence, resolved by the sad yet spiritually necessary departure of the man. "That's my idea of a good movie," Alvin said, half to himself.

Feeney handed the bottle back to him. "You sure you don't want a slug?" he urged.

Alvin said no and continued staring out the windshield, the snow firing out of the darkness into the path of the car. Without looking, he put the bottle back into the glove compartment.

They drove a ways farther in silence, through Crawford Parade, along the road to the Center, past the fairgrounds, with the river on their right, iced over, the ice whitened by the snow, following alongside the car as the vehicle wound a careful way home. Driving into the Center, they approached

Feeney's house, dark and dilapidated, looking beyond anything desperate, like an old railroad hobo, and Feeney asked Alvin if he wanted to come in and have a drink and maybe watch some television or play some cards awhile. "Christ, it ain't even eleven yet," he said in a whining voice, pulling nervously at one thick eyebrow with the thumb and forefinger of his right hand while he steered the car with his other hand.

"No thanks. I might's well go on home. This snow's starting to build up now and I'd probably have to walk if I stayed at your place. Nights like this, I start to thinking about my grandpa, y' know," he added half-jokingly. But half-seriously, too, because it was true that he never remembered any of the stories of how the old man, his father's father, had died, except on nights like this, when there was a hard, cold snow falling in drifts, and he remembered, pictured, a man he'd never actually seen stumbling home in the dark, drunk, angry, snarling at the wind and snow, and halfway home falling over a stone frozen into the dirt surface of the road, and tumbling off the road into a high drift, forgetting in that second of spinning collapse his anger, the hard, ancient center of his focus, coming softly to rest in the drift and letting go there, falling backward into sleep, at last — to be found there in the morning, rock-hard, with his hands and arms and legs extended, splayed, as if, when he had died, he'd been dreaming of swimming easily underwater, or as if he had been hurled to earth by a god. It was the reason Alvin's father did not drink, or so his mother had told him.

"Okay," Feeney said slowly. "I'll take you up the fuckin' road. But hand me that bottle one more time, will ya?"

Alvin once again retrieved the flat, brown bottle and passed it to his friend, who took a quick drink from it and blindly passed it back, bumping the bottle against Alvin's beefy shoulder in the darkness, spilling rye whiskey down the front of his wool loden coat and over his lap. Alvin grabbed the almost emptied bottle from his lap and cursed. Feeney apologized thickly, and they drove the rest of the way to Alvin's house in grumpy silence, passing no other car on the road, barely making it up the hill from the Center.

Alvin got out, said nothing, and walked through the snow to the house, stamped his feet noisily at the door, and walked in as Feeney drove off, the red taillights of his car swiftly disappearing behind high fantails of snow.

His mother heard him come in. "That you, Alvin?" she called from the kitchen. "I was worried, with the snow and all . . ."

"Yeah," he said sourly. He was standing near a table lamp in the living room, holding part of his coat out in front of him as he studied the whiskey stains on it. "Shit," he said in a low voice.

"Will you come and have a cup of tea with me, son? I'm glad you came home early," she called. Alvin could hear her get up from her chair and walk quickly, eagerly, to the cabinet over the sink for a cup and saucer.

Oh, well, why not? he thought. Maybe she'll know how to get the stain out of my coat. "Yeah, sure, I'll have a cup of tea with you." And he walked out to the kitchen, shedding his bulky coat as he entered the room.

She stood next to the counter by the sink, pouring him a cup of tea. Picking up the cup and saucer, carrying it across the room by pinching the saucer between thumb and forefinger, she walked past her son, tiny next to his enormous size, and suddenly, as she passed, she groaned, "Oh-h, Alvin!" With an expression on her face that joined disgust with self-pity, she placed the cup and saucer on the table in front of him, sat down opposite, and petulantly pushed the sugar and milk at him.

"What d'you mean, 'Oh-h, Alvin'?"

"You *know* what I mean!" she exploded at him. *"You! You're* what I mean! *You're* what's the matter. *Look* at you!"

"You think I'm drunk?"

"Think!" She kept stirring her spoon in the cup of tea, her hands shaking as she moved, her rage barely contained by the act. Her dark eyes glowered at him, her head twitching nervously from side to side, her feet tapping against the linoleum-covered floor. "You, you're nothing but a bum, a drunken bum! That's all! I don't know why I even bother to . . . to hope. You'll probably end up like your grandfather, the way you're going now."

"Not that one again. Jesus. My grandfather. As if ending up like my father is an improvement. Anyhow, I'm stone sober, Ma," he said quietly.

"You're a drunken bum! You smell like a brewery. You come in here smelling like a brewery, and then you have the gall to tell me how sober you are, and making cruel cracks about your father, too. You're a drunken bum, no good for anything. And now you're a liar, too."

"Ma, I am not!" he cried, and he stood up, facing her.

She wouldn't even look at him then, talked into her teacup instead and made him overhear her. "I work and I slave year after year, for what? For *this?* A drunk who can't even speak kindly to me? A thankless bum who can't say anything kind about his father?" She continued talking loudly at the teacup and about him, as if he were in an adjacent room, and he moved erratically away from the table, then back again, and finally grabbed her shoulder with one huge hand and shook her, which made her scream directly up at him, "Leave me alone! Don't you touch me! Get away from me! You're *drunk!*"

At that instant his father came crashing into the room from the bedroom. The man was dressed in a wildly billowing flannel nightgown, he was barefoot, and the gray hair on his narrow head stuck out like a spiky crown. His face was knotted in fury, and as he rushed for Alvin, he roared, "You son of a bitch, I'll *kill* you! Raising your hand against your mother! I'll *kill* you for that!"

Alvin turned, releasing his mother's shoulder, and caught the full force of his father's rush. Falling backward, he broke his fall with one hand and tried to ward off his father's punches with the other. The older man was swinging at him like a windmill gone berserk, hitting him on the head, face and shoulders, slamming him in the chest with his bony, naked knee, trying to keep him down on the floor while he beat him with his fists. Alvin reached behind him and knocked the cupboard door open, and with no conscious thought, or none that he would remember later, he reached into the cupboard, yanked out a large cast-iron skillet, and swung it at his father, hitting him squarely on the forehead. There was a thick, crunching sound, like that of an apple being broken in half by two strong hands, and the old man's body went limp and collapsed on the floor.

Alvin, dazed, dropped the skillet, stood up, heard as if from a great distance his mother screaming, "Alvin! You've killed your *father!* You've *killed* him!" and he ran from the house, grabbing up his coat as he ran.

Outside, it was dark and snowing hard. The wind had dropped, and the snow was falling straight down, like a gauze curtain. For a few moments he ran, then walked — down the road to the town, then through the darkened town to the highway, where the first vehicle heading south, a truck, stopped and picked him up.

"Where you goin'?" the driver asked from behind the red glow of his cigarette. He was a fat man a few years older than Alvin.

"Boston. Tonight."

"Okay by me. Your old lady kick you out or something?"

"Yeah," Alvin said, instantly constructing a scene that would justify his words. "Yeah, I came home too late and too drunk once too often, I guess. And she flipped her fuckin' lid. She'll probably cool off in a few days if I leave her alone. You know."

"Yeah, they always do," the driver said cheerfully as the truck picked up speed, plowing heavily, powerfully, through the falling, drifting snow.

(*Here ends the excerpt from the novel.*)

CHAPTER FIVE

Back and Fill: In Which the Hero's Ditch, Having Got Dug and the Pipe's Having Been Laid Therein, Gets Filled; Including a Brief Digression Concerning the Demon Asmodeus, along with Certain Other Digressions of Great and Small Interest

AN ANONYMOUS CALL to the chief of the two-man Barnstead Police Department, the large, barrel-chested, crew-cut man named Chub Blount, who happened to be Hamilton Stark's brother-in-law, brought the chief, as he preferred to be called, out to Hamilton's house early one morning in February. The call had come in to the chief's home around one A.M., waking the burly man from his peaceful, nearly dreamless sleep. His wife Jody, Hamilton Stark's sister, punched her husband's side with one of her sharp elbows and woke him.

"Chub! Answer the phone!" she ordered crossly.

"Whut, whut, what?" His hand clumsily groped for the telephone in the darkness above his face. Then he realized that the instrument was beside him on the nightable, and at last he stopped its shrill ringing by picking up the receiver. "Yeah?"

"*Barnstead Police?*" It was a man's voice, hurried, thin, slightly overarticulated.

"Yeah. This's the chief."

"*Good. There may have been a murder in your town. I thought you should know.*"

"Whut the hell . . . Is this Howie? Who the hell is this?" The chief sat up in bed and looked into the mouthpiece in the dark, as if trying to see who was talking into it at the other end of the line.

"Who is it, Chub?" Jody impatiently snapped.

"*Never mind who this is. I just thought you might like to know that Hamilton Stark may have been killed this afternoon. You ought to look into it, that's all.*"

"What kinda crap you handin' me, pal? Hey, is this Howie? C'mon, Howie, is it you?"

"What on *earth* is going on, Chub? Is Howie drunk?"

"*This is an anonymous phone call.*"

"Yeah, well, I don't believe you, pal. It's Howie Leeke, I know your voice, Howie, and I don't think it's funny, I gotta get up in the fuckin' morning and I don't like getting pulled outa bed in the middle of the fuckin' night to play games with a drunk."

"*No, seriously, this is an anonymous phone call.*"

"Hang up, Chub."

"Howie, look, whaddaya doin', pullin' my chain like this in the middle the fuckin' night?"

"*You don't seem to understand. I'm anonymous. I'm not Howie Leeke or anybody else, either. I'm anonymous.*"

"Chub, hang up on him."

"Bullshut you're anonymous. It's Howie."

"*No, really. I'm dead serious. I think Hamilton Stark has been murdered.*"

"Chub, will you hang that thing up!"

"Hey, Howie, ol' pal, where're you calling from? you calling me from a bar? You over the Bonnie Aire?"

"Why? Why do you want to know that? I'm anonymous."

"Jesus, Chub, it's one in the morning!"

"Shaddup, Jody. Howie . . ."

"Seriously, why do you want to know where I am? Are you going to try to trace the call? Go ahead, I'm calling from a public booth. It's only a waste of your time, though, because I'm calling to give you an important message about Howie, I mean Hamilton Stark . . ."

"Yeah, sure. Now listen up, Howie, whyn't you tell me where's that booth you're callin' from, you know, so's I can come on over an' have a drink with ya." Covering the mouthpiece with his hand, he said to his wife, "I'll get the bastard to tell me where he's calling from, see, and I'll send Calvin down there to pick him up for Drunk and Disorderly or Driving while Intoxicated. Teach that gabby bastard a lesson . . ."

"Listen here, now, this really is an important message. I think you ought to drive out to Hamilton Stark's place and look for him."

"Yeah, sure, that's all I got to do is drive around lookin' for that silly asshole. Now, c'mon, Howie, where ya callin' from? I'll come on down an' having a drink with ya. How's that?"

"I'm not Howie Leeke. I'm trying to remain anonymous, and you're not making it very easy for me, Mr. Blount."

"Okay, Howie, ol' pal, thanks for the tip about Ham," he drawled, reluctantly giving up the attempt to entrap his friend. "But one of these fine nights I'm goin' to catch you drivin' drunk or D and D, ol' buddy, and when I do, I'm goin' to hang your fuckin' ass from a fuckin' tree."

"No —"

The chief cut him off and hung up the phone. He flopped

down into the warmth of his bed, bumping against his wife's bony knees and elbow as he squirmed back into the gully he had been sleeping in earlier, and quickly, with no further words, the two of them fell asleep.

But the next morning after breakfast the chief remembered the call, and saying to himself, What the hell, I haven't got anything better to do, he decided to drive out to his brother-in-law's house. He hadn't seen the man in several months, so they'd probably be able to think of things to say to each other, and what if the bastard *had* been murdered? It wouldn't be a shock to anyone — there were plenty of people in the world, hell, in the whole state of New Hampshire, who would be happy to see Hamilton Stark dead. Hung up on a tree with flies clotted around his mouth and eyes. Down a well, green in three feet of water, his body swollen like a jelly doughnut and held there with concrete blocks. Tied to a tree, with KILL THE PIG carved into his chest, his boots filled and overflowing with the blood from the carving job they'd done on him.

It wouldn't be any great loss, as they say, but even so, it would be murder, Murder One, right here in Barnstead, New Hampshire, where there hasn't been a genuine killing for several generations — not since the one over in Gilmanton, the one that woman wrote the filthy book about, *Peyton Place*. They should have burned that damned book. Maybe someone would write a book about this one, too. Killings up here are unusual. A few accidental shootings, hunting accidents, suicides, that sort of thing, sure, but no real live killings, he thought as he drove out of town, along the river, and turned left at the Congregational church, the only church in town, onto the dirt road that led to the narrow end of the Suncook Valley, where, in the shade of Blue Job Mountain, Hamilton Stark lived.

It was a cold, dark gray day, with the sour sky sagging down almost to the treetops. Along the sides of the narrow, winding road, the tin trailers and tarpaper-covered shacks seemed frozen into the several feet of old, leathery, late-winter snow that surrounded them, the vehicles outside and the leaning, dilapidated outbuildings scattered around them. Behind the dwellings and vehicles lay the woods, the dark, tangled, third-growth pines and spruce — twisted, erratically spaced trees and groves laced together by the ruins of ancient stone walls and low, scrubby brush, a forest for squirrels and porcupines, creatures that run close to the ground or high above it.

As he drove, the chief squared his Stetson on his head, checked himself in the rear-view mirror, and hated his brother-in-law. He had not forgiven him. Although of course he told everyone that he had forgiven him long ago, which usually made the listener shake his head with surprise and admiration, for many of the things that Hamilton had done to the chief — not so much to the chief himself as to his wife Jody and her mother Alma Stark — were generally thought to be unforgivable. The chief usually explained the generosity of his spirit by saying, "Look, hey, the bastard's just not right in the head. I mean, what the hell, you don't think the bastard's *happy*, do you?" And no, no one thought for a minute that Hamilton Stark was happy, which proved the chief's assertion that the bastard wasn't right in the head. The chief liked being right, especially when he could prove it logically.

Two miles beyond the church there was a large cleared field on the right and, at the far end of the field, a driveway that led from the road along the edge of the field to a white-painted metal gate and, a little ways farther, the house. The chief turned off the road onto the driveway and in a few seconds pulled up at the gate. Easing his bulk out of the car, he walked around to the gate and unlatched it, stopping for a few seconds to study the piles of trash, most of them half-buried in snow that lay in the field in front of the house. Shaking his heavy head with disbelieving disgust, he squeezed back into his car and drove through the gate, following the driveway to the front of the house, where he came to a stop behind Hamilton's pale green Chrysler limousine.

Shutting off the engine of his own car, a Plymouth station wagon with the standard blue bubble on the roof, the chief slid out, zipped up his storm coat, slowly approached Hamilton's car from the driver's side, and immediately saw the three bulletholes in the window, which caused him to unzip his storm coat and draw his revolver from the holster on his left hip. It was a smoothly executed series of moves. For a large man the chief was fast and balanced, and he practiced all his moves diligently in his free time. Poised on the balls of his feet, his head laid back and slightly to one side, and holding his revolver with his left hand, he switched off the safety and reached for the door handle with his right hand, slowly, as if he were trying to catch a butterfly without damaging its wings. He whipped open the door, shoving the snout of his gun down into the space where the driver's head ordinarily would have been situated.

Nothing. Empty. No blood on the seat. Slugs probably in the upholstery someplace — send the lab boys out to look for them later. Course, the slugs might be buried inside Ham's body. Hit the bastard clean and fast, got the body out of the car right away so they could wipe it down, dumped the body in the trunk of the hit car, then took off to where they could drop it into some open water. The nearest open water would be the Atlantic Ocean, the Chief figured. Kittery, Maine. This was going to be a tough case to crack alone, he thought grimly. He was going to need some help.

Jamming his gun into the holster, he walked back to his own car and sat down in the driver's seat. He slammed the door behind him and started the motor and the heater, after which he slid a few inches to the right of the steering wheel to a position on the seat from which he could operate the radio comfortably. He stretched out his legs, plucked the microphone from the hook, and barked into its face. "Hawk! Come in, Hawk! This's Eagle! Come in, Hawk. This is Eagle, come in, Hawk!"

After a few seconds of answering static, a high-pitched voice cried, "*Hawk here, Eagle! Come in, Eagle!*"

"That you, Calvin?"

"*Sure is, Eagle What's up?*"

The chief scratched at the nest of curly blond hairs where his throat met his chest. "I'm over to the Stark place, where Ham Stark lives? You know the place?"

"*Sure. The place up on Blue Job Road, used t' be his mother's place —*"

"Yeah, yeah. Well, listen," the chief interrupted. "I think there's been some kinda trouble up here. Looks to me like there's been a little shooting." Suddenly, as if the bank of clouds had parted and the sun had come out, the chief became frightened. Terrified. His head was located in his car precisely where he supposed Hamilton's head to have been when he had been shot. Whoever had shot Hamilton could as easily shoot his brother-in-law. The chief flopped down on the seat, his right cheek pressed flat against the cool upholstery, and went on talking into the microphone. "Look, Calvin, get over here right away, will you? Where the hell are you now, for God's sake?" he puffed. He was lying on his side, facing the glove compartment, and it was difficult for him to breathe.

"*I'm over on Route Twenty-eight, on my way to that guy*

Yanoff's, you know the guy, takin' his goddamned dog home to him. Herb Kernisch says he seen it runnin' deer last night and he'll shoot it next time it's out loose, you know Herb . . ."

"Yeah, yeah, sure. How long will it take you to get here?" The chief was terrified. He'd walked into a trap. Shit, shit, shit. Those were rifle slugs for sure. Hit men from Boston. Probably Cosa Nostra. Mafia. Italian. They'd as soon kill him as pick a flower, and they could do it, too, the way he'd set himself up. They could pick him off from fifty yards, and all he had was his damned service revolver.

"Oh . . . I dunno, twenty minutes, I guess, if I come straight over an' don't take this mutt back to Yanoff's. I ain't there yet."

"Well, for Christ's sake, hit your fuckin' siren an' get the hell over here!" he cried into the mike.

"You okay, Chief?"

"Yes. Yeah, sure. Just get the hell over here, will you, Calvin?" The chief was sweating, and his eyes were darting wildly back and forth across the narrow slab of leaden sky that he could see from his position on the seat. It was everything he could see — a rectangle of low, dark sky — but he expected that any second even that would go black on him, as three soft-nosed slugs penetrated his large, soft body.

"Ten-four, Eagle."

"Yeah, yeah. Ten-four." He looked for his hat, the white Stetson he'd bought last spring at the police chiefs' convention in Dallas. It was on the floor in front of him, getting dirty. He retrieved it and started brushing it clean with his hand. That goddamned Ham Stark, he fumed, as he brushed his hat with his thick fingertips. Getting me into this. Why does he always have to . . . whatever it is he does. I ought to just get the hell out of here, drive off and forget the whole thing. Not even mention it to anyone. Not even Jody. Except that

Calvin's already on his way over here. *He* knows. Shit. Never should have called him. Jesus Christ, why don't things go right for me? Shit, shit, shit. Who the hell made that phone call last night, anyhow? *That's* who probably did it, got me into this in the first place. He studied his hat. It was white again, sparkling white, without even a bruise of dirt from the floor.

Taking a long-handled plastic windshield scraper from under the seat and sticking the wide end into his hat, the chief slowly raised his hat above him, hoping that, if they shot at it, they would miss. But no one shot. Silence. He held the hat in what he assumed was plain view for a minute, joggled it temptingly, and then slowly sat up beneath it, took the hat off the scraper, and squared it on his head, checking himself out in the rear-view mirror. He tried a little smile, the one that started with a sneer and ended there too, the smile he used to answer backtalking out-of-state speeders. He'd started practicing it when state troopers caught Ethel Kennedy, the murdered senator's wife, speeding on Route 93 on her way home from a ski weekend at Waterville Valley. The smile looked good. Tough, smart, mean. A smile that said he'd seen it all, seen it all twice last week.

How the hell had Hamilton got himself mixed up with Mafia hit men? the chief wondered as he settled back into his seat to wait for Calvin. Ham was a *plumber*, for Christ's sake, a pipefitter. Not a bookie or something. Maybe he was mixed up with a woman of some kind. Maybe this time the bastard went too far, got himself involved with a woman who belonged to someone who'd kill him for it. Serve the bastard right. Serve him right if some tough little wop in a three-piece suit kicked him in the nuts three or four times and then shot him in the face. Some women a man has to steer clear of. The chief thought of his own wife, Jody, her long, angular body, her grim mouth and flat voice. He studied the house in front of him, and as he hoped, forgot his wife. It was a nice place, he observed, a handsome white house, square, well kept, large but not too large, situated well off the road, with the mountain behind it and the valley in front. No wonder Ham was so attached to the place, he thought.

The house was a two-hundred-year-old, traditionally proportioned Cape, with an ell at one end that was connected to a small barn Hamilton had converted into a garage. Behind the house was another, larger barn, several outbuildings, and then the woods. Behind the woods was the mountain. The main house and the small barn had been built by Josiah Stark, and the place had remained in the hands of the Starks until now, which of course was a mightily significant fact about the place. But not to the chief. He could see only that it was a solid-looking, attractive and well-kept place, and that alone made it desirable. Oh, he knew that Hamilton had been born and raised in the house, and he imagined that that, too, probably made it desirable, at least to Hamilton. I can see why the bastard wanted the place so bad, he conceded. But I'll never know why he couldn't wait for his mother to die first. Never.

Though the chief had been a visitor to the house for decades, though he had courted and eventually married a woman who had been born and raised there, and though afterward for years he had visited his in-laws there, nevertheless, whenever he saw or thought of the house, he remembered only one event, a single night, the night Hamilton had taken possession of the house. Here is how it happened.

Or rather, here is the version of what happened that was generally accepted as the truth, accepted by all but one of the participants in the events of that monstrous evening, accepted as well by the townspeople of Barnstead, and accepted by hundreds of others who were told the story only because it could be said to have a certain universal "human interest," or because it was an example of horrid behavior, say, or of long suffering, or of a bizarre turnabout.

At any rate, almost any native of Barnstead, New Hampshire, the librarian, perhaps, or the town clerk, visiting a cousin named Mattie in Daytona Beach, Florida, might look up from her knitting and say, "Well, if you want to talk about your bizarre turnabouts, *here's* one for the books." Or, "If you think *that's* one of your long-suffering parents, let me tell you about Alma Stark . . ." Or, "Now that's horrid, all right, but I can tell you something so horrid, Mattie, that it'll make you never want to have a son." And this is what she'd say:

"Up to Blue Job Road, oh, maybe a mile, mile and a half from town, you've got the Stark place, which has been in the family since it was built, probably some two hundred years, though of course it's lots different now, different from the way it was when it got built, because the Starks have always been hardworking and mostly in the building trades, the men, so they've fixed the place up quite a bit over the years—not so much the land, I mean, which is over five hundred acres, at least that's what they always got taxed for, 'in excess of five hundred acres'—no, they didn't so much fix up the land as the house and barns, putting on a dormer here, a new porch there, sort of constantly renovating was how the Starks have always taken care of their place, so by the time poor Alma and Horace Stark were up in their seventies and their children were all grown and married—there were three, the son Ham and the daughters Jody and Sarah—well, by that time the place was all modernized, you know, with electricity and aluminum storm windows and a new oil furnace, and the plumbing was just about the best you could imagine, because Horace was a pipefitter, like his father, who died pretty young in a sad way, but that's another story — anyhow, if there was one thing the Stark house was going to have, it was good plumbing. Oh, I guess Horace'd got to be about seventy or maybe seventy-one, and Alma was about the same age, when he got his first heart attack and had to retire from the pipefitting and stay in the house all the time, though of course he wouldn't do it, wouldn't stay in the house all the time, he was outside working on that place as soon's he could walk again, no matter he couldn't move half his face and couldn't even talk right anymore, though he never talked much anyhow. But now he couldn't even remember what you'd told him five minutes ago. Anyhow, all that man knew about life was work, work, work, and if he couldn't keep on working, he was dead, so he kept on working, putting in the garden, shingling the barn roof, building fences, cutting firewood — just about anything needed doing around the place, and lots that didn't need doing too. Poor Alma. She couldn't keep that man in and down the way the doctor had told her to, 'You keep that man in and down,' he told her, and Horace'd never been the easiest man in town to live with anyhow, kind of cross all the time, not very talkative and then grouchy when he did talk, but after he got the heart attack he got even crosser, scowled all the time, even when he didn't know you were looking at him. And because he couldn't talk right anymore, he stopped talking completely, left it up to Alma to do the talking for both of them, wouldn't even answer the telephone, would stand right there beside it and let it ring and ring and ring. He'd look at it like it was a design on the wallpaper or something. And the cost. Well, I know that heart attack of his cost them a pile of money, because Alma let me know with a few well-chosen words, she said, 'It's twice as expensive to be sick when you're old,' she told me one day, and I could have just cried for her, the poor thing. So proud, you know. But at least they owned the house clear and free, I told her, trying to comfort her, and at that time they did own the house clear and free, no mortgage, no debts of any kind, the way I heard it, so all they had to do was make do from month to month on Social Security, and I guess for a while that's what they did. Then Horace went and got his second heart attack, this time one of your real strokes, and he had to have surgery this time, so when he come out of it he couldn't even leave his chair without help from Alma, and all he could do now was sit in the living room in his rocker or his armchair, he liked to switch around, and watch the wrestling on television, a nice twenty-one-inch color set his son Ham, who was living over in Concord with his new wife, had bought him for Christmas. Ham was nice about that, the color TV, because he really didn't have to, they already had a black and white, but when it come to the question of how they were going to pay all the doctor and hospital bills, Ham told his mother, who was now the only one capable of making a decision, he told her to borrow the five thousand dollars from the bank and take out a mortgage on the house to guarantee it. Now naturally there was no way that poor old couple was going to be able to make the payments on a loan that size, so the son, a pipe-fitter like his father, but young, of course, and making good money working heavy construction over to Concord, he offered to make the payments for them, but so's he'd feel covered — that's how he put it, so's *he'd* feel covered — they should sign the deed of the house over to him, and he and his new wife would move into the house right off, 'to help take care of Pa,' he said. Now if you knew

Ham's wife, you'd know how likely *that* was—she was his second wife, a fancy New York City tap dancer, used to be one of those June Taylor Dancers on the *Jackie Gleason Show*? You've probably seen her on TV, but it's hard to remember one from all the others. Anyhow, I can't blame her, not after what I know now, but that's how Ham put it: 'Annie and I want to be able to help take care of Pa, and we can do it a lot easier if we're living right there in the house with you,' he told his poor old mother, who naturally was terrified by all those bills and by the idea of having to take care of a man who'd become practically a vegetable—no disrespect, but that's truly what he'd turned into since the second heart attack, kind of leaning all the time off to one side there in his chair while he looked at the wrestling and the cowboy shows, which is what he liked the best, the wrestling and the cowboys, with the whole left side of him stiff as a door and the rest of him spastic as a cat with distemper. It was something horrible to see, so I used to go over there twice a week, to visit Alma and try to cheer her up some, and naturally I'd have to see Horace too, and even though he'd turned a lot sweeter, a whole lot, since the second attack and the operation, it was kind of sickening, if you know what I mean. I used to almost wish he was still all sour and grouchy, so he wouldn't try to talk to me, because now when I'd go over to spend the afternoon with Alma, he'd try to talk and smile, but all he could do was make these pathetic moans like a cow and toothy kind of crazy-looking smiles, which I know must have embarrassed Alma so much that probably even she was wishing the old man would get cross and silent again. I don't know, maybe Alma didn't have any other choice, because after all, Ham was her son and she *had* to pay those bills; so anyhow, she agreed to sign over the house and take out the mortgage and let Ham make the payments — he paid her a dollar, a single dollar bill, for the house, because when they signed it over there had to be some money change hands — and she also agreed to let him and his second wife Annie move into the house. They sold this little ranch over to Concord they'd owned and moved right in that same week, going right to work fixing up the second floor entirely for themselves with a new bathroom and converting two of the little bedrooms up there into one 'master bedroom' — that's what he called it, a 'master bedroom' — and his mother and father went on using their old bedroom and bathroom downstairs. That was when the big dormer in back of the house got put in too, because Ham and Annie wanted a view of the mountain from their 'master bedroom.' It wasn't enough they already had a view of the mountain from the kitchen; no, they had to have one from their bedroom too. But of course all this time everyone, Alma too, thought that Ham was being kind to his mother and father. No one knew what he had in his head. No one knew that when the old man finally died, as he did that spring — very peacefully, thank heaven, just went to sleep and didn't wake up again, just like his own father died, only that was in a snowbank and he was dead drunk at the time — anyhow, when Ham's father finally died, no one knew six months later everything would blow up like it did. Ham went and put in a garden like his father had done every summer, and Annie got herself involved a little bit with the town, joined the Ladies' Aid Society and so forth, and Alma seemed happier than I'd ever remembered seeing her, because everyone knew that Horace had been a difficult man to live with. He was so cross all the time, even as a young man. Anyhow, as fall comes on, Annie stopped going to Ladies' Aid, and Ham was seen drunk a lot in town, and ever since he was a boy in high school, practically, he's been nasty when he's drunk, and he was being nasty all right, scrapping and fighting in the Bonnie Aire over to Pittsfield, wrecking his car one night by driving it dead drunk into the Civil War Memorial down to the Parade. So people started getting the idea that things weren't going all that smooth at the Stark place. And they sure weren't, as we later found out. What was happening was that Annie had decided she didn't like living way out in the country with no one but her mother-in-law for company all day, and so she'd started nagging Ham about moving to Connecticut or someplace where she could have the kind of life she preferred, and like I said, I can't really blame her. After all, being married to that man must have been no picnic, like they say, and since she was a big-city girl, a famous dancer and all, living way out at the end of a dirt road in an old house with an old woman must have been pretty boring for her. She was sort of a pretty woman then, and she was actually a nice woman when you got to know her, and she couldn't help it if fate and Ham had put her in a place that could only be boring to a woman like that. So they did a lot of fighting, she and Ham, and one of the ways she got around being so bored and doing so much fighting was to take week-long trips down to New York City, where she stayed with her aunt in an apartment in the Bronx, she once told me. That made it easier for everyone, I suppose, probably even for Ham, though who can say what makes things easier for that man? Anyhow one night in October when Annie was down to New York, Ham came home drunk and late, around nine o'clock or so. Alma'd made supper for him, and so she was ticked off that he'd come in so late and drunk, and I guess she must have let it out a little, because he got to fighting back at her, yelling that this was his house and he'd come home when and how he damned well pleased to come home, and so forth, until finally she said, out of anger, you understand, not really meaning it, 'All right, then, I'll leave,' and he said, 'Fine.' He went and phoned up his sister Jody, who thank God lives in town with her husband Chub, the chief of police, and Ham told Jody to come pick her mother up, she was moving out. Jody was shocked, naturally, but what could she do, so she drove up to the house and picked up her mother, who had refused to show that man any emotion over the thing and had gone right ahead and packed her bags, and Jody drove the old woman back down to the Center where she and Chub and their twin boys have a trailer, and lucky for everyone, it's one of those two-bedroom trailers, so they had room for Alma. Then Chub went and called Ham and asked him what was going on, sort of man to man, and when Ham told him to mind his own GD business, Chub got mad — and he's not the kind of man you want to get mad — so he hopped into his car and drove up to the house and stormed in, but when he got into the house he found Ham standing in the middle of the living room with a rifle pointed at him. I mean it. A rifle. Pointed right at Chub's heart. That's the kind of man Ham Stark is. Or was. I really wouldn't know now, because I haven't seen the man to talk to, even assuming I would talk to him, which of course I wouldn't, for what, twelve years now, ever since that night . . ."

There are two versions of what happened following the moment when Hamilton confronted his brother-in-law with a 30.06 rifle. Both are widely believed. Here is Chub's version:

"I come in there and the bastard's got his thirty-ought-six aimed and cocked. I can see he's drunker'n a fiddler's fart, so I start trying to humor him, you know, because your drunk man can pull the trigger when your sober man won't. So I start saying things like, 'Hey, Ham, ol' buddy, you don't want to shoot your ol' buddy, get yourself in all kindsa trouble.' You know, stuff like that, just talking to him, while all the time I'm circling around the room and closing in on him, trying to look real casual, like I'm just checking out the furniture or something, but with each step getting closer to the guy, not being obvious about it or anything, of course, until finally I'm maybe only two feet from the tip of the barrel. That's when I make my move. I look quick off to my left, like there's someone at the window, and he follows my look, and I grab the barrel of the gun and yank the thing out of his hands, and then I throw it on the couch behind me with one hand and reach around his neck with the other arm, yank his head back, and throw a hammer lock on him until he blacks out and goes limp. He's a pretty big guy, bigger'n me, but he doesn't have my training, of course, so there's not much he can do against me, especially since he's drunk and all. Anyhow, after a few seconds he comes to, and realizing what he's done, the guy starts bawling like a baby, pounding his fists on the floor and everything, just like he's a little kid. I can see he really isn't right in the head, so I says to him that he ought to get himself to one of those psychologists or something, a head doctor, only he tells me to go to hell, starts laying me out like that, so I say the hell with him and I walk out, and I haven't seen the bastard, not socially, since that night."

The second version of that confrontation was, naturally, Hamilton's own, which he conveyed by means of a typed post card to his daughter Rochelle, when in a letter she asked him specifically what had happened at that particular point in the evening, "the night you and your family quarreled," was how she delicately put it. Here is his post card:

Big Chief broke into private domicile. H. S. ordered him off property with aid of 30.06 Winchester. B. C. eagerly complied. Nothing else. Later phone call from B. C. threatened H. S. with bodily harm. Promises never kept. Boring story. Tell about how your great-great-great-great-grandfather stole 700 acres from Abenookis. You need some humor in your book.

Her father's literary advice, offered gratuitously, was not followed, which is perhaps unfortunate, because possibly the only significant flaw in Rochelle's novel is its lack of humor.

At the time she received the above card from her father, she was especially unlikely to heed the kind of advice he was offering, for at that particular moment in the writing she was exploring and expounding her theory that her hero, Alvin Stock (Hamilton Stark), was actually possessed by a little-known demon named Asmodeus. Although, to be sure, Rochelle later on gave up this somewhat bizarre notion, so that in the completed manuscript there is not a single reference either to demons or possession (with one possible exception, in her Chapter Two, "Conversion," where she describes a vision of the archangel Raphael that was experienced by the hero, Alvin, at the age of sixteen one night after a high school dance in the Pittsfield High School parking lot), nevertheless, the terms of her theory are significantly revealing, not only of how Rochelle perceived the extremity of her father's behavior, but also of the man's behavior itself.

While in many ways a courageous and rigorously rational young woman, Rochelle, especially during the period when she was writing her so-called novel, was nonetheless capable of profound superstition, and further, was capable of structuring her superstitions to help her evade uncomfortable truths. Of course, she was very young at the time (still is), and besides, one can hardly blame her. Even if she had been drawing on nothing more than her own direct experiences of her father, she would at some point have been forced to confront the facts that he had mistreated her mother, that he had deserted her in her infancy, that later, as she grew into young womanhood, he had mocked her attempts to express her love for him, and that he had rejected outright her final attempts as an adult to create a friendship with him. Additionally, he had done all this as if he had intended to do it from the beginning! As if nothing could have pleased him more! His villainy was all of a piece. Thus, no matter how much one would have liked to, one could not have forgiven Hamilton Stark for his weakness, nor understood him for his stupidity, nor sympathized with him for his pathology — because he so consistently had insisted that everything he did was intentional, was deliberate, and in the long run was happiness-producing. And if all this, which was no more than her own direct experience of the man, were not sufficient to send her flying to the warm solace of superstition, at the time of her novel-writing Rochelle was interviewing and corresponding with many other people who had been involved with her father, either as wife, sister, brother-in-law, or even friend, and thus she was being literally overwhelmed with tales of selfishness, of rage, drunkenness, lust, greed, of eccentric violence and destructive manipulation, of betrayal, disloyalty and deceit. She could find people, men as well as women, who said they had loved him, who even seemed to be obsessed with him, but she could find no one who could tell her tales of sweetness, of gentleness, kindness and generosity, of affectionate big-heartedness, humility and steadfastness. And yet, oddly, the more of the man's nature she uncovered to herself, the more she loved him and the more her obsession with her father dominated her thoughts and actions.

How else, then, to explain to herself (or to others) such a compelling attraction to a man she knew in all ways to be morally obnoxious — unless she could believe that he was possessed? An otherwise sweet, gentle, kind and generous man, she decided, an affectionately big-hearted man, a humble and steadfast man, was tragically possessed by a demon, she believed, and he had thus been transformed into a wholly selfish man, a raging, drunken, lustful man, a greedy man, a man of eccentric, unpredictable violence and pointless manipulation, a master of betrayal, disloyalty and deceit.

And it was not unnatural, once she had determined that her father was possessed in the first place, that Rochelle would happen on the demon Asmodeus. She had what might be called a lively religious curiosity, possibly the guilt-motivated residue of an adolescent conversion experience and the falling away that had followed. She had been raised rather casually as a Presbyterian, southern (and therefore highly emotional regardless of how casual one might be in keeping the rituals), and when she underwent what in those sects is referred to as the "conversion experience," whereby Jesus Christ, heretofore a mere abstraction, becomes one's "personal savior," she brought with her the intellectual apparatus and energy that were her genetic birthright, and as a result she succeeded in making herself into something of a biblical scholar before, at the age of eighteen, she commenced to fall away from the organized forms of religion. Thus, later on, when the young woman began looking around for the proper demon, she had little difficulty remembering Asmodeus. (It might be worth noting also that in the meantime, between her falling away from her religious faith and her "discovery" that her father had been possessed by the demon Asmodeus, she had undergone almost a year of Jungian psychoanalysis, and consequently it was not especially difficult for her to credit non-Christian deities and other mythical figures with immense power in determining the behavior of individuals who in all ways were unconscious even of the mere existence of such deities.)

Rochelle knew that Asmodeus, or Ashmedai, though imported from Persian mythology into Palestine, showed up rather frequently in Jewish literature, where his original function was to cause frustration in marriage, usually by provoking rage and violence. There was a crucial link with lust, however, a particularly non-Jewish and non-Christian (although perhaps not non-Protestant) link between rage and lust. Rochelle's adolescent studies had shown her that the Jewish Asmodeus had probably originally been the Persian "fiend of the wounding spear," sometimes Aeshma Daeva, from the root *aesh*, meaning "to rush forward" or "to be violently self-impelled." He was a storm spirit, a personification of rage, one who took deep pleasure from filling men's hearts with anger and desire for revenge. In contrast to the modern world, where anger is regarded as a thing of great value, as something not to be suppressed but rather as a "feeling" to be experienced as a type of ecstasy, in the ancient world anger was regarded as something pre-eminently evil and nonhuman and, therefore, dependent upon interference from outside forces for its visible expression.

According to Jewish stories, Asmodeus was the son of a mortal woman, Naamah, either by one of the fallen angels or possibly by Adam himself before the creation of Eve. In the testament of Solomon, written between A.D. 100 and 400, he is reported to have remarked, "I was born of angel's seed by a daughter of man." Described there as "furious and shouting," he not only prevents intercourse between husband and wife, but also encourages adultery. "My business is to plot against the newly married," he boasts, "so that they may not know one another . . . I transport men into fits of madness and desire when they have wives of their own, so that they leave them and go off by night and day to others that belong to other men with the result that they commit sin. . . ." A peculiar function: to frustrate desire so that he may arouse it elsewhere. In another account, the book of Tobit, written around 250 B.C., Tobias marries Sarah, who has had seven husbands before, all of whom were strangled by Asmodeus to prevent them from lying with her. On the advice of the archangel Raphael, Tobias cooks the heart and liver of a fish, and the smoke repels the demon and drives him off.*

For Rochelle, the peculiar sequence of the demon's evolution — from a demon of rage to one who infected men with uncontrollable lust to one who meddled with the mainsprings of marriage — was sufficient to qualify him as the one responsible for her father's equally peculiar combination of what she had no choice but to regard as social and moral inadequacies. Of course, to connect Asmodeus to the life of her father, Rochelle was also forced to ignore or to explain away as "corrupted sources" and "mistranslations" long chains of bizarre imagery and anachronistic, minor attributes of the demon. All she cared about was the fact that he was the only figure who combined rage with lust and loosed these emotions onto the institution of marriage. To do this, she

* The Latin version of Tobit adds that Tobias and Sarah defeated the demon by successfully remaining chaste for the first three nights of their marriage, which was the beginning of the later custom of "Tobias's Nights." In fact, right down to the nineteenth century in parts of France, Germany and the Balkans, it was customary to follow the example of Tobias and Sarah, and in medieval France, husbands were often permitted to pay a fee to the Church for a license to disregard the rule.

had to overlook, for instance, the efficacy of the smoky fish liver. She also had to sidestep all ancient attempts to describe the demon physically, because his attributes, if she visualized them, would have made her suspect herself of having drifted into "imaginative zeal," which she abhorred in others as much as in herself. How, for instance, could she have pictured her father as being possessed by a figure who was said to have the enormous feet of a cock (a bird, one might note, well known for its indiscriminate sexual vigor)? How could she have accommodated herself to those several Jewish tales that have Asmodeus as the king of the demons and residing on top of a mountain from which he regularly journeys to heaven where he takes part in the learned discussions that supposedly go on there? How to make peace with the tale that has the master magician, King Solomon, force Asmodeus and the other devils to construct the Temple at Jerusalem,* after which Asmodeus takes his nasty revenge by seizing the ring in which all Solomon's magic power resides and, tossing the ring to the bottom of the sea, sends Solomon into exile and reigns in his place until, miraculously, Solomon recovers the ring from a fish's belly and proceeds to imprison Asmodeus and all the other devils in a large jar? And how to honor the source called the *Lemegeton*, a highly respected magic textbook, which, providing a long list of demons, asserts that when Asmodeus shows himself to human eyes he rides a dragon, carries a long spear, and has three heads, that of a ram, a bull and a handsome youth, asserting further that only a bare-headed magician may sum-

* Oddly, when asked which of his many construction jobs had given him the most personal satisfaction, Hamilton replied, "The Temple at Jerusalem," which remark, at the time, was interpreted by the interrogator as meaning that none of his many jobs had given him personal satisfaction.

mon the demon, whereupon the demon will respond by making the magician invisible and will lead him to great treasure? How indeed? And what is meant by "bare-headed"?

Nevertheless, despite such pathetic imaginings, Rochelle successfully managed to incorporate the demon into her vision of her father and, for a single, early version of her novel, her vision of Alvin Stock as well. Happily, she saw the irrationality and the personal psychological use such a vision implied, and because she is as brave a woman as she is intelligent, she purged the novel of all references to demons and possession, and though she did not in that way simplify the character of her father, she did succeed in seeing him more clearly, more *realistically*, one might say.

On the other hand, perhaps by coming to regard her father in such a critically analytical light, she lost something, too — a depth, the shuddering, vibratory quality that a proper description of his character required, especially if the reader were to understand the intensity with which Hamilton Stark (Alvin Stock) could simultaneously attract and repel people who, for whatever reason, came close to him. One is left, with regard to Hamilton Stark, with the two-dimensional vision of the chief of the Barnstead Police Department, Chub Blount, who, unable to imagine (or if he imagined them, to care about) the qualities of life associated with the Stark house simply because it had been owned and lived in by the Stark family for over two hundred years, and not mentioning those qualities to himself, thus saw the house in what may be called a "realistic" light. To continue the analogy, one would be forced to deny oneself any vision of the house that explained how a man could commit irrational acts of loyalty to a mere wooden structure. One would not be capable of understanding why a man, who from adolescence had resolutely refused to pray for anything, suddenly had found himself on his knees one night next to his bed in his modest ranch house in Concord, steadfastly praying for ownership of the same house his ancestors had owned. No, if the reader relied on the chief's view of the relationship between Hamilton and the house his ancestors had owned, he would see a merely selfish, aggressive man using the occasion of a deed and his old and sick parents' desperation to work out his hostilities and gratify his greedy whim to own the house outright and exclusively.

Knowing about the patina of time and family that in Hamilton's mind had surely been laid over the image of the house — an inescapable aura, when it's available, for any imaginative American of our time — knowing that, however, the sensitive reader may add to the chief's opaque view of the dispossession the vision of a man obsessed and terrified, a man determined to attach himself to the one thing in his life that seemed capable of connecting him to the thread of time that potentially runs through the fabric of every family. In most cases, especially in this country and among the members of all classes but the most privileged, this thread is broken at every turn. Given geographic relocation, eager divorce, homes for the aged, distant, private schools for the young, housing developments for the middle-aged and insistence by all generations that the adult life of one generation will not be repeated as a life again, it should be no wonder when, having endured all that discontinuity, a man who sees a possibility to attach himself to his familial past by means of a two-hundred-year-old farm and house will grow desperate and impatient beyond reason. He will conceive plans and schemes, will see potential heirs (such as his two younger sisters) as threats to his very life, will even see his own mother as a likely breaker of the thread, and will see his father's death as a piece of great good luck. Who then is to say this is mere selfishness and aggression? For a man such as Hamilton Stark, emotionally severed from his parents and sisters since childhood (and perhaps, because of the conventions, since birth), a man unable to attach himself to the life and history of a wife or even, at the deepest level, of a friend or of his only child, a daughter he can barely remember and for whom he is unable to create any loyalty except in terms of conventional guilt, which he rejects as both inappropriate and insufficiently personal — for a man such as this, it seems natural that an old frame house and seven hundred acres of rocky, overgrown hillside would become, for all practical purposes, mystical emblems, badges which, if his, would connect him to the rest of the universe.

Obviously, while the chief sat in his patrol car in front of this very farmhouse and let his mind drift across the unpleasant details of his near-violent (or possibly violent, in fact) encounter with his brother-in-law, even though the encounter had taken place some eleven years ago, nothing like sympathy or understanding organized his thoughts. They merely drifted across the surface of the remembered event, and if a question were raised about any possible deeper motivation lying behind Hamilton's outrageous behavior, he answered it immediately, saying to the questioner with complete confidence that what happened is what happened, and what happened is the kind of man Hamilton Stark is, a guy who's mad at the world and wants as much of it for himself as he can get, no matter who gets in the way, no matter if it's his mother or his sisters or anybody else. That's how the chief would probably put it. In fact, that is pretty much how he did put it when, one afternoon, he was asked about that particular evening by Rochelle.

Poor Rochelle. Even though she loved her father, she still did not understand the potentially mystical aspect of real estate in New England (the reader may recall that Rochelle was raised in central Florida), and thus she was unable to understand what storms of emotion Hamilton had been responding to when he had dispossessed his own mother. Naturally, this created a sharp conflict for her. No matter how diligently she analyzed the details of that evening, no matter how many interviews she conducted, visits to the house, careful reconstructions of the minutes of the evening and the months that preceded it, she was unable to get around the conclusion that her father had behaved in a wholly reprehensible way. And as a result of her examination, she (unlike the chief, who had no need of, nor interest in, neutralizing all emotions but love for the man) experienced considerable pain. If the chief were to read the final version of her novel, which describes in agonizingly honest detail her pain in this regard, he probably would agree fully with her description of the events that prompted her painful judgment of her father, but he would not understand why that judgment, once she had made it, gave her any trouble. As far as he was concerned, when you love somebody who turns out to be a bastard, you stop loving him. And not without a certain relief, probably.

Some of this was going through the chief's mind that gray February morning while he sat in his car outside the Stark house and waited for his assistant to arrive. I.e., When you love somebody who turns out to be a bastard . . . Yes, even for the chief, it was difficult to look at the house and not drop into examinations and speculations concerning the kinds of love and hate these Starks bore for each other and for themselves. They were no noisier than any other family in town, nor were they unconventional by way of education, travel or economics, and except for Hamilton, they were as careful to avoid eccentricity or drawing attention to themselves as practically everyone else in town. All this made it difficult to explain the intensity of their feelings — not so much the fact of the intensity as the fact that people were allowed to see that those feelings existed at all. It was unusual to know that much about a person or a family, especially when the family was as reticent and close-mouthed, as *ordidinary*, as the Starks.

Suddenly the chief's ruminations were intruded upon by the whining voice of his assistant, Calvin Clark. "Hey, Chief!" the man cried through the closed window of the chief's car. "What's up?"

The chief squeezed his large belly past the steering wheel and got out. "I got an anonymous tip last night that Ham Stark might've been shot," he said, "so I come up here this morning to check it out. I figured it was just Howie Leeke calling me drunk from the Bonnie Aire or someplace — you know Howie, how he does — or I would've come out here last night."

"Sure, sure, Chief." Calvin was gulping air, a habit that made it almost impossible for him to lie successfully. Whenever he became even slightly insincere, he found himself unable to keep from gulping while he talked, as if he were about to be beaten for his insincerity. Luckily for him, or perhaps merely as a result of his habit, he rarely lied outright. Politeness, however, often made it necessary for him not actually to lie but rather to speak with little or no sincerity, and since he was a polite man, he frequently found himself gasping like a fish out of water.

"Yeah. So anyhow, I come out here this morning. Just to check it out, you know?"

"Sure, Chief, sure." Gulping.

"And I found *these*," the chief said dramatically, pointing with a thick finger at the trio of bulletholes in the window of Hamilton's Chrysler.

"Holy shit!" Calvin gasped appropriately. "What are they?"

"Bulletholes. Thirty-thirty, I'd say. Maybe bigger."

"Yeah, sure, sure. Where's Ham? He seen these yet? Boy will he be pissed. You know Ham."

"No, you . . . *Jesus!*" The chief stomped back to his car and got into it.

"Where you going, Chief?" Calvin called.

"Nowhere," he answered, almost whispering it. Then, with authority, "Listen, take a look in the house for Ham. I'll poke around out here and in the garage."

"Right, Chief," Calvin said, promptly jogging toward the front door of the house. It was locked, and in a second he had disappeared around the corner of the house, checking the side door at the porch. The chief, sweating, restarted the engine of his car. After a few moments, Calvin appeared at the front of the house again, spreading his empty hands to show that he'd been unable to find Hamilton.

"Not out here either!" the chief hollered out the car window. "It's probably just some kind of crazy . . . Let's head back to town, you can check by here late this afternoon!"

Calvin walked slowly up to the chief's open window. "You don't think somebody *shot* him, do you? I mean, *somebody* hadda shoot them holes in his car," Calvin reasoned.

"The bastard probably did it himself. You know Ham."

"Yeah. Then who was it called you last night?"

"I dunno. Probably Ham. It still could've been Howie, but I kinda doubt it now. Probably Ham made the call, just to get me pissed."

"Yeah," Calvin gulped. He was shivering from the cold. The gray sky had seemed to tighten and lift a bit, and flecks of snow were drifting slowly down.

"I'll see you later, back at the office," the chief announced.

He cranked up the window, dropped his car into reverse, and backing around Calvin's car, entered the turnaround behind it, spun the wheel hard to the left, and fled down the long driveway to the road.

By the time he reached the center of town it was snowing hard, as if blankets of the soft flakes were being tossed against the ground. Boy, snow in February is depressing, the chief thought, and then he decided to go home for the rest of the day. He figured, with the snow and all, he'd be out on emergency calls most of the night, so he'd better catch some sleep while he could.

CHAPTER SIX

Chapter Beginning as "His Second Wife Speaks of a Man She Calls 'Your Father' (from a Tape Recording)"

HIS SECOND WIFE speaks of a man she calls "your father" (from a tape recording):

"Yeah, my mother, she used to sit back in her chair and she'd clap her hands together, like this, and she'd say to me, 'Annie, oh, Annie, you're so pretty with that smile and those legs. With those legs, honey, you, you're going to the *top!*' She said, she said it often enough, boy, once a day at least, and she wasn't the only one saying it, either. My God, Uncle Zack, my Aunt Harriet. I mean, even old Grover said it, old Grover the janitor in our building on East Eighty-sixth, even he said it, so by the time I was, say, oh, I dunno, twelve, thirteen, by that time I really believed it myself. I really, I believed it was gonna be *true*. I was going to the top. And you know what that meant to us, 'getting to the top,' it meant Show Business. SHOW BIZ. I guess because we were New Yorkers. You know. But also because we were all jokers, all of us, the whole family — comics, singers, mimics, like that. This was before television, of course, back in the forties and all, so to us Show Business didn't mean TV, it meant the stage. The Musical Stage, honey, right up there in front of a live audience, people who really love ya, and you can feel 'em loving ya, nobody cares if you feel it, so you just take it in like the sun's rays, and the more you get the better you get, no kidding, that's how it works, Show Business. With the stage, I mean, not TV or movies. It's different there, TV, the movies, because the audience there hates you if you look like you can feel 'em loving ya. They want to see you as if you're all alone in the world or something, you know, as if they're looking at you through one of those one-way mirrors that department stores have for detectives. Anyhow, to be good, *really* good, on the stage, you have to get special training, of course. No matter if you're talented — talent's as cheap as daisies and'll do you about as much good as a dozen of 'em — unless you get the training, because you might, you maybe wouldn't think so, but it's not so easy to stand up there and let 'em love ya and let 'em know you can feel it, let 'em know you love it. Which of course is what keeps them doing it, loving ya. It really is not easy. I don't care what you might think. It's work. Hard work, honey. You wouldn't believe — you've never been in show business, have you? I can tell. Never mind, I mean, I can tell from the way you walk and how you're sitting, stuff like that, though of course you've got the looks, you could do it, I mean if you had the training and all, though you might be too old for it now. I was only a kid when I got started. I had the looks too, but like I said, talent's cheap. Nothing. Nuth-ing. So I had to get started early, before I was ten, even, I got started. At first all I could do was sing, you know, like a little kid, but cute, I mean cute enough to get me on 'Uncle Bob's Rainbow House' eight times in one year, and then when I started taking lessons it didn't take long before I was good enough to sing with Major Bowes, and after that I did the 'Rinso White' commercial on radio. Did you ever hear that one? 'Rinso *White!* Rinso *White!* Happy little washday *song!*' You're too young for radio. Another radio show I was on was 'Our Gal Sunday,' where I had a singing part for thirty-six weeks running. And all this time I'm taking voice lessons, training to be *heard,* honey, not seen, not yet, anyhow. First things first, you know what I mean? But around the time I was eleven my mother says I ought to start getting ready to be seen, people are really starting to talk about how good-looking I am anyhow, so she starts me taking tap and modern ballet, and three afternoons a week the accordion. Things you can do out in front of people. Not like the piano or the cello or something like that, that hides you. My mama really had it figured, she really knew what she wanted for me and how she could get it for me. She wanted me to be seen, and naturally, to be loved for it, for being seen. Oh yeah, my mama just knew it, people were going to love me for letting them see me — and I was going to let them see everything I had, too. I was going to turn myself into a beautiful girl gracefully dancing up there on the stage, long white legs shining in the lights, feet in silver shoes tapping miraculously fast in complicated rhythms while the whole upper body and the accordion would swing back and forth in a slick kind of counterpoint! *That* girl was going to be *me!* That girl up there tap-dancing and playing the accordion, her fingers and arms moving as fast and as graceful as her feet and legs, with the music of the accordion and the crackle of the taps joined by the sweet sound of her own singing — *that* girl was going to be *me!* 'Lady of Spain I Adore You.' Sure. I was going to become an entire musical production, with the movement, the rhythm and the melody all together in a single body placed in the exact center of an enormous stage! I mean it, she meant it. That was my mama's dream, God rest her soul, and naturally, before I was very old, it was *my* dream too. I guess when, I guess you're more likely to do that, make your parent's dream into your own. You know, when your parent dies young. Maybe, I don't know, to work off the guilt or something. You know. Hell, I don't know. It doesn't matter. Why, I mean. Anyhow, it sure became my dream awful fast, and especially after mama died, which was the summer I turned sixteen and was starting to take voice with Estelle Liebling—you probably know who that is, Beverly Sills studied with her, though I didn't know her then, even though we were about the same age. I guess we had our lessons on different days or something. I could hit a high G above high C then, would you believe, and that's as good as Beverly Sills, though like I said, talent's cheap, you have to have a lot more than talent to be a Beverly Sills. Anyhow, when my mama died I was sixteen. Cancer. My father died when I was two. Car crash. I went to live in the next block, over on Eighty-seventh, with Uncle Zack and Aunt Harriet and just threw myself into my lessons, tap-dancing and singing and playing the accordion, all of them, practicing eight and ten hours a day, probably driving everybody in the building nuts, but no one ever complained, because just like my mother, they were all sure I was going to the top. They all knew that someday I would make it big. Big. And then they could remember when. You know how people are. They like to be able to remember you when. And if you yourself are a true believer, I mean really believe, even to the point where it's never actually occurred to you that you might not make it big, never even once occurred to you, pretty soon everyone who knows you starts thinking the same way. It never even occurs to them either that you won't become a star. So long as you're not a complete idiot, of course, so long as you've got *some* kind of recognizable talent. That's the one thing you really need talent for, to convince people you're not crazy because you happen to believe you're going to become a star. It's what makes them *believe*. In you. People, strangers practically, would start telling me on the elevator, 'Annie, I just *know* you're going to make it big! I can already see your name up in lights on Broadway!' they'd say to me. Stuff like that. Only, the trouble was, pretty soon I was, I not only had to live up to my poor dead mother's expectations for me, but the expectations of everyone who lived in our building too, and all my teachers, even my friends. So if the thought ever did occur to me that I might not make it, get to the top and become a world-famous tap dancer and accordionist — or the even more horrible thought that I might not really *want* to become it — well, you better believe those were thoughts I put out of my head in a hurry. I can remember lying in my bed in my room on Eighty-seventh, my legs and ankles stiff and aching from ten hours of practice, and suddenly I'd be thinking, I might not make it. I might not be good enough. I might not be lucky enough. Stuff like that. And pretty soon I'd start to think that those were thoughts that were being put into my head by my poor dead mother's restless spirit, just to sort of test me. To discipline me. No kidding, that's how I got around any doubts I felt in those days. I just figured it was Mama, doomed to wander through purgatory or someplace until I made it to the top, Mama somewhere out there helping to guarantee my becoming a star by toughening me up with bad thoughts. So I'd give the right response, I'd say, I'd tell myself, 'Not a chance I won't make it, not this kid, not me, not Annie Laurie!' And then I'd roll over and fall asleep, probably with a smile on my face . . ."

If I may, I'd like to state now that the above is a partial transcript of a tape recording made by Rochelle Stark during a series of lengthy interviews with her father's second wife, Annie Laurie Stark, who now resides alone in a shabby tenement in Manchester, New Hampshire, middle-aged, depressed (I'm sure) and angry in ways she herself can never know, or she would probably try to kill someone — her ex-husband, a randomly selected stranger, or even herself.

I will try to explain. I have not offered the transcript in its entirety here because the whole tape is too long, too painfully depressing and, finally, because of the several secrets she must keep from herself, a little confusing to the listener. Also, unless you happen to know the woman personally, boring.

For one thing, if you do not actually *hear* the tapes, if you must read them, you cannot hear her tough, New York accent, its glitter, and thus cannot hear it cut against the enervated, listless quality of her language, the words she uses. It makes an interesting conflict, creating an effect of stoic bravery, that accent and those words. And then, of course, there are the secrets, what she cannot mention, cannot bring herself to talk about to anyone, not even to patient, kind Rochelle, who, sitting across from her in the dusty, cluttered living room, knows what those secrets are. For while, naturally, you who read this account cannot see Annie, Rochelle, in interviewing the woman, could see her, and among the several things she could observe was that Annie Laurie is obese, is almost grotesquely fat. And because she will not speak of it under any circumstances (and no interviewer would be so callous as to force her), Annie's obesity remains a secret. Well, not anymore.

But there is a second secret which I cannot bring myself to reveal. Not yet, at least. At least not with this character. Perhaps never. (This is a *novel*, for God's sake, not a court case.)

Anyhow, the tapes of her interview with Annie Laurie Stark are among the documentary materials that Rochelle chose to use in the making of *her* novel. How they happened to come into my possession is not worth going into here, but it is enough to say that she made them available to me, with full knowledge of the use I would make of them. I have tried to give credit to Rochelle and her materials wherever in my novel I have consciously drawn from them or from her novel itself. And because her novel will never be published (for reasons that I will go into later), I do not feel any particular misgivings over certain of my appropriations — even though I am sure there are people, literal-minded readers with a facility for legalistic short division, who would construe my truly creative operations as plagiaristic or, at best, as derivative. To such readers, I offer neither apology nor explanation. To the rest, the above ought to be sufficient as both apology and explanation.

But the tapes. When I first sat down in my chair and listened to them, a process that consumed an entire evening, long into the winter's night, I was astounded. Appalled. Aghast. Amazed. (I can see now that I'll be unable to keep Annie Laurie's second secret to myself. It's fast becoming part of the novel. Oh, Annie, Annie, I'm sorry.)

Immediately, I called my friend and neighbor C., the thinker, a man whose sense and sensitivity I trust explicitly because both sense and sensitivity happen to be driven by a deep curiosity about the nature of the universe rather than by any purely personal considerations. "I have something here that I want you to listen to," I explained to him, after first apologizing for calling so late.

"*Now?*" he petulantly asked me, understandably, for it was three A.M.

I assured him that it could wait until the following morning, that I had just got carried away by a rush of perceptions that had led me to a state of extreme agitation and, as a result, moral confusion. An orderly progression of perceptions makes the moral life easier to accomplish. When a flood of perceptions washes over one, however, one's moral certainty gets swept violently away. This is possibly why it's so rare and difficult for the aware man to be much of a moral example to others. One is always safer if one can save that role, the role of moral example, for the dull and the stolid, the insensitive, the practically insensible.

But to return, I explained to C. that I needed an objective response to some tape-recorded interviews I had recently obtained, materials that I wished to use, in a much modified form, of course, in my novel about Hamilton Stark, which C. well knew to be in fact about A. I told C. that the reason for my excitement and my need for him as an objective listener derived from my bewilderment, which in turn was a consequence of my inability to trust any longer certain conclusions I had drawn prior to my having heard these tapes, conclusions which, of course, had to do with Hamilton Stark's character.

"I thought I *knew* this man!" I exclaimed to C. "I thought I had a clear idea of the quality of his attractiveness, its limits and uses. I thought I knew how he had been perceived by the people who loved him as well as by those who hated him, and thus I thought I knew how to perceive him myself and to make him available, visible, known, to people who knew nothing of him except by what they got through me. But now . . . now I'm just not sure anymore. I've heard some things in these tapes that simply don't belong there. Or rather, they don't belong in the same moral universe as the one I have cast my novel into. I'm finding myself tempted to break into that universe, like some kind of sneaky rapist climbing through a bedroom window, with secrets, information, data, stuff I had wanted to keep out. I need someone to confirm or deny what I think I'm hearing on these tapes before I can go on. Am I making myself clear?" I asked him.

"*Not at all,*" C. answered.

"Please bear with me. I know it's late. But this may be the most important chapter in the book. It'll be either the final chapter or the sixth of eleven," I explained.

"*Well, what are you hearing?*" He yawned noisily onto the mouthpiece, letting me know that he wished to go back to bed.

"I'd rather not tell you until after you've told me what *you* hear." I didn't want to prejudice him any more than necessary. I told him only that the tapes were an interview made with D., who was A.'s second wife, the one he now and then refers to as "the hussy" and sometimes as "the actress." He once told me, concerning D., that the trouble with a woman who has been an actress is not that she will lie but that you will never be able to believe her.

"*Ah,* that *one,*" C. said.

I decided to tell him nothing more until he had heard the tapes himself. I promised him that I'd have two bottles of a fine California wine, a pinot noir from a small vineyard outside Sonoma that we are both especially fond of, and he gladly promised that he would come over to my house and listen to the tapes tomorrow evening after dinner.

He arrived at about nine, still sucking his teeth, as was his habit following an enjoyable meal. It was a blustery cold night, clear and starry, the kind of night that sometimes occurs in mid-February when a spring wind stirs the midwinter cold. I helped him out of his overcoat and escorted him into the library, where I had a large, cheering fire crackling well along and the wine and glasses set out next to the armchair.

He descended into the hug of the chair, taking possession of it as if with great physical need, lit one of his thin cigars, capped a light belch with his gopherlike front teeth, and indicated that I should pour the wine. Our visits are characteristically embellished by a certain ritual, a ceremony. This was a typical one. The purpose of our little ritualistic parading around, our wheezing, sighing, genuflecting, our litanies, and so on, which either would go undetected by a stranger or, if detected, would be thought curious yet boring, is that we both are trying to create as much as possible of the atmosphere that we assume prevails at meetings in, say, London or Brussels, or Belgrade even, between two wholly civilized intellectuals. The underlying assumption, of course, whether held consciously or not, is that by creating such a particularized atmosphere (no matter that we must imagine the model for it), we will therefore find it easier to behave as wholly civilized intellectuals ought to behave — not a simple feat for two middle-aged, middle-class, American men living in a village one hundred miles from even a minor seaport or a major university. But this kind of imitation has always been characteristic of American intellectuals, I suppose. We are, in our own odd way, neoclassicists, regardless of our low opinion of other neoclassical people or ages and in spite of the fact that we have never enjoyed a specifically classical period in our cultural development. Perhaps it's too late to have one . We have lost our innocence. We must imitate, and we also must imagine what we imitate. Thus we always seem to be at least twice removed from true sincerity, true, innocent authenticity. It's hard to tell if that's a problem or a solution to one.

I poured the wine, standing next to C.'s chair while I poured, as if I were the wine steward and my library our club library.

C. tasted the wine, just a sip, almond-sized, and made a slightly dissatisfied face. "Cheese. A small slice of Gouda to neutralize the taste buds."

I strode to the kitchen and returned with a wedge of Gouda on a small wooden plate, which I placed on the table next to C.'s chair. Then I filled both our glasses.

C. sliced a sliver off the wedge, popped it into his mouth, quickly chewed and swallowed. He cleared his mouth, as if to make a speech, and tasted the wine again.

Still standing, I waited through the sniff, the flip of tongue, the hold, and the drop.

"Excellent," he pronounced.

As if relieved, I crossed the room to the fireplace, where, my glass held casually in one hand, my free arm draped like a sweater across the mantel, I assumed a posture that in the dim half-light of the carpeted, book-lined room would make a disinterested viewer think of Oliver Goldsmith. I watched C., legs crossed at the ankles, one hand flopping across the thick arm of the chair, the other posing his wineglass beneath his nostrils as if he were holding a long-stemmed rose, his cigar building a white tubular ash in the ashtray beside him, assume a posture in his chair that would make that same disinterested viewer think of my friend as Ford Madox Ford. Sometimes it was Paul Valéry, but usually, especially in winter, for some reason, it was Ford Madox Ford.

"You said something about listening to some tapes?" C. wheezed at me. Ordinarily he affected the wheeze when he was unsure of the direction of the conversation. It seemed to settle him down, make him the center of the room regardless of where the conversation might wander.

The recorder was inside a cupboard next to the fireplace. Leaning down and switching the first reel on, I quickly told C. that what he was about to hear was an unedited interview made by Rochelle Stark (whose real name C. of course was familiar with) with Hamilton Stark's (A.'s) second wife, to whom I am referring here as Annie Laurie. "You've never met this woman, and I don't believe we've ever discussed her before, have we?" I suddenly realized that I was speaking with the voice of an attorney addressing a jury. I couldn't tell, however, if I was the prosecuting attorney or the attorney for the defense. I wasn't even sure who the defendant was.

"No, although you *have* alluded to the fact of her continued existence. Somewhere in New Hampshire, I believe."

"Yes. Manchester."

"Ah. The Queen City."

And here the tape began:

"What, what's that thing you got there, a tape recorder? Is it on, is it turned on, honey? You aren't going to *record* this, are you? Listen, honey, if you're going to put this on tape I'll have to be a lot more careful of what I say, especially with you being his kid and all. I mean, you know what they say about how blood and water don't mix, don't you? I'm not interested in a feud, starting some kinda family feud, not anymore, not now. On the other hand, I mean, what the hell, maybe it doesn't matter anymore, I mean to him. Or anyone else either. There's a lot of water gone under the dam, you know. What can it matter now, after all these years? I mean, so what if he happens to hear what I've got to say about him now, there's plenty others who could say lots worse by now, I'll bet. Besides, he can't hurt me any, not anymore, not anymore. And it's not like I was interested in making a good impression on him, if you know what I mean. Pretty hard to do now, ha, ha, ha. It's been what, ten years now I've been sitting around thinking about what happened between your father and me, and you know what? Most of what I thought was true back then, ten years ago, when I divorced him, I really don't think is true anymore, not that I'd do it all over again if I had the chance, believe me. I wouldn't marry that man again in a million years, and I wouldn't divorce him either. What's done is done, and marrying and divorcing a man like your father is something you only want to do once. Jesus, isn't it amazing how you never know what's happening to you when it's actually going on? You have to wait until it's all over and done with before you can find out, and then it's too late, you've forgotten too many things, you can't remember what people said, or what they even looked like, or even the order, you can't remember the order of things anymore, if you ever knew the order of things in the first place, for God's sake. Makes you feel kind of helpless. I guess you can never know what really happens to you, not even afterward. Right? It's kind of crazy. Think of all the trouble you'd save, though. I mean, if you knew what was happening at the same time as it was actually happening. Hah, it's probably a good thing you don't You'd probably just kill yourself and save yourself the trouble of your whole life. Here I am, look at me, running on about nothing, old motormouth, that's what your father used to call me. Old Motormouth. I'm sorry, honey, I know I talk too much, I'm really a great talker, or at least I used to be a great talker. I don't get too many chances anymore, so I don't know now, I mean, maybe I'm just a lady running off at the mouth . . ."

"How old was she when this was recorded?" C. asked in a flat voice.

"Thirty-one."

"Not old."

"No."

". . . twenty when I first met him, about your age, a few years younger, even. Jesus, we were a beautiful couple, I was really thin then, no kidding, I had to be, I was dancing with the June Taylor Dancers on the *Jackie Gleason Show* every week, national TV, and they did a weight check every Thursday night, like they do with boxers, because after all, our bodies were our meal tickets, honey, our livelihoods, and if we put on a pound more than we were allowed, there was a dozen girls standing right behind each one of us ready and able to take our places on a moment's notice. It was a grind, lots of pressure. Once you stepped out of that line-up, honey, you stayed out. We worked harder than anyone who hasn't done it can know, new routines that the choreographers more or less made up on the spot and as we went along, practicing seven and eight hours a day right up to the dress rehearsal, which really wasn't your actual dress rehearsal at all as much as it was just the first time we could do the entire number all together from start to finish, and usually there were half a dozen last-minute changes that we'd have to fit in before Saturday's show, and then we'd have Sunday off, and then on Monday the whole thing would start over again. The life of a chorus girl isn't all it's cracked up to be, honey. We really were a lot like your professional athletes, like boxers or something. Except that we had the summers off, but not many of us could afford to loaf, or wanted to anyhow, so most of us took summer stock and chorus line jobs in musicals or nightclubs, which is how I met your father. I was in the chorus line, with a singing part, too, at the Lakeside Theater up in Laconia. You know the place probably, it's pretty famous, over there by the lake, at that place they call the Weirs. Anyhow, your father went to see the show one night, alone, and he picked me out of the chorus line, so he says, and sent me a dozen yellow roses and a note backstage after the show. Believe it or not, it was the first time that had ever happened to me. A stage-door Johnny! Imagine! Me, little Annie Laurie, singled out of the chorus line by a man in the audience! Remember, honey, I was only twenty years old at the time, and sure, I was a big-city girl and he was supposed to be a country rube, but I'd been raised like a flower in a hothouse and he'd been brought up like a piece of moss on a rock, a chunk of lichen or something, so when he tried the old dozen-roses-and-a-note routine, I fell for it. Hook, line and sinker. Also, I was pretty lonely, spending the summer like that in the sticks, away from home for the first time, really, because back in New York I was still living with my Uncle Zack and Aunt Harriet, who had raised me after my mama died. So here I am, backstage in this dingy little barn theater beside the lake, taking off my make-up, and one of the stagehands comes knocking on the dressing room door with a dozen yellow roses and a note for "The Tall Blond Singer in the Chorus Line." That's how he'd addressed the card, and since I was the only one in the line with a singing part, one short number, which I had because it was a six-girl line and I was the only one who wasn't completely stone-deaf, I knew the note was for me. I can still remember pretty well what it said. It was in that style of his, the way he wrote all his notes or letters or anything. Even the way he talked, most of the time. *Flowers a token of esteem from member of audience. Would you have drink with sender. H. Stark.* The note was typed, you know, with a typewriter, but it's strange, I didn't even notice that, or if I did, I certainly, I didn't think anything about it, you know, like, What's a member of the audience doing with a typewriter in his lap? I should have, of course. Thought about it, I mean. I guess he must've typed the note out at home before he came to the theater and brought it with him, and that's strange, don't you think? I mean, it was opening night. He couldn't have known who he was going to send the flowers and note to until after he'd already got to the theater. The note on the flowers were in handwriting, somebody's, probably the stagehand's. I should've thought about stuff like that, at the time, I mean. I sure have since then, but a lotta good it's done me. If I'd thought about it then I would've been able to know quite a lot about your father before I even set my eyes on him, but I guess I was too flattered and lonely to notice even. All I cared about was whether or not he was going to be young and handsome, so I asked the stagehand, and he told me sure the guy was young, you know how stagehands talk, and yeah, the guy was handsome. "Okay-looking," was probably how he said it. "But the guy's pretty big," he told me. I remember that clear as a bell. I remember picturing to myself this tall, handsome stranger, as big as John Wayne and handsome as Robert Taylor, so when, when I walked out the stage door and saw your father, I had to pinch myself on the arm to be sure I wasn't dreaming. He was very gallant, like they say, I mean at first he was. Real old-fashioned, kind of making these little bows when he'd open a door for me, attentive to every detail of the evening, like making sure that when he brought me a corsage, which he did every time we went out, at least at first, but making sure too that he had on a lapel flower that was the same as was in the corsage. Jesus, what a Romeo he was, that guy! But not one of your Latin lover types. Different. All the time serious as a preacher or something, talking like some kind of weird professor in that flat metallic voice of his about things that usually were pretty interesting, if you listened close, like about the history of Lake Winnepesaukee, which is the lake the theater was located on, or maybe discussing the fine points of the show, pretty well informed on theater, he was too, almost like one of those critics for the *Times*. I was really, I was surprised, up here in the woods like that, and all of a sudden here comes one of the local yokels, and it turns out he has this interest in theater and travel and history, all kinds of stuff, stuff I thought only New Yorkers were interested in. Jesus, honey, what a sucker I was. Twenty years old, getting sweet-talked by some big hunk of country meat. And by the time I let him sweet-talk me into bed with him, I was pretty much in love with him. He wasn't my "first," but he *was* the first man I fell in love with, really deep, you know? That was also the first time I saw him drunk, too, but it was too late for me to get out by then, the bastard. He had me hooked, so when he started getting mean and wild and drunk all the time, instead of running away from him, which is of course what I should've done toot sweet, I tried to comfort him. You know, to soothe his fevered brow, like they say. Wrong thing to do, honey. Dead wrong. You know, to soothe his fevered brow. All my hand on his brow did was jack up the temperature about ten degrees. Jesus. I'll never forget his face, the way I saw it then, that first night in the motel with him, like the face of some kind of beast, all the time roaring and shouting stuff that didn't make any sense at all to me, stuff that didn't have anything to do with me, although he'd stare right into my face when he shouted, so naturally I thought at first he was shouting at me, that's what anyone would've thought. It was the most frightening, scary thing I'd ever seen, I thought he was . . ."

C. was refilling his glass. "Old A. doesn't seem to've been able to hold his liquor, eh?" He smiled tolerantly. "Not really a man's man."

"So it would seem," I said. "But listen, this is interesting here."

". . . until finally he flopped onto the bed and passed out, and afterward, after I was sure he was out cold, I crawled into the bed next to him, but under the covers, he was lying on top of everything, and I tried to sleep, which I guess I eventually did, for a while, anyhow. I woke up, I woke up before he did, and in the early morning light looked at his face. Oh, Jesus, it was like a baby's face. Peaceful, innocent, curious, good-natured. You know what I mean? Like a baby it was. The exact opposite of what it had been six or seven hours before. I'd never seen such an incredible switch. I wondered if maybe I'd imagined the whole thing, you know? But anyhow, even though I was wondering this, I still expected him to act all hangdog and guilty as hell when he woke up. Naturally. I mean, I was all set to forgive him. I'd even rehearsed a couple of speeches where I forgive him for getting drunk the first night we spend together and we talk a while about his childhood and he promises never to drink like that again. That's the sort of thing I figured would happen. No kidding. I never expected him to do like he did. To wake up and just act like nothing had happened. It was something weird, honey. One for the books. He acted like I was an old pal or something, just somebody who happened to be there in the morning after a night out with the boys shooting pool or bowling or something. He brushed his teeth and shaved and got his clothes back on — one of the last things he'd done before passing out was take off all his clothes and pound on his chest like Tarzan, no, more like a scowling gorilla, the real thing — and then, all the time humming and cleaning up the room, he waited for me while I dressed too. Finally I got up the nerve and I put it to him, I asked him straight out, "What about last night, Ham?" And you know what he did? Get this. He winked at me! Real slow and sexy. Just crinkled up his cheek, smiled a little, and *winked!* Then he pats me on the ass and pushes me gently toward the door, saying as we go out that he's hungry as a bear. That was the first time your father made me feel I was crazy . . ."

I reached down and snapped off the recorder. In the sudden silence that followed, I placed another log on the fire and refilled both my and C.'s glasses.

"I don't . . . I don't quite understand," C. said slowly

"No?"

"No. There's something . . . *peculiar* about her tale." He held his glass by the stem and twirled it slowly. "There's a gap between the story she's telling, all that business about a man she was married to long ago, a man she met over a dozen years ago, for God's sake, a gap between that story, as data, and the way she's telling it. She's in no way still in love with the man, that's obvious. Not like A.'s first wife. This woman is brighter, more conscious of herself, than the other. Tell me," he said, peering over the rim of his glass, "is this, this *gap*, what you were so eager for me to hear and speculate on?"

"Well, yes, but there's more." I was alarmed that he'd picked up the distance between the content of her story and its formal elements. It meant that for him to be able to respond intelligently to the tape he would have to know the secrets about Annie Laurie that I had hoped to keep out of this book. Her obesity, already revealed, at least to the reader, was but one of several pieces of information concerning her that I was loath to expose — for several reasons. First, it would make it easier for some readers to identify Annie Laurie's model, D., if they happened to see her on the streets of Manchester or in one of the local department stores, say, or coming out onto the stoop of her building to get her welfare check from the mailman. And if one of my readers happened to be her mailman — oh, almost too cruel to imagine!

When I began this project I was under the impression that I would be able to keep certain secrets, an impression that increasingly looks false. I wanted my story to seem true-to-life, as it were, which meant to me that a great deal of it had to be redundant. Also, I was aware from the start that Hamilton Stark in many ways could be seen as a grotesque, an exaggeration of a merely neurotic human being, and to ground him sufficiently in everyday life (as well as to justify my view of him as something quite superior to a merely neurotic human being formed and contained by his social circumstances), I felt it necessary to surround him with plain fare, pea soup and porridge people. Not exotics. Not three-hundred-pound ex–tap dancers whose sadly diminished lives are spent reminiscing over a few tattered clippings and an unpleasant night spent years ago in a lakeside motel. I had to go this far, however, to reveal this much: there was no way I could keep it out of Rochelle's novel, after all, and certainly there was no way I could legitimize my altering the transcripts of her tapes. And as for revealing Annie's great weight, I could not withhold that fact without misrepresenting Annie's narrative altogether. What if the reader were to infer, as he naturally would, that Annie was still beautiful, still slender and long-legged, that her memories and childhood ambitions were not mocked outright by her present physical condition? That reader would have heard something quite different from what I and C. and the rest of us have heard. But . . . was it sufficient that I reveal only her enormous belly, arms like the legs of a hippo, throat like a tire tube, cheeks and forehead smooth and round as basketballs, hands swollen like sausages? Was that alone sufficient? Well, I hoped my friend C. would tell me. If C. heard nothing odd, nothing that was not mildly moving and interesting, then I would probably not even bother to tell him as much as that the woman he had been listening to was an almost impossibly fat woman. If C. found himself slightly bewildered by the tapes, however, if he detected, as he did, a "gap" between form and content that was not quite comprehensible, then I had decided I would reveal the fact of her obesity. If still he was not relieved and was not permitted comprehension of her testimony, if he was neither moved nor interested by it, however mildly, then . . . well, then I would probably have to reveal more.

"Would it clear things up for you," I said to C., "if you knew that the woman is unusually obese? A frightenly fat woman?"

C. thought for a moment. "You mean like the fat lady at the circus? Freakish?"

"Yes."

"Well, no. No, not unless *this* makes no sense to you . . . or to me, of course," he said, indicating with his diction and furrowed brow, pursed lips, index fingertips pressed to chin, that he was about to launch a speculation, a ship of theoretical thought. "We are, all of us, so unsure of what is real and not real, that whenever we encounter a person, especially one of the opposite sex, for some reason, who behaves as if the question of what is real and not real were a simple one to answer, and further, when that person then proceeds to proffer an answer that completely denies the simple evidence of our senses, we are, all of us, likely to forsake our senses and cleave to the other. Essentially, that's the role our parents play for us when we are infants and small children. They define what is real and what is not real, and quite often, *usually*, in fact — because as children we don't understand even the basic physical laws of the universe yet, not even the laws of perspective or of Newtonian physics — quite often what our parents tell us is real denies completely what our senses have indicated is in fact the case. We say, for example, 'The moon is bigger than the sun.' It's obvious to us. But our parents contradict us: 'The sun is thousands of times bigger than the moon.' Often they even laugh at us, and they always explain away the contradiction with some piece of nonsense, like, 'It only appears to be smaller because it is so much farther from us than the moon is.' So even though we're presented with a contradiction that is then justified only in terms of nonsense, we nevertheless accept it wholly. At that time, the power of the contradiction seems to depend on two things: the physical size of our parents compared to our own tiny displacement and their self-assurance. 'Ho, ho,' they say, 'the sun is thousands of times bigger than the moon!' We as children have neither size nor self-assurance.

"Now, my friend, here's the point. Evidently certain women, and possibly a number of men as well, when encountering a man of A.'s enormous physical size and self-assurance — which to my mind borders on the psychotic — find themselves reduced back to the level of children when it comes to their ability to separate what's real from what is not real. Your man was apparently able to induce in Annie Laurie the emotional equivalent of a child's relation to its parent, in particular as regards the parent's having been thrust into the position of arbiter of reality, a kind of metaphysical supreme court of no appeal. That's evidently what made our Annie Laurie, I mean D., think she was crazy. Unfortunately for her, she was made dependent upon him, and her dependence increased in geometrically multiplying degrees every time such an encounter as at the motel occurred. I'm curious. Did his denial of her reality in so absolute a fashion take place only after one of his episodes of drunkenness and rage?"

"The fact of her obesity doesn't really alter your comprehension of her words?" I queried hopefully.

"No. Of course not. Don't be silly. But tell me, did A. deny D.'s perceptions of the world only after one of his episodes of drunkenness and rage?"

Somewhat relieved, I answered him. "Apparently what he could not remember simply did not happen, as far as he himself was concerned. According to the tapes, portions you haven't heard, he could not remember *anything* he said or did while drinking, and he could never remember what he had said when he was enraged, which was often, and he could not recall what he experienced during sex. I'm summarizing, of course, but there's no point in your listening to seven hours of tape. Most of what's there is self-centered trivia and small talk between two women who don't know each other very well. The important facts about Hamilton Stark, A., though, are, one, he believed passionately that if he had no memory of a particular act, speech, or emotion, he did not commit it, speak it, or experience it. It wasn't his. It was someone else's. And two, he never remembered what he did when he was drunk, said when he was angry, or experienced when he was copulating. A third fact of consequence might be that he was often drunk, frequently enraged, and regularly had sexual relations with women."

"You speak of him in the past tense," C. said with a smile, "as if he were dead."

"It's a narrative convenience. Ignore it."

"Fine. But it is odd," C. opined, and again my heart fluttered with dread, "that the man would seem so deliberate about his offenses. Do *you* think it was deliberate on his part? Is that why you want to immortalize this cad? Do you think his awful personality was the expression of a consciously held idea, a philosophical idea, about the world and how to be in it? That is, after all, what's fascinating about religious leaders, isn't it?" (That's one of the things I love about C. — he refuses to deal with personalities; he goes straight and deeply into the abstract, historical heart of the matter. It's why I referred to him earlier as a thinker.)

"Oh, I don't know, I'm no longer sure," I said sadly. "I feel like Saint Peter making one of his denials." For the first time in my celebratory examination of my hero, I was aware of the strong possibility that he was not only a churl, but a nonconscious churl. A true churl. I was suddenly afraid that my man's life was out of his control, when my original perception of him, the very reason I had decided to celebrate him in the first place, for heaven's sake, was that he, of all people, had gained control of his life without suppressing his life. For an instant I thought of telling C. about the cataclysmic end to Hamilton's marriage to Annie, and also the final secret. But then, like Peter after the cock crowed and the prophecy had been fulfilled, I felt a sudden surge of belief — possibly welling from my knowledge of how C. would interpret the information and the secret, possibly for an even less defensive reason — but regardless, like Peter, I was once again rocklike in my steadfastness, and I was no longer ready to give up on my man, my Roarer, my Crank, my Colossal and Cosmic Grouch and Bully Boy, my Man Who Hated Everything so as to Love Anything, my Man Obsessed with a Demon so as to Avoid Being Possessed by One — my one last possibility for a self-transcendent ego in a secular age!

Our conversation dawdled on into the late evening, but we, neither of us, could add anything substantial to what has already been described here, especially since I had by then decided to withhold a quantity of specifically cruel qualities demonstrated by my man, and by eleven o'clock, C. and I decided to have a nightcap and end the evening's conversations with a . . .

CHAPTER SEVEN

Ausable Chasm

THIS IS THE STORY of how Hamilton Stark almost went to college. Unavoidably, it will be the story of numerous other events as well — other people, other missions, other conflicts resolved and unresolved — but mainly, it will be the story of how Hamilton Stark almost went to college.

Not many people know it, know that he even wanted to go to college in the first place or that he actually came close to doing so in the second. Naturally, you'd never have heard it from the man himself — he carried a number of odd, perhaps even (now that we know what we know) defensive prejudices against people who had gone to college.

"You take your college-educated man," he frequently proposed, "and I'll show you a capitalist dupe. Not that I mind your capitalists. Shit, no. I *admire* capitalists," he said. "It's your *dupes* I can't stand. I'll stomp a capitalist dupe before I'll stomp a communist true believer, and you know what I think of your communist true believers," he reminded me.

Needlessly, it turned out, for I did indeed know what he thought of people he chose to designate "communist true believers." I knew that he despised them. Possibly despised them to the point of violently attacking them, for, though I personally have never actually *seen* him physically assault a so-called communist, nevertheless I have heard stories that, frankly, I'd rather not relate here. Let it suffice to say that Hamilton Stark, in the barrooms of central New Hampshire, was a well-known, militantly forceful anticommunist. Every morning he read the Manchester *Union-Leader*, a newspaper widely regarded as the nation's most rabidly right wing, a newspaper with red-ink headlines such as MUSKIE WEEPS WHEN SHOWN HIS OWN WORDS and HALDEMAN AND EHRLICHMAN QUIT UNDER LEFT-WING PRESSURE. That sort of garbage, which Hamilton, oh, my Hamilton, seemed to choose to believe.

There was a brief period when he and I were still willing to argue politics. I am a moderate Christian Socialist and at the time of this writing have cast my presidential ballot for the following individuals: Adlai Stevenson, Adlai Stevenson, John F. Kennedy, Rogers Morton (write-in), and Morris Udall (write-in). Hamilton, though he has voted in every presidential election since 1948, has voted for only one man — Ezra Taft Benson. At least that is what he tells me. And I have no reason to doubt that if Hamilton votes in 1976, he will vote yet again for Mr. Benson, even though by then Benson may well be dead and out of the running altogether. And who knows, Hamilton may write in Benson's name anyway. He used to quote Benson to me until, my ears burning, I begged him to stop. "You want to hear what a *wise* man said? 'It's just too bad, it's really sad, but there has to be a loser.' Now that's *my* idea of presidential wisdom!" Hamilton would exclaim. "I *love* that . . . 'it's really sad,' heh heh heh. You talk about your Kennedy wit. What about the *Benson* wit?"

I suppose in a certain perverse light Benson's remarks could have been seen as witty, but to me they seemed cruel and shallow. The difficulty in arguing politics with Hamilton was that I could never tell for sure whether or not he was being serious. It was never clear that, by taking such an extreme position and then defending it with quotes from someone like Ezra Taft Benson, he wasn't mocking me. Here are some other sentences Hamilton quoted and claimed were uttered by the man: "There's no way a man can live a useful life without stepping on a few people's toes." "It's in the nature of freedom not to know what a man will do with it." And, "The best defense is the one you never have to use." Actually, this last sentence I heard myself as it came from the crinkled lips of the ancient parchment-skinned Ezra Taft Benson. He gave the graduation speech at Ausable Chasm College of Arts and Science, Ausable Chasm, New York, in 1969. I was in the audience because Hamilton Stark was in the audience; he was there, first, because his hero Ezra Taft Benson was giving the graduation speech, and second, because his daughter Rochelle was giving the valedictory speech. Frankly, I think Benson's speech meant more to Hamilton than his daughter's did — Hamilton either fell asleep or pretended to fall asleep during the latter — but for me, that day was momentous. It was the day I first met Rochelle, Hamilton's daughter. Benson could have collapsed from a heart attack during his speech and I wouldn't have noticed or cared. And the only reason that today I can recall the merest scrap of his speech — "The best defense is the one you never have to use" — is because Hamilton quoted it to me a dozen or more times during the drive back to Barnstead.

I had never met Rochelle, though of course I knew of her existence, had listened to Hamilton talk about her for years, and had seen pictures of her, first her grade school photographs, then junior high school, and most recently, four years ago, her high school yearbook photograph. So, in a manner of speaking, I knew what to expect. I had seen her image change, gradually, year by year: from that of a bright-faced, wide-eyed, mischievous three-year-old (taken at nursery school), in which she wore a kelly green daysuit that contrasted beautifully with her then flame red hair; to the image of a gap-toothed seven-year-old grinning proudly into the camera, her now deeper red hair in braids tied around her head, her green eyes flashing with innocent affection; to the image of a sober-faced, sexually serious adolescent, an intense face already full of intellectual grace and sensual force, with a touch of the bewilderment that such rare presences in such inordinate quantities must have caused her; and on to the most recent image, the tall, almost statuesque, even though delicate and slender, young woman, her deep red hair now tumbling roughly, densely, over her shoulders, her eyes warm, intelligent, disciplined, her mouth in a slight smile as if about to speak, full and promising, her neck long, proud, elegant. And of course, because these photographs were all inscribed to her absent, never seen nor even directly remembered daddy, I was able to trace the development of her character over the years by studying the changes in her handwriting and the language she used to inscribe her photographs. From her nursery school photograph (precociously, I thought):

And then, sadly asserting her relation to him, a six-year-old who could no longer even recall the presence of the man, who knew him only as a name and burning need:

WITH all My Love TO My Father
FROM His DAUGHter
ROCHeLLE

Here she is at ten, obviously after having read a bit of Shakespeare (one wonders what her mother made of the little girl's reading habits: a fifth-grade child poring over Lear?):

from Cordelia to her lear, with love
and loyalty forever

And here, in her own, mature, self-aware hand, at the age of seventeen, describing the true nature of her relationship with the man while at the same time offering him its positive denial, which was, of course, the nature of her daily experience of the man:

... love, even from such an inhuman distance, for my father.
Rochelle

It was never clear to me why Rochelle was graduating from college in Ausable Chasm, a small tourist town, once a mill town, located in upstate New York a few miles from Lake Champlain. I could not imagine anyone sending his child to such a college for academic reasons (unless the child were unable to matriculate anywhere else), and so far as I knew, Rochelle's mother still resided in Lakeland, Florida, as had Rochelle, at least through her senior year of high school. It didn't make sense to me that she should attend a small, nondescript college fifteen hundred miles from home, especially when there were so many right around home to choose from. I asked Hamilton about it during the drive west and north from his home in Barnstead. He had called me the week before to ask if I would accompany him to his daughter's graduation, mentioning, as if it would help me decide to come, that the featured speaker would be Ezra Taft Benson. He did not mention, of course, that his own daughter would give the valedictory speech, or that it would be in Latin (of her own choosing — the first time in the history of Ausable Chasm College of Arts and Science that the graduation speech had been given in Latin!). He told me about that, offhandedly, in Burlington, Vermont.

"Why," I asked him as he drove his car onto the ferry at Burlington and we began the crossing of Lake Champlain, "why does your daughter happen to be graduating from a small, obscure college in upstate New York, when all along I thought she was living in central Florida with her mother and presumably would have gone to either a well-known, prestigious college in the New England states or else one near her home? Did they move north while she was in high school?" I prodded. I suspected there was a story here to be told me by someone.

It was a beautiful, sunshiny, mid-June day stuffed with bright yellows and jade greens. The mountains, the broad valleys, the almost giddy blue of the lake — it made me want to be either a farmer in this valley or a tourist. I could not decide which role would give me more of the place. It's an ancient dilemma: we can never choose between the experience itself and our memory of it.

Hamilton's answer didn't make much sense to me. Not then, anyhow, except to let me know that he didn't wish to discuss it. He simply told me that the girl was obviously trying to get closer to her father now that she was no longer wholly dependent on her mother, but that Ausable Chasm was as close as she dared come to where he happened to be. So I let the subject drop and tried to enjoy the day, the smooth lake, the immense sky above it.

At the campus, a complex of half a dozen small, square, brick buildings that from the outside resembled a munitions plant, we met Hamilton's daughter, Rochelle, he for the first time since she was an infant, me for the first time ever. As we got out of his car — he was driving an air-conditioned, dark brown Cadillac Coupe de Ville at that time, quite luxurious — I asked him if Rochelle knew he was coming. He grunted that in response to her invitation he had sent her a post card so indicating.

"Is this the first time you will have seen her since she was an infant?" I asked him.

Again he grunted his answer, which was yes. I could tell from his grunts that he was somewhat tense and possibly even a bit frightened of the occasion. One could hardly blame him. I'm sure that, although he never mentioned it, her acceptance of him was fully as important to him as his acceptance of her was to Rochelle. What if she saw him and, flooded with memories of her mother's angry descriptions of the man, said to him, "No, I have changed my mind, I don't want you here, I don't want you to come to my graduation!" Would he try to comfort her, try to convince her that he truly wanted to be there, reassuring her with his kind, soft and urgent words? Or would he simply spin on his heels and walk away, back to his car, and go home?

Luckily, when Rochelle came up to him and introduced herself, saying that she recognized him from snapshots her mother had shown her, he smiled graciously — one of the few times, perhaps the only time, I've seen Hamilton Stark smile graciously — and he took her hand in his and thanked her for inviting him. Rochelle was already six feet tall, a young woman with electrifying beauty, and as she stood there in the parking lot outside the auditorium in her royal blue gown and mortarboard, her hand in her father's hand, her green eyes staring directly, searchingly, into his brown eyes, which were squinting from the bright sunlight, I felt tears running over and down my cheeks.

Though she and I barely spoke, except for the moment when Hamilton introduced us to one another, it seemed to me then, and was later confirmed by her own testimony, that we both felt a deep bond between us. Years later, six, to be exact, I was able to ask her about that first meeting at Ausable Chasm, to ask her how she had perceived me then. We were lying in bed together, drifting languidly from passionate peaks through hazy valleys all the way to the gray light of dawn, the time of night and first intimacy when lovers ask one another how they were seen before, when they were not lovers. It's an ancient form of talk, one of the few reliable ways of finding out how one actually is in the world.

I lit a cigarette for her and, naked except for my socks and garters, walked across the room to the dresser — we were at my home, in my own bedroom, this the conclusion to an evening that had begun as a literary discussion on the subject of the modern novel — and fixed her a drink, cognac and soda. "Tell me," I said to her, returning to the bed with her drink, "on that day we first met, your college graduation day, the day you told me about your father's wanting to go to college and how he had failed to satisfy that desire and how that was all tied up with your desire to attend Ausable Chasm — on that first day, how did you see *me?* How did I seem to you? Can you remember?" I asked, handing her the glass. "You don't mind telling me this, do you?" I asked, suddenly worried that I might have embarrassed her with my question. I still did not know how to anticipate her reactions to anything I might say or do, nor do I even today. She is more intelligent than I, but her thought sequences are linked in patterns and systems that are not as logical as mine, and consequently she is unpredictable to me. Excitingly so, however! I find myself enlarged, enriched, and challenged by her unpredictability. She accomplishes it, expresses it, in our relationship in such a way that it never makes me feel arrogant or humiliated (the two most conventional responses in a male to a female's unpredictability).

"No," she said in her low, early morning voice, "I don't mind." She was tired, I knew, as was I, but we were both nonetheless stimulated by the occasion. It produced in her a kind of languid animation that, whenever it appeared, made me want to make love to her again. But I resisted the impulse and attended her words.

"I saw you immediately as an ally," she told me. "I looked into your face and watched how you watched my father. I knew then that you were probably the only other person on earth who was obsessed with him in a way that corresponded to my own obsession with him." Then she stopped a second. "But you don't want to hear about my *use* for you, do you? I mean, after all, as an ally you were useful to me. You were going to become a way for me both to justify and satisfy my obsession with my father. I did have other perceptions of you, perceptions that had nothing to do with any possible *use* I might make of you. Wouldn't you rather hear those?" she gently asked me.

Indeed. I had an erection to cope with now. The milky light of dawn was entering the room like a thief, stealing the nighttime and our disembodied, anonymous voices, thrusting us back into our particular, constraining bodies, those vessels, those jugs, those ridiculous, pajama-shaped symbols of our true identities. (I believe this, I have always believed it. I have never regarded myself as anything more than my disembodied voice and have never thought of myself as more clearly seen, known, than when I am heard. This, of course, lies behind my need to pursue and understand Hamilton Stark — at least it's what presents me with a rationale for my pursuit — for he is the only human being I have known who did not seem to exist solely through his disembodied voice.)

That day at Ausable Chasm College of Arts and Science, though, I almost gave up on Hamilton. I came closest then to believing that the entire view I held of him was nothing more than an objectification of my own psychological and philosophical needs. For the first time, and, I hope, the last,

I seriously entertained the notion that I had, in essence, made up Hamilton Stark, had invented him, had taken an ordinary man with an unusual personality disorder and had structured his numerous symptoms into an image that satisfied a set of secret, shameful needs in me.

My true weaknesses always seem to derive from my sympathies. Hamilton has told me this, and it's true. You will recall my sympathy for his second wife, the one he called "the actress," and how my sympathy for her made me question his very authenticity. Well, the same thing happened, only in a more extreme fashion, that day when I first met Rochelle, discovered that she was giving the valedictory speech, saw her reaching out for her father's love and part of his life, and saw him yank both back. I was horrified. This was going too far, I thought. Surely, cruelty has its metaphysical use and meaning, but there must be a point where it is simply and purely cruelty and has no use or meaning except for the perpetrator.

"I'm glad you came," she said to him in a voice that, to me, seemed remarkably calm.

He squinted into the sun and, expressionless, said that he had come to hear Ezra Taft Benson speak, a privilege that heretofore he had been denied.

Rochelle asked him if he understood Latin.

He shook his head no and asked, surprised, if Benson were going to speak in Latin.

"No, not that I know of," she said, smiling easily. "But *I* am. Would you like to have a translation of my speech," she asked him coyly. "I've copied it out for you."

Again he shook his head no.

The half-hour that followed was extremely strained. The three of us strolled around the parking lot, Hamilton in the middle, Rochelle on one side, and me on the other. We looked at the automobiles, commented on the makes and the number plates, and asked one another questions that could not be answered. At least not by any of us.

Rochelle: "Are you happy to know that your daughter is graduating from college?"

Hamilton: "Seems like a good idea."

Me: "What are your plans, now that you're graduating from college?"

Rochelle: "Everything depends on one thing."

Me: "And what is that?"

Rochelle: "I'm not sure yet, and I can't tell you what I *think* it is."

Hamilton: "What kind of a car is that, the little convertible sports job with the raggedy roof?"

Rochelle and Me: "I don't know. Custom made, maybe?"

Hamilton: "Don't you hate custom-made cars?"

Rochelle: "I don't know. I never thought about it."

Me: "Why?"

Hamilton: "Who knows? Maybe I'm just trying to make conversation."

Me: "Oh."

Rochelle: "Have you been friends with my father for a long time?"

Me: "Relative to what?"

Hamilton: "Yeah, relative to what?"

Rochelle: "I don't know. Forget it. I was just trying to make conversation."

Me: "Oh."

Hamilton: "Where are we supposed to sit?"

Rochelle: "I don't know. Anywhere in the auditorium, I guess. Wherever you want to sit."

Hamilton: "All right if we go and sit now?"

Rochelle: "If that's what you want."

Hamilton: "That's what we want. Right?"

Me: "I guess so, you're the host today. Or are *you* the host, Rochelle? I mean the hostess."

Rochelle: "I'll show you where the auditorium is. Then I'll have to leave you and join my classmates for the march. I'll be sitting up on the platform."

Hamilton: "With Benson?"

Rochelle: "I don't know. I presume so."

Me: "Well, should we wish you luck, Rochelle? Or are you the overconfident type?"

Rochelle: "Who knows? Relative to what, eh?"

Me (laughing): "Right."

Hamilton: "Let's go find a seat."

Me: "Okay."

Rochelle: "The auditorium's right through those doors, straight ahead and to the right. Think you can find it all right?"

Hamilton: "Sounds simple enough."

Me: "No problem. Right, Hamilton?"

Hamilton: "No problem. Right, Rochelle?"

Rochelle: "No problem. Right?"

Me (laughing again): "Are you making fun of me?"

Rochelle: "I don't know. See you after the speeches."

I realize that I'm not explaining many things that the reader doubtless would like explained. Please believe me, I'm not leaving these questions unanswered merely because I have a perverse love of mystery. Quite the opposite; in fact, I despise mystery. Mystery is the last resort of the hysteric. It's a frantic, final attempt to organize chaos, or rather, to give the *appearance* of having organized chaos. None of that for me. It's too easy and too cheap a way out for a man who feels, as I do, morally compelled to abide with chaos all the way to the end, until either he has succeeded in answering all the questions at hand, unraveling all the tangles, explaining all the puzzles, solving all the riddles, or else he has succumbed to the snarl of chaos altogether. For such a man, for me, the middle, where "mystery" lies, is definitely excluded. I am an *emotional* man, yes, but I am *not* a romantic man. And though I may never ascend quite to those airy levels of pure reason where, for example, my friend C. strolls about so comfortably, at least I am clear about the nature of my goal and can measure with accuracy the distance I remain from it. This particular clarity and the measuring that results therefrom comprise, for me, the only possibilities for a moral life. All else is either fantasy or determinism.

For this reason, that day at Ausable Chasm I persisted in trying to find out why Rochelle was graduating from college here in the North. Ordinarily, if Hamilton indicated that he didn't wish to discuss a subject, I deferred to him and changed the subject, never bringing it up again unless and until he indicated readiness. But my fascination with Rochelle, then, at the actual sight of her, drove me to push in ways I would have otherwise found rude, if not downright boorish, in myself as well as in anyone else.

"What's the story?" I asked him. "What's the explanation? How come?"

All of which he answered with a shrug, a downturned mouth with pouting lower lip, like a carp's, a helpless flop of open hands at his sides. And after a while it occurred to me that he didn't know the answer either, that it was likely, when he had learned that his daughter was graduating from Ausable Chasm College of Arts and Science, that he had been as surprised and puzzled as I.

I therefore ceased asking the man about it and promised myself to ask Rochelle instead. Unfortunately, whenever I was with her, I became so addled by her physical and spiritual presence that I forgot my promise altogether, and now, six years after making that promise, I still have not kept it, and thus I do not know why Rochelle graduated from an obscure college in upstate New York rather than one in central Florida. This distresses me. For now it is too late to keep that promise. Rochelle is gone from me except in memory and imagination. I will never know the answer to my question, and the reader will never know either.

To return: I handed Rochelle her drink and joined her in the bed. (This happens to be the imaginary point from which I can most easily recall the events of the day I spent in Ausable Chasm.) We were talking about the day we first met each other and how we had perceived each other then. She said that she had thought of me as a small man, short and slight, but later, after having seen me numerous times alone, realized that it was because I had been in the company of her father that first time and thus, when compared to his great height and overall bulk, had appeared much smaller than, in fact, I actually was. She was pleased, she told me, when she discovered that I was the same height as she and that, while my musculature was not exactly overdeveloped, I was nevertheless wiry and in quite good shape for a man my age.

Waving her compliments away, I gently asked her if she had seen her father and me from the speakers' platform while she had been giving her speech. I wanted to know if she had seen my attentiveness. I confess it. Hurt somewhat by the comparison between her father's and my physical size, I wished to have her compare my rapt attention with her father's cruel inattention. So I risked causing pain. I risked the chance that, by invoking thc image of her father sitting in the audience and apparently sleeping through her speech, with me perched on my chair, rapt and admiring next to him, she would feel again the pain that moment must have caused her.

"You were an angel," she said, smiling into my face. She had cut through my ruse in one stroke, had comforted me without mocking me and at the same time had spared herself the pain of the memory. What a woman! Then, with laughter, she began to talk about Ezra Taft Benson's speech. "Remember it?" she asked me. "That funny little old man with all that crazy fervor?"

Actually, I recalled nothing of Benson's speech, except for the one line that Hamilton had continally quoted to me all the way back home in the car. I promptly related it to her: "The best defense is the one you never have to use," I said.

She giggled, then reminded me that when Benson had uttered those words Hamilton had broken into applause, mortifying me, perhaps astonishing Benson, and inducing a few scattered, sheeplike souls in the audience to join him. I had completely forgotten that awful moment and for a few seconds relived my embarrassment, which had been quite painful. I wasn't so much embarrassed because I was sitting next to a person who seemed to be reacting to a banality with inappropriate enthusiasm, as I was embarrassed because that man happened to be my hero. I did not point this out to Rochelle. I didn't have to. After all, he was her hero too.

I may not have listed it among my earlier encomiums, but Rochelle's memory is prodigious, photographic. Mine, of course, is ordinary. But she could recall details, entire conversations, books, films, any text at all, things and events in their entirety that I could but barely invent. Catalogues of things passed by on an afternoon's drive in the country, newspaper articles and editorials verbatim, entire chapters from the Bible, the first paragraphs from novels she had read years ago, news accounts from radio or television that she'd listened to but moments before — it was unnerving, slightly otherworldly, and at all times not quite believable. I could never rid myself of my initial response to one of her recitations, which was that there must be a trick to it, a crib, a way of faking it somehow. At any rate, on this morning, when she noticed that I had preferred being amused by the Benson speech itself to being embarrassed by the associated image of Hamilton's suddenly applauding a remark of, well, questionable morality, she quickly and kindly proceeded to recall for me the introduction given Benson by the president of the college, a Mr. Carlisle Bargeron.

"Remember," she said, "in President Bargeron's introduction, this bit of deathless prose: '*Ezra Taft Benson was conditioned early in life for the political buffeting that was to come. In fact, he experienced mob abuse early in his life.*' " Rochelle giggled and put on a pompous expression that mocked President Bargeron and continued. " '*Secretary Benson is not a ministerial man in appearance.*' " She was recalling his words effortlessly; they came back to me as she spoke them. Surely she was making them up; but if she were, how could I recognize them as she spoke? " '*He could be taken for a well-groomed businessman, over six feet tall and weighing two hundred pounds. He greets you with a pleasant smile and has an easy laugh.*' " She smiled at me. "He must have written that speech from old publicity handouts from the Eisenhower administration. Because there was old Benson, sitting right next to Mr. Bargeron in a folding chair, tiny, shriveled, scowling like a Puritan minister!" she laughed. "Do you remember the crescendo of the introduction?"

I shook my head no. Good God, until she had started quoting it, I had forgotten that there had even been an introduction in the first place.

" '*Secretary Benson stands at the crossroads, seeking to turn the tide!*' " Then, wrapping her long arms across the front of her body, she broke into goodhearted laughter. Utterly without malice, her laughter seemed to enfold the very object of her mockery, President Bargeron, and even Benson himself in a hug of compassionate understanding. For a second I felt that her laughter included as its object Hamilton too, and even me. Swinging her long, tanned legs over the edge of the bed, she got up and, naked, un-self-consciously crossed the room to the dresser and made herself another drink.

I must tell you that I was happier at that moment than I could remember ever having been before.

When she returned to the bed, she went on quoting, this time in a wheezy, high-pitched voice designed to affect the quality and tone of Ezra Taft Benson's aged voice. " '*We need*,' " she said sternly, " '*as we need no other thing, a nationwide repentance of our sins! In our rush for the material things, we have, indeed, forgotten to serve the God of this land. We must look beyond the dollar sign! Our greatness has been built on spiritual values, and if we are to survive we must find again what we once had and now have lost. I am speaking of the inner strength that comes from obedience to divine law!*' "

Taking a sip from her drink. Offering me a sip. Then, amazingly, going on. " '*At least twenty great civilizations have disappeared! The pattern is shockingly similar. All, before their collapse, showed a decline in spiritual values, in moral stamina, and in the freedom and responsibility of their citizens. They showed such symptoms as excessive taxation, as bloated bureaucracy, as governmental paternalism, and in general a rather elaborate set of controls and regulations affecting prices, wages, production, and consumption.*' "

She paused again, and then she began a recitation that to me was indeed beyond belief (I could not believe that she had merely heard the speech once; she had to have read a copy at some point), for she was now quoting Benson as he quoted yet another speaker, and she was quoting both exactly (as far as I knew): " '*After reviewing the decline and fall of these great empires and appraising the lessons taught, the historian Glover of Oxford University makes this cryptic comment: "It is better for the development of character and contentment to do certain things badly yourself than to have them done better for you by someone else.*" ' "

Her voice, ordinarily low for a woman and tender, had tightened in her mimicry and had risen and, to be sure, had harshened somewhat. I was struck dumb by her ability not only to remember the man's exact words but also to mimic his voice and mannerisms. What a woman! I said to myself.

"And remember how he ended his speech?" she reminded me.

I had not remembered at all, of course, until she began to quote it, and then as she spoke there returned to me in a rush a second embarrassing image, the image of Hamilton's second outburst, which, fortunately, had not been perceived by Rochelle. It came as Benson was reaching the rhetorical peak of his message. The little man, visibly trembling with the emotion of his message to these young graduates, had cried out to them, "*I love this nation! It is my firm belief that the God of Heaven raised up the founding fathers and inspired them to establish the Constitution of this land! This was ingrained in me as a youngster by my father and mother and by my church! It is part of my religious faith! To me, this is not just another nation! It is a great and glorious so-*

ciety with a divine mission to perform for liberty-loving people everywhere!" Here he hesitated a moment to wipe the spittle from his lips with his handkerchief. Then, continuing with fervor, he shouted, "*Freedom is a God-given, eternal principle vouchsafed to us under the Constitution! It must be continually guarded as something as precious as life itself! It is doubtful if any man can be politically free who depends upon the state for sustenance! A completely planned and subsidized economy weakens initiative, discourages industry, destroys character and demoralizes the people!*" At precisely this moment as Benson stepped away from the microphone, Hamilton had leaped to his feet and, brandishing one huge fist like a club, had bellowed, "Live free or die!" It was the New Hampshire state motto!

The rest of the audience had begun to applaud and a few individuals had risen to their feet, to prove their patriotism, perhaps, but possibly because of their genuine enthusiasm for the secretary's words, and thus, luckily, Hamilton's cry was lost on most of the people in the auditorium. Not on me, however, nor on the dozen or so people seated near us. And not on Ezra Taft Benson, either. The old man, by a quirk, happened to have been looking straight at Hamilton as he finished his speech, so when Hamilton leaped to his feet and bellowed the New Hampshire state motto, Benson must have thought an enormous fanatic, an outsized Puerto Rican or some kind of Balkan anarchist madman, was about to attempt a suicidal assassination. The old fellow went white and staggered backward, clutched at his chest, clawed at it, and fell to the floor, where he began kicking his feet like a child having a tantrum.

In a second Mr. Bargeron, Rochelle and the minister who had offered the prayer at the beginning of the ceremonies had reached Benson and had pulled him back to his feet. Apparently they had not seen the cause of his fall and assumed he had tripped over a microphone wire because they were, all three, apologetic and concerned mostly that he might have hurt himself. The secretary, who by this time had realized he was not about to be assassinated, smiled painfully and limped from the stage, disappearing quickly behind the curtain, ashen-faced, shaken, mumbling to himself.

Rochelle and I must have been remembering the same image — old Benson staggering backward, grabbing at his chest, falling over and kicking his feet on the floor, then being helped off the stage — for suddenly she looked at me in the gray, melancholy light and in a soft voice asked, "What *really* happened? What made that old man act like that . . . so *terrified* . . . as if someone were going to kill him? Did something happen that I, that I didn't see? Did my *father* do anything?"

I knew that she wanted me to say no, to keep it a puzzle, but I couldn't lie to her any more than I could lie to myself. So I told her, told her how her father had stood up fiercely with his enormous fist raised and had cried out the New Hampshire state motto, which, as she could tell immediately, was indeed threatening. To a timid listener it could sound like, "Live free or I'll kill you!"

"Did he do that because he was so carried away with enthusiasm for Benson's speech?" Her voice was shaky, frightened, pleading.

"Oh, God, I don't know. I just don't know anymore. But he has a way," I explained, "as you probably know all too well, of praising a thing by condemning it and of condemning a thing by praising it. He has a way of making a positive statement from a double negative, and a negative statement from a double positive. The first skill is not rare, but the second is. You aren't a native New Englander, as I am and as your father is, so you're probably not as aware as I of the degree to which this skill operates in the culture as a means for self-expression. Practically any old Yankee farmer will let you know how cruel and relentless his winter has been, not by condemning it, but by smiling and perversely praising the facts that his thermometer has frozen, that his cattle and pigs all froze to death in January, that there was still ice on the lakes in mid-June. It's almost an ironic point of view, an extremely highly developed form of sarcasm that they're not even aware they possess. The late Latin poets possessed it, consciously, of course, and certain eighteenth-century English authors owned it also, again quiet consciously. But rarely, if ever, has it been characteristic of an entire people. Hamilton, your father, seems to have developed it to an extremely high degree, mainly because at some early age he must have become conscious of it and realized that, if he pushed it to a still more extreme point, he could gain a much wider range of reference for it, could use it to criticize matters more complex than last winter's awful weather. At least that's my theory, Rochelle. And because I love the man, I choose to believe it. So I guess it's more than a theory, it's also a rationalization. I wish it were more than a rationalization, though. I wish it were a description."

"I know," she said softly, in almost a whisper. "If it *were* a description, you could believe that he despised Ezra Taft Benson, had utterly rejected him, and yet had managed at the same time to avoid subscribing to your and my liberal notions. Wouldn't that be a profound and mature politics?" she said in a voice filled with wonder. "To be free to criticize and even to despise the old man's reactionary position without, as a result, having to endorse any other. To offer yourself essentially as a *critique*, to be able to trust yourself that much! Why, you'd have to be a political genius to accomplish it!" she exclaimed. "Or some kind of Kierkegaardian ironist," she added thoughtfully.

"That's precisely what keeps me from deserting your father's side at moments like that, like the time he shouted the state motto at Benson or when he fell asleep during your valedictory speech or mocked me for voting for people like Morris Udall . . . or all the other things he's done that, on the surface, seemed mindless, cruel or intolerant." Our enthusiasm for the man was growing again. Our fear and mistrust were on the wane. With bright eyes and rapid words we cheered each other on, and before long we were both loving and admiring him without qualification again.

It was more than merely possible that he had intended all this, had even foreseen it, and that it was his method of teaching us to see and understand the world more independently and with steadily increasing clarity. He was in many ways like a Sufi master or a wizened old peyote-chewing Indian shaman or a Zen Buddhist teacher who by indirection points direction out. But we are so naïve and ill-formed that, in our search for wisdom, we run around expecting to find it only in stereotypical figures — like desert-browned Sufis or raucous old Indian grandfathers or crisp Buddhist monks — never realizing that it is more in the nature of true wisdom that, for us, wisdom reside in the familiar form of a New Hampshire pipefitter who can't seem to get along with people.

Reaching over, I took her by her smooth shoulders, pulled her to me, and felt her cool breasts press against my chest. "Oh, Rochelle!" I cried. "We must be strong! And I do believe that we're stronger together than we are alone! Your father is probably the greatest man either of us will ever have the good luck to meet in our lifetimes. Alone we weaken, we forget how difficult and tangled is the path to true wisdom. But together we are strengthened, toughened, encouraged to push through the intellectual and emotional tangles and our own most private fears and insecurities and conditionings to the end, where we, too, can offer ourselves as critiques, as double positives, and finally, in the largest sense, as human beings!"

Needless to say, I was hovering somewhere between ecstasy and hysteria when suddenly, and thankfully, Rochelle taught me the utter ridiculousness of my feelings, showed me how far I still had to go before I could claim to possess a shred of the cloth Hamilton wore. She showed me also how much further along that path she had gone than I, showed me that while I might have glimpsed the master's garment, she had actually touched it.

"I don't think you understand the nature of religious experience," she said evenly. "I'm sorry, but when a person reaches the point where he or she can claim to know what you are now claiming to know, he or she should be free to enact it. If he or she can't, if he or she still needs help, then he or she really cannot say that he or she has the requisite knowledge. I'm sorry, but you're much closer to the path when you're greedily interrogating me about my father, when you're splicing together your own personal knowledge of him with my personal and acquired knowledge of him, making of the man's life a text, if you will, that will guide you straightway into the invention of your own life." Gently, she pulled away from me and took a last sip from her glass. Then she smiled. "If you'll fix me another drink, I'll tell you how my father almost went to college."

"What?" I was stupefied by the sequence — first a collusion, then a collision, and now a collusion again.

"Sure," she said brightly. "I'll tell you everything I know about him. And it's quite a lot. I've done four years of research on his life so far, for that 'novel' of mine. You know,

The Plumber's Apprentice. I don't feel possessive about that material anymore. I'm no more a professional novelist than *you* are, for heaven's sake!" she laughed, and I had to laugh with her. "Go ahead, honey, fix me another drink and I'll tell you all about how my daddy almost went to college." She smiled and spoke with a southern accent that, as I rushed across the bedroom to the dresser where I had placed the cognac, soda and ice, nearly made me swoon.

"After all, honey," she drawled from the bed, "you told me something this mo'ning I didn't know about before, that stuff about how Daddy stood up and shouted the state motto and all? I oughta do the same thing for you now, shouldn't I?" And she winked at me. *Winked!* What a woman!

I was certainly very confused. How, *how* had I lost control of the situation like this?

Then I remembered: it was the ecstasy and the hysteria — or rather, it was my having reached the point halfway between the two. After that, everything had gone haywire for me. Rochelle had taken complete control of the conversation, and of me, until there I was fetching her a drink in exchange for a tale I hadn't even particularly wanted to hear anymore, and to make matters worse, I was doing it in a swoon. How would I ever be able to remember the tale, let alone determine its importance to my own tale? Oh, reader, dear reader, remember this, and let it be an example to you. In the book of your life, never permit yourself to invent a woman or a man who is capable of bewildering you while he or she seduces you. You will lose the thread of your argument, you will find your story line impossibly tangled, your plot utterly overthrown, and your faith in your powers of observation and analysis sliced to limp ribbons of insecurity. Call it love, call it whatever you will, but know the risk. If you must, as I must, think of your life as a novel and of the creatures therein as "characters," then unless you can keep yourself from falling in love with one of those creatures, you will have to give up the idea of control. You will have to become not an inspired author, but one who is simply not in control of his own novel. It happens, it happens frequently.

"I'm sorry," I said, my voice hushed with contrition. "You're right, you're quite right, of course." I handed her drink to her, and holding on to my own as if it were a kitten, I sat down next to her on the bed. "Please. Please tell me how Hamilton, how your father almost went to college. It's a chapter in his life I know nothing about. I'd even forgotten it existed, that you had mentioned its existence that day after your graduation ceremonies, until you mentioned it again tonight, I mean this morning."

"Yes, this morning. It's late," she yawned, stretching her long white arms in the milky light, and once again I found myself having to deal with my own tumescence.

"Tired?" I asked.

"Yes," she answered. "But still, I want you to hear this. It might help you to know important things about him. It's a short story, I can tell it to you in a few minutes, and tomorrow, later today, I mean, I'll let you have the chapter from my novel that describes the adventure. As a matter of fact," she went on, "I've been thinking of turning the entire manuscript, even my notes and tapes, over to you, to let you use in any way that pleases you." She yawned again, as if with disinterest in my response.

I was shocked. "*What?* What do you *mean?*" Her novel, the obsession-driven activity of her last four years? Give it up, just like that?

"Yes. I've made a decision. I think it's a waste of my time to be writing a novel about the man — I mean that kind of self-consciousness, that kind of objectification. It all seems to run counter to what I'm trying to learn from the man. From what I am learning. It's hard to describe. *You* write the novel. If you can. I can't. And even if I could, I'd never bring myself to *publish* it," she added with a wry smile.

I was twice shocked. She sat there, looking straight ahead into space, apparently close to emotionless, as if she had once witnessed a glory or a horror that I hadn't, announcing as she was to me in a passionless voice that she was canceling out the work of four years of her young life, hard, diligent work, boring research, arduous travel, careful visioning and revisioning, until she had nearly perfected a style and had mastered the content. I, her most confirmed admirer, could not believe that she would cancel this enterprise, that she, simply and practically without feelings, would turn the manuscript over to me for my grimy use. (Relatively speaking, of course. I can't pretend to be *that* self-deprecating.)

"Listen," I said to her, "I *love* your novel!"

"*Do* you?"

"Yes!" I exclaimed. "It's so . . . so . . . *realistic!*"

She said, "Well, you've still got a lot to learn, I'm afraid. But *I* can't teach you. I'm still an initiate myself, you know. Here, here's the story," she began, and leaning back against the pillows, as the new day's sunlight spilled into the room for the first time, she took a sip from her drink and told me the story of how Hamilton Stark almost went to college.

She was right. It wasn't much more than a short story (she told it at one sitting), and, to fully understand the event, its subtler aspects, I did need the manuscript, which she delivered to me late that same afternoon. It was entitled "Fighting It, Giving Up," Chapter Four, from *The Plumber's Apprentice*. I've included it here, rather than try to summarize it or provide my own version, for the usual reasons: her handling of the material seems so much superior to what I could accomplish that only an insensitive egoist would proffer his own version instead. The name changes are the same as indicated earlier, when other portions of Rochelle's novel were quoted. There is, however, one additional character here, the youth called Feeney, and though he appeared briefly in a chapter quoted in my Chapter Four, Addendum C, Rochelle's Chapter Eight, "Return and Depart," at that time I said that no one corresponded to Feeney in Hamilton's, A.'s, life. It now appears that I was wrong. Rochelle, through diligent, wily research, has uncovered the prototype for Feeney, a man named F., who now works as a machine operator in a tannery in Penacook. He and A. rarely see each other these days, and then only by accident.

CHAPTER 4

Fighting It, Giving Up

It positively amazed Alvin that he could get in his car and drive it over the hills for four hours roughly north and west, stop the car, get out, walk into a bar, order a drink, and be served legally. Well, not quite legally, even here in New York State, because he was only seventeen, but even so, it was still enough to astound him when he and Feeney strode through the door of the Valley Café in Ausable Chasm, New York, and each ordered a Seven-and-Seven, that the bartender merely served them and took their money.

It was a Friday in November, Alvin's senior year in high school. He was a football star and a good student, "especially in math." Everyone said so. He had driven to Ausable Chasm this day for an interview with the dean of admissions of the little-known engineering institute located at the edge of the small town. Feeney had gone along to keep him company and "for laughs," he'd said, and while Alvin was being interviewed, he'd taken the car and had driven around the town looking for a bar that he thought, from its appearance, would serve them without asking for IDs. "I got a sixth sense for these things," he had explained as he drove off in Alvin's Ford.

It was a raw, rainy day, blustery and dark, and Alvin wore only a lightweight cloth raincoat over his charcoal gray flannel suit, and he carried no umbrella, so by the time he had located and entered the brick, armorylike administration building, his clothes, hair and shoes were soaked through. Miserably uncomfortable and smelling like a wet, long-haired animal, he sat through a painful fifteen-minute interview with a blond crew-cut young man who never once smiled as he asked Alvin questions about the size of Pittsfield High School, the percentage of the graduating seniors who went on to college, and the range of courses offered there. "We've never had an applicant from your school before," the somber young man explained.

"Oh, I see," Alvin said.

A few minutes later, when, in answer to the dean's inquiry as to the possibility of Pittsfield's football team winning the state championship, Alvin had laughed and said, "Never!" it was the dean who said, "Oh, I see."

It had gone on like that, the two of them saying soberly, "Oh, I see," perhaps half a dozen times each, ending with Alvin's pointing out that he would need a scholarship, a full scholarship, to go to college, because his parents were unable to help him financially. "My father's a plumber," he added helpfully.

The dean had said, "Oh, I see," one more time and then, "Yes," and then, "Well, yes," and had ushered him back to the outer office, where they shook hands and grimly parted.

By the time Alvin reached the coffee shop near the campus where he'd arranged to meet Feeney, he was again soaking wet and he was growling. He was still growling when he sat down across from Feeney in the plastic-seated booth, and Feeney laughed.

"Let's get the hell outa here," Alvin said. "I gotta get *plowed!*"

Feeney went on laughing. He always laughed when Alvin started growling. That Alvin Stock, what a crazy guy! He gets pissed at something, he starts growling like some kinda mad dog or something. Really growling, and loud. Anybody can hear it. Like he was gonna tear somebody up with his teeth. What a crazy guy!

The growl was new — or rather, it had only recently been noticed by others. Alvin himself was still not quite aware of it, not even when it was timidly pointed out to him. He wasn't sure what people heard when they laughed and said, "Hey, man, calm down! You're *growling*, for chrissake!" But he knew what he felt — a knot, at first tightening in his chest, high up, and then slowly loosening as it rose in his throat and finally, between clenched teeth, squirted from his mouth. For him, the sound was merely that of his breath exhaling under pressure from below, scraping against resistance from above, the physiological opposite of a sigh.

But what others heard was a frighteningly literal growl. For them it began with a deep rumbling from Alvin's chest that thinned, tightened, and rose in pitch as it moved up his throat. Then, finally, after resonating in his mouth, the noise would flow like a metal ribbon between his teeth, usually driving anyone near him back a step or two in surprise and, for a second, fear. Then, when it was apparent that Alvin was not conscious of his noise, came the nervous laughter, the light mockery. In turn, his response was usually one of irritation and slight embarrassment — irritation that he was being distracted from expressing his anger, embarrassment that he was not fully aware of how he was being perceived. And too, from some corner of his mind, embarrassment that he was angry at all and had been found out, betrayed, almost, by a noise his body seemed to make involuntarily.

The Valley Café was a neighborhood tavern located in a row of wood tenements south of the center of Ausable Chasm at the edge of the Ausable Chasm River, which, a few miles downstream, emptied into Lake Champlain. It was a small place, a storefront, actually, with a dark bar along one side of the room and a dozen or so red plastic-seated booths along the other. At the back were three doors, one leading from behind the bar to the small kitchen, the second leading to a pair of filthy, unventilated restrooms, the third, marked by an Exit sign, leading to an alley. At the front there were two large plate glass windows painted dark green from the low sills to eye level, with a small red neon sign in each pane that rapidly blinked VALLEY CAFÉ.

The place was quiet, dimly lit, almost empty. In its own toughly cynical way, the bar was friendly. It worked hard at seeming to be no more than what it was, a neighborhood bar. Anything that was deliberately atmospheric, as if to attract strangers, would not have made sense, no more to the patrons than to the owners. A juke box was allowed, was not thought pretentious or, worse, naïve, but only if the songs were the type of melancholy love songs that celebrated stoical loss, songs ten years out of date sung by middle-aged crooners who'd broken in with the big bands in the thirties and forties.

Alvin and Feeney walked up to the bar and ordered Seven-and-Sevens from the beefy, T-shirted bartender. He was a chinless, balding man in his fifties, his thick arms covered with faded red and blue tattoos. His T-shirt was stretched tightly across a belly that clung to the front of him like a tortoise shell, below which he had tied a white apron like a bib. He served the boys quickly and went back to his post at the front of the bar, where he had spread his newspaper. Planting both elbows on the counter, his chin resting against his knuckles, he resumed reading, slowly moving his lips as he read.

In a few seconds, having grown accustomed to the semi-darkness of the room, the boys took a look around them to see where, in fact, they were and who was there with them. At the far end of the bar, in a bank of shadows, hunched a man in his late sixties, a serious afternoon drinker with a shot of blond whiskey and a glass of flat draft beer arranged precisely in front of him. In one of the booths, with his back to the bar, a young man in khaki work clothes was arguing in a hissing voice with a tubby, bleached-blond, middle-aged woman who was barely listening, but now and then making a low-voiced comment that would set the young man off and hissing again. He chain-smoked from a pack of Camels in front of him, and she affectionately studied her pink-painted fingernails. For a minute Alvin wondered why the young man was haranguing her. Were they married to each other? Lovers? Brother and sister? He gulped down the last of his drink and called for another.

Maybe she was a prostitute and he was her pimp. Naw, impossible. The guy's wearing work clothes. Besides, she's too old and fat to be a prostitute. What's it like, he wondered, to fuck a woman that old and that fat?

She was looking across at him then, not quite staring, but openly, undeniably, looking at him. Alvin returned her gaze.

Feeney, staring down into his glass, went on chattering, something about California, L.A., swimming year-round, beautiful cars, a '49 Olds 88 . . . Alvin noticed that the woman's face was not unattractive. She had bright, dark, heavily made-up eyes that were wide apart and low on her face, and a full mouth that she had painted pink, to match her fingernails. Her hair was short and curly, fluffy almost. The color of vanilla ice cream, Alvin thought. She was wearing a maroon short-sleeved sweater and a navy blue wool skirt, both of which clung tightly to her bulky, round torso. Her arms and breasts, though exceptionally large, looked firm to Alvin. Maybe she's not really that old, he thought. In her late thirties, maybe. And the guy is her brother-in-law and he's complaining about something that his wife, her sister, did to him, and she really doesn't give much of a shit because she doesn't like the guy much in the first place and he's constantly whining in the second place. And anyhow, what she's really interested in is *me*. Finishing off his drink, he ordered another.

Feeney ordered another too. "Gimme a coupla Slim Jims, will ya?" he said to the bartender.

Other people, mostly men, came into the bar, drank awhile, and left. It grew dark outside, and the bartender turned on a set of rose-shaded lights. Alvin played the juke box, half a dozen Frank Sinatra songs, and while the records played, Alvin, back at the bar, snapped his fingers to the beat. He drank, ordered again, and drank again.

Feeney started talking about the drive home, four hours, and Alvin said, "Yeah, yeah, sure. Later, later," and because it was Alvin's car, Feeney forgot about it. What the hell, he could always sleep in the back and let Alvin worry about the driving. He was only along for the laughs, he explained — but Alvin didn't seem to hear him.

A pair of sailors, quite cheerfully drunk, wandered into the place and took stools next to Alvin and continued their drinking. The young man with the woman in the booth started to get up to leave, but as he rose from his seat, he saw that the woman was looking intently at Alvin, who was leaning off his stool in her direction, like a tower about to fall, and the young man quickly sat down again.

One of the sailors, a thin, red-headed boy with freckles swarming across his face, elbowed Alvin in the side and, grinning good-naturedly, said to him, "You got somethin' goin' with Blondie over there, ain't you?"

Slowly Alvin turned and looked at the sailor. All he could see was the red-headed boy's huge grin, a tooth-filled half-moon, and to Alvin at that moment the sailor's great, good-hearted grin was the silliest, weakest thing he'd ever seen, so he said, "Whyn't you mind your own fuckin' business?" and watched with pleasure the collapse of the grin.

"Fuck you," the sailor quietly offered, and he turned away.

Satisfied, Alvin resumed watching the woman in the booth, who had now placed herself so that Alvin could see her legs, crossed, halfway up her thighs.

By this time Feeney, too, had realized that Alvin's attention was focused solely on one person, and also that the person's attention seemed to be focused on Alvin as well. "Go easy, Al," he warned. "We're a long ways from home, y'know."

Alvin brushed his friend's warning aside with a crooked smile, and the next thing he knew he was standing beside the booth, staring down at the blond woman. "Buy you a drink?" he asked, flashing the same crooked smile he had given Feeney a moment before.

The woman looked up at him, her face wide open and

pleased, but before she could answer, the man seated opposite her snarled, "Screw, kid. Get fuckin' *lost*, will ya?"

In a dead voice Alvin said, "I didn't offer to buy *you* a drink." And for the first time he saw that the man was actually quite a bit older than he'd thought, was in fact the same age as the woman, probably in his late thirties. Up close, Alvin could see that the man was large, and muscular too, red-faced from working outside, with large tanned hands crossed with pencil-thick veins.

The man jammed an unlit cigarette between his thin lips, and with one motion he snapped open his lighter and lit the cigarette while with his free hand he pointed first an index finger at Alvin's chest and then a hooked thumb at the barstool Alvin had just left. Inhaling deeply, blowing the smoke from flared nostrils, the man repeated his instructions: "Screw, kid. The lady's with me. Now get fuckin' *lost*, will ya!"

The woman smiled helplessly up at Alvin and remained silent.

Alvin looked coldly into the man's pale blue eyes. "Shut up," he said evenly. "I'm talkin' to her, not you."

"Lissen, honey, maybe some other time, okay?" the woman said to him in a husky voice. She was still smiling up at him.

"I'm from outa town, I'm leavin' tonight, so whyn't you let someone who's just passin' through buy you a drink? Whaddaya drinkin', anyhow?" Alvin peered down into her glass, as if peering down a well.

"Gin and tonic."

"Gin and tonic!" Alvin called over to the bartender. "An' another Seven-an'-Seven!" He started to sit down next to the woman, who quickly slid over to make room, when suddenly the man reached across and clamped onto Alvin's wrist, stopping him.

"Kid," he hissed, "if you don't turn around an' get the hell outa here I'm gonna take you apart."

Swinging his other hand around in front of him, Alvin wrenched the man's hand free of his wrist and threw it against the table. "You ain't takin' anybody apart tonight, pal."

Alvin felt wonderful. Like a tractor or bull or tree. And fast, like a cobra or lariat or chain saw. And fearless, like a block of ice or a surgeon or the wind. Here was a big man who was older than he, a tough, wiry man facing him with threats and anger, yet to Alvin the man was like a curtain that could easily be brushed aside. So he turned all his attention to the woman, asking her name and did she live around here.

The man stood up and grabbed Alvin's right shoulder. "Let's go. Out." His voice was hurried but low and smooth, almost pleasant, as if he were putting his cat out for the night.

At the bar, Feeney, the sailors, the bartender, and three or four other customers, all older men, were watching intently. Only Feeney looked frightened. He got off his stool and took a step toward the booth, then a sideways step toward the door that led out to the street and Alvin's car. From the juke box at the back Frank Sinatra was singing "On the Road to Mandalay," but otherwise the place was silent, still, and waiting.

Alvin looked down at the man's hand clamped to his shoulder. He said, "You wanta step outside *with* me, pal? 'Cause that's the only way I'm goin'."

"Some other time, kid. I ain't got time to play games with punks like you. Now get outa here."

"Screw you. Either you step outside with me, mister, and get the shit pounded outa you, or you just pick up your little lunchbox there and trot home alone. I plan to sit here awhile an' have a drink an' a talk with Mary. Is that your name, honey? What's your name?" he asked the woman with the vanilla ice cream hair.

"Helen."

"Terrific. Terrific. What's you say you were drinkin'? Gin an' tonic?"

"Yeah."

"Okay, honey. Bartender, let's have a gin an' tonic an' a Seven-an'-Seven over here!"

"Okay," the man in khakis said. "You want your head beat in, you're gonna get it. Let's go, sonny. Outside," he said, and he let go of Alvin's shoulder and strode angrily for the door in back that led to the alley.

Alvin grinned and slid out of the booth without looking back at the woman.

Feeney grabbed him by the arm. "C'mon, Al, let's get the fuck outa here. Whaddaya doin', for chrissakes? That guy'll kill ya!"

Pulling silently away, Alvin started for the exit to the alley, and Feeney shrugged his shoulders and followed his friend, averting his eyes as he passed the woman in the booth.

Jumping from their stools, the pair of sailors followed. "I hope the bastard gets *creamed*," the red-headed one said.

The bartender, wiping up the bar with a dirty gray cloth, shook his head as if disgusted and slightly bored by the whole thing. "Fuckin' kid drinkers," he mumbled to one of the men at the bar. "Who needs 'em?" Then he called over to the woman, who was lighting a cigarette from a lit butt in the ashtray in front of her. "Hey, Helen, you still want that drink?"

"Yeah."

"Who's payin' for it?" the bartender asked, winking to the men along the bar.

"Whichever one comes back, Freddie. Whichever one

comes back." She laughed and started studying her pink fingernails again.

The man in the khaki work clothes was at least six feet tall and broad-shouldered, but still he wasn't as tall as Alvin or anywhere near as wide. He was thick and compact, though, one of those men whose muscles are flat and short, an efficiently built, heavy-boned man with thick wrists and large hands.

When Alvin stepped out of the bar into the alley, he saw the man standing, facing him, a half-dozen paces away at the edge of a circle of light thrown by the single bulb burning over the door. In back of the man was a cinderblock wall about nine feet high, and beyond that was a belt of the dark gray, almost black sky that rose straight up from the river below. Next to the back door of the bar on either side were overflowing garbage cans and collapsing, rain-soaked, cardboard boxes. The ground was puddled and muddy, and a nasty, erratic wind was blowing.

Alvin shed his suit jacket and handed it to Feeney, who tried to lean himself casually against the side of the building. The sailors came out and stood next to him, grinning, their arms folded over their chests. With one hand Alvin unknotted his necktie and passed that too to Feeney.

Feeney said, "Thanks."

Alvin said, "Yeah."

The man said, "C'mon, kid," and crouched slightly, his fists in front of him, his head pulled down into his bulky shoulders, his feet planted firmly on the ground. A puncher.

Taking two quick steps forward, Alvin drew his fists up in front of his face, quite high up, leaned slightly off the balls of his feet, and then, for the first time in his life, he started to fistfight. As if he were in a trance, thinking consciously of the mechanics of what he was doing no more than he would if he were eating a meal, he slid to his left, feinted once, and jammed his right fist, twice, as if firing it, under the man's left arm, crashing his fist against the rib cage, driving the man off-balance to his side, where Alvin caught him with a knee slammed into the crotch as the man fell away. The man grunted and swung a couple of slow punches at Alvin's head, both missing weakly, and Alvin started moving swiftly in and out, his fisted hands attacking the man's neck, chest and belly, like a pack of dogs tearing at the sides of a wounded deer, moving too fast, too relentlessly, too automatically, for the man to avoid them. As he started to collapse backward toward the cinderblock wall, with Alvin driving on like a crowd, the man, spitting blood, groaned, "Enough!" Alvin grabbed him by the shirtfront, held him at arm's length, and whacked him, hard, across the temple with one enormous paw, flipping the man out of his grasp into a heap in the mud. Walking over to him, he picked him up again and threw him back down again. He kicked him once on the shoulder. Then he left him alone.

"Jesus Christ!" Feeney yelled. "You did it! You really took the guy!" He was clapping Alvin on the shoulder and staring down at the man on the ground.

Alvin pulled his jacket and tie out of Feeney's other hand and shoved his arms into the jacket and slung the necktie around his neck without knotting it. He turned and started straight down the alley toward the street.

"Hey! Where ya goin'? What about the broad? Where ya goin'?"

"Home," Alvin grunted and kept on moving, head down, for the street.

"Okay, I'll get your raincoat. You left it inside," Feeney called to him.

"Yeah." Then he was gone from sight.

Feeney turned around, a puzzled but still exhilarated expression on his face. "Jesus." The sailors had gone back inside. The man on the ground was slowly, awkwardly getting to his feet. "You okay?" Feeney asked him quietly.

The man was bleeding from the mouth and nose. He stood, bent over, clutching his left side, breathing laboriously. His clothes were smeared with mud and fresh blood. "I gotta . . . busted . . . rib. I think . . . . Tell Freddie . . . C'mere. Th' bartender . . ."

"Sure." Feeney walked somberly inside, told the bartender he'd better check the guy out and maybe get him a doctor or something, the guy seemed pretty busted up. Plucking Alvin's tan raincoat from the coatrack, he pointedly avoided even a glance at the woman in the booth next to it and started walking out the door at the front.

"Where's the other one?" the bartender asked. He had come out from behind the bar and was on his way toward the back door. "I don't wanta see him in here again. You tell him that."

"No sweat," Feeney said, grinning. "No sweat at all." Then he looked down at the woman. Serious-faced, she was sipping from her gin and tonic. She caught him staring, and without removing her pink lips from the rim of the glass, gave him the finger.

Feeney laughed and strolled happily out. When he reached the car and got in, he looked over at Alvin behind the steering wheel. He was smiling and the car motor was running.

"Feelin' pretty tough, ain't ya?" Feeney observed.

"Yeah. Like a bucket full of nails." Then he jammed the car into gear, and they headed back to New Hampshire.

I was grateful for the story, grateful to Rochelle for having delivered it to me, for having written it in the first place. But the story complicated things for me far more than it simplified them. I asked Rochelle if it complicated things for her, too, and she said no, not really, which surprised me.

"But he sounds so *ordinary*," I pointed out to her, "like almost any young man already determined at adolescence by social and familial past, one of those angry American youths locked into patterns of violence, drunkenness and sexual expoitation. Even if he eventually raised his consciousness to the point where he could direct his anger politically, rather than mutely against himself," I observed to her, "he'd still be little more than another feeble example of the type called 'working-class hero.' " And both Rochelle and I were claiming much more for him than that.

It was not exactly what I had been looking for in a story about Hamilton's brush with a college education. I had wanted him to be offered a full scholarship, say, by Harvard or Princeton or Yale, and after visiting one of those campuses and encountering there for the first time an example or two of the academic mind, to reject the offered scholarship with some sort of truth-telling gesture of defiance. It would have made a marvelously effective vehicle for social satire.

"My father is *not* Holden Caulfield all grown up," Rochelle said, sounding a little hurt.

I couldn't tell if it was her author's pride that had been bruised or the pride of a daughter who believes that she understands her parent better than any stranger can. In either case, though, she was justified in feeling hurt, so I apologized, first for my persistently soft-headed expectations that Hamilton's past could be anticipated any more than could his future, and second, for not having immediately expressed my enthusiasm for the skill and restraint with which she had told her story.

"As always," I explained to her, "your literary gifts amaze and delight me. Especially when placed next to my own awkward attempts."

She smiled politely.

"Look," I brightly said, "the sun has risen above the trees! Shall we go downstairs for breakfast? Or would you like to let me make love to you?"

"Oh, you devil. Don't you ever get tired?"

"Eventually," I confessed.

"You some kind of billy goat, honey," she purred in that southern accent of hers, the one that stiffens me with lust.

CHAPTER EIGHT

100 Selected, Uninteresting Things Done and Said by Hamilton Stark

1. He drove past a hitchhiker without picking him up. The hitchhiker was a long-haired youth in an army field jacket whose stance and bulky physical proportions reminded him for a second, as he later said, of the author's younger brother, now dead, whom Hamilton had met only once, several years before.

2. He bought a new saxophone (tenor) but still preferred the old one.

3. After placing a classified ad in the Concord *Daily Monitor*, he sold his new saxophone for $25 less than he had paid for it. He considered the loss not bad at all. "Self-knowledge always has a price."

4. Between his second and third wives, he perfected a technique for getting out of bed in the morning in such a way that he had to make the bed only once every ten days or so. The technique involved spreading his legs under the covers to the far corners of the bed and then dragging his long body toward the top of the bed, where, springing his weight with his arms against the brass rail headboard, he lifted himself to the floor. When he married for the third time he ceased this activity, but when the woman left he resumed it until he mar-

ried again. He also employed the technique between his fourth and fifth wives and after his fifth wife had left.

5. He changed his brand of cigarettes twice in his life — from Chesterfields to Camels to Lucky Strikes, which he now smokes at the rate of one pack a day.

6. He never learned to fly an airplane, though he often expressed a desire to do so.

7. When he was twenty-six years old he learned to drive a bulldozer, an activity he still enjoys. So much so that when he was thirty he purchased his own bulldozer, a small Caterpillar that he painted black and keeps waxed and shiny, even the blade, which he retouches with black enamel after each use.

8. In winter he usually wears a navy blue woolen watchcap. He rarely covers his ears with it. They are small and turn red from the cold, but he doesn't seem to notice or care.

9. He cut down a dying maple tree behind his barn and that winter used the wood for his fireplace. He remembered having looked at the tree from his earliest childhood, and he thought of this while he was cutting it into fireplace-length pieces. He used his chain saw for the cutting, used it expertly, especially for a man who was not a bona fide woodcutter.

10. He never in his entire life wore a pair of sandals. Never even tried them on in a shoestore.

11. He never defaulted on a debt, and his checking account was never overdrawn. Once, however, he was tempted to default on a television set he had bought on time from Sears & Roebuck. He made his payments punctually for fourteen months, and when the set broke down for the fifth time, he threw it away in anger, tossed it over the fence into the field

in front of the house. With ten months remaining, and no television set to be repossessed or repaired, he threatened in a letter not to make any more payments, but instead sent his checks in nine days late each month until the balance was paid. After that he was reluctant to purchase any more appliances on time; he said it made it more difficult for him to get rid of them when he wanted to.

12. At the end of each year he threw away the old calendar and posted a new one, making a careful point of using a different calendar altogether, different size, picture, advertiser, etc. He preferred calendars from plumbing and heating wholesale supply houses. The pictures were usually of New Hampshire winter scenes, though sometimes they were of bathrooms or furnaces.

13. One winter morning, as he prepared to leave for work, he observed that he always put his left glove on before his right. He reasoned that this was because he was right-handed. For the same reason, he reasoned, he always shaved the right side of his face before the left.

14. One summer afternoon, a Sunday, he tried to draw a picture of his house from the field in front of it. He made three careful attempts but wasn't satisfied with any of them, so he threw them away.

15. "If I was governor of this state, I'd let them all go to hell. That's the only way to govern." (He was speaking of Democratic and liberal Republican critics of the present governor's policies.)

16. The most horned-pout* he ever caught in one night was twenty-two, on June 17, 1964, on Bow Lake, alone.

* A local, smaller, coldwater version of the well-known catfish.

17. Because of his size, he often had difficulty buying clothes until he was about thirty, when he came across an L. L. Bean catalogue in a privy. After that he always bought his clothes by mail order from L. L. Bean.

8. This is the sequence in which he read the several sections of the Sunday newspaper: comics; sports; obituaries; headlines and front page; editorial page; letters to the editor; classified ads. He followed this pattern with the weekday editions too. On Sundays, however, he was more conscious of there being a pattern and of his being free not to follow it if he so desired.

19. He talked to dogs in a gruff voice that seemed to send them cowering away. Once, however, he was almost bit by a friend's unusually courageous dog, which ended the friendship, such as it was.

20. Drawn into a leather-goods shop in Concord by the attractive window display, he was about to purchase an eighty-dollar briefcase, but at the last minute he changed his mind and bought a new wallet instead. "I like the smell of new leather," he later explained.

21. To an insurance salesman as the man stepped from his car: "Get the hell outa here! If I'd wanted to buy anything, I'd have sent for you!" The frightened salesman drove off quickly enough to satisfy him.

22–39. Once a week, at various, though unvarying, times, he performed the following chores:

a. dumped his rubbish in the field in front of his house;

b. buried his garbage in a pit in the field in front of his house (except in winter, when the ground was frozen solid, in which case he simply permitted the garbage to freeze solid, until spring, when he would cover the moldering heap with earth);

c. swept out the barn and cleaned off his workbenches;

d. added a quart of STP additive to the crankcase of his car;

e. checked the tire pressure of all four tires, plus the spare, of his car;

f. in summer, mowed the lawns; in winter, chipped off any ice or snow that had accumulated on the gutters and scraped away any ice or snow on the walks and driveway that he had missed during the week (he shoveled and plowed out his walks and driveway immediately after every snowstorm, but often, because of the lateness of the hour or other responsibilities, had to leave the finish-work for the weekend); in the fall, raked any leaves that had fallen that week into a pile, which he burned (the ashes he piled next to the garden in back of the house until spring, when, before turning the soil, he spread them); in the spring, worked at least three hours cutting and pruning in the wooded areas surrounding the house and along the path up the mountain.

g. drove to Pittsfield, where he bought groceries at the IGA for the coming week, filled his car with Shell gas, stopped at Maxfield's Hardware Store for any tools, nails, screws or other items he might need or had run out of during the previous week, stopped at the state liquor store for a half-gallon of Canadian Club and at Danis's Superette for a case of Molson ale, and returned home;

h. except in winter and late fall, tended his flower beds and vegetable garden, usually between 4:00 and 6:30 P.M. on Saturday; in the late fall and winter, during these same hours, he cut and stacked firewood for the fireplace and the two wood stoves in the kitchen and barn;

i. read the New Hampshire *Times* (the Sunday edition of the Manchester *Union-Leader*);

j. repaired any furniture, appliances, tools, machinery, lamps, cupboard doors, faucets, shutters, shingles, gates or fence posts that, during the previous week, had broken or had begun to malfunction, leak, buzz, flap, or lean;

k. drank half a gallon of Canadian Club and a case of Molson ale, one shot and one bottle at a time;

l. watched one, and no more than one, sporting event on television;

m. sharpened, on the wheel in his workshop, all his butcher knives, axes, hatchets, and handsaws; sharpened his Swiss Army pocketknife while he was at it;

n. fired at least twenty rounds from his Winchester 30.06 rifle — at bottles and tin cans in the field in front of the house; sometimes he shot idly at crows in the field in front of the house; sometimes rats and woodchucks, and when his garden was up, rabbits;

o. as a spiritual exercise (though he never called it precisely that), once a week went twenty-four hours without uttering a word to another person; because of the requirements of his job, this usually took place at home on Sundays, where it was easier to accomplish without complications;

p. walked to the top of Blue Job Mountain behind the house and looked out over the land below, wished it were his as far as he could see, all the way to the limits of the horizon;

q. checked all the above items off his list, one by one, as he performed them, and when necessary, revised the list to accommodate the upcoming week and any changes in routine that might be necessitated.

40. As a matter of course he tossed all mail addressed to Occupant into the trash can in the kitchen or in winter directly into the wood stove. Once, though, as if on a whim, he opened and read a plea for contributions to Boys' Town. After that he resumed tossing all such mail into the trash can or wood stove, as before.

41. He liked to open the glove compartment of his car and find it neat and orderly. Flashlight, registration, New Hampshire roadmap, sharpened pencil, matches, extra fuses tightly rolled in a strip of electrician's tape.

42. To his third wife (Jenny): "I'd as soon wipe my ass with a corncob as this damned stuff. Can't you buy better toilet paper than *this?* It's like sandpaper, for Christ's sake!" To his fourth wife (Maureen): "You trying to give me piles or something? How much d'you save, buying this cheap shit? It feels like emery cloth!" To his fifth wife (Dora): "This stuff feels like pie crust, for Christ's sake! What *gives?*" He figured that, because of his size, he was more sensitive to the texture of toilet paper than normal-sized people were. He also knew that made no sense, but he didn't care. Whether a thing made sense or not had nothing to do with whether it was true or not.

43. He didn't like dogs. "All tongue, lips and flapping tails. No sense of their own worth. Which makes them worth*less*."

44. He didn't like cats. "Sneaky bastards. They love dying even more than death. Which in *my* book makes 'em unreliable."

45. He didn't like horses. "Should've gone extinct forty or fifty years ago, when they couldn't compete with tractors or trucks anymore for work or with cars and bicycles for transportation. Besides, they're ridiculous-looking. Bodies're too big for their legs. I'd like 'em if they were the way they used to be, before the Arabs started screwing 'em up — dog-sized things, like white-tailed deer, only smarter. Probably made good eating."

46. He hated domestic fowl of all kinds. "I don't even like to eat one of the bastards, unless it's cut up so I can't recognize what kind of animal it was when it was still alive."

47. He liked pigs. "Now you take your typical pig. That's an animal with a developed understanding of its life. No delusions. Not like cows. Cows are under the impression that people keep them around because they *like* them. Pigs never make that mistake."

48. What he hated about sheep was the way most people regarded them: "Most people think sheep are sweet and gentle. The truth is, sheep sleep twenty-four hours a day. As far as being alive goes, they're located only one step this side of lawn furniture. Three stomachs covered with a woolly mitten. Personally, if it wasn't for the mutton, I'd rather see a flock of cotton bales."

49. "I'd make a lousy farmer," he confessed. "Plants are okay, though. I don't mind being around plants, long as they don't get too cute, if you know what I mean."

50. He claimed not to know his birth date. "I was barely there, for Christ's sake." When asked how old he was, he would answer, "About thirty-seven," or, "About forty-two," or whatever, always, of course, giving his correct age. He claimed his sense of time was different from most people's in that it was more precise. Doubtless he knew his birth date and, when required to by law, provided it, for he possessed a driver's license, union card, Social Security card, and so on, like the rest of us.

51. Whenever in conversation the word "Florida" came up, he would interject, "Coney Island with palm trees."

52. He did not believe in God. He said that when God believed in *him*, then he'd believe in them *both*. He made this statement somberly, with care, apparently with full awareness of its theological, philosophical and psychological implications.

53. He had lifetime subscriptions to *The Farmer's Almanac*, *Reader's Digest*, and *National Geographic*. Frequently, however, he sneeringly referred to an individual as, "The type of man who has a lifetime subscription to *The Farmer's Almanac*," or, ". . . to *Reader's Digest*," or, ". . . to *National Geographic*." Once, when someone had the temerity to point out that he himself owned lifetime subscriptions to these very periodicals, he answered, "Of course. How else do you think I'd know the types?"

54. He woke at six o'clock every morning of his adult life, even when he did not have to go to work. He did not own an alarm clock and could when necessary wake himself earlier than six and at exactly the time he wished to waken. He seemed to require no more than five hours' sleep a night. In providing this information, he explained that this was because when he went to bed he went to sleep immediately and when he slept he concentrated on it. "Like a machine," he explained. "No, like a rock," he added.

55. Exposés and public scandals seemed to make him sad, as if he were suddenly reminded of some great loss from his childhood.

56. "I hate a melee. If you want a fight, you ought to make it personal. Insult somebody. Insult his mother, his girl friend, his manhood, whatever it is he thinks needs protection."

57. He never permitted any of his wives to make breakfast for him. Once Jenny, attempting to curry his favor, got up an hour earlier than he and prepared a breakfast of fried eggs,

pancakes, sausages, fresh biscuits, coffee and melon, and when he came downstairs and discovered this lovely meal, he was enraged and stormed out of the house. Later, when describing the event, he explained his rage by pointing out the control a woman can obtain over a man if he lets her imitate his mother. "Good intentions can't dull a sharp knife," he aphorized. In fairness, he also pointed out the control a man can have over a woman if she lets him imitate her father. "It's how I kept all my women in line. While I kept them."

58. He despised throw pillows, bric-a-brac, knickknacks, and souvenirs, scatter rugs, doilies, and imitation chandeliers, flower decals, pink appliances, the color off-white, and whitewall tires, decorated mailboxes, and lawn sculpture, and David Susskind, and game shows, and television weathermen. He believed that you are what you love, and therefore he despised people who loved any or all of these things. He also believed that you are not what you despise, and since you cannot very easily control what you love and thus cannot very easily control what you are, you therefore ought at least to make a concerted attempt to avoid being what would disgrace you. For him, then, the most interesting person was the one who hated more things than anyone else, and the least interesting was the one who loved more things than anyone else. Errol Flynn, he thought, was an example of an interesting man. Lee Harvey Oswald and Arthur Bremer were interesting. Gerald Ford, Marilyn Monroe and the Beatles were not.

59. He loved compression when, as a quality, it was joined to symmetry — as in algebra or symbolic logic, a portable tape recorder, a double-bitted ax, or a Maltese cross. In fact, his favorite design was a Maltese cross, and he frequently left it doodled behind him, on restaurant tablecloths, condensation on windows, sand, snow and dust.

60. He wore no jewelry and carried no watch. "On principle," he claimed. As with so much else.

61. He did not wear glasses.

62. The men were unloading a truckload of twenty-foot lengths of six-inch galvanized pipe. He was the foreman on the job site, and because it was only eight-fifteen in the morning and the four men unloading the truck were moving very slowly, two men to each length of pipe, he grew annoyed and left the shanty, where he had been laying out the day's work on the blueprints, and told the crew they were unloading the pipe as if their intent were not to get the truck unloaded but were instead to avoid hurting themselves or tiring themselves out too early in the day, as which point he himself began unloading the pipe, yanking a length by himself from the pile, hefting it to his shoulder and carrying it to the stack twenty feet away, and there laying it gently, so as not to damage the threaded ends, down. The men looked at the sky and the ground. He came back to the truck and did it again. Then again. The men stood aside and watched him work, confused as to the point he was making. After he had unloaded ten lengths of pipe, he stopped before the men and calmly said to them, "You have to lift until everything turns black. Lift till you black out. You have to do it every day. The job will always be more than you can handle, anyhow, so the only point is to lift until everything turns black." Then he walked back into the shanty and resumed laying out the day's work. The men turned to each other for a second, grinned good-naturedly, and went to work unloading the pipe, as before, two men to each length, and moving slowly, with care, pacing themselves.

63. He suddenly remembered his father's walk, his stride, efficient and regular, like a dog's involving his body only from

the hips down. He tried to imitate it and discovered that to do so he didn't have to alter his own stride in the slightest. The discovery gave him a moment's extreme pleasure, not because it meant that he resembled his father even more closely than he had thought (which would not have pleased him at all), but rather because he believed that his discovery of the similarity between his imitation and the remembered image had led him directly to a momentary awareness of the nature of *all* human beings. And who, indeed, would not experience such awareness, however momentary, with pleasure?

64. He visited his father's grave only once after the funeral, the following summer, when the grass had returned. He walked about the plot for a few moments, admired the view of the river from the hilltop cemetery, and got back into his car and drove home. From the top of Blue Job Mountain behind his house, he could see the cemetery, three miles distant. His ancestors for two hundred years were buried there, and once, when this was pointed out to him, he seemed surprised and confessed that it had never occurred to him, even though he made it a habit to climb to the top of Blue Job once every week.

65. To Trudy, his first wife: "I can't tell you I love you because I don't know what the word means. I mean the word 'I,' not 'love' or 'you.' "

66. To Annie, his second wife: "I can't tell you I love you because I know what 'you' and 'love' mean and I don't know what 'I' means."

67. To Jenny, his third wife: "I can't tell you I love you because I know what 'you' and 'love' mean."

68. To Maureen, his fourth wife: "I can't tell you I love you because I know what 'you' means."

69. To Dora, his fifth wife: "I can't tell you I love you."

70. With regard to all five wives, he observed one evening that it would have been possible for him only to have told them he did *not* love them, because he would then be lying and thus he would know what he meant. He meant to lie. By this it seemed that he believed that the only statements a person could make, and also could attribute meaning to, were statements known by the speaker to be falsehoods.

71. Asked by a friend why he continued to marry, feeling as he did toward women in particular and things in general, his response was to shrug helplessly and say, "When you don't despise a thing, you let yourself be powerless to resist its advances, when and if it advances."

72. He disliked most curtains and drapes, all venetian blinds, overhead lamps, tools that were not kept in immaculate condition, and collections of any kind. "I believe in sets of things, not collections."

73. " 'Everything implies its opposite.' I read that. The writer didn't understand what he was writing. He thought it was about logic instead of the world."

74. He refused to return the greetings of his immediate neighbors, the people who lived along the road to his house, and after a while they ceased greeting him or waving to him when he drove past their homes on his way to and from town and work.

75. He seemed to attract the adulation of adolescent boys, and as long as they remained in awe in silence, he did not discourage it. But as soon as anything more was asked of him, a declaration of loyalty or affection, say, or a simple explanation, he in turn asked more of them, and this inevitably drove

the boys away, usually hurt, often angry, and always confused as to who had failed whom.

76. On a number of occasions, with something like glee, he quoted a well-known Jamaican proverb: "Me no send, you no come." He claimed that it meant, "If I didn't send for you, then you're not here."

77. He combed his hair the same way all his life — straight back without a part, cut fairly long, trimmed by a barber every three weeks. Even in his forties, he had no gray hair, and as a result it was difficult to guess his age. People took him for anywhere between twenty-five and fifty-five, depending on their opinion of how old they themselves looked.

78. He kept himself physically very clean, and every morning he shaved himself meticulously, using no cologne or after-shave lotion on his face other than coarse rubbing alcohol. He used a straight razor, which he honed daily on a two-inch-wide leather strap, and a mug and brush. The razor, strap, mug and brush had all belonged to his father, and every morning while he shaved he thought of his father every morning shaving who must have had some other way of calling forth his father, for the grandfather, the one who had died drunk in a snow-bank, had been a bearded man. In that way, every morning while he shaved he was able to think of his grandfather, a man he had never met and who had never shaved. This process satisfied him doubly because it demonstrated for him the way he believed everything worked.

79. He participated in no sports, had not played a game of any kind since his adolescence. The only kind of fishing he did was what is called "bottom-fishing," and though he owned numerous firearms, both rifles and handguns, he hunted only what he called "pests," crows, woodchucks, rats that scavenged

his rubbish and other used-up household articles dumped in the field in front of the house.

80. Where other people saw only white, he claimed to have recognized twenty-one different shades of the color of snow. What he said he saw were eight shades of gray, seven of yellow, and six of blue. His favorite snow color was "blue number four." Black and white, as colors of anything, were unknown to him, he insisted.

81. Drunk, regardless of whether he was speaking to a stranger or to an acquaintance, he usually spoke in accents — Irish, Southern, Italian, and so on. Then after a few more shots of Canadian Club and bottles of ale, he would begin to speak in foreign languages, or what the people around him took for foreign languages. If a French-Canadian were present, he would speak a bit of French. Occasionally, if it came out that the person he was talking to was fluent in some other foreign language than French, in Spanish, say, or German, he would start dropping sentences, phrases, words, as well as entire paragraphs, that seemed to be in Spanish or German. No one ever challenged him on his proficiency, and surely no one dared to challenge his veracity. The people usually just smiled and nodded, the way they would if someone had merely introduced a pleasant non sequitur into the conversation, which by then would have been drunken, loud and digressive anyway, full of fits and stops, starts and interruptions. What matter, then, if some of the fits and stops came in foreign languages that no one in the group, except the speaker, seemed to understand? In this way, he had spoken in recent years with dozens of French-Canadian lumbermen, millhands, and fellow construction workers, an Italian-American formalist painter from New York City with a summer home on Bow Lake, four Creole-speaking Jamaican transient farmworkers, a Portuguese

fisherman visiting relatives in Fall River, a pair of Russian chemists at a convention in Breton Woods, a Venezuelan student at the University of New Hampshire, many Greek cooks, restaurant managers and waitresses, a Chinese Bible salesman, and six Japanese tourists. Additionally, in what he claimed were the original languages, he had made references to and quotations from numerous works of literature written in ancient Greek, Latin, Sanscrit, and Hebrew. As he rarely bothered to translate these into English, it was not known how accurately he was quoting the original, if at all. And of course, always at these times he was extremely drunk, and the personality he was exhibiting was so vivid that, while it could not be ignored, neither could it be taken seriously — that is, as literally a personality.

82. He wore size 13 EEE shoes, over-the-ankle, mocassin-toed workshoes with a steel-reinforced toe and heel. At all times he owned three pairs of these shoes, one brand-new, one two years old, and one four years old, all of them purchased by mail from L. L. Bean in Freeport, Maine. These were the only shoes he owned, and every two years, when he bought a new pair, he threw away the oldest pair, just tossed them over the fence into the field in front.

83. He sent the apprentice pipefitter, his very first day on the job, to the toolshed for a glass-stapler. After a while the boy returned, saying he couldn't find it, and then, timidly, asked him what a glass-stapler looked like. He stared at the boy with apparent disgust and after a moment told him it looked just like it ought to look. "Keep in mind the function, and you'll figure out the form," he said grumpily and walked off. The boy asked the other men, who smiled and sent him on several wild goose chases before the boy finally figured out what was happening, and then everyone had a good laugh together.

"You can't find what doesn't exist," he advised the boy. "But remember, you can't lose it, either." The boy nodded somberly, as if understanding, and the men looked from one to the other and grinned knowingly. Later in the day, one of them said to the boy, "He's a little crazy, y'know. But don't let it worry you none, because he never lets it interfere with his job."

84. He picked up the phone and dialed the first three digits of his sister Jody's telephone number. He had prepared one sentence; it was: "Hello, let me speak to my mother." From there on he planned to improvise. He had, however, forbidden himself to explain or apologize for *anything*. All else was permissible, depending on what she or his mother said. Then he stopped dialing and put the phone down. "If I'm not going to explain or apologize for anything, then I have no reason to be calling her. She should be calling me," he later reasoned.

85. Inside his house, he walked around in his stocking feet. His shoes were always neatly set on a wicker mat next to the door.

86. He could find the cube and square roots of extremely high numbers in his head with nearly the rapidity of an electronic calculator. He dismissed the feat as a trick of concentration that any fool could teach himself if he weren't so happy being a fool.

87. He owned no photographs of himself. Whenever one came to him, he threw it away, just tossed it into the trash can under the sink without even examining it to see whether it was a good likeness or not.

88. Nor did he own a single photograph of anyone else, not a snapshot. If one were presented to him (as by his daughter Rochelle, numerous times), unless it was personally inscribed

(as were all his daughter's), he pitched it into the trash can under the sink. His explanation (no apology) was that he already knew what the subject of the photograph looked like; he didn't need any machine to tell him what he already knew. If he were going to save any photograph, it would have to be of a person he'd never seen before, but he'd never found any reason to do that yet, as evidenced by the fact that he even threw out pictures of himself.

89. Suddenly everyone noticed that he was growling, his lips curled back, his eyes gone cold, his scalp drawn back from his face. A moment before, everyone had thought he was speaking in what he said was an Ashanti dialect of Twi, still spoken, he had told them, in parts of Ghana. He had seemed to be directing his utterances to a black woman reporter for the Detroit *Free Press* who was in the state to cover the presidential primary election. In fact, he had been directing all his attention toward the young woman in the gray-tinted aviator glasses, as had she to him, and here he was now, growling like some kind of trapped beast. The others at the table all started talking at once, each of them trying separately to change the subject, whatever it was. Soon he had ceased growling and his face had returned to normal. By then someone in the group was telling the others how little he thought of this guy McCarthy's chances of beating LBJ in the primary. The black woman avoided looking at him, and when she spoke to anyone at the table, it was only to answer a quiet yes or no to a direct question. He in turn seemed to withdraw into himself, and after a half-hour, he got up silently and left the bar for another.

90. In his lifetime (thus far), he had made love, as it were, to nineteen different women. The first was when he was seventeen years old. The woman, five years older than he, a French-Canadian down from Quebec for the summer, work-

ing as a waitress in a resort hotel on Lake Winnepesaukee, was "experienced." He was drunk at the time. The most recent was a forty-seven-year-old divercée who works as a compositor in a Concord printing plant. He met her at the leather-upholstered bar of a cocktail lounge and took her back to her dingy apartment where they made love, as it were, on a Murphy bed. He was drunk at the time.

91. He saved all personal correspondence — all letters, post cards, telegrams, inscriptions, memos and notes — everything directed to him that was in the slightest way personal. Then he filed everything alphabetically by sender (he called it "author").

92. Though he was married five times, he never wore a wedding ring. His reason was that in his work he might catch the ring on something that would rip his finger off. He'd seen it happen, lots of times.

93. He worried about diseases of the rectum, though he had never suffered from any such disease or affliction. He used his size as rationalization: anyone his height and weight made things hard on the rectum.

94. Whenever in conversation the words "New York City" came up, he would snort, "Babylon!"

95. After any act of violence, however minor (or major), he was extremely calm, clear-eyed and physically relaxed. Indeed, much more so than anyone else in the area. It didn't give the effect of release as much as it seemed he had regained something precious that had been lost, something he had luckily plucked from the flux.

96. Every year he received four Christmas cards: one from each of his sisters, one from the union business agent for the

Concord local, and one from the chairman of the New Hampshire Republican party. The first two were always signed in ball-point with just the first name of the sender; the other two were always unsigned, with the name of the sender printed by machine. The first two he filed alphabetically by author; the other two he promptly threw away. He himself sent out no Christmas cards, although his wives had all participated in the rite, secretly, however.

97. When other men told stories from their experiences in the military, he never contributed any stories from his experiences in the Army Engineers Corps, although, if questioned directly, he would not deny that he had had such experiences. In that way he usually gave the impression that he had been involved with "security matters" that simply could not be discussed without clearance from above. He did nothing to correct that impression, naturally. The same was true when the men he worked with told stories from their childhood or adolescence; he merely would not deny that he, like other people, had gone through a childhood and adolescence. The impression given was that either his childhood and adolescence had been totally uneventful and bored him to think or talk about now, or else he had suffered so profoundly that it was extremely painful for him to think or talk about now. Again, he did nothing to correct either of these impressions.

98. One rarely spent an evening or afternoon with him without his at some point asking this riddle: "If you can hold six eggs in your right hand, how many can you hold in your left?" Most people, whether they knew the "right" answer or not, said, "Six," whereupon he placed six eggs one by one into the person's right hand. Then he placed six more eggs in a group on a tabletop and instructed the person to go ahead and hold them in his left hand — without, of course,

first emptying the right. His riddle answered (i.e., three or four, depending on how many eggs the person could pluck and hold with the fingertips of his left hand), there followed a demonstration of the denial of that very answer. He deposited the dozen eggs onto the tabletop, and then, as if plunging both his hands into a vat, he placed them simultaneously over all the eggs, covering them completely, and when he lifted his hands and turned them over, he was holding six eggs in his right hand and six in his left. On his face was a broad smile of triumph, as if he had proved, not to his audience but to himself, something that couldn't be believed.

99. He knew that if he had been a small man, people would have behaved differently toward him. But he also knew that if he had been a small man, he would have behaved differently toward them. "Different solutions create different problems," he concluded.

100. One night, shortly after his mother had moved out, he discovered a photograph album that she had accidentally left in an upstairs closet in a dark corner of the overhead shelf. Most of the pictures in the album were snapshots of him as a child taken in the summertime at the river, by the sea, in the sun-dappled meadow. He studied each picture for a long time, and when he had finished, he took the album downstairs and walked outside, coatless in the cold night air, and heaved the album over the fence, sending it in a long, fluttering arc into the darkness.

CHAPTER NINE

The Uroboros: Being a Further Declension of the Central Image

"Sometimes there is such a thing as
too much integrity."
—Errol Flynn, *My Wicked, Wicked Ways*

It had occurred to me, on my own, that in my apparent need to justify, to myself if not to anyone else who cared to listen, the peculiar nature of my relation to Hamilton Stark, I may very well have been guilty of misrepresenting Hamilton's peculiar relations to others, in particular to his mother. This would not be an unusual error or failing on the part of an author in my position. In fact it's almost normal for those who come after a great man to distort that man's relations to others, his parents, friends, other disciples, and so on, in order to cast one's own role in the great man's life in as interesting and favorable a light as possible. One wishes not only to spread the word, as it were, but to establish one's version of that word as the authoritative one as well.

Thus, one evening when my friend and neighbor C. told me flatly that I had so far slighted Hamilton (A.) by my failure to address the question of his treatment of his mother, I had to agree.

On this particular evening C. had come over carrying a paper bag containing his bath soap, shampoo and towel. Every late August and September he visits me once every three days to bathe and later to drink a little wine and chat.

His well, a dug well, goes dry every year at this time, whereas mine, a drilled well several hundred feet deep, continues to provide water, and naturally, it pleases us both to turn this neighborly service into a social occasion. While C. splashes about in the tub like a walrus, I often pull a kitchen chair up to the closed bathroom door and converse with him. I think at times like this, if someone could see us, he would believe that we were lonely men, and he could be right, except that we are not lonely at all. One way in which Hamilton has helped me in my well-known solitude, incidentally, is his insistence on maintaining the distinction between solitude and loneliness. And I believe that I, in my turn, have taught it to C. A solitary man is not necessarily a lonely man, unless he permit himself to fuzzy the distinction between his particular solitude and loneliness in general. That fuzziness inevitably results in self-pity, and self-pity necessarily drags along loneliness for its escort. It insists on its oppressive company, because self-pity, as if compulsively, always slaps at the presence of anyone who might offer pity and understanding instead. We are always alone, but we need not ever be lonely. What Hamilton demonstrated is that our recognition of the former, which is true whether we believe it or not, makes possible the reality of the latter, which is true if and only if we believe it so. Far be it for me to presume, but it made sense of some of his otherwise inexplicable enthusiasms, homeopathy, for instance, whose main maxim is, "Like cures like." If you are lonely, he would say to me, don't run out and fill your life with friends and acquaintances. Instead, direct all your attention to the inescapability of your solitude, your absolute oneness. The only way to cure a glutton of gluttony is to force-feed him. Starving him will only increase his appetite.

Most of us can understand and respect the logic of such a

position, but few of us are strong enough to enact it. Hamilton, of course, by his example, shows us simultaneously both the price of exacting it and also the rewards. What more can one ask of his teacher? I ask you. And what less?

These thoughts, however, were not part of my conversation with C. He was sloshing about in the tub and shouting through the closed door about Hamilton's (and A.'s) mother, Alma Stark (M.), and how, by my having neglected to present in any detail or believable complexity the nature of her relationship with her son, I had not merely been remiss as an author of a novel, but I had also invited the reader to deal superficially with my characters. "An otherwise excellent and amusing novel," he warned me through the door, "can be robbed of its *significance* if you make it easy for your readers to deal superficially with your characters."

I'm afraid that at first I found his theory specious, but I knew he was right about my having slighted poor, long-suffering Alma Stark. It kept her two-dimensional, robbed her of the true human complexity that I had granted, say, to Hamilton's wives (so far). And I also knew C. was right in that by my slighting Alma, describing her as merely victim, I had also slighted my hero, Hamilton. I had made him appear as merely victimizer, insofar as I had described his relationship with his mother at all.

No, C. had me all right. I was going to have to stop in my accelerating rush toward the climax of this novel and go back, not to the beginning, but at least to Chapter Five, "Back and Fill," and bring to bear a more scrupulously observant point of view than the one offered there, the town librarian's, as I recall.

Let me try my own point of view. I don't really know the woman very well, have not met the woman she's modeled after, A.'s mother M., more than twice, and casually at that, and of course I was not there the night Hamilton threw his mother out of what everyone thought was her own home. But I do know Hamilton (or rather, A., the man *he's* modeled after) quite well, as well as anyone, with the possible exception of his daughter, knows him. And I've had numerous opportunities to discuss that evening with him, to draw out of him as much of his own point of view as he's willing to share with anyone else. I think, therefore, I can give a fairly reliable account of what led up to and what followed from that evening, thus creating a somewhat different account of what actually transpired *during* that evening, the particulars of which, because they've been included in an earlier account, the librarian's, and referred to several times, by Police Chief Blount, for instance, the reader is already doubtless quite familiar with.

Hamilton's mother Alma had a habit of wringing her hands and, when they seemed to have been wrung out, of tweaking with her thumb and forefinger the loose skin under her chin. Wring and tweak, wring and tweak. I don't know when she developed this habit, but Hamilton told me that he never recalled her to his mind's eye without seeing her first wringing her hands and then pulling at her throat. He never recalled her with her hands in the air, palms out, in glee or happy surprise, or down at her sides, empty and disappointed. He could not remember her clapping her hands in excitement. Always they were wringing and tweaking, wringing and tweaking.

This image did not make him feel particularly happy. As a youth, he had responded to the gesture with shuddering, deep waves of guilt for nameless offenses, sins of omission as much as commission. In general, other people than Hamilton, strangers even, tended to respond to Alma Stark in much the same way. One had to ask oneself, even when meeting her for the first time, if one had not somehow, inadvertently, injured this woman, disappointed or deprived her, imposed on her, if one had not added, somehow, to her already unfairly heavy load of woe. For most people, the answer to the question of culpability was a simple denial. After which one tended to regard her through a skeptical lens tinted with pity. For, to most people, she proved immediately to be potentially manipulative, which was why most people felt justified in objectifying her somewhat by pitying her.

In a patriarchy, or any male-oriented society or household, husbands and sons are especially vulnerable to the trap that results from real or imagined injuries to women. It's one of the very few routes to power for their wives and mothers, which, naturally, invites them to specialize in it, and, through disuse, all the alternative routes gradually get broken up and overgrown, until soon they are impassable altogether. Thus, Hamilton and his father were especially vulnerable to Alma's particular specialization. They were both willing and conscious participants in a patriarchy, they were both raised, as conventional New England Protestants, to prove their moral and spiritual worth by the nature and extent of their works, that is, by their worldly success, and they were both reared, in the Victorian manner, to be ashamed of human bodies. Since neither the father nor the son, for various and different reasons, had experienced much of what is conventionally called worldly success, and since both father and son had human bodies, they were forced into employing extreme and often cruel-seeming means of resisting the trap Alma's generalized woe had created for precisely them.

To neutralize the effect of her wringing and tweaking, her sighs, her constantly wet eyes, her self-denying anticipation of needs he himself never even knew he had, Hamilton's father applied the old male strategy of grim condescension.

He disregarded her point of view, treated it as he would a simple child's. She thinks *she's* suffered, he would snort. Hah, she doesn't even know what suffering is. She doesn't know how lucky she is!

But this strategy couldn't work as well for his son, because for Hamilton she was someone whom he first knew and continued for several years to know from the point of view of utter dependence. Condescension comes hard to sons, no matter how easily it comes to them later as husbands or fathers. For him to neutralize his mother's wringing and tweaking, her long-suffering wet eyes, her whole series of practically irresistible invitations for him to draw on his guilt quotient, Hamilton had to devise a different and even crueler-seeming strategy. It was to affirm, as much as possible, his mother's point of view. Let his father deny it, condescend to it, reject it any way he could. Hamilton would honor it, would validate it, would meet all its most stringent demands on him. If she felt injured or disappointed or deprived somehow, if she felt that her unfair burden of woe had been unfairly added to, he would do what he could to justify her feelings — to provide an objective correlative, as it were — by injuring her, by disappointing and depriving her, by adding, even if only slightly, to her burden of woe.

His description of the process by which he validated and honored her point of view went something like this: "When a lady makes a request, a gentleman has no choice but to meet that request. Sure, he can ignore it, but he wouldn't be much of a gentleman, would he?" He was smiling, but the smile was characterized more by resignation than good cheer.

I had asked him pointblank why he had behaved toward his mother in a way that the rest of the community had regarded as a heinous way to behave toward one's mother. He had first obtained the power, legal and financial, to evict his mother from the home she had lived in all her adult life, the house she had raised three children in and where she had lived in wedlock with a man, his own father, for over forty years, the house that had become the source and final resting place for a lifetime's most personal memories and associations. He had obtained the power to evict her from this house, had obtained it under the guise of helping to care for her in her dependent old age, and, *horror*, he had *used* that power. He had gone ahead and evicted her. He had forced her to accept the extra room in her daughter Jody's small and crowded trailer and to have the costs of her room and board paid by her other daughter, Sarah. Hamilton had forced Alma into becoming her daughters' burdens of woe, he had forced her into deepening their sense of having been injured. He had given them, thereby, control over her. For he had forced her into the role, for the first time in her life, of victimizer, of depriver, of oppressor.

This was not, of course, what the community saw in it, but it is what eventually I came to see in it. Gradually, as I pondered Hamilton's cryptic, seemingly irrelevant answers to my questions, I came to believe that his eviction of his mother that night was an almost inevitable consequence of the years in which he had honored her need to be injured. Doubtless, in time she had gradually come to realize that he did not feel guilt for his role as injurer, at which point she played her last card, so to speak. She would force him to reject her altogether. She would up the ante. Which, from Hamilton's point of view, gave him no alternative but to raise her bet and force the next round of the game into play. Did she want him to be *that* ungrateful a son? All right, if that's what she wanted, it's what she got. After all, she was his mother and he could do no less for her than try to provide for her what she really wanted.

"I learned something about women from that experience," he told me one evening at the Bonnie Aire, where we had gone for a few drinks. It was a hot, overcast, Friday night, the July following his eviction of his mother.

What had he learned about women? I asked him (having at the time intimations of some future troubles with women, whom I then understood almost not at all).

He learned, he told me, a woman's greatest power over a man is her ability to turn her suffering into a virtue. She converts the one into the other, completely. She makes a condition of being female — and a wife and mother — into an ethical feat, which feat we as men have no choice but to reinforce. Most men don't understand this conversion, he explained, and that's why most men, rather than reinforce the conversion, deny that it's even taken place. They treat their women as if they were still suffering. But what we're *supposed* to do, what they *want* us to do, is to reinforce the conversion by acknowledging it and making it possible for the process to continue. So, naturally, what they want is for us to increase their suffering, to build their supply of it back up at least to where it was before they managed the difficult task of converting it into something that gave them power, the power of possessing virtue.

He paused and chugged down his glass of ale as chaser to the shot of Canadian Club he had tossed down right before speaking. I remained silent. Hamilton seldom spoke at this length (not to me, not about a subject that he knew was important to my understanding of him), and I didn't want to distract him with my presence.

"And I'll tell you something, something that I've not told anyone else," he said, looking down at the empty glass, turning it in his huge hands. "It ain't easy, giving them what you know they want. Especially when it's your mother. Because the spring the whole thing, the conversion thing, works off is guilt. Male guilt." He explained that it's only to a man that a woman's suffering looks like an ethical feat. Other women look at it with envy, or, if they're a little protective of their own brand of pain, they see it as pathetic, or maybe they look at it with fear, because they know a woman who suffers more than they do cannot honor their own conversions. But a man sees it differently. Only a man can admire the pain, can acknowledge the bearer of it as virtuous. And the reason a man sees it this way is because he bears with him a quantity of guilt, nameless because he's born with it, having been born male in this world where one-half of the species dominates the other half. Hamilton wasn't saying it was right or wrong, that domination. He was just saying that it exists. The dominant one in any pairing off feels guilty for that fact, whether he knows it or not. And because most men don't know they feel guilty, guilty in general, rather than in the particular case, most men don't see what's being asked of them by the particular cases before them.

He was sweating across his forehead and upper lip. Two large fans, one in each of the back corners of the tavern, were not cooling the place much, The temperature outside was the same as the temperature inside, and all the fans accomplished was to create movement in the heated air, which was sufficiently close to body temperature as to be incapable of cooling anybody. The bartender leaned morosely on his elbows and stared at the front door. There were no customers aside from Hamilton and me. The waitress, a tubby woman with frizzy orange-dyed hair, sat on one of the barstools, her tray plopped on her lap. Hamilton and I were in a booth close to the door.

A man's guilt, he told me then, wants him to eliminate the suffering of the particular case in front of him, so gradually he tries, and sometimes he thinks he succeeded, only to see it reappear a moment later, in her face, her hands, her voice. Some men, after a while, realize that the particular case has nothing to do with their generalized guilt, and what they do is to dismiss the particular case, to deny its hold on them. As Hamilton's father had done. He had ended up ignoring Alma's virtue and had treated her suffering "as a plain pain in the ass," to use Hamilton's words. It's easier on the man that way, he explained. But harder on the particular case, the woman. The only honorable thing a man can do is, first, realize that this particular case's pain has nothing to do with his guilt. That lets him deal realistically with the particular case, but it also means that he can't kid himself about there being any easy removal of his generalized guilt. "No," he declared, "you've got to learn to live with it. You're not going to change society, so you just have to learn to live with it. Right?"

"Right. Right."

"But that doesn't mean it's easy, any of it. You've still got to face down that guilt every time some woman comes up to you wringing her hands in despair," he went on. It's hardest, he explained, when the woman is your mother, because if she practiced "smotherhood" on you while you were young and helpless and completely dependent on her for information about the world, then she's going to have a strong hold on your guilt. She won't be able to help it. "Smotherhood," he said, glossing the term for me, is a self-defeating, usually unconscious way of deluding a son into thinking that all his guilt is directly related, as effect, to his mother's pain and apparent powerlessness. And this delusion gets set into the son's mind long before he can think for himself. So that later on, when he tries to respond rationally to the demands some woman's pain is putting on him, if that woman happens to be his mother, he's still got to deal with the old, deep-seated delusion that his only honorable response is the guilt-ridden one. In the particular case of Hamilton's own mother, he felt that he had been put to the ultimate test. She had made it clear to him that the only way he could honor her conversion of generalized suffering into particularized forbearance was to kick her out of her own house. Which, after a lot of tugs in the opposite direction, he did. "It wasn't easy," he sighed. Then he waved to the waitress for another round.

"I bet it wasn't," I said admiringly. Perspiration was running off our faces. I unbuttoned my cuffs and rolled up my sleeves to the elbows, then loosened my collar and took off my necktie. I had long since removed my sport coat. Hamilton was wearing a clean white T-shirt and work pants — not that it matters, except peripherally with regard to what happened next.

The waitress, whose name was Linda, a cheerful type who seemed resigned to spending the rest of her life doing just what she was doing then, brought us another round, our third or fourth, I can't recall, and slowly, her tray slapping her thigh, walked back to the bar and hitched herself up onto a stool and resumed staring at the front door. The bartender, whose name was Lee, a town "character" who played Rudoph the Red-nosed Reindeer every year in the Kiwanis Club's Christmas Pageant, went on peering morosely into the hot empty space a few feet in front of him. He was obviously lost in thought, puzzling his way around a bit of supper caught behind a tooth, his mind a single, low-frequency hum of passive attention that, having fallen upon his tooth, seemed glued there. In the corners of the room, the two standing fans whirred uselessly away at the heated air as the screen door swung open and a woman walked in from the street, alone. The door banged behind her, and she looked around the room, smiled at Hamilton and me slightly, and walked directly to the bar, where she ordered a gin and tonic.

She was around forty, a good-looking woman, more handsome than pretty, wearing a sleeveless blouse that exposed her muscular arms and drew attention to the amplitude of her bosom. Her corn-blond hair, long and healthy-looking, was wound into a Teutonic bun behind her head. Her white Bermuda shorts were tight and made of such heavy cloth that they seemed to armor her lower body rather than merely to cover it. Though she had been in town, living in an apartment over Paige Realty, for no more than two weeks, certain things about her were already known by just about everyone else in town: she was the new school nurse, she was from Concord, the capital, where she had previously worked in an old-age home, she was unmarried, probably had never been married, she had a loud, commanding voice and a hearty laugh and she liked, on these hot evenings in July, to come out of her sweltering apartment around nine for a couple of gin and tonics and a little conversation with "the boys." Her name was Jenny, and within two weeks she was Hamilton Stark's third wife.

"Well," I said to C., "that ought to make things more 'significant.' " We were in my library on the ground floor. C. had finished his bath and dressed, and we had adjourned to the library where we could drink a little wine, an excellent California burgundy that C. had not yet tried, and warm ourselves by the fireplace. It was a chilly evening, not yet cold enough, of course, to turn the furnace on, but quite cold enough to welcome a room's being heated by an open fire. C. was seated in his favorite armchair, resting from the exhilaration of his bath, as was his wont, and I had taken my accustomed place by the fireplace, standing with one elbow resting on the mantel.

C. was wheezing slightly. "Ah, yes. Yes, that's fine, fine." He uncrossed and recrossed his feet at the ankles on the ottoman. "Tell me, if you don't mind giving things away, tell me," he wheezed, "do you *personally* agree with Hamilton's rationalization for his . . . behavior toward his mother in particular . . . and women in general? After all, it implies an attitude toward women that's not exactly fashionable, you know." He almost chuckled. "You may get yourself into deep trouble with your female readers, heh-heh."

Letting himself sink back into the chair, he went on. "Two questions. Did you indeed have 'trouble with women' later on? And did the understanding of women that you gained, apparently through Hamilton Stark, help you out of your trouble? Obviously the two questions become one, and obviously, again, that single question is an attempt to determine if your novel can be used as a pragmatic guide. For we all, if we are men, have 'trouble with women' from time to time and wish, especially at such times, that we understood them better." C. smiled benevolently and nipped off the end of his cigar with his front teeth. I don't think the burgundy suited him.

"Yes, yes, of course. But that was just a personal aside there, that business about my intimations. It really refers to nothing that should concern my readers.* Probably, be-

* It might be worth noting, however, that the intimated troubles did occur later, very recently, in fact, and naturally enough concerned the only woman in the author's life (at the time of this writing). That woman was Rochelle Stark, and the author's "troubles" with her arose from her gift, and his literary use, of the voluminous materials and several texts of her novel, *The Plumber's Apprentice*, which, the reader will recall, were formally presented to the author in his Chapter Seven, "Ausable Chasm." For, when it became apparent to Rochelle that the

cause it does intrude on the narrator's locus of attention, and therefore the reader's locus of attention as well, I'll revise it out of the final version of my manuscript. I will say this much, however: If you want to use this novel as a guidebook, then you'll have to accept Hamilton Stark as your guide. That's the only rule for reading it, the only condition I'll attach — except of course that you know the language well enough to recognize a persona when you hear one."

"Ho, ho!" C. laughed.

I refilled his glass. That should quiet him, I thought. I had expected him to respond, not to my slip of a reference to my own, later, personal difficulties (which are well outside the scope of this book), but rather to the peculiar juxtaposition of Hamilton's confession regarding his mother in particular and women in general, and the sudden appearance in the narrative of his third wife, Jenny, the nurse. After all, if it's specifically the custodial compulsion of some women that you find most disturbing, one would expect you to be especially wary of women who are custodial by profession — nurses, housekeepers, babysitters, prison guards, and so on, professions that have

author intended to incorporate extended pieces of her more or less completed narrative directly into the body of his own narrative, her reaction was surprising to the author. He had taken her at her word, that her research materials and other texts were his to use, however he wished to use them, in the writing of his own novel. Thus he had hoped that she would be pleased by what he regarded as his imaginative use of those texts, especially since he had credited her for them and had so elaborately praised their qualities (even when, naturally, with this fastidious an author, there were sections that displeased him somewhat). And if his hopes of her gratitude and delight could not be met, then he fully expected her, at the least, to provide him with an objective appraisal of his use of those materials, as one craftsman to another. In other words, the author hoped she would be flattered by his deployment of her help, and if he couldn't get that much from her, then he expected *more* help, this time in the form of critical analysis. Instead, as the reader may have guessed, Rochelle's reactions were more complex. She would not criticize. No, indeed, quite the oppono product as issue. It certainly surprised me — Hamilton's speedy courtship and marriage to Jenny, I mean, and, that night at the Bonnie Aire, his quick switch from the painful (to him) description of his relationship with his mother to his moves on Jenny. For, no sooner had she sat down at the bar and ordered a gin and tonic than Hamilton arose from our booth and joined her at the bar. He opened his conversation with a discussion of the weather, the evening's dominant fact, and moved quickly to questions about her — where she was from, her job, her impressions of the town and its people, what she did with her evenings — to a suggestion that they dance (Hamilton is well known as a dancer, an excellent dancer), whereupon he played "On the Road to Mandalay" by Frank Sinatra on the juke box in the corner, and the two of them danced, slowly at first, in the oppressive heat, then in large, graceful circles around the small room, between tables, from the door in front to the bar at the back. They played "Moonlight in Vermont" by Andy Williams, and danced again, serious-faced, athletic, the two of them, a pleasure to watch, certainly, but somehow embarrassing, for, in

site; she lavished him with praise for his imagination and wit. And she would not let him believe that she was sincerely flattered. "Oh, my goodness! I'm so happy that you were able to take so *much!*" she exclaimed. "And that you had to change so *little!*" This was the beginning of the author's "troubles" with Rochelle. A sensitive person, he was able immediately to break her code and perceive that her exclamations were actually whimpers of pain, a woman's pain, the kind of pain no self-conscious man can perceive without recognizing its cause — man himself, or rather, that aspect of himself which is characterized by gender (as opposed to sex or any other personal manifestation of manhood). At first the author permitted himself the standard, expected reaction of personal guilt. After all, her suffering certainly seemed personalized enough, a particular kind and dose of pain caused by a particular person's offense. He therefore apologized. She told him not to apologize. He sounded ridiculous. She was honored. Why should he apologize for having honored her? He apologized again. She rejected his apology again. He tried to minimize his actual use of her

this heat in the all-but-deserted tavern, with their somber yet intent expressions, it was a rather intimate dance they were doing. Then they played the theme from the movie *Picnic*, and I think we all, the bartender, the idle waitress, and I, became extremely self-conscious and turned away from the dancers, the bartender to a chore in the kitchen in back, the waitress to painting her fingernails pink, and I to a copy of Peterson's *Field Guide to North American Birds* that I happened to have in the pocket of my sports jacket, which I had removed some time earlier.

It was several minutes later, when, as I was committing to memory the call of the brown creeper (*Certhia familiaris*), whispering to myself "see-ti-wee-tu-wee," that Hamilton interrupted and informed me that he and Jenny were going for a walk to the top of Blue Job, where it would be cooler, and if I wanted a lift back to his house, where I had parked my own car, he would provide it. I smiled hello politely to Jenny, who was sweating profusely, and said no, that I'd stay here awhile and would catch a ride out for my car later in the evening.

---

materials. She agreed, ashamed of their irrelevance. He came back and defended his need for them, their utter relevance. She didn't believe him. He insisted. She believed him, and again, honored, she rejected his apology, this time in advance of its being offered. He grew suspicious of her expectation that he apologize. She must think he had something to apologize *for*. He denied having done anything wrong. She agreed, nothing wrong. He said lots of novelists had done it. She was happy to know there was a tradition for this sort of thing. He demanded to know what she meant by that. She said nothing. He said he knew irony when he heard it, and sarcasm too. She doubted that. He laughed sarcastically. She apologized — for misleading him, for having been unclear. She had been perfectly clear, he said ironically. She wrung her hands. He stalked about. She apologized. He told her not to be ridiculous, he felt honored by her gift. Why should she apologize for having honored him? She apologized again. He rejected her apology again. She began to deprecate the materials, pointing out his good judgment in deciding to use so little of them. He agreed, de-

Hamilton seemed relieved, or at least he did not scowl as he usually did when I abridged or altered one of his suggestions with a plan of my own, and the two of them left together, as silently and intently as they had been dancing.

The next time I saw Hamilton, not three weeks later, he had married her. "Well, I married her," he said.

"Who?"

"Jenny, the school nurse," he said, as if I should have expected it. I did not, of course. Quite the opposite.

C., however, was not surprised.

"Well, let me tell you, it surprised *me!*" I fairly shouted, startling him back into his chair.

"Goodness!"

Certainly it surprised me. Hamilton had but barely shed his second wife, Annie, and he had only just met this new one. Also, because of her profession, as I have mentioned, and because of her rather ordinary life so far, which, I assumed, gave her a rather ordinary mind, and because of her appear-

pressed by what he feared was their irrelevance. She came back and defended their relevance to his novel, especially the way he had integrated them. He didn't believe her. She insisted. He believed her, and again, feeling honored by her gift, he rejected her apologies for the meagerness of the gift. What, she asked him, made him think she wanted to apologize for her gift? He must think her ashamed of her work, especially in relation to his work. She told him hers was just as beautifully done as his. There was nothing wrong with it. He agreed, nothing wrong. At least, she informed him, she was working in a tradition. He was happy for her, as for so many other writers, that there was a well-established tradition for them to work in. She demanded to know what he meant by that. He said nothing. She said she knew irony when she heard it, and sarcasm too. He doubted that, judging from her work. She laughed sarcastically. He apologized. He said he was guilty of having been unclear. After all, he depended on a tradition as much as she did. Oh, no, he had been *perfectly* clear, she told him, wringing her hands. He stalked about. She wept. He apologized.

ance, this new one did not, to me, seem to be Hamilton's "type." She was a handsome woman, in an athletic way, but her overall appearance was Prussian, almost manly. Both of Hamilton's previous wives had been physically delicate by comparison, even Annie, who did not start to gain weight until after she had married him. This woman seemed invulnerable, which surely only reinforced what I assumed (from her profession) was a custodial temperament. How could Hamilton have thought he would be happy with such a woman, especially so soon after the dissolution of his second marriage and that final encounter with his mother and the insights into what he called "smotherhood" gained there?

It wasn't difficult to understand or to predict, my large friend assured me. According to him, though my even larger friend, Hamilton, might well be conscious of a particular image dominating his relationship with his mother, he might even be conscious that the same image had dominated his relationships with his other wives, and possibly his relationships with all women (an awareness, C. pointed out, that so far I had not granted Hamilton); in spite of this awareness,

---

And so it went, around and around again, like a uroboros. They had been transformed, and two separate people, hitherto linked solely by their love for one another and their shared obsession with a third person, had suddenly found themselves capable of connecting only viciously, autocannibalistically, wearing a single body, yes, but a body with its tail in its mouth. And since neither the author nor Rochelle could distinguish the head of the beast from its tail, they could not break this self-devouring connection, and rapidly their love for one another turned to fear for their own survival, then desperation, then hatred of the other. Their old shared obsession broke apart also, and they began to attack each other's viewpoint and interpretation. Where one found meaning, the other saw projection and egoism. Where one found sublimity, the other saw wishful thinking. Each began to think the other soft-headed, sentimental and self-indulgent on the subject of Hamilton Stark. Yet they could not separate. The uroboros is a mesmerizing image. It is, in spite of the entrapment it signifies, a securing, containing, utterly stable image, and if the author had not

this self-consciousness, the man might still be compelled to go on living in its dominion.

At first I didn't understand, but then C. explained that it depended on the image, its qualities. A uroboros, for example, is an image of closure, a frightening image of compulsive, ritualistic repetition. To have one's life organized under the dictates of a uroboros would be painful, indeed, and if one were unfortunate enough to be conscious of that image, one might find it even more painful, for all one could do would be to raise the repetition to a higher level, hoping to avoid it there, only to find oneself once again repeating oneself. What one would have in that case would be a spiraling uroboros, as it were. In Hamilton's case, by becoming conscious of his compulsive attraction to women who wanted to "smother" him and his resultant revulsion at the indebtedness incurred, that is, his "guilt," his only recourse seems to have been to introduce "wrath," so as to speed up the process, to spin the wheel a little faster, hoping thereby (one must assume) that the pain for the woman and confusion for himself would be lessened.

---

recalled his earlier conversations with Hamilton and had not decided to enact certain of the aphorisms learned there (and set down earlier in this chapter), it's possible that their lives, the author's and Rochelle's, would be locked together even today by the image of the self-swallowing serpent. For the author, as the reader doubtless knows by now, bore a typically heavy burden of typical male guilt, despite his years of study with the master of neutralizing precisely that guilt. And Rochelle, in turn, bore a typically heavy burden of typical female pain, despite her relative freedom from any oppressive relationships with particular men (heaven knows, her father had never participated in any such relationship, and her love affair with the author had been essentially the connection between two acolytes, with nothing in their role as acolytes to permit an inequality between them). Thus, by the time the author finally remembered Hamilton's advice and example and their applicability to his own situation, he had grown feeble and confused, and it took an enormous effort of will for him to face down the forces that conspired to keep him from applying that advice and

Rochelle's demon Asmodeus was not a wholly imprecise way of perceiving her father's behavior, C. reminded me. It explained a great deal — his fervent seductions, his cold withdrawals, and, finally, his wrathful rejections. If you concede sincerity to such a man, then his behavior does indeed seem possessed. The difficulty with the image of Asmodeus, however, is that it holds out the possibility of exorcism. Magic. The right combination of aspects of the moon, chants, artifacts and fetishes, and *voilà!* he's free. A daughter's love, a *spurned* daughter's love, explains her attraction to it.

But I, as C. quite rightly pointed out, I was no man's daughter, spurned or otherwise. Which was doubtless why I had chosen to describe the same man with the image of the holy man, the man outside all social prescriptions for meaningful behavior, the man who uses his life as allegory, who, to demonstrate human ordinariness, heaps ashes on himself, who, to demonstrate the vanity of human wishes, forgoes all normal access to praise and achievement, the man who, to demonstrate the possibility of self-transcendence, denies the claims the rest of us honor.

---

example, the forces of his own conventions, the threat of public disapprobation, his fear of loneliness, and naturally, his love of Rochelle. There was a further consequence that threatened him: he doubtless would end up unable to use the materials of her novel in his own novel, either because she would forbid it or because he would be too ashamed, purely and simply, of a cruelty that, at such a point, would be merely gratuitous. And possibly illegal. But even so, he was at last capable of meeting this coercive array of forces head-on. One afternoon following a particularly vicious turn of the wheel they were locked into, he went to his desk and drew out of a drawer all the notes, tapes, genealogical charts, maps, photos, and all the carefully typed manuscript pages of *The Plumber's Apprentice*, wrapped the materials fastidiously in brown paper, and drove to the post office, where he mailed the package to Rochelle, who at that time was still living in a boarding house in Concord. To the top sheet of her manuscript, he had clipped a typewritten note, which read: *I have read your manuscript and related materials with care, and, as you know, with a predisposition to enjoy them*

We are the only creature that does not know what it is to be itself, C. went on. We are the only creature that must perceive itself through the use of images. The limits and the possibilities implied by those images, then, are the limits and possibilities for our perceptions of ourselves. And because we can hardly be expected to exceed the morphology of our perceptions, then it's clear that our images of ourselves determine the morphology of our very lives. Rochelle saw her father through the image of a particular kind of demon-possession, one that combined and thus explained his peculiar juxtaposition of drunkenness, lust and rage. I had tried to convert her to my point of view, which depended on her coming to see him as a holy man. C., in his turn, was recommending that I see Hamilton as a spiraling uroboros. We were all three trying to perceive him, to imagine him into a reality in our own lives, by means of a coherent image. Yet he persisted in resisting our imaginations. The demon had fallen away in the face of Hamilton's obvious intentionality. No man possessed could be that willful. And the holy man was rapidly being secularized by what appeared to be compulsive

---

because of the person your character Alvin Stock is based on. I have found, however, that, whether taken as a work of imaginative fiction or as a roman à clef, *the manuscript fails to interest or amuse, and I am therefore returning it to you with my thanks. You are obviously quite intelligent and at times show evidence of talent, and I would not wish to discourage someone who is at the very beginning of her career as a writer, but it occurs to me that you might consider trying some other aspect of writing than fiction. Have you ever thought seriously of writing articles for women's magazines? This can be extremely lucrative, and you would be free to travel. In any case, I am flattered that you cared to solicit my opinion of your work, and if you wish to have me read any of your future writings, I would be delighted to do so. Good luck to you in your career.* She never knew, of course, that as he typed this letter the author wept. Nor would he have told her or even hinted at his pain if they ever happened by chance to meet again. It was the end of Rochelle's lovely presence in his life, he knew that. He also knew how she would remember and imagine him from

behavior rather than self-conscious, exemplary behavior designed to be taken as allegorical. And now this somewhat pathetic and depressing image of the self-devouring serpent had come to control my perceptions of the man. The time had come to try to discover how Hamilton perceived himself, if at all. And if this could not be determined, to ask oneself if, indeed, one had invented him altogether.

Thank heaven for C.! If it hadn't been for his presence in my life, his very presence that evening in my library, I would at that moment have felt wholly alone.

---

that day on — as a senselessly cruel man, possibly psychotic, a man unable to give love because he was unable to accept love, a *dangerous* man. And he knew that, in so describing him, she would bring him closer to the way most people described her own father, and that possibly her experience with him, the author, would lead her finally to view her father as others did. Her inescapable image of him, the author, as villain would, by its similarity to the other, lead her to accept an image of her father that she had resisted so bravely these many years. He knew that this conversion, or lapse, would deprive no one of any particular truth — not Rochelle, not Hamilton, and not the author. And finally, he knew now that he himself was going to have to research and write all those sections of his hero's life that he had originally counted on being researched and written by Rochelle. That meant work. Hard work. He did not enjoy reading realistic fiction; still less did he enjoy writing it. But he had no choice. Rochelle was gone, used up and thrown out with the rubbish of his imaginative life. And her novel was gone with her. He was alone in his book now, a solitary. (Except, of course, for the company of his friend C. and Hamilton Stark himself.)

CHAPTER TEN

Graveside

THIS IS A PAINFUL CHAPTER for me to write. Before I'm through with it, I will have lost my best friend, will have sent him from my house into the snowy cold, leaving me behind, remorseful and, to counter remorse, desperate for justification. A dangerous state for a rationalist: it's when he is most tempted to depart from reality and fly off into the soothing heavens of reason.

It began with the death of Alma Stark — not the actual fact of her dying, but later, in my describing it. It's possible that it began earlier, of course, in Chapter Nine, where I told of Hamilton's meeting and consequent marriage to Jenny, but I was not aware then of any irreconcilable differences between my and C.'s points of view. At that time, despite the differences between us, I was still able to use C.'s point of view to inform my own, as I had been doing all along. So that at the end of Chapter Nine, while I may have seemed disconsolate at having to lose Rochelle, I could still console myself with the continued presence of C. But all that was before I had told of the death of Alma Stark.

The death itself was not especially poignant or wrenching. It was expected. She had been ill for most of the previous winter and had fended off an attack of flu and then pneumonia, but clearly she was weakening and, in fact, had not been expected to survive the winter at all. She was eighty, still mentally alert, but no longer able to resist ordinary onslaughts against her body. The following November, she came down with a strep throat, and despite massive doses of antibiotics, she developed double pneumonia and had to be hospitalized in Concord, where, after struggling on for two more weeks, she died, quite peacefully in her sleep, of heart disease.

Though her last years obviously had been scarred by the wound Hamilton had inflicted on her when he had evicted her — a wound she could close only by refusing after that night ever to see her son again, refusing and regularly renewing that refusal, for the cut was deep and could be staunched only with difficulty — those last years, nevertheless, had been relatively comforting to her. She was able to convert her dependence on her daughters, Jody and Sarah, into something which caused *her* to suffer, and thus the integrity of her personality was sustained. Her daily round of activities included helping Jody with housework, cooking and cleaning up after the children (twin boys entering adolescence, people who, to her tongue-clucking satisfaction, seemed to regard her presence as they would a maid's — or at least that's how, sighing, wringing her hands and tweaking her throat, she would put it to her friends at the Ladies' Aid Society, always adding, of course, "It must be hard for them, having an old lady suddenly come to live in a crowded little house with them"). After the first year, Chub had added a small bedroom to the trailer, off the back at the middle, like an awkwardly placed appendage, and she spent most of her evenings there, and while her daughter, son-in-law and their two children watched TV in the living room, she crocheted, wrote letters to the Barnstead boys in Vietnam, and read the Bible. It was a nice room, pine-paneled, with a single window that faced Chub's gravel pit (a supplementary source of income for the family). She had her own bed, a dresser, a small desk under the window, and even a closet of her own, which she had filled with the rest of her possessions — her clothes, photograph albums, Christmas tree decorations, and the quilted spread that she had made the spring she married Hamilton's father and that she had used on their bed for over forty years. But now she slept alone on a narrow, cotlike bed. It would look foolish, she remarked, if she used the quilt to cover this little bed. But she couldn't bring herself to give it over to Chub and Jody, to lay it across their wide Hollywood bed in the master bedroom. She thought maybe she'd just leave it to them in her will. She'd leave the photograph albums to Sarah, who seemed more interested in them anyhow, perhaps because she was childless. At least that's what she told the ladies at the Ladies Aid Society while they knitted, sewed, crocheted, and wove handy, warm articles for the Barnstead boys in Vietnam. As it turned out, however, she wrote no will; Sarah ended up with the quilt and Jody took the photographs and Christmas tree ornaments.

During these years, between Alma's loss of her home and her death, no one in the family spoke to Hamilton or saw him socially. If one or several of them accidentally came up against the fact of his presence, at a bean supper or the Fourth of July Band Concert or in McAllister's General Store, for instance, they ignored that fact and would not acknowledge its existence even to one another. Once Chub had backed his cruiser — his own station wagon, actually, outfitted at the town's expense with a siren, blue glass bubble on top and two-way radio — into one of Hamilton's cars, a year-old Cadillac, the one he'd driven to Rochelle's graduation in Ausable Chasm, New York. Hamilton had parked it outside Danis's Superette and was inside at the time, picking up the week's groceries and ale. Chub had driven up without noticing Hamilton's car and had parked next to it, both cars facing the store, and then, recognizing the dark brown Cadillac, he had realized that the owner doubtless was inside the grocery store and that they would unavoidably pass in the aisle, so he had immediately dropped his cruiser into reverse and had backed out quickly, clipping with his right front fender Hamilton's finny taillight. While the glass was still tinkling to the ground, Hamilton had emerged from the store and had stared, expressionless, as Chub spun the wheel of the cruiser, tromped on the accelerator, and roared away.

No one ever spoke to Hamilton of the event that for all intents and purposes had severed him from his family, and naturally, he never brought up the subject himself — not necessarily because he was ashamed, however. It just was not his way to discuss his personal life, not even with people who happened to participate in his personal life, his wives, for instance. In fact, none of his wives learned of the split in the family from Hamilton himself, and there were three of them (wives) who came to live with him in the very house that had been as much the symbol of that split as cause. They found out from their friends and other associates in town, usually when someone, eager to obtain and circulate Hamilton's point of view, would ask Jenny, the school nurse, or, later, Maureen or, still later, Dora why on earth her new husband had kicked his mother out of her own house. Jenny, or Maureen or Dora, would demand to know what on earth the person was talking about, whereupon she would hear the generally accepted version of the story, so that the interviewee became interviewer, first of the friend or associate who happened to have made the query in the first place, then of Hamilton himself.

"Why on earth did you kick your mother out of her own house?" she would ask him finally.

His answer always went something like this: "A, it wasn't her house. B, it was my house. And C, I didn't kick her out against her will." And that's all he would offer as explanation or description of what had happened that night. If his wife of the moment persisted with questions, he would simply announce that his mother was the only person to whom he would explain or describe what had happened, but only if she first indicated to him that she neither understood nor remembered what had happened. "And so far," he would say, "she's given no such indication of stupidity or lapse of memory." At which point it was clear that the interview had ended. Hamilton would go back to reading the paper or weeding the garden or repairing the toaster, and his wife would promise herself that she would inquire further into the matter, to be sure, but she would ask other people than her husband.

His first wife, of course, never heard as much as a rumor about the event, but his second wife, Annie, "the actress," who had been visiting her aunt in the Bronx at the time, had been forced to rely on the town's version of the story as much as any of the wives who came later. When she came back from the Bronx and her mother-in-law was no longer living with them in what Annie had regarded as her mother-in-law's home, Hamilton had refused to tell her any more than he later told Jenny or Maureen or Dora: "A, it's not her house. B, it's my house. And C, I didn't kick her out against her will." This, to Annie's bewildered, "Where's your *mother?* Where are her *clothes?* Her *things?*" Though she never actually judged him for what had happened (she always said, "Whatever it was that actually *did* happen that night"), it nevertheless was one of the things that she cited later when she chose to list her reasons for eventually becoming so frightened of him that she left and divorced him.

His third wife, Jenny, however, left and divorced him for no other reason than his supposed treatment, his mistreatment, of his mother and his refusal to confirm or deny the local description of that mistreatment (there was no local *explanation* for it, of course). It was assumed by the townspeople that because Jenny was middle-aged, childless and, it was discovered, an orphan, she had married Hamilton with the hope of obtaining thereby a ready-made family. When it appeared that he was as orphaned and childless as she, and thus could not deliver what she desired of him, she had swiftly returned to her previous way of life as the school nurse and, later on, as athletic director of the girls' sports program. Some people thought that Jenny may have been a lesbian and that her marriage to Hamilton had been a last, vain attempt to kindle and warm herself with a "normal" sexual relationship, but to believe that, they would have been compelled to attribute "normal" sexual proclivities and needs to Hamilton, which by then no one was willing to grant him. Not that anyone suspected he was homosexual. Rather, no one could imagine his being tender. People could easily understand why women were initially attracted to him — "After all," they said, spreading their hands and lifting their eyebrows, "he *is* good-looking, in a largish way, and he makes a decent living, and he has a nice house, now. And he *is* a beautiful dancer. He's a smooth talker, too, when he wants to be. So if you'd just met him, and if he wasn't drinking too much, not drunk, I mean, well, who knows, there's lots of women who might think he'd be a good catch. At least at first." And indeed, five women in Hamilton's lifetime so far had thought so and, as a result, had pitched themselves into his lap. And he had married them for it. As he put it when, after each divorce, he was asked why he had married the woman in the first place, especially as with each consecutive wife the courtship and marriage became more and more abbreviated: "Hey, what's a man to do? When a woman tells you she loves you, you can't tell her not to. And if you don't particularly dislike the woman, there's no point in telling her you dislike her. No woman wants to hear a lie like that, even when it's true. And frankly, I never met a woman I disliked." In recent years, however, he would add, "Course, I never met one I liked, either. Maybe if I had, I wouldn't have gotten married so many times, heh, heh, heh."

His fourth wife, Maureen Blade, only eighteen when she married him, probably was too young to be able to evaluate her new and much older husband's past behavior, or even his present behavior, for that matter. That's both the advantage and disadvantage, for the elder, of choosing a mate who is still not much more than a child: she has not yet been exposed to enough adult behavior to recognize when it is abnormal. The whole idea of "normality" depends on the availability of a fairly large sampling, which would necessarily be unavailable to an eighteen-year-old girl, no matter how precocious. And Maureen was not thought to be especially precocious. By the time she had been Mrs. Hamilton Stark for six months, however, she had aged considerably, if not matured as well, and the whole question of precocity was no longer relevant. After her divorce from Hamilton, she resumed the use of her maiden name, Blade, but to no avail. No one could think of her as a maiden anymore. She was a young divorcée, a woman with a complicated past.

But Maureen was the only one of Hamilton's five wives who already knew the story of his break with his mother when she married him. A psychiatrist might suggest that, in marrying him, she was working out, through identification with his well-known acts against *his* parent, her own desires to behave similarly toward *her* parent, a drunken lout, Arthur Blade, a chronically unemployed lout who had mistreated his eldest daughter for years, beating her and, it was rumored, even making sexual advances against her. One might, if one were that same psychiatrist, also suggest that in marrying Hamilton she was seeking a replacement for her father, for, not more than a month before the marriage, Arthur Blade had been committed to the New Hampshire State Hospital in Concord, where his extreme alcoholism could be treated, at least temporarily.

In any case, Hamilton refused to act the father for her, no more the kind father than the cruel; he treated her the way he treated any other adolescent, tolerating her enthralled presence, exchanging goods for services and vice versa, and whenever she asked for something more, some direct expression of his personal affection, say, he responded by demanding more of her first, such as more room in which to move without having to explain or justify his moves. "If you think you can make a man report back to you who he is, where he goes and where he cannot go, and that by doing so he will be acting out of love for you, you're dead wrong. A man will do these things for you only if he is afraid of losing you. And fear of losing a woman and loving her are not the same thing. Actually, they may be opposites," he told her, and immediately Maureen fell into confusion and despair, a state he encouraged and she endured for six months, until she at last realized that she would be rid of her confusion and despair only when she had got rid of her husband. She knew that she would then, as a direct result, have many other unpleasant thoughts and feelings to live with — such as what it meant to be an eighteen-year-old ex-wife in a small New Hampshire town — but she no longer cared. Besides, she could always say that he had treated her no better than he had treated his own mother. Then everyone would understand her leaving him, especially those people who had not been able to understand why she had married him in the first place.

So she told him that she wanted a divorce. He said, "Fine with me, if that's what you want." He would not contest it, as he had not contested any of his divorces ("I never contested the marriage, did I? Why should I contest the divorce?"), as long as there were no demands for alimony and no demanding property settlement. She could take whatever she wanted of what she had brought with her. Anything else she wanted he would sell to her at one-half the market value. So she packed her clothes in her battered suitcase and went back to live in her father's house, to care for her five younger brothers and sisters until her father was released from the state hospital, at which time she hoped to move down to Manchester or some other city, maybe Boston, where she could find a job in a factory and get an apartment of her own and maybe buy a red car.

His fifth wife, Dora, on the other hand, until Alma's actual funeral, knew nothing of her husband's break with his family. Naturally she knew about his other wives and his daughter Rochelle, for he made no secret of their existence. (Oddly, for such a talked-about man, he made no secret of anything; there was no question he would not answer; it's just that very few people knew what to make of his answers or how to avoid having their next question manipulated by the answer to the preceding one.) She had asked, as did all but his first wife, if he had ever been married before, and he had answered, "Of course." She asked him how many times. "Four." So many! Were there any children? she wondered. "Yes." And how many children? "One." Hamilton never offered information gratuitously, so if you didn't know ahead of time precisely what your question was, and then asked it, it was likely that he would never provide the answer. For instance, in the above interrogation, what Dora really wanted to know was, "Who, if anyone, do you love more than you love me?" To that question, he probably would have simply said, "No one." Whether or not she felt comforted by his answer would depend on whether or not she had been able to assume that he loved her in the first place. Dora, however, believed that when a person told her he loved no one more than he loved her, he had already answered the question of whether or not he loved her in the first place. Thus it was not till later, after Alma's funeral, that it even occurred to Dora to ask her husband if he loved her at all. "I can't tell you I love you," was his answer. Her next question, even though they had been married for no longer than a few months, was, "Would you give me a divorce if I asked for it?" And, once again, he said, "Fine with me, if that's what you want." And by then, indeed, it was what she wanted. She had seen enough, heard enough, by then. The form of the interrogation, more than its content, and Hamilton's strict and what seemed to some his almost fanatically pure adherence to the form had trapped her. As she would later say, "He didn't exactly tell me to leave, but it was obvious to me that I had no choice."

When she first met Hamilton, Dora knew nothing of the stories about him that had circulated for years in and around Barnstead, mainly because, until she married him, she had never been to Barnstead. She had been living in Concord at the time, in a small and rather drab apartment. And since her divorce six months earlier from her first husband, Harry Franklin, a man she had loved deeply and loyally for twenty-three years, she had lived there alone, extremely depressed, quietly trying to heal the deep, suddenly inflicted wounds that had precipitated the divorce. What had inflicted the wounds was her accidental discovery that her husband Harry Franklin had been a lifelong philanderer, and she alone, of all the people who had known him these many years, she alone had been unaware of this aspect of his character. In fact, to her great embarrassment, she had thought of him as sexually cold, almost unresponsive, not just to her but to all women. She had even developed a kind of condescending, maternal affection for his nature, often referring to him as a cold fish, a stodgy haberdasher on whom, she felt, all sexual innuendoes and provocations were lost. And when finally his true nature came out (broadcast hysterically by one of his girl friends, who, not as trusting as Dora, had trailed him and had discovered that he was betraying her, too), she had felt as if he had yanked her legs out from under her. And when, through some perverse determination to "clear his conscience once and for all," Harry had revealed to his poor wife the names of all the many women he had slept with over the years, continuing for weeks to remember and then to confess yet another old and all-but-forgotten liaison, when his confessions were finally over, Dora felt as if her life had been cut to pieces, the pieces cast into the sea, like so much garbage, to float there, swelling in the sun, picked at by gulls above and nibbled by passing fish below. It was in such a state, then, deeply depressed, beaten — a woman so deceived that any further deception would be meaningless, for there was now nothing left to "protect" her from — in such a state, one night after work, she had stopped for a drink alone in a cocktail lounge next to the typesetting shop where she was a compositor, and she had met Hamilton Stark.

They were seated at the leather-covered bar in the artificial gloom; he was a little drunk, and soon so was she. Perhaps she was attempting to put a little cynicism into her life, to see if it could lift her spirits a bit, even if only briefly, and when he had idly mentioned his displeasure with the place, what he called its "ad-man décor," she had just as idly suggested that they adjourn to her apartment for the evening, where, she said, the décor was "early Woolworth's." He had asked her if she had a television set; she had said yes, a color set, and he had been delighted. There was a Frank Sinatra special on that night that he wanted to see. "Ol' blue eyes," he had called him. "You know that song he sings, 'I Did It My Way'?" he asked her. She thought she knew the song. "Well, that's me," he said.

She married him within the week. The reasons were obvious to everyone who knew her. "She's marrying the pipefitter because of what it'll do to Harry," they said. It was presumed that she did it so Harry Franklin would regard her new marriage as the act of a broken, possibly deranged woman, and therefore, people reasoned, he would feel guilty. "As well he should," they clucked. It was, of course, no less possible that her marrying Hamilton after knowing him over drinks and color TV for only a week was the act of a broken, possibly deranged woman, in fact, and that how Harry the haberdasher might feel about it had never once occurred to her. But no one thought of that possibility. People tend to see ulterior motives everywhere these days, even in grief and woeful distraction.

They were married by a justice of the peace, a man who ran a large dairy farm and ice cream stand in Northwood, and a few days later, Hamilton's mother died. Dora had barely unpacked her clothes and color TV. The kitchen set and bedroom suite they had purchased together, as a cynical nod to the forms of sentiment, had been delivered that afternoon, and she had just finished tucking in the linen, placing her combs, brushes, make-up and jewelry neatly on the dresser, moving first one article, then another, then removing them all and starting over again, trying to make these dozen articles look as if they had been on top of that dresser for twenty-three years, when the phone rang. It was the first time it had rung in the three days since she had moved in, and she rushed out to the kitchen to answer it.

It was Sarah, Hamilton's sister, she knew, even though they had never met, calling to inform her that her new mother-in-law, after a lengthy illness, had died in her sleep the night before. Funeral services would be held at the First Congregational Church in Barnstead at 1:00 P.M. on Saturday, December 1, two days later. Dora started to respond to this news and the, to her, peculiar way in which her new sister-in-law had conveyed it, but before she could utter a word, even a stammer of sympathy, Sarah had hung up.

That evening, when Hamilton came home from work (he was then the foreman for the plumbing, heating and air-conditioning systems on the new Tampax factory being built in the southwestern part of the state and was driving forty miles each way to work every day), she told him, word for word and in the same tone of voice, what Sarah had told her. She prefaced her bulletin, naturally, by telling him that his sister had called him that afternoon with some "shocking" news.

"Oh? Which sister?"

"Sarah."

"What was the news?"

She told him.

"Anything else?"

"No, nothing else. Just 'click,' " Dora said, miming the act of hanging up a telephone receiver.

" 'Click,' eh?"

"Yes. 'Click.' "

Hamilton sat down slowly at the kitchen table in the chair

that faced the window. It was where his father had always sat. At breakfast he could see Blue Job as it caught the day's first light, and in the late afternoon he could watch it lose light and slowly turn gray until finally it loomed darker than the sky that surrounded it.

He asked her to tell him again when the funeral was to be held, and she repeated Sarah's message. It *was* a message, she assumed, even though it had come in the form of an obituary notice. She wanted to ask him about Sarah, about his other sister, Jody, and about his mother, too, but she did not dare, not now. Until this moment, she had not once wondered about these people; she had been too preoccupied with how her marriage to Hamilton fit or did not fit into her own private, truncated past. And now that she wanted to know about his past, if for no other reason than to be better able to comfort him at such a bad time, she was afraid to — for he had begun to growl, low in his chest and throat, like a large and vicious animal. He sat there, looking dead-eyed out the window at the gathered darkness, his hands fisted heavily on the tabletop, and growled.

Very slowly, one silent step at a time, she backed away from him, and then left the room altogether. In seconds she had left the house and was outside in the front yard, standing next to the car, a green Chrysler airport limousine he had recently purchased, wondering if she should flee down the road in his car, which so far he had not allowed her to drive, or return to the house and try to comfort him. She had never heard anyone growl aloud like that, and she had never seen a person's eyes go dead before, and she was terrified. Harry Franklin, when *his* mother had died, had cried like a baby, she remembered with sudden affection. And she had held him in her arms and crooned soothingly to him while for hours he had catalogued his childhood memories of the woman. What could this woman have done to Hamilton to have evoked such an enraged response? Clearly, it was rage — those eyes, that growl, the enormous fists on the smooth Formica-topped table — but rage at whom? Somehow it did not seem directed at his mother. No, the rage belonged elsewhere, and that was why Dora was so frightened that, rather than try to comfort him, she had fled from him, had tiptoed out to stand coatless by the car in the cold November twilight and wonder if she should flee still farther from him.

Suddenly he was there, standing at the door, his bulk filling the doorframe, his face burning darkly across the yard at her. He slowly reached one hand out and pointed a finger at her, as if it were the barrel of a gun. "Where the hell are *you* going?" he demanded in a low voice.

"I . . . well, I don't know. I thought . . . I thought you wanted to be alone." She started to wring her hands. The ground that lay between them, freshly frozen but already as bleak as tundra, seemed to undulate in slow waves, and she knew she was weeping. From across the field a wind chipped at her back, and she began to shiver from the cold.

"Get in here," he ordered. "One woman already left me today. Don't make it two." He turned slowly around and disappeared into the darkness of the living room, leaving the door wide open for her.

She hesitated a second, then, still wringing her hands and shivering from the cold, quickly walked across the dead yard and followed him into the house.

He did not speak to her again that evening, nor did she attempt to engage him in conversation of any kind. As swiftly and unobtrusively as possible, she prepared their meal, a frozen sirloin that she broiled, frozen french fries and peas (his favorite meal, he had told her one evening the week before at her apartment in Concord when, quite by accident, she had presented him with the very same fare). And after they had eaten in silence, she had quickly cleared the table, washed the dishes, and had gone into their bedroom, which had once been his parents' bedroom, adjacent to the kitchen. Off that room was the cold, unused front parlor, empty of furniture, curtainless, with a fireplace that he had blocked up years before. A few days earlier she had looked on this house as having what she called "marvelous potential," and she had imagined redecorating it, starting with that old, tomblike parlor, which, because on fair days it filled to brimming with morning sunlight, she had thought would make an attractive master bedroom, then converting his parents' old bedroom into a large and luxurious bath and dressing room. The upstairs, where there were two bedrooms and a connecting bath, she planned to use for guests. Her mother could come from Chicago and visit them, and her sister in Pittsburgh could come, and her father and his second wife, and her friend Gladys from Massachusetts could drive up during her vacation next summer. She had imagined new curtains, new carpeting, fresh paint. The house was squarely built, meticulously maintained and spacious, and it coaxed out all her most hospitable fantasies and plans, even though for the last six months she had been a woman who had felt that all her life's plans had been for another, a previous life.

But that night, as she sat on the edge of the double bed that she and her new husband had purchased a few days before, she looked around her, and all she saw was hopelessness and dark retreat. It was not the kind of hopelessness that was characterized by disorder or sloth, but the kind that makes itself known first by the ruthless paring down of the elements of a life to its essential, molecular units, then by a compulsive ordering of those units, a deliberate placement of remnants in self-referring relations that were abstract, geometric, intellectually pure, controlled. The house and its contents seemed suddenly, hopelessly, cold to her, like an arctic wind, and she began to think with fond nostalgia of her small, crowded apartment in Concord, its warm disarray and thoughtless clutter. (She did not dare to think of the house she had lived in before that, the house she had shared for twenty-three years with Harry Franklin.) She snapped off the light next to the bed, got slowly undressed in the dark, and slipped into the bed. She began to think that she had made a terrible mistake. It might not be too late. Harry was a good man, though flawed, cruelly flawed . . . and he had cried when she left him, cried like a baby. . . .

Hamilton did not come to bed that night. Or at least not to their bed. Possibly he had slept in one of the upstairs rooms and had made the bed when he got up, but when she came into the kitchen at six-thirty, the ceiling light above the table was burning and his coffee cup and breakfast dishes, as usual, were soaking in the sink, and his car, as usual, was gone.

She heard the furnace kick over and start its low hum, and she checked the thermometer posted outside the kitchen window. Fourteen above zero. She hoped it wouldn't snow for the funeral. Oh, God — the funeral. What should she do about the funeral? As the gray cold day wore on, she worried more and more fixedly about it. How was she supposed to act? What was expected of her? She could not understand how such a thing could have become problematic, but it had. She was surprised that she actually did not know what was the proper and appropriate thing to do. Funerals and weddings and birthdays — these were events in a life that were such integrated parts of its overall texture that one almost never questioned what was expected of one as a participant in those events. One simply knew. They were rituals of the culture, and she was one of the people who lived inside and sustained that culture. Why, then, was she so unsure of herself, so incapable of deciding what was expected of her by her husband, her sisters-in-law, the townspeople they lived among? She felt as if she had accidentally wandered into an alien land, where the rituals were obscure and exotic, where a wrong guess could be disastrous for her because outrageous to everyone else.

Around four that afternoon, as it grew dark and the temperature began to fall again, she called the only florist in Barnstead, Herb Cotton, and ordered a large arrangement of white chrysanthemums to be sent to the church the next day in time for the funeral. She knew that she should have sent the flowers to the funeral home, but Sarah hadn't said anything about which funeral home her mother's body was lying in or whether there was to be a service there, and she didn't dare call Sarah now and ask her.

"*What should the card say?*" the florist, presumably Herb Cotton, asked in a high, thin voice.

"What?"

"*The card. What should we put on the card?*"

"Oh . . . Well, I suppose . . . the usual, I guess."

"*The usual?*"

"Yes . . . you know, 'From Mr. and Mrs. Hamilton Stark,' " she said with hope in her voice.

"*This Mrs. Stark speaking?*"

"Yes."

"*I see,*" He paused. "*Ham's wife, eh?*"

"Yes."

"*Yep. Wal, don't you an' ol' Ham worry yourself. We'll get these over to the Heywoods' Funeral Home tonight. They'll still look good at the church tomorrow.*"

"Oh . . . Well, thank you."

"Good woman, y'know. That Alma Stark. That's Ham's mother, y'know."

"Yes, I know. I . . . I never knew her."

"*Yep. Bye, now,*" he said sharply.

"Good-bye," she said, and she hung up the phone.

That evening, Hamilton arrived home three hours later than usual, only slightly drunk, but dark and glowering and filled with smoldering silence. She bobbed around him, gave him food, and stayed in the bedroom for the remainder of the evening, listening to him as he tramped heavily in and out of the house from the barn. Every now and then she could hear sounds that told her he was sorting out tools, equipment, materials — "a place for every thing and a thing for every place." One minute she imagined him doing something that was wholly intentional, deliberate, no matter how bizarre-seeming. She imagined him, for instance, building a coffin for his mother, a hearse from his car, a graveside marker. But a minute later she could only imagine him doing something that was determined wholly by forces outside his conscious will, compulsive acts, no matter how ordinary or normal-seeming — and she imagined him sorting out jars of nuts and bolts, inventorying pipe and fittings, stacking kindling endlessly.

That night she slept alone again, and again she didn't know where her new husband slept or if he had slept at all, for when at seven-thirty she went out to the kitchen, even though it was Saturday and not a workday, once again the light was burning and his breakfast dishes were in the sink and his car was gone. Around nine he returned, with the newspaper and the week's groceries, ale, and Canadian Club. He had begun his regular weekend routine. Dora, of course, did not know this yet, but by eleven, when she had watched him several times perform some menial or trivial task in the yard or house and then pull a pen and small black notebook from his shirt pocket and make a mark in the book, she realized that he was indeed performing a weekly ritual. That's when it occurred to her that the man had no intention of attending his mother's funeral. She could not say with confidence, however, that it was his intention, actually, not to go, for she also believed that he was *unable* to go, that forces beyond and stronger than any of his intentions were keeping him at home on this day, notebook and pen in hand, checking off his chores, one by one, as he did them.

She decided it was safe to tell him, simply and straightforwardly, that she would be going to the funeral. Whatever ritual he was going through, she knew that it did not include her, at present, in any way, and that she was free to attend the funeral or not. So, as he strolled whistling through the door with an armload of split wood for the kitchen woodbox, his face red and dry from the cold, she told him that she wanted to go to the funeral but had no way to get there.

"I'll get you there," he said cheerfully, clattering the wood into the box next to the large black stove. "What time's the service?"

"One."

"Well, you'd better hurry. I'll drop you off on my way to Pittsfield," he said, as if he were agreeing to drop her off at the library. "I forgot to stop at Maxfield's this morning for some eightpenny nails and friction tape. By the time I get back from Maxfield's, you ought to be ready for a ride home, so wait outside the church and I'll pick you up as I come by," he instructed her, and then he made another mark in his notebook and walked out to the barn.

Grateful, though somewhat perplexed, she quickly put on a dark gray, simply cut wool dress, hat and coat. By then it was a quarter to one, so she went out to the barn and presented herself. "I'm ready," she announced.

When she came in, he had been filing the points on a circular saw blade, and when he saw her, he quickly put down his file and the blade, strode from the barn, got into his Chrysler, and started the motor. She slipped in next to him and tried to draw herself back and down into the seat. Somehow she felt he was doing a great favor for her, and in spite of his apparent cheerfulness and easy manner, she believed that the less space she took up the better.

They rode in silence for the mile and a half along the road to town, past the bleak, leafless maples and elms and clustering pines and spruce at the edge of the fields. The day was clouded over again, and everything was cast in shades of gray and tan — the dead grasses, the brush and weeds, the bony branches of the trees, even the houses and barns, trailers and cabins, that huddled in shabby groups alongside the road.

The First Congregational Church, located at the center of the village and facing the Parade, a square patch of open ground, was shaped like a long barn with a bell tower at one end. Though it was painted white, in the chill light it looked cement-gray and somber, more like a mausoleum than a barn or church. A dozen or so cars and pickup trucks, and a single black hearse, were parked on the road outside the church, and Hamilton had to pull out into the middle of the road to get past. But as he started to slow and stop at the end of the line of cars, a short, stout woman, then a tall, gaunt woman, followed by a thick man and two brittle-looking teen-aged boys, got out of a station wagon with a blue light on top. Hamilton drew in just beyond the car and came to a stop.

"That group getting out of the cruiser?" he asked her. "That's Sarah, the short one. Jody and Chub Blount are the others, and their boys, Alfred and Alvin. Twins. If you want to go to the graveyard for the burial, ride out with Sarah and her husband, Mooney. Sam Mooney. He's probably inside the church, getting set to ring the bell. He's a deacon."

"Is it all right?" She had opened her door and had one foot on the ground.

"All right? Well, I guess you'll have to ask *them*. Sarah and Mooney. *They're* the ones to tell you if it's all right. Not me."

She decided to risk it. She had got out of the car completely and was peering in at him through the open door. "Hamilton, I'm sorry, but *please*, tell me why you aren't going to the funeral."

He gripped the steering wheel with both hands. "Go," he said stiffly, not looking at her. "Go on. You haven't imagined being dead, so you go on. It'll help you keep from imagining it a while longer." He paused a second and pursed his lips as if he were about to whistle, then went on. "To me, not imagining being dead is like believing in Santa Claus, you ought to do it as long as you can. So go ahead, you deserve it," he said, suddenly smiling into her puzzled face. "We all do."

So she did go, as he instructed, first to the funeral service, which was appropriately somber and brief, and, after the ceremony, she left her seat at the back and paraded with the others past the coffin and looked down, once, at the embalmed, parchmentlike face of the old woman, and then filed out of the church, where she joined the rest of the people at the roadside and where she introduced herself to the stout woman Hamilton had pointed out and who had by then been joined by her husband, also stout and as short as his wife.

When Dora asked if she could ride with them to the

cemetery, it was the man, Mooney, who smiled and said, "Of course," and when they had driven the three miles out of town to the cemetery on the hillside overlooking the frozen, lead-gray Suncook River, it was the husband, Mooney, who briefly told her what she by then suspected, that Hamilton and the rest of the family had been engaged in a "feud" for over ten years, "maybe even longer, maybe since he was born," Mooney added. But he hadn't enough time to tell her much more than that, so in many ways, and in a few new ways, as she got out of Mooney's car and crossed the narrow cemetery lane to where half a dozen people she recognized from the church and the pallbearers and the minister were gathered around the casket and open grave, she was as confused as she had been back in front of the church when she had first stepped out of Hamilton's car.

There was a sharp, steady wind blowing off the river. The mourners had positioned themselves at the head of the grave, behind the waist-high granite gravestone, with their backs to the wind. Dora walked quickly around the grave and the four or five floral arrangements at the foot, noticing as she passed the large fan of white chrysanthemums among them, and took a place at the end of the line, next to Mooney, who, like most of the others in the group, had jammed his hands into his coat pockets and was staring at the ground. One or two of the men had folded their arms over their chests and were staring into the sour sky, but all of them were standing in postures that to Dora seemed more defiant than mournful, more angry than grieving. Mooney's face was set, his soft chin and cheeks held tightly back, almost as if he were wincing. Next to him Sarah, far from indulging in the expected filial weeping, was scowling darkly down at the bleached-out ground, and beyond her, Jody, too, scowled and worked her lips against her teeth. Chub was one of the men whose thick arms were crossed over their beefy chests and who looked up at the sky and flexed the muscles in their jaws. Even the twin boys, Alfred and Alvin, in their awkward way, stood angrily at the head of their grandmother's grave and looked as if they were about to have a tantrum.

Dora didn't know what to make of this show of apparent anger. She felt as if she had walked into the middle of a play, one of those modern plays where the characters never speak and act in the ways you expect them to speak and act. Even the minister looked angry, standing there at the foot of the grave, his Bible in his hand, glaring down at the gravestone and then scowling into the book as he read the half-dozen sentences that committed Alma Stark's mortal remains to the earth. Was this how the people of this town expressed their grief? Who were they angry at? It almost seemed they were angry with God Himself for having taken the old woman from them. But she knew that couldn't be true — surely, Alma had not been that passionately loved a mother and grandmother, that steadfast and selfless a friend and neighbor. Surely, she could not have been so desperately mourned that her survivors would blaspheme the God who had taken her from them.

The minister, having completed the requisite benediction, gave the signal to the two men from Heywoods' Funeral Home to lower the casket, and then he spun around and stalked across the roadway to his car, with the others immediately following. As the casket hissed hydraulically into the cold, dark earth, Dora suddenly found herself alone, and she started to rush after Mooney and his wife Sarah, who were already grimly getting into their car. Glancing back at the gravestone as she passed alongside the grave, she saw with mild surprise that the single large stone had been put there to mark two graves, not one. On the left of the polished face of the stone it read Horace Moore Stark, with the dates 1892–1963, and on the right half of the face it read Alma Braithwaite Stark, with the year of her birth, 1893–   , and a blank space left for the year of her death, 1973.

Was there something about this stone, Dora wondered, that had angered them? Why? What was wrong with the stone? It seemed perfectly appropriate to her — the husband, Horace, had died first, in 1963, she could see that, and naturally the wife, knowing she would someday be buried next to him, had placed a single stone to mark both graves, leaving blank the place where the year of her own death would eventually be carved. Dora was sure that many surviving wives and husbands handled the matter precisely in this manner. The alternative, she thought, as she got into the back seat of Mooney's car, was to employ two separate stones and to leave the selection of each stone and its placement entirely in the hands of the survivors of each partner, which, she reasoned, would probably be a slightly more expensive and complicated way of doing it, but at least it would have the advantage of not trying to anticipate the order in which the various members of a family would die, who would be the survivors and who would not. And one would not, year after year, every time one came out to the cemetery, to pay one's respects to the memory of one's dead husband, have to look on one's own gravestone, with that blank space for the date of one's death beckoning to one, impatiently reminding one who was next, suggesting by its very incompleteness that one was late, was overdue, urging one to rush, to come down sooner to the earth.

They were almost back to the church, and none of the three in the car had said a word. Then, in a low, frightened voice, Dora asked, "Did Hamilton have that gravestone installed on his own?" knowing that the answer would be yes, and knowing that he had done it without ever having mentioned it to any of them, not to his mother and not to either of his sisters, and knowing, too, that they had discovered its presence one afternoon, doubtless one Memorial Day, when they all had gone out to the cemetery with Alma to place flowers on the old man's grave, which up to then had probably been marked by a modest brass plaque laid flat in the ground, the conventional way for survivors to put off the expense and the usually painful negotiations with one another that accompany the selection and purchase of a large, permanent, granite marker.

Mooney stopped in front of the church. Hamilton's green Chrysler was slightly ahead of him and on the other side of the road. Dora had reached for the handle to open the door when suddenly Sarah spun in her seat and faced her. Her wide face was torn unexpectedly with furious weeping and she bellowed into Dora's shocked face, "You *fool!* You *fool!* I don't even feel *sorry* for you!" Then she began to sob and turned away, burying her face in her hands. Her husband said nothing. He reached one hand across and patted his wife's knee; it was a practiced gesture, a fruitless one, but one he could not let himself forgo.

Slowly, silently, Dora got out of the car, crossed the road, and started to walk to Hamilton's car. She knew the woman was right, Sarah, her husband's own sister. For she *was* a fool, a pathetic, middle-aged, solitary fool, and she deserved no pity for it, none at all. Opening the heavy door of the car and holding it open for a second, she looked in at her husband, the man whose name a week ago in a dark haze she had attached to her own, and she decided, as she got into the warm interior of the car and closed the door behind her, that she would leave him, she would flee this man as soon as she dared, as soon as she no longer feared he would kill her for it.

The ringing of the telephone next to my bed clanged into my dream and woke me. I groped for a second, half-blind in the semidarkness, and found the receiver and finally stopped the ringing. As I drew the receiver to my ear I checked my watch — Was it morning or evening? What day? What night? As if by answering these questions one might know who would be calling and breaking so unexpectedly into one's sleep. And while my eyes, fixed on the luminous face of my watch, told me that it was 6:25 A.M. and that the day was Monday, February 5, and that the year was 1975, my ear, pressed to the cool, smooth, plastic face of the receiver, told me that it was my friend C. who was calling me at this early hour, still a half-hour before sunrise.

He spoke sharply, before I myself had said a word. "*Did I wake you?*"

My mouth felt sourly dry — too much cognac and too many cigars the night before. "Well, yes, but it was time to get up anyhow. I was up late last night," I said, as explanation for my still being in bed a half-hour before sunrise. (C. sleeps almost not at all, or rather, never for longer than two or three hours at a time; over a period of twenty-four hours, however, he probably averages eight full hours of deep sleep — but as a result, he has lost touch with normal, if not exactly "natural," sleeping habits, and thus I never know when he will call me and I never know when not to call him.) "Working," I added guiltily.

"*Ah, yes. On your novel.*"

There was no point in my denying it, so I said nothing. The room was filled with soft, dark shadows, as if it were under water, and I sensed a snowstorm coming.

"Well, I wanted to know if she's all right."

"Who?"

"Oh, sorry! Dora. Or the one you call Dora. I've been reading your Chapter Ten and sitting here pondering her fate, and I must confess it, you've given me cause for concern, even alarm."

"Alarm?" This surprised me. "For whom?"

"Why, for Dora. Or whoever she is — A.'s fifth ex-wife. Is she all right?"

"All right? Well, yes, yes . . . I mean, I suppose so. She left him over a year ago, you know. Why, what's wrong?"

"Is she back with her husband, the haberdasher?" he asked nervously.

"Oh, yes, certainly. They were married again, the day her divorce from Hamilton, A., came through. Sometime early this winter, as I recall. No. C., Dora's fine now, fine. She's even gone back to her old job at the typesetting company. I imagine her time with Hamilton, I mean A., seems like a bad dream to her now. Which, of course, is a shame."

"How's that aagin?"

"Eh? A shame. I said it's a shame that she considers her few months with A. as she would a bad dream."

"Well, if you asked me, and I'm beginning to think that you wouldn't, but if you asked me, I'd tell you that I think she's damned fortunate to be able to think of it as a bad dream. She's lucky to be able to think at all!"

"Wha . . . ?"

"The man's dangerous. And surely you *see that,"* he said, his voice suddenly lowered.

"Ha, ha, ha, ha, ha!" I laughed. "Dangerous? Perplexing, yes. Frustrating, certainly. But dangerous? No, my dear friend, I think not."

"You sound irrational, man," he informed me quietly.

Was there a tainting touch of condescension in his voice? I couldn't tell. Perhaps he actually believed what he was saying, perhaps to him I did sound irrational. But to me, his assertion that Hamilton was dangerous, and was dangerous specifically to Dora, his ex-wife, was, well, hysterical. No, if anyone sounded irrational this gray predawn, it was my old friend C., the man I was accustomed to regard as an almost pure thinker.

"C.," I said calmly, "what's got you off on this 'dangerous' tangent? If you're afraid for Dora's welfare, for heaven's sake, or her physical safety, you might as well be afraid for mine as well," I said.

"*Indeed.*" His voice was still low, and then very carefully he began to try to "reason" with me, as he put it, though I must say right here and now that what he had to say did not sound particularly reasonable at all. I will concede that he was sincere, however, and that he was not condescending to me. And I do believe that the man was genuinely afraid that Dora, and possibly I myself, were in danger of being killed by Hamilton Stark. Yes, that's right, *killed*. By Hamilton, *my* Hamilton, good old Ham Stark. My *hero*, for God's sake!

The way C. saw it, he told me, the very inability of practically every intelligent or sensitive person who came into close contact with Hamilton to determine with confidence whether the man's behavior was deliberate and intentional or out of control and compulsive — that very inability made the question of whether Hamilton was dangerous or not a very real question, one that any responsible person, as well as any other kind of person who chose to associate with Hamilton, had to try to answer. Then C. went down a quick list of people who, close to Hamilton in various ways, had been unable to determine whether his behavior was intentional or compulsive — Rochelle, who tried so hard for so long, and for all I know may still be trying as she reads this, and Rochelle's mother, and Annie, Hamilton's second wife, and probably Alma, his mother, although, from the evidence, one couldn't be sure, and Dora, and then, of course, me. On the other hand, people like Jody and Chub Blount, probably Sarah and her husband, Sam Mooney, too, and Hamilton's third and fourth wives, Jenny the nurse and Maureen the waif, and most of the townspeople who knew Hamilton considerably less than intimately — these people all were convinced that the man was stark raving mad, out of control, dangerous. They had no doubts. Whether they could come up with a sure diagnosis or not didn't matter; they believed he was ill and that the nature of his illness put them in various kinds of danger.

The rest of us, according to C., couldn't decide whether the man was ill or transcendently healthy. We were attracted to him quite as much as we were repelled. And that, according to C., made the question of his potential danger a real one. He went on briefly to cite a few famous cases that he thought were historical parallels — Juan Perón, Howard Hughes, Mary Baker Eddy, and several others I've forgotten. In all these cases, C. insisted, the very thing one person used as evidence of the hero's madness, his illness, another person cited as evidence of his genius, his transcendent good health. Usually, this produces a stand-off, a static situation, which no responsible person should abide. (I thought C. did sound a bit self-righteous there, but basically I agreed with him.) At which point, according to C., the person recognizes that he or she is faced with the choice of either becoming one who follows the hero or one who flees from him, and because of the nature of genius on the one hand and this particular type of illness on the other, one is forced to forgo one's reason, one's reliance on objectively considered evidence, and rely instead solely on one's intuition, which, C. said, was precisely what all of us — Rochelle, her mother, Annie, Dora, and I — had attempted to do.

Apparently it was easier for people like Rochelle's mother and Annie and, eventually, Dora to trust their intuition. Though they never actually were able to conclude, in a syllogistically sound way, that the man they had married was insane, they nevertheless had ended up acting as if they had so concluded. Though they had all three decided, after the fact, to regard certain bits of his behavior and certain physiological manifestations as evidence of his madness, it was wholly on an intuitive basis that they had reached their conclusion. After all, C. pointed out, the very same bits of behavior and physiological manifestations these three people used to prove their ex-husband's madness, Rochelle and I had cited as evidence of his genius — the cryptic, self-denying, aphoristic utterances (which, C. reminded me, I had once regarded as "double positives" and a higher form of wisdom); the absurd ritualization of petty tasks and minor events (to me, the absurdity was admirable and was in fact the whole point); his inability to demonstrate "normal" feelings toward others (a willed characteristic, which, I had claimed, functioned mainly to make us more conscious of our "normal" feelings); his growling out loud, the "dead eyes" cited by Dora (to me, evidence of a yogic state of meditation employed by Hamilton to help him cope with deep frustration without having to resort to simple repression); and numerous other minor acts and behavior patterns. The point C. wanted to make, apparently, was that none of this was evidence that could justify our feeling one way or the other about the man. For on that level Hamilton resisted penetration or analysis. One could not confidently project oneself onto him, which, said C., is indeed as much a characteristic of genius as it is of madness, for we are, none of us, one or the other. Rochelle and I, C. believed, had taken longer than the others to decide one way or the other, had continued to entertain the question, letting one ambiguous, open-ended image of him fold into another just as the first image seemed about to close, because we were probably slightly more intelligent than they, or at least were more worldly-wise in the way of paradoxes.

Up to this point I had not found it especially difficult to agree with my old friend, and actually, as the conversation progressed (it was more a monologue than a conversation), I had felt grateful to him for taking the time and thought to put the matter in this particular perspective. In my quest for an understanding of Hamilton Stark, C.'s point of view was still of value to me. The bedroom had gradually filled with a milky light, and because of the peculiar stillness, I knew that it would soon be snowing. I lay back down and propped the receiver against the pillow next to my ear and continued to listen.

But, unfortunately, this was where C. started to assert a point of view that, to my mind, not only revealed an intolerable intellectual arrogance but actually undermined his carefully stated previous position as well. Essentially, what he started to do was cite what, to him, was clear-cut evidence for the madness of Hamilton Stark, what he, C., called, "*a particularly virulent form of madness.*" I listened with dismay as he described Hamilton's absurd overritualization of petty tasks and acts as a compensatory device for his failure to participate any longer in his society's "normal" social rites. Then C. went on to recall for me Hamilton's youthful belief, "*on rather suspiciously flimsy evidence,*" that he had killed his own father in a quarrel. That, plus his unseemly rush to supplant his father later, after the old man's first stroke, by taking over legal title to his property, indicated to C. the presence of a "*deep and unresolved oedipal conflict*." As further evidence of this unresolved oedipal conflict, he also pointed to what he described as Hamilton's strong need to keep his mother at a safe distance, even going so far as to "*toss the old woman out into the cold*" and to withhold all expressions of feeling for her, even at her death.

By now, quite frankly, I was too appalled to stop him. And thus C. went on uninterruptedly, dragging out one bit of so-called evidence after another, each time reasserting his diagnosis of "*unresolved oedipal conflict*," sounding more and more like a college psych major. I could barely believe what I was hearing! There was the pattern of Hamilton's passively aggressive stance toward the women who became his wives — why there were so many of them, C. insisted. There was his inability to declare his love for any one of them, which, conjoined with his inability to say that he did *not* love any one of them and his apparent belief that the only alternative to loving someone, in particular a woman, was to hate him, or, in particular, her. And then there was "*that gravestone business*," as C. called it, which indicated to him that the man was by now dealing with only barely repressed desires to remove the object of his obsession, the object of his "*unresolved oedipal conflict*," by wishing her dead. And so "*naturally*," C. had felt a rush of concern for Dora's welfare, for with Hamilton's mother finally dead and buried, his dark obsession would turn to the next closest substitute, his wife, and even if she were his most recent ex-wife, she would still be the next closest substitute for his dead mother. "*Murder, my friend, is always the madman's way out of an overpowering love-hate relationship*." Hamilton was giving evidence, to C., at least, of an increasing inability to sustain any relationship at all with a woman, as shown by the increased pace of his marriages and divorces. "*How can I not be deeply concerned with the welfare, even for the very life, of any woman who falls prey to the charm of his enigmatic ways and his manipulative passivity, especially now, when he seems so close to losing what little ability he has had in the past of repressing his murderous impulses?"*

How, indeed? I thought sarcastically. Yes, how? Oh bitter disappointment! Oh solitude! Oh inevitable betrayal! Oh silence, exile and cunning!

"You there?"

Oh lost and by the wind grieved point of view!

"Are you still there?"

Oh deep-wounding reason! Oh overreaching Apollonian perspective!

"Hello? Operator? Anyone there? I think I've been cut off. Operator? I think I've been cut off. I think the connection's broken. Operator? Is anyone there?"

CHAPTER ELEVEN

An End

" 'A fine setting for a fit of despair,' it occurred to him, 'if I were only standing here by accident instead of design.' "
—KAFKA, *The Castle*

"Let me lie here in the snowfield and die warm."
—STONE-PEOPLE-LONG-SONG, Stave 12
(Abenooki Creation Epic, LaFamme and Brôlet, trans.)

THERE WAS NOTHING LEFT for me to do but return to A.'s home in the town of B., locate the man, seek him out and face him there, and gather from that confrontation the evidence and information, the data, that would let me rest easily with my having at last rejected C.'s point of view. I was extremely distressed, perhaps even desperate. Everything was either falling apart or else was about to come together. I felt that if I stayed at home this bleak morning and continued to write my novel, for instance, or cooked a ham or read a bit of Livy, by nightfall everything indeed would have fallen apart. If, on the other hand, I drove myself across the center of the state to the town of B. and scrupulously searched A.'s house and adjacent grounds, I just might be able to discover a clue to where he was, and then I could follow the clue to where he was and meet with him there, my mind wracked by dread and paradox, and the meeting would somehow set me at ease again.

Surely, I thought, as I lay there in my bed and slowly put the receiver back on the telephone base next to me, surely, this is the final test of my faith. Never again will I ask myself to question the very sanity of my hero, and thus my own sanity as well. Never again, I swore, would I permit myself to be so torn, so divided, so alone. By the end of this day, I would have committed myself to following and, to the best of my abilities, emulating the man, or else I would have purged myself of him forever, would have freed myself at last from the glittering beauty of his image.

Thus my desperation and dread and fatigue were mixed with a certain gladness, for I knew that after today, one way or the other, my agony of self-division would be ended. For a second I wondered if the whole thing had been engineered by A. himself, as a final test of my loyalty and spiritual insight. But I quickly shoved that thought away. After today I would no longer be asked to plague myself with such fearful speculation, and knowing that, I also knew that any speculation today was pointless, was but the idle habit of my deeply troubled mind. Once a divided mind foresees resolution as inevitable, it no longer has sufficient cause to be divided.

I bounded from my bed and got dressed quickly in a woolen shirt and heavy flannel trousers — after having first glanced out the window at the cold, overcast day. It hadn't yet started to snow, but clearly it was about to. Neglecting to shave or even to brush my teeth, I hurried downstairs to the kitchen, where I sat down and laced on my boots, pulled on my overcoat, cap and driving gloves, and walked quickly, briskly, to the garage.

By eight-fifteen I was in Concord, headed west toward the town of B. As I skirted the downtown area and began the gradual climb away from the Merrimack Valley to the Suncook just beyond, the snow started falling, scattered flakes, hard and wind-blown. They came like bits of ash at first, tiny, dry flakes, isolate, drifting slowly to the ground as if settling to the bottom of a motionless sea. Soon, though, the snow was falling in swirls and waves that blew from the roadside in powdery sprays and fantails as the car, winding downhill from the ridge west of Concord, reached the Suncook River and brushed along the road that followed the river north and west toward the narrow uplifted head of the valley, where, near the horizon, I could make out the dark gray hump of Blue Job Mountain. Here the river, where it meandered, broadened, and then slowed, was frozen from bank to bank. The ice was invisible beneath the thick blanket of old snow. Sledges, sleds, snowmobiles and people afoot had left trails, paths and tracks across the smooth white skin of the river, scribbles and doodles that, from the road, looked random and pointless. Doubtless, when they were first laid down, the tracks and trails had followed a deliberate pattern, had logically sought a goal — just as had the black, curling ribbon of the road itself, which, seen from a map, would also look random, pointless, dropped from the sky to lie however it fell, as if only accidentally tying together two distant, named points on that grid. But, in fact the road had not been randomly drawn. It had been laid down atop the still narrower, unpaved, wagon route that nineteenth-century Yankee traders had built to carry granite and lumber from the mountains to the sea, and that road in turn had been laid down atop the old market road built by eighteenth-century farmers in the valley, who, in their turn, had been following the still older footpaths that the earliest settlers had worn smooth, their paths laid atop the Indian paths, which had followed the migratory movements of the animals, the deer and moose, the bear, and even, before these, the bison. And the animals had been following the river, this very river before me now, its smooth white surface crisscrossed and scribbled over, like a used sheet of paper, with the tracks, trails and footpaths following the invisible rivers, valleys and ridges of the makers' whims and impulses.

Far out at the center of the river, where beneath the ice the water ran deepest and coldest, there were several clusters of tiny windowless huts. Inside each hut, a fisherman sat hunkered over a head-size hole cut in the ice, drinking whiskey and warming his red hands over an oil heater, each man closed into his own kerosene-lit world, as shut off from the others by the cold and the wind as planets in separate solar systems. And though their huts were clustered together in the same galaxy, the fishermen were together for no reason of comfort or sociability, but only because here, in this region, the river ran deepest and coldest and the fish would take the bait.

A little farther on there is a place, where the river is at its broadest and makes a long, slow sweep around a gently rounded plain, that has been marked by a plaque placed by the state historical society beside the road as it curves along the arm of the river. The plaque tells the traveler that there, in the spring of 1703, the first party of settlers in the town of B. spent their first night in the valley. There, on this slight swell of land, they made camp, and the next morning, as dawn broke and the mist lifted from the river and the trees turned gold in the hazy sunlight, the settlers were surprised by a war party of Abenooki Indians and in the ensuing battle lost one of the original incorporators, a man named Lemuel Stark.

By the time I reached the outskirts of the village, where the river narrows to rapids and the mills were built, the gristmill, the sawmill, and later, in the nineteenth century, the shoe factory, now a storehouse for a local well-drilling company, the snow had started to fall densely, in semitransparent curtains down and across my field of vision like veils dropping away first to reveal a face and then to cover it.

At the Parade, the large common square of ground at the center of the town, as I approached the Congregational church and the turnoff to Blue Job Road, I saw the police chief's car, Chub Blount's Plymouth station wagon with its blue glass bubble on top, come out of Blue Job Road, turn onto the main road, and pass swiftly by me, heading in the direction I had just come from. The snow was falling too heavily now for me to have seen his face as he passed, but I recognized his white Stetson hat and saw that he was alone. A few seconds later, I was passed by another car with a blue glass bubble on the roof, this one driven by the chief's assistant, Calvin Clark. I assumed that the two had come directly from A.'s house, and I responded to the fact that they both were alone with a peculiar mixture of relief and disappointment — relief that they apparently had not found A., or if they had, that they had not arrested him; and disappointment because, if *they* had failed to locate him at his house, then how could I expect to succeed? Of course, it was also possible that they *had* found him after all, had found his body, that is, and thus had no reason not to be alone as they drove back to town. But then, I reasoned, I would have seen only one of the two police officers, for surely Chub would have left Calvin back at the house to watch over A.'s body and to make sure no one tampered with or accidentally disturbed the evidence.

But evidence of what? I asked myself. How do I know a crime's been committed? Maybe nothing unusual or disastrous had happened to *anyone* — not to Dora, not to A., not to Chub Blount, not even to *me* — and maybe the chief and his assistant had not even been at A.'s house in the first place but had been out on Blue Job Road this snowy morning on some other and wholly unrelated police business. Quickly, I ran down the bits of evidence — the three bulletholes in the car window, the strange circumstances of the car's presence and A.'s absence, with all the doors of the house locked, the gate closed, and even though yesterday had been a Sunday, week's end, the absence of any freshly tossed out trash at the edge of the field in front. Yes, it's true, I thought. It's true. The evidence points with equal force to numerous conclusions, and many of the conclusions do not constitute crimes or disaster or even anything especially unusual whether in A.'s life or Dora's or Chub's, or my own. As I slowed the car to make the turn at the church onto Blue Job Road, I finally admitted to myself that, yes, I may have made the whole thing up. I may have imagined everything.

But then, as soon as I was on Blue Job Road, I started to laugh at myself, not out loud, but with a low, ironic giggle. An hour before I had been wondering seriously if the whole thing, this very thing I was now afraid I had imagined, had been engineered by A. I felt light-headed, almost giddy. This was self-mockery taken to the edge of hysteria.

By then the snow had covered the road sufficiently to obliterate any trace of its surface, and I was only able to keep to it by following the high banks of old, ice-hard snow on either side. The windshield wipers clacked back and forth, cutting a pair of half-moons for me to peer through. In a few seconds I entered the short stretch of the road where the conifers grow to the very edge of the road, their branches interlacing between them and across the road above me, making a rough, dark tunnel, and it seemed suddenly that it was no longer snowing and a great arching space had opened around me. The woods here, mostly Scotch pine and dark spruce, grew scruffily into the shaggy wall of an outdoor cathedral, and I remembered then that it was there, just yesterday afternoon, that I had looked hopefully for the figure of Rochelle, as if she were a sister or daughter whose recent death I still mourned and had not yet accepted as real, whose familiar form and hair and green, hooded loden coat my eyes still habitually searched for.

Then, as quickly, I was out of the wood and into the snowstorm again, peering anxiously through half-moons, aiming the car rather than driving it, for the road was slightly slippery under my tires. I passed several battered house trailers and tarpaper-covered shacks, the homes of A.'s neighbors, barely glimpsing them through the falling snow, noticing only that, covered with the layer of fresh snow, the buildings and the cluttered yards looked cleaner, more orderly, as if the snow could tend to them more capably, more energetically, than could the inhabitants.

A few seconds more, and I slowed the car and turned onto the lane that led to A.'s house. I glanced over at the large, hummocky field in front of the house and saw that it, too, had been transformed by the fastidious care of the falling snow, had been made over to look more like a natural, cleared meadow in winter than an open dump, a private trash receptacle.

When I drew up to the gate and prepared to stop so that I could get out and open it, I saw, with surprise, that the gate was wide open already. Hadn't I remembered to close it the day before? It was enough of a habit that I didn't have to think consciously of it in order to close it after passing through, therefore I couldn't be sure. Was this "evidence" of anything — that the gate, normally closed, was now invitingly wide open? I looked up the long driveway to the house and garage. Everything was as I had seen it yesterday afternoon — A.'s Chrysler parked facing the closed garage door, the house darkened and apparently empty, the large expanse of smooth, freshly whitened yard encircling the house from the fence down in front to the woods in back, and beyond those woods, the rising shape of the mountain. No, except for the new pelt of snow and the open gate, everything was the same. Everything.

Very slowly, the snow creaking under my tires, I drove up to A.'s car and parked directly behind it. Then I got out of my car and walked around to the window at the driver's side of the Chrysler. There they were, the three bulletholes connected by a network of tiny cracks, like spider webs. I touched each of the holes with my finger. One of them unexpectedly crumbled at the edges from the pressure, and my finger poked into the cold interior space of the car, startling me. Frightened by something nameless, I quickly withdrew my finger and nervously yanked on my gloves.

It was totally silent, windless, the snow falling straight down, as if being drawn to the ground by the ground itself in some guilty need to hide itself. I left the car and checked the garage door, which was locked. Then I crossed the yard to the front door, determined that it was locked, went up to the side porch and yanked on that door too. Leaning close to the glass to block out my reflection with my shadow, I peered into the kitchen. It was dark inside, but when my eyes had grown used to the darkness, I could see the outlines of the stove, sink, refrigerator, and the small, wooden table and single stool A. had built to replace the Formica-topped table and chairs he had once owned with Dora and that now lay beneath a foot or more of old snow in the field in front, the chromium legs rusting, padding from the seats spilling from rips torn one afternoon last April by high-powered rifle slugs. I could see the calendar on the wall near the telephone. Below the four-color photograph of an oil burner was the sheet for the month of February, for the year 1975 — just as it should be. Yet somehow I was surprised. Somehow I had expected to see some other year, some other month. The house seemed to have been deserted long, long ago.

Slowly, I stepped down from the porch and took a few steps into the yard. The only sound was the constant rattle of my own voice inside my own head. The snow was still softly falling, and I couldn't see clearly more than a few feet in front of me. There was nothing left for me to check, I thought, except the footprints, and that was quite impossible now. Everything was buried under several inches of soft, fresh snow, so that the only footprints I could see were my own. They dribbled along behind me, tiny, crumbling craters slowly filling with new snow. I knew that in a few minutes even these, my own tracks, would disappear. And that would be the end of the "evidence." Any further pursuit of A. would have to be based solely on abstract reasoning, speculation, empty theory. Or else I simply would have to *guess* at his whereabouts, randomly placing him here and there, then rushing to seek him here and there, and if he was not to be found at either place, to guess again. I did not want that. No man wants to believe that his life has finally gotten so out of his control that he either must theorize about it or else be forced to *guess* at its nature. He'd rather believe in magic, fetish objects, totems, dreams. This is how a real life becomes a fiction, I thought, dismayed.

Suddenly, as if remembering a scene from a dream, I remembered driving through the cathedral-like woods on my way over this morning and how, for a few hundred yards, where the branches of the trees wove themselves together overhead, the snow had seemed almost not to be falling. If there had been old tracks on that ground, I thought, footprints laid down beside the road yesterday or the day before, anytime back to the last heavy snowfall, then they would still be visible. Like the faces of type in a printer's matrix, they could be returned to after the type itself had been destroyed and read again. With a matrix, yesterday's or last week's newspaper could as well be today's or tomorrow's.

Stepping quickly, almost bounding, around the side of the house to the back, where the second barn and an old chicken house and tool shed were located, I reasoned that if A. or anyone else had decided in the last few days to walk into the woods, for whatever reason, his tracks would probably still be visible near the trees and would remain so until the wind came up and blew the new snow into obliterating drifts. I knew that A.'s habits and routines seldom led him into the woods, so I knew that any trail I saw would be a sign that something out of the ordinary had occurred — and I desperately needed just such a sign at that moment to break the impasse, the painful balance that hung between all the signs of normalcy and all the signs of variance. Of course, I also knew that his habits and routines led him at least once a week to walk up the path to the top of the mountain, so any variation from the tracks that the habitual walk up and back ought to have left would be meaningful, too.

With a hunter's eye, I scrutinized the exposed, old, packed snow that lay in corrugated sheets beneath the tall pines, cedars and spruce growing along the cleared ground behind the barn and outbuildings. Nothing. Several times I walked back and forth along the edge of the clearing, looking into the woods. Nothing. An occasional rabbit's trail, the scattered scratches from birds, the small spirals left by squirrels — that was all. Then, as my spirits sank, I came to the path, the narrow defile between the trees and bushes that slowly switchbacked up the gradually rising incline all the way to the top.

And there they were — A.'s tracks, his easily recognizable 13 EEEs, each one a yard from the next, leading swiftly from under the smothering blanket of new snow on the yard directly into the woods and on. This I had, of course, fully expected to see, especially after a weekend, when I knew that A. had made his weekly trek to the top of his mountain, Blue Job, two thousand feet or so above sea level, a huge lump of granite and glacial till that had been his family's property since the days of the earliest white settlement in the valley. It comprised almost the whole of seven hundred acres for which they had been taxed these two hundred years, that mountain and the three- or four-acre apron at the base of its south face, where the house and fields were located. Except for its lower half, where every fifteen years or so timber could be harvested, the land was not arable. The upper thousand feet of its height, at this latitude, was so close to the tree line and so free of loose soil that it was almost completely clear of vegetation — a gray gnarl of rock and bony plate and crevice.

I took a short step onto the path, and the snow suddenly seemed to cease falling. My vision cleared as if a screen had been removed from before my eyes. I straightened and peered around for the second set of tracks, A.'s return set. But there was none! How could that be? If he'd gone up, he must have come down, and if he'd left tracks going up, then he must have left tracks coming down. There was no other route for him, up or down, especially at this time of year. The northern slope was precipitous and notched with crevices and sheer drops of hundreds of feet onto ledges and broken shards of stone. The east and west slopes, once you got off the knob, no easy descent, and entered the trees, were practically impenetrably dense with low scrub brush and face-whipping birches left from the last timbering. Besides, they eventually flattened into fields that were owned by other people, people A. had refused to permit to trespass on his property. He was not very likely to trespass on theirs, not unless he was in the direst of circumstances, and probably not even then.

But how to explain the presence before me of tracks leading up the mountain, and no tracks leading down?

I could not answer my own question. Emphatically I decided again that there would be no more speculation. I would follow the tracks through the woods to the rock, and I would follow what I knew was A.'s usual path across the rocks the rest of the way to the top. I knew that my answer lay there, at the wind-blown top of the mountain, not here below, in the shelter of the forest.

I pulled my cap over my ears, gave my gloves a tug, and started trudging uphill along the path, first easterly, then westerly, switchbacking through the trees. As I ascended, the trees became shorter and more twisted, and soon I could see patches of gray sky over me and fresh snow falling on the path. In a short while, the trees were not much higher than my head, briary Scotch pine and dwarfed and gnarled spruce, and when I looked down to check for A.'s tracks, I could no longer see them, for the snow was by then falling heavily on me and on the path, erasing my own tracks behind me as quickly as, a few minutes before, it had erased A.'s. But I was familiar with the path, had walked it many times before, and I knew that A. had come this far and that he must have gone on, so I continued to climb. It became more difficult, for I was out of the trees altogether, and the path was rougher and more circuitous as it wound around huge boulders and skirted short but dangerous drops. The new snow on the old, hardened snow below made my footing less sure. Several times I slipped and almost fell, and once I kept myself from tumbling back down a steep stretch of the path only by pulling myself forward with my hands on a long, jagged outcropping adjacent to the path. The wind was high now, and it whipped the snow against me in wet, adhesive sheets, plastering my hat and coat and face. I could not see more than a dozen feet in front of me and then only when the wind momentarily hitched or shifted and blew the snow from behind me. My progress was slow, I knew, but I didn't have much farther to go. I had reached the crown, where the path abruptly steepened for a final hundred and fifty feet and then leveled off at the top. Increasing my effort, even though I was panting like a racer and, despite the cold and the wind, sweating heavily, I made the final scramble to the top, where I finally came to rest on the table-sized ring of flat stone there. I could see nothing that I could not reach out and touch. The snow had covered my entire body and had turned all but the red sun of my face as white as the whirling white space that surrounded me. If there had been another human face on that high flat tabletop, that altar, I would have seen it, I would have fallen to my knees before it, for I would have seen nothing else but that face. But there was no other human face there to match mine. I was alone, completely alone. I knew that if I took another step, I would walk off the altar into empty space, a swirl of white, and then nothing. Nothing. *Unimaginable nothing.* I turned slowly around and began the descent.